Praise for RICOCHET

"Nick's story will break your heart. It will make you feel. It will grip you by the throat from the very first page and keep you at the edge of your seat the entire time... Keri Lake is a master of her craft and she wrote a sexy, dark and twisted tale filled with unpredictable plot twists that will make your head spin."
-Dirty Girl Romance Blog

"Oh man, this book had my emotions all over the spectrum : anger, outrage, sobbing like a baby, steamy-go find the hubby-hot, sadness , surprise. You name it, this one has it!"
-Wendy S., Goodreads

"Revenge is a dish best served dark, twisted, and ohh-so-steaming-hot! Be prepared to dance the line between love as both savior and destroyer and don't expect to emerge unscathed."
-K.L. Schwengel, author of the Darkness & Light series

RICOCHET

Eye for an eye, Heart for a heart

KERI LAKE

Michele —
Thank you
For reading!

RICOCHET
Keri Lake
Copyright © 2015
All Rights Reserved.

ISBN: 978-0-9848517-9-9 (ebook)
ISBN: 978-1514635537 (print)

Cover Art © Ryan Whalen
Photo © Chris Davis, Specular Photography
Model: Chris Williamson
Editing by Julie Belfield
Layout provided by Polgarus Studio

Books By Keri Lake

Sons of Wrath Series (Paranormal Romance)

Soul Avenged (Book 1)
Soul Resurrected (Book 2)
Soul Enslaved (Book 3)

The Fallen (A Sons of Wrath Prequel)

But from each crime are born bullets that will one day seek out in you where the heart lies. -Pablo Neruda

SPERAMUS MELIORA
RESURGET CINERIBUS.

For SNL and AJL.
You are the best chapters of my life.

*****

And for Julie Belfield.
Because every writer needs a kick in the ass sometimes.

Dear Reader,

First, thank you so much for picking up my first contemporary romance. I typically write paranormal, and admittedly, venturing into a new genre was a bit daunting. However, I enjoyed writing about mortals, as much as my beloved immortals, and look forward to crafting more contemporaries in the future.

If you're picking up one of my books for the first time, I want to caution that I'm one of those *show versus tell* kind of writers. Therefore, I'm not just *telling* you that my hero is a ruthless killer and a sexually charged alpha. You can expect to find graphic violence and strong sexual content throughout the book.

Trigger warning for self-harm, and drug abuse. Not recommended for readers under the age of 18.

This book would not have been written without the help of my beloved musical muses. Check out my website at http://www.kerilake.com/playlists/ for all of my playlists!

Thank you for your interest in my writing.

Much love,
Keri

PROLOGUE

You never forget the sound of gunfire. How the ringing drowns the screaming inside your head. No matter how loud, it's always louder, until the bullet hits its mark in an explosion of pain. Unrelenting fucking pain that sears through the flesh and leaves a gaping hole in its wake. Blackness settles in, and for one fleeting moment of bliss, all is silent.

You become numb, traipsing the fine thread between life and death.

I wish the bullet had killed me.

At least, if it had, I'd be certain of three things:

I could forget the dullness of her eyes as the blood drained out of her body.

I'd no longer hear the promise that I whispered in her ear.

And the barrel of my gun wouldn't be crammed down the throat of a man who'd begged for his life just moments before I cut out his tongue.

But that's what happens when you shoot at something impenetrable.

It ricochets.

CHAPTER 1
Nick

Cull: transitive verb
1: to select from a group; choose
2: to reduce or control the size of (as a herd) by removal
(as by hunting) of especially weaker animals; to hunt or
kill (animals) as a means of population control

According to Newton's Law, for every action, there is an equal and opposite reaction.

You punch a brick wall, your knuckles bleed.

You shoot a gun, it recoils.

You destroy a man's life, he seeks revenge.

An eye for an eye.

So, there I waited, beside a broken window, ten stories in the air, fingers stretching and clenching to a fist, while the early October winds whipped past the abandoned building where I'd hidden.

The place must've been a classroom at one time. Desks stood spaced and lined, some tipped, a few standing.

Dirty, weathered books lay plastered to the floor, splayed open like dead crows in a snowfield of papers. Like an apocalypse had stricken the city and the workers had been forced to flee with no warning.

Outside the window, broken and abandoned husks dotted the landscape, set against a gray, dishwater sky. Scarred and beaten, the perfect metaphor for the people who lived within its forgotten neighborhoods, Detroit was like an abused kid, just waiting for the day someone would come along and give a fuck about it.

The third world city of America.

In any other part of the country, what'd happened would've been an atrocity. There would've been a candlelight vigil, stuffed animals set outside the ashes and rubble where my home used to stand. Parents would've clutched their kids a little tighter at night, given thanks they weren't me.

Instead, the murder was never reported. Not even the fucking neighbors bothered to call the fire station to report a burning house.

I tugged the black hoodie forward to conceal my face and tipped the barrel of my M24 below the windowsill, out of sight.

On the streets below, a crowd had gathered around two white vans packed with care packages for the homeless. In the throng, a white couple, casual but too clean-cut to belong so far east, passed out the large clear bags with easy smiles plastered on their faces, pausing every so often for the camera.

Michael and Aubree Culling.

Care packages. The mayor didn't give a shit about the city, let alone the scum homeless who littered his streets and left a blemish on his blue prints. I wouldn't have been surprised if those packages had been laced with rat poison by the asshole, or his obedient little wifey, always there to stroke his shoulder and smile for the camera.

I could've killed them from my vantage point. Watched their brains paint the pavement, while the crowd dispersed in a ripple of panic.

The arguments for *not* pulling the trigger seemed to diminish with each day that Michael Culling was able to forget he'd ever given the order to murder my family.

Whereas, my memories continued to churn.

With every nightmare that plagued my sleep, a greater need burned somewhere in the darkest corners of my mind—one that left me questioning my own humanity. I *needed* to see the devastation on Michael Culling's face as I took everything from him. I wanted to watch him curl into himself, cursing the heavens, as the pain of watching his entire world slowly drift from his fingertips mercilessly ripped his heart from his chest.

I needed Culling to feel what I'd felt in those final moments. To know that the crushing blow of reality existed behind a thin veil of hope that'd burn down at any moment.

He'd know my pain. My suffering. My desolation.

No quick bullet would deliver vengeance to that bastard. I intended to gift to Culling the understanding of true hell. The realization that what he wanted most, the very reason he lived, was gone forever.

Revenge.

The word simmered in my head, a steady boil of seething that'd kept me from blowing my own brains out the last three years. Like the word held some kind of sanity. A purpose.

The crowd below dispersed, as two men, dressed in rags, fought over one of the packages.

Police guards, who'd maintained a halo of space between the Cullings and the mob of homeless, shifted closer, drawing their guns. Shouts erupted, and a visual of Michael and Aubree being torn to shreds in the shithole neighborhood had the opportunist in me bubbling up from the darkest depths of my soul, urging me to slip the rifle through the hole in the window and shoot.

Done. Over.

I'd never have to see their fucking smiling faces again.

I took a step back from the window just to prove to myself that I could, that I wasn't stupid enough to be fooled by the chimera of a quick kill. It would be a total suicide shot, anyway. The whole fucking plan would be out the window, and all the men who'd carried out Culling's orders would remain free.

Alive and free.

Besides, it wasn't the first time I'd had the opportunity to kill them, and it wouldn't be the last. For three years, I'd watched Michael and Aubree Culling parade the streets like saints. Both of them smiling those bright, fake smiles that begged to be knocked to crags while handing out promises to the poor, despondent souls who lapped them up and followed like rats behind the Piper.

A glance down at my forearm revealed the iron cross with the snaking scorpion where James Nicholas had been tattooed, as well as the quote below it:

Anyone who injures their neighbor is to be injured in the same manner: fracture for fracture, eye for eye, tooth for tooth. – Leviticus 24:20

The cross was a reminder that I wasn't always a monster.

There had been a time I didn't believe in them—monsters. Sometimes, my son would wake from nightmares, screaming of them under his bed. Like all parents, I told him they didn't exist.

Except, monsters did exist. They didn't hide under the bed, though. They stormed through the fucking door and stole away everything we loved.

To defeat a monster, I had to become one.

I often wondered what kind of man I'd be, if they hadn't robbed me of everything that night.

Snapping from my absent musing, I refocused on the scene beyond the window. Aside from a few residual pushes, both men had stopped fighting, the bigger of the two taking his package and pushing though the crowd, as if to get as far away from them as he could.

My gaze trailed back to the Cullings, and pain stabbed my skull, casting a flash of jagged light behind my lids as I clamped my eyes shut.

Clutching the side of my head did nothing to dull the needle-like spasms chipping away at the bone. When I lifted my lids, a yellow haze clouded my vision.

Not again.

Last time I'd seen a doc, about a year ago, he'd told me I could expect headaches— side effect of a fucking bullet to the brain, I supposed. Sometimes, I lost whole stretches of memory, too. Blackouts. A real pain in the ass on the occasions I'd snapped out of it and found myself standing in the middle of a goddamn crack house with no memory of how, or why, I was there.

"Beautiful, isn't she?"

In spite of the throbbing at my skull, I twisted to find a figure, nothing more than a ghostly outline, cloaked in shadows. His voice was unmistakable, though.

Alec Vaughn.

Where my voice carried a deep, gruff quality, Alec's was lighter, like a gentleman's, betraying the fact that he happened to be a ruthless mastermind who'd made quite a name on the streets over the past few years.

I snarled at his question, grinding my teeth as I worked out a tingle in my jaw.

"Come now, hatred and vengeance aside, she's a stunning creature. Surely you can appreciate that." He stepped into view. Even smack in an abandoned shithole, Alec never failed to look meticulous with his three-piece suit and fedora.

Though our styles differed, Alec and I shared two similarities: we both knew a thing or two about computers and both of us carried an unquenchable thirst for revenge—only, I'd yet to discover the root cause of his. The only thing Alec had divulged about himself, aside from his name, was his talent for hacking and his penchant for hiding stolen money.

He'd come to me a while back with a proposition, one I couldn't refuse—a well-constructed plan that was better than anything I had at the time. To exact revenge on the men who'd destroyed my life, and, ultimately, the smiling couple who mocked it every day.

I huffed at his intrusion, coaxing the lingering ache in my head with the heel of my hand. "How the hell do you always find me?"

"Public affair involving the Cullings. The only abandoned building with a sweet vantage point. It's not rocket science, my friend."

I smirked at that. "I look forward to the day I actually pull the trigger."

"I'm surprised you haven't done it yet." A click preceded the warm scent of tobacco, and Alec moved beside me at the window, a thick Cuban cigar making my taste buds pucker. I'd never been one for smoking cigars, but damn, if every time the bastard lit up, I didn't suddenly taste that smoky flavor. He flipped the cigar, and blew on the end of it, before tipping it back and putting it to his mouth.

"The bait worked," I reluctantly confessed. "I'm sure you had no doubts."

His eyebrow winged up. "You'll do it, then?"

"Do I have a choice?"

A wicked smile danced across his face. "No." He blew a plume of smoke into the air, parking the cigar between his teeth as he crossed his arms behind his back and paced. "I trust you've read the files."

"Every word."

A month earlier, Alec had handed off a chip, all smug and proud of himself. Police files. Criminal records for each of the men who broke into my home three years prior. Not just any men, though. Around Detroit, they were known as the Seven Mile Crew—the most ruthless band of contract killers the city had ever known. In a matter of just a few years, they'd snuffed the most dangerous gang members, quickly climbing ranks and banking cash. But they got greedy. Brandon Malone, their leader, and his brother, Julius, decided they didn't want to be hitmen anymore. They wanted to be the bosses. So, they partnered with Culling in a quiet operation that would reduce the kingpins in the city, level some of the shit neighborhoods, and propel Brandon and his crew to an untouchable status.

The gangs and Culling's closest confidantes knew it as *The Culling*, and it happened once a year, on the city's most feared night of crime.

Detroit had always been notorious for shit going down on Devil's Night. Arson, vandalism, murders. It waxed and waned with the enforcement method of each mayor, and had been at an all time high just before Culling took office. Under the guise of making legitimate arrests,

Culling assembled a task force of *Angels*, to combat the crime on the surface, while underhandedly paying off the gangs to kill other gangs. Level a neighborhood and eliminate the smaller fish, all in one sweep.

To the rest of the public, it was a mysterious method that'd somehow begun to transform the shittiest neighborhoods in the city into something its people only saw in the surrounding suburbs. From trash to class, including fancy apartment complexes far too expensive for most of the existing Detroit natives.

For that very reason, I couldn't just let the city's justice system deal with the bastards. No way could I sit idly by after what they'd done, what they'd stolen from me.

For a price, a man could find any information he wanted in the underbelly of the internet, known as the deep net. 'Place was an online convention of the world's scum. Pedophiles, contract killers, serial killers—name it and it'd be there, in all its depravity. It was in that carnival of crooks that I found out it was Culling who'd paid the Seven Mile Crew to scour my old neighborhood, and the Chief of Police who supplied the names of drug dealers living nearby. Alec was able to cut a deal for access to the files—ones he was all too happy to deliver, damn near gift-wrapped, to me.

"And?" Alex prompted.

I knew what he referred to. His offer came with one stipulation that didn't exactly blow my fucking skirt up, though. A task that'd been added to a perfectly good plan a couple months back. "I'm to kidnap Aubree Culling," I said. "For what?"

He nudged his head toward the window. "Look at the way he looks at her."

Below, Culling stood beside his wife , and even at that height, it wasn't difficult to catch the adoration in his eyes. The way he gripped the back of her neck as the two stood off from the crowd talking to the news anchorwoman. The endless glances and smiles he gave every time Aubree spoke.

He leaned in and kissed her, the gesture curling my lip in repulsion. They'd been dubbed *political sweethearts* by the press—how fucking perfect—an image I'd have liked to blow away with a hollow point bullet.

"Don't you remember that feeling?" Alec's voice cut through my thoughts. "A man who'd kill for the woman he is clearly obsessed with. That's the real pain." His whisper drifted through my head, fogging all the images of the two of them lying in blood-soaked clothes. "Perhaps you might agree, death would've been easier. Living … now, that's where the bullet hides its poison."

The air turned thick, suffocating. My throat tightened, begging for a shot of whiskey, but I swallowed past the dryness. "Why not kill both of them? End it. Walk away with a smile, right here, right now."

Alec's chuckle bounced off the wall. "You know I can't do that, Nick. I've too much at stake, for one sloppy kill." As something of a masked marauder, Alec had developed a bit of celebrity status. A genius when it came to computers, with knowledge of even the most secure computer systems , he was known amongst hackers as the infamous Achilleus X, a trouble-making hacktivist with a talent for evading the authorities. "Besides, there's the matter of a promise you made. Or have you forgotten?"

Motherfucker. Like knives twisting in my gut, his words cut deep. I'd vowed my own death to keep the promise I'd made to my dying wife. My teeth clenched together, trapping the anger parked on the tip of my tongue.

"We're not enemies, Nick. This isn't me threatening you. You can easily just give me the files, and we'll part ways."

I couldn't, though. He knew I couldn't. If I walked right then, I'd be dead by morning. A man without purpose was a danger to himself, and the only thing that'd kept me alive so long was one painful hard-on for revenge.

"I'll do it. What's the plan?"

"I'm not going to lie to you." He reached into his pocket and pulled out a coin the size of a gold dollar, flipping it into the air. "They've branched off. Expanded operations from the small crew of hitmen that invaded your home three years ago." Every one of the crew had gone on to bigger and better things. And why not? They were financed by the mayor and protected by the police. They owned the fucking city. Entrepreneurs in crime. "It'll be you against the most ruthless collection of underbelly scum there ever was. Drug dealers. Sex traffickers. Arms dealers. And they've got connections. The odds of you surviving this ..." He opened his palm to a completely blank side of the coin—an anomaly.

"Uncertain."

"What's it matter in the end, anyway?"

Alec's jaw ticced. "You of all people should know the difference between a mercy and a vengeance kill. Perhaps I should leave you to face the latter on your own."

It all came down to one night. One night I would make that corrupt motherfucker Culling remember the family he'd slain, the lives he'd destroyed. I'd take whatever pathetic, tiny heart may be beating inside his chest, tear it out, and watch his world fade all around him, while he took his final breath.

"I said I'll do it." I'd do it by stealing away the very woman that gave him breath to begin with. "Now tell me the goddamn plan to kidnap her."

"Personally, I think you're crazy for doing this alone." His eye squinted as his cheeks caved with a puff of his cigar.

"Certifiable, Brother. Now what the fuck's the plan?"

Blowing the smoke in one lazy exhale, he tipped his head back. "A celebration at the new hospital, the opening of the cancer center, Friday night. She's to accompany him. He's dedicated the Healing Arts Center in her name. Masquerade Ball ... how perfect." He sniffed, scratching his cheek with the thumb of his cigar-toting hand. "It's a closed, black tie affair. Only one bodyguard. Hospital security, but they won't be anticipating trouble. You'll slip out through the underground passageway that connects the hospital to the old dorm rooms."

The hospital had been closed down and abandoned for

years, before Michael Culling provided the much needed funding to reopen its doors. One of the largest trauma centers in the city. How sweet. If only the city knew the majority of Michael's business dealings were signed in blood. "And the cameras? Crowd?"

"Idiots practically use the default settings. I've hacked through a hole in their security system. You won't have a problem. As for the crowd …" He puffed on his cigar. "I've arranged a distraction."

"What kind of distraction?"

His lips stretched into a smile. "A party crasher."

"I don't like the sound of this."

"A little trust, if you will." In truth, Alec's brilliance would guarantee success of the kidnapping. No doubt, he'd already thought of every angle, every loophole. Every possible scenario had probably been teased out with immediate resolution. I trusted Alec because of that. "Culling's preoccupation with his missing wife will render him careless. Keep him from focusing on the big picture."

"And then what?"

"You're to hold her while negotiations take place."

My stomach knotted at that—a detail we hadn't discussed when he first proposed the ridiculous idea. "Babysit the bitch? 'The hell did I ever do to you?"

"Fret not, my friend. If Culling refuses, and he will surely refuse, you'll have the pleasure of killing both of them." He blew another plume. "Jack off to that thought for a while."

"Good. I'm looking forward to giving the two of them

the same slow and painful death that I've suffered every night for three fucking years."

Alec's gray eyes bore into mine, and goddamn if I didn't get a sense he was about to say something punch-worthy. "There *is* an alternative."

"No." I shook my head at the sinister lift of his brow. "I know what you're going to say. No."

"It's not weak to move on, Nick. You could start over."

Lurching forward brought me at arm's length from him, just enough room to knock out that perfect row of teeth he sported. "I've done the legit life once. And what about you, Alec? Why don't you just move on? Pretend shit never happened."

"What makes you think I haven't?"

Impossible. A bluff, no doubt. Alec's thirst for bloodshed rivaled my own. No woman could possibly get in the way of that.

"One of these days, the light is going to flip on, and you'll realize the hits you've suffered in darkness were your very own shadow. Honor your family with vengeance, but don't make yourself one of your own victims."

Alec had a problem with the final act, the part of the plan where he put a bullet straight between my eyes and let me fall with the rest of them. A mercy kill. It was the only way I'd agreed to carry out such an insane act of revenge.

"That's the deal." I sniffed. "No renegotiating. You know it's this, or Lithium, for me—either way, I'm casket-bound." I rubbed my hand down my face in frustration, the same argument rearing its ugly head the closer we approached D-day. "You got my back, or not?"

"I always have your back, Nick. Are you ready for this shit?"

I took one more look out the window and strapped the gun across my chest, knocking Alec in the shoulder as I passed him on my way out. "I'm ready."

CHAPTER 2
Aubree

My father once told me, of all the delusions in the world, that hope was the most dangerous follower of insanity.

I'd have liked to believe that, as a widower, he saw something in me that refused to be torn down by the death and suffering that surrounded me as a kid. Or that, as a father, he prided himself on the tenacity he'd instilled in me.

After all hope, once ignited, was impossible to extinguish. I knew that firsthand. Because hope was all I'd clung to, for the last five years I'd been married to the bastard Michael Culling.

Looking back on his words, I think my father feared early on that I would always have too soft a heart, too strong a mind, and that my desire to seek out the good in others would ultimately destroy me in the end.

How right he was.

Hope allowed the serpent to breach the wall my father had spent decades constructing for our safety, and hope turned that slick devil into my husband.

Too-white teeth stole my attention, as I entered Michael's home office with the trepidation of a mouse that'd unwittingly landed in a snake's pit. His eyes were always warm, inviting, in spite of the blackness deep within their depths. Even then, as quickly as I'd seen them turn cold, it made sense how they might lure someone with a first meeting. The smile happened to be his best feature *and* his greatest disguise, while his eyes very effectively concealed the slippery killer buried behind them.

To the public, Michael was calm, logical, soft-spoken, as a psychopath should be. That same impassive, fluent speech, devoid of emotion outside of the pedantic points of inflection, was precisely what made Michael dangerous.

I took a seat across from him, my throat suddenly in need of cool water. In silence, we stared at one another, but the subtle tracking of his eyes told me he was analyzing my face, like a robot that could pick up on the slightest disruptions in the universe.

Those dark brown, almost black eyes trailed down to my arms and the corner of his lip kicked up into a half-smile. "You're nervous, darling. After five years, I still make you nervous?"

A bright flash of his perfect smile drew my focus away from those evil eyes, while his fatherly tone had me stifling the urge to curl my lip. I imagined smashing my knuckles into those teeth, reveling in the crack of veneer as his perfect mask crumbled to the floor. After all, it was that flawless face, with his smooth, shaved skin, and those warm inviting eyes, that allowed him to survive. Without it, he'd have starved. A psychopath's diet consisted of domination, power, and control. The only way Michael could achieve such a thing was with charisma—something he only understood on a superficial level.

"I'm cold," I replied, because why give him the satisfaction, even after all those years, of thinking he did anything more than make me feel dead?

I hated those kinds of interactions with him—his attempt to assert himself, to remind me that he still had the power to make me feel as meek as the girl he'd met years ago. As much as he'd laid me out like a specimen beneath his microscope, though, I'd also watched him in return. Studied his behaviors to the extent that I could, in most cases, predict them.

Charming and calm happened to be two red flags.

"Perhaps I might offer something warm." He rose from his chair, undoing his belt as he rounded his desk, and leaned against the front of it. With his palms planted on either side of him, he tipped his head, a movement I only happened to catch out of my periphery.

An upward glance showed him staring down at me, anticipation dilating his pupils like a cat high on catnip. He loved to think that I craved him as much, that I couldn't control myself at the yanking of his dick from his pants. Right. The mere thought of his cum in my mouth made me want to wretch.

A dryness hit the back of my throat and I desperately

needed to swallow, but he'd mistake that for my mouth watering. Maybe it was. Maybe I'd become like Pavlov's dogs, or a lab rat, knowing that if I performed well, if I got him off, I'd be one step closer to the illusion of freedom.

Hope, you delusional cunt.

I should've been broken after all those years. Torn open on the inside, thinking of ways to get him to love me, because men as powerful as Michael Culling offered two options when it came to relationships: submit entirely or die—neither of which held any more appeal than the other. He'd told me a number of times, the only path out of his heart lay along the edge of a blade.

The game was what kept the sadistic bastard going, though. The cat and mouse and the uncertainty that he'd conquered me.

"If that's what you want, Michael," I said.

I should've felt stuck. Helpless. As beaten as the bruises that marred my body. I'd known freedom once, and every day since I gave my vows, I'd fought for it, would do anything to have it once again—even pretend I could take his dick in my mouth without the urge to gag, or smile in front of the camera and act like I didn't dream of blowing his head clean off his shoulders.

Cage a bird born in captivity, and it'd happily die with clipped wings.

Cage a bird that once felt the wind through its feathers and the world beneath its feet, and you'd find that insane glint of hope in its eyes that enticed it to escape every time the door swung open. Even if it could no longer fly, it'd never stop vying for its freedom, and neither would I.

It was such stubborn hope that kept me alive.

Michael's head cut to the left, and he nabbed a pen from his desk. "Did I show you my new pen?" The black and gold object spun between his manicured fingers. Odd thing, the psychopath, how he could so easily weave something totally benign into an otherwise perfectly dysfunctional interaction. "Best pen in the world, if you ask me. A Montblanc Meisterstruck. The craftsmanship is … remarkable. Here, hold it." He offered the pen, holding it out toward me, as if I had any other choice but to receive it. "You won't believe how it feels in your hand."

Every instinct told me *no*. That was the cruelty of Michael. Whether I accepted the pen, or declined it, the end result would be the same.

Pain.

However, my father also once told me that to instill fear was power, so I lifted my hand, holding my steady palm out to him.

"I have to say, the design is sleek for such an obnoxious price. But what I love most is …" His fingers curled around mine, tightening his grip, and my muscles tensed in alarm.

As he hammered the tip of the pen toward my palm as if to stab it, but stopped short, even I was surprised when I didn't flinch.

For a moment, his jaw fell slack, before sliding into a wide grin. "You see?" He licked his lips and set the pen aside. "It's like we're … *soul mates*." He released my hand

and clutched my chin, peering deep into my eyes. "If you ever try to leave me, Aubree ..." His words hushed to a whisper. "I will hunt you down and stab you a thousand times with that pen, until you bleed out of every hole I've punched in your body. And when you're on the brink of death, I'll dump you in some cold and abandoned shithole, where you'll *drown* in your own blood before the rats can eat you to bone." Like a lunatic, his mask flipped back to cordial, eyebrows winged up in a smile. "Understand?"

He could have any woman he wanted. It just so happened, I'd have left in a heartbeat if I could've, which made him *want* to keep me. Not because of love. The asshole didn't know a damn thing about love. It was control. The more I longed for escape, the happier he was to keep me chained.

With my tongue caught between my back teeth, I swallowed the salty blood and nodded.

"Good girl." He hooked a finger beneath my chin, lifting my gaze to his, and brushed his thumb along my jaw. "Now, suck my dick." Shoving his tight briefs down to his thighs sprung forth his pathetic cock—flaccid, as usual.

Opening my mouth, I leaned forward and damn near puked at the sensation of his flimsy organ passing my lips—like one of those gel-filled snake toys. Disgusting. Taking his weak shaft in hand, I cupped his balls.

He jerked, releasing a small gasp, while I took some pleasure in the discomfort of my ice-cold hands on his skin.

A whack to the back of my head had my nose slamming into his groin and the tip of his cock hitting the back of my throat. The gag reflex set in, and I tried to hold it back. I'd once made the mistake of throwing up on him, a meal he attempted to force me to consume twice, until he'd walked away with a nice fat split to his lip, and I a broken rib.

"Next time, blow on your fucking hands before you touch me."

Wrenching my head away from him, he stepped out of his pants, grabbed a drink and his cell phone, then sprawled himself out on the leather couch at the opposite side of the room. He jerked his head for me to follow, and I did. Hell, if I could justify a good enough reason, but I did. While scrolling through his phone, he casually took a sip of his scotch. "Get me off. And be sure to lick every drop of cum."

I took a seat in the small space he'd given me between his splayed legs and lowered my face to his groin, acid gurgling in my stomach as I clamped my lips around his shaft.

"Bet you'd do anything for a gun, wouldn't you?" He exhaled a hiccup of laughter. "Pretend my dick's a pistol and blow me away." The wet gulp, as he sipped his drink while stroking me, grated on my spine. "Ah, good girl. You're such a good girl." Fingers threaded through the back of my head, gripping tight to my crown, and he pushed with each bob.

For years, I'd dreamed of biting down and tearing the flesh clean off of him. Fantasized the spray of blood in my face and the victory of watching his features twist in pain.

Doing so would mean death, slow and painful, but I knew the opportunity would come. I held out for it every day. *Patience*, I reminded myself, as his fingers dug into my skull.

"I didn't tell you ..." A quiver to his voice reminded me of a high school kid getting his first blowjob. "You were lovely today. Daddy's good kitten. If you play nice tonight, I'll reward you."

Michael's phone rang over the sounds of his grunts and moans. He ignored it, slamming his hips upward as he fucked my throat.

It rang again.

"Motherfucking cocksucker!" He lifted his cell to his ear. "How can I help you, Chief Cox?" After a minute's pause, his body planked beneath me, rigid as stone, while he tucked the phone against his shoulder and patted the floor.

Chattering voices erupted across the room, and I sat back onto my ass.

"What the fuck am I looking for?" The irritation bled through his voice as he flipped through the internet channels of the Smart TV and landed on his email.

The chill of leather brushing against the back of my thighs hardly registered, as my gaze remained fixed on the wall-mounted TV screen behind Michael's desk. Because there was only one thing the corrupt son of a bitch, Cox, would dare interrupt Michael's beloved office time to report.

Another video had leaked.

Achilleus X.

A tingle climbed my spine at the chime of his name inside my head.

Dramatic music, like something out of a horror movie, accompanied the vertical movement of numbers zipping over a three-dimensional skull overlay that appeared to be talking. Blackness crawled over the white bone, engulfing the numbers, morphing into a ski mask with red stitching across the mouth, before the screen faded to black.

The same intro to all of Achilleus's videos.

He was what was known as a hacktivist. A cyber terrorist who'd somehow managed to evade the FBI. Due to being an indirect target in each video, Michael preferred that the feds not find him first, anyway, lest they'd be knocking at his door—a thought I'd fantasized about many times.

Achilleus had grown a large following on the deep web and amongst the many anti-government groups out there. Each time a video leaked, it spread across the net like flames, and Michael was forced to stamp out the blaze before it got out of control.

Onscreen, lights flipped on in a boxy room, revealing a black ski mask like the one from the intro, the mouth of which had been stitched with red thread. As usual, his head remained cloaked by the hoodie he wore, leaving two black holes for his eyes. I stared at the screen, waiting for some slip when those eyes might've become apparent, allowing a small glimpse of how intense they must be. Achilleus was careful, though. Too careful.

Behind him, a poster that read, *Never Be Silenced,* glowed in the darkness. Already my adrenaline pumped in time to the fast beat of my heart. I knew what was coming.

A computer-generated voice said, "Good evening, citizens of Detroit. I am Achilleus X." With controlled movements, his head bobbed and his gloved hand gestured with his words. "In October two thousand and fourteen, a party took place at the home of councilman Leonard James." Images flashed on the screen, of a group of boys clustered around a girl who appeared to be passed out. "The names you see across the screen below are the men who took part in the kidnapping, rape and murder of a seventeen year old girl. One of the young men was James's son, Eli. This video serves as proof for the masses, as the city of Detroit has been very thorough in keeping this case quiet."

Phone still propped at his ear, Michael sat beside me. A growl rumbled in his chest, as the names flashed across the bottom of the screen, including his own.

"This young girl was taken from her home during *The Culling* on Devil's Night, then drugged and raped, and did not wake from her comatose state. Pathology reports show she died from the drugs she was given. This bastardization of laws designed to protect you, the citizens of Detroit, is unacceptable. Mayor Culling ..." He shook his head and tsk'd, waving his finger in disapproval. "... has once again failed you. As you watch this video, the personal information, including addresses, cell phone numbers and social security numbers of all the young men listed, as well as their parents and anyone involved in covering up this crime, is being compiled. This information will be released, unless you come forward and acknowledge your crime. You have forty-eight hours to confess. As for Mayor Michael Culling, I'd advise you to watch your back—or, more importantly, what you find most valuable in the world. Speramus meliora resurget cineribus. Operation *Culling* … engaged."

Trance music punctuated a non-distinct robotic voice announcing a call to action.

A threat. A promise to steal what Michael loved most.

Michael sat up, lip peeled back like he might snap at any minute, and the anger plastered to his face had me stifling a smile. The targets in each video could be linked to Michael. Members he'd personally appointed to his staff. It'd only be a matter of time before the mysterious vigilante uncovered the truth behind the fake façade of Michael's smile. The deals, the bribes, the exorbitant amount of money to which I would never be privy.

As mayor, Michael had connections to powerful politicians, but also some of the most brutal leaders of organized crime. Yet, only one man got him flustered. One man had him waking in the middle of the night with cold sweats. The only man who had the smarts to expose him, ruin his career, and only because Michael had no idea who the hell he was or what he wanted.

Achilleus X.

In truth, I had no idea whether Achilleus was a man or a woman. I'd become obsessed with him just the same. Behind that mask was a mastermind of the most notorious computer hacks the city had ever known. His bold threats, his willingness to take on my psychopathic husband, had turned him into my own personal fantasy. I dreamed of the day Achilleus X would drop some major revelation about Michael's illegal deals and send my shitty half straight to hell. Every video sent pulses of excitement through my body, clenching my stomach, and drenching my panties. I'd fallen in lust with a complete stranger, strictly on the basis that he happened to scare the shit out of my husband.

The men he'd called out would come forward because they had no choice. They always came forward after Achilleus's threats, because he never bluffed. The FBI had nothing on Achilleus.

The hacker community had dubbed him a mysterious hero.

I'd dubbed him a beacon of hope. My freedom.

"Why the *fuck* hasn't he been brought down yet?" Michael's voice barely hid the ire that'd undoubtedly spread like a volcano deep inside of him. His will to keep calm must've been spinning like a hamster wheel. "This isn't good for any of us, Cox. *Any* of us." He spared me only a quick glance before turning his attention back toward the TV.

Following a brief pause, a flashing 'Call to Action'

banner danced across the screen over the blaring din of an air raid. Something inside of me thrilled at the sound—a warning, loud and clear, to my corrupt fuck of a husband that justice would be served.

"I know what the fuck dark net is, I don't need a goddamn lesson! You find him, Cox. You find out who this motherfucker is, and you bring him down, hear? Bring him down to the depths of hell and then cut his fucking balls off. Better yet, bring him to me." He shot up from his seat, paced a few steps, and collapsed back onto the leather couch again. "He is going to ruin us. Do not fail me. You do not want to fail me, Cox."

Michael threw the phone across the room, where it slammed into the opposite wall before crumbling into pieces of plastic. He let out an angry bellow, and goddamn it, I had to choke back a laugh. It was rare for him to be pushed beyond the calculated and controlled psychopath I'd come to know.

Like Achilleus, though, Michael made threats he was only too happy to deliver. It was why no one crossed him. Why I hadn't gone screaming to the FBI myself. Even if Michael died at my hands, he'd have three hitmen lined up to take my ass to the grave alongside him.

Achilleus X could've brought an end to my husband's regime. Exposed Michael's darkest secrets—ones not even I'd had the pleasure of knowing. For five years, I'd worked my way into my husband's trust, to let him think he'd broken me. All in the name of finding one hole that could secure a ticket out.

"Come here." My heart sank at Michael's words, particularly because of his mood at being shown up again.

With some hesitation, I slid along the couch, closer to where he sat, and piercing pain stabbed the back of my neck where he dug his nails into my nape.

"You want to fuck him, huh? Like all these other bitches? Does he get you hot?" His game. He looked for any sign, any flicker or flinch that might suggest I'd been even remotely enthralled by Achilleus's threat. His way of justifying the pain he wanted to inflict right then.

If there was one thing I'd learned after five years with the asshole, it was not to give any reason to piss him off— so I remained silent. There were days when that approach worked, and like night and day, he'd snap back to being relatively gentle. The twitch of his eye and the rubbing of his thumb along my nape told me something inside of him was building, though.

"Did I tell you, darling …" He placed lips to my ear, and my heart kicked up. "The last time we were together, I recorded it. Every humiliating moment was caught on video." His chuckle had my hand flexing beside me. "I can't help but think, by the look on your face, that you enjoyed every minute of it."

"Fuck. You." A twinge of rebellion lit my blood and I resisted the push of his hands clamped to the back of my head, toward his flaccid cock. Getting him hard again would mean pain and punishment for me, because that was the only thing that got Michael off. Control.

His nails dug harder, and he gripped the crown of my

head, twisting my hair in his fingers. My muscles buckled under the pressure, and his groin slammed into my face. He finally released my nape, held his dick, and smashed my mouth over it, cramming my head to the base of him while his erection grew, hitting the back of my throat and tripping my gag reflex. "You're nothing but a whore, Aubree. A dick-gobbling whore."

Bracing my hands against the leather couch, I pushed against his hold, trying to keep dinner from spilling out, as he ground himself into my mouth. My muscles trembled with the effort, until, at last, he released my head. Falling backward, away from him, I muttered, "Asshole," and wiped my mouth of his pre-cum.

One sharp blow to my shoulder sent me sprawling to the floor, and I kicked at his stomach when he advanced up my body.

Gritting his teeth in a wicked smile, he gathered my legs between his, locking them together, while I clocked him in the jaw, but my stomach twisted when he paused, the glint of insanity dilating his pupils, telling me pain would follow. Daubing the blood from his lip onto his finger, he shook his head. "This. This is why I chose you, Aubree. This is why you'll always be mine." He gave one hard slap to my thigh and flipped me over onto my stomach.

I pushed against the floor to slide from beneath him, but his full weight crushed down onto my back.

"You constantly give me reason to punish you. And you know how much I *love* to punish you." Stuffing both of my arms beneath my body, he vised my arms with his thighs, pinning them between me and the floor.

I squirmed and screamed in defeat, but no one would come. Not even the security guard manning the door. For the staff who might've passed by outside, hearing me scream was nothing new.

"Do you wish to attend your class tomorrow?"

His words had my muscles sagging, and I panted with frustration. He knew I'd want to go. Knew I lived for the moments when I could escape my fucking prison for a few hours and feel like a human being.

"Answer the question."

"Yes," I gritted out, and bile rose up my throat as his stiffened cock slid between my ass cheeks.

"Shhhhh." He licked the shell of my ear. "It's been some time since we played, Pet. I've been so busy lately. I can hardly see the bruises on your flesh anymore. I think it's time we bring out the toy box."

Dread consumed me, and at his thrust, a scream tore from my throat.

CHAPTER 3
Nick

Long stretches of bright lights zip above me, like cars passing in the night. I want to shield my eyes, but can't seem to move my limbs. The world is slipping by in my periphery, too fast to latch onto some comprehension of where I am.

Masked faces glance back at me. I hear a voice announce an open room. More bright lights flash in my eyes, these ones much more intense, and my head throbs a rhythm of relentless agony. Everything is sterile. Cold. Bright.

The masked faces talk to one another but I can't hear what they're saying.

The biting taste of metal coats my tongue, and a smoky scent overpowers the strong odor of alcohol.

"Where's my wife? My son?" I think I've spoken aloud, but none of them answer. "Lena!" I bellow, and her name crashes against my skull in searing pain. "Lena! Jay!"

Writhing does nothing to free me from what's bound my wrists. I catch sight of a mask covering my nose, before my field of view begins to narrow into a small circle, and the masked faces, no more than shadows, stand over me, watching, waiting for me to die.

Their voices turn distant, drifting farther and farther away, until all I hear is the swishing of blood in my ears.

Easy now, a voice breaks through the barrier. The pain dissipates. The circle of view closes.

***

A well-groomed dark-skinned man stands over me, wearing a white lab coat. His murmurs reach my ears, but I can hardly make out what he's saying. Something about surgery. Taking things slow.

"I … want … to see … my wife." Flames lick my throat, and pushing the words past my lips forces me into a coughing fit. "Son."

His eyebrows come together in a frown, and he bows his head before lifting his gaze back to mine. "Do you … remember anything about them? Your name? What's your name?"

The words don't sink in at first, because why doesn't he know my name? Didn't he have my ID? How the hell did I get here?

A tidal wave crashes over me with the memory of stumbling along the side of the road. Cold. So fucking cold, I thought my heart might freeze inside my ribs.

An explosion of pain rips through my skull, like tiny bits of glass shattering inside my head. I slap a trembling hand to my face and let the all-consuming misery pull me under. Pain churns in my gut and I weep. I still don't know if the images in my head are real, or if this is just an everlasting nightmare I'm trapped inside, but I can't stop sobbing behind the shield of my hand.

Clenching my jaw, I drop my fist to my side, and through gritted teeth, I say, "Kill me."

"I'm afraid I can't do that."

A spear of pain strikes my chest, and the cold frost branches inside my veins. It feels like death all over again, but it's not. It's defeat. Hopelessness. As if I'm sinking in the middle of the ocean, watching the light at the surface fade out of reach.

***

Sucking in a sharp breath, my eyes flipped open. I jolted upright, kicking my feet over the edge of the bed, and clutched my skull. Tremors spread through my body, jarring my muscles. The dark room of the abandoned mansion I'd taken as a home for the last six months stood quiet. Empty. As lifeless as I felt inside.

The glint from my long blade called to me, and I swiped it off the nightstand beside me. Closing my eyes brought images of black, thick poison pulsing through my veins, searing them from the inside. It tore through my organs and flesh, as my heart pumped faster, diffusing the darkness to every part of my body—until it burned. Hot! So fucking hot. Goddamn it burned, like acid snaking through my vessels, as it crawled up my arm, sinking deep inside my bones. I had to get it out of me. The poison would consume me. Turn me mad, insane, violent.

Did I want to be one of those sorry motherfuckers staring out the window of an asylum, drooling, waiting for death to take me?

No.

My hand trembled when I placed the blade to my forearm and made a long cut there. Kicking my head back, I let out a hiss, as the poisoned blood seeped from the cut, falling onto my jeans. A cluster of skinny red, some white, lines marred my forearm—small slits that released the pressure inside of me, kept it from building, combusting into a fit of rage.

I had them sometimes, crazed fits, on the occasions I'd thought about my family. The blackness crawled through my body, into my eyes, stealing away my sight. A complete blackout, from which I'd awake to destruction.

It used to be I'd dream of my wife and son a few times a week, see their comatose faces staring back at me, hear the constant ring of gunfire over their muted screams. I'd wake up with that awful metallic taste in my mouth and the smoke in my nose, sweating like I'd run a marathon in my sleep, needing to slice the blade into my skin.

The dreams eventually lessened, though nothing I noticed immediately, because Lena and Jay remained at the forefront of my mind.

The hallucinations were the worst. They'd appear so vivid, almost felt like I could touch them again, could hear their voices calling out to me to save them.

Alcohol had always numbed my body, and the drugs cleared my mind. I'd slip into a comatose state of being alive and functioning, but having no awareness of anything around me, so much so, I couldn't even say, exactly, how I stumbled upon Alec. Could've been in one of those group therapy sessions, or maybe while I was teetering on the parapet of Book Tower with a gun in my mouth. I had no recollection of any human interaction in that first year, no connection that kept me grounded. I'd been a zombie, moving through the human experience as if I'd had any place there.

I'd always thought it funny, the way therapists tell someone how to deal with death and half the bastards didn't even have a family. How the fuck could they tell me the right way to deal with losing everything I loved, when they'd never known the devastation of having their son collapse just a few feet out of reach, watching the blood pool and knowing it was too much, too much fucking blood for a body so small. At the same time, hoping to God to be wrong. Maybe it wasn't too much after all, maybe he could survive it.

Hope. A cruel bitch who kept me alive when I should've burned alongside my family. She hoisted me up on my elbows, when I could hardly keep my head from dragging on the floor, and drew me to my son's dead body, only to find what I'd feared all along—it was too much blood.

A therapist once told me there were five stages of grief, with the bright marquee of acceptance hanging over the finish line. I'd chosen to spin my tires in anger for a while. Anger was where I felt alive. I needed it to survive, to feed some twisted, charred part of my soul with which I'd been waiting for a plan, craving something I couldn't formulate inside my own head.

Alec whispered the word *revenge*, and like a rich liquor, it cooled that burning thirst inside me. He'd constructed a plan, so elaborate, so meticulously well thought out, I couldn't say no. Death to every one of them, and at the end, the bullet would bounce back on me and put an end to my own misery and suffering. Alec had agreed—he'd pull the trigger himself.

So, how could I refuse?

Weeks turned to days, days turned to hours, until I found myself so consumed with vengeance, the hours I thought about the murder turned to minutes. Short flashes that came on without warning, but failed to break me entirely. Only on rare occasions did I wake shaken and sweating, the echo of the promise I'd whispered to Lena as I clutched her still-warm hand alive in my head.

Every one of them will die—painfully and mercilessly.

The promise fueled my will to survive.

Through the dark drapes, a beam of sunlight hit my hand, so warm the heat dispersed beneath my skin, a wake of comfort penetrating my tired bones. I lifted my hand, mesmerized by the specs of dust drifting along the ray of light, slow and directionless, suspended by a moment in time.

"It begins today," I muttered, pushing myself up from the bed.

***

Blue, my full size Cane Corso, had been the only piece of my life that'd managed to survive the fire set to my house. His bulky head blocked my rear view in the back seat, while I drove in the direction of Esteam's Coffee Shop in downtown, just as I had every Wednesday morning for the past two years. It was probably the only place in the city that'd allow a Cane Corso to sit at the table like he had any business there.

The parking lot stood empty at ten thirty in the morning, well past the morning rush, and I parked in front where Lauren sat waving at me through the window. The pale brown of her mixed heritage gave off a glow, set against a pretty smile and bright green eyes. I could easily imagine the same beautiful face staring back at me from the cover of some French magazine—too damn pretty for a nineteen year old who'd grown up on the streets most of her life.

Warm hazelnut hit me as I entered the coffee house with Blue in tow.

"Blue!" Lauren jumped up from her seat and knelt to give the dog a hug.

"I see how it is." I smiled down at her pouty face, as she rose to a stand and wound me in a tight hug.

Lauren was the first person, besides Alec, that I bothered to connect with after the murder, though only because she'd taken it upon herself to care for Blue during my stay in the hospital. In fact, I owed her my life. She'd found me, passed out and bloodied on the side of the road, and called 9-1-1. For months, I was nothing more than John Doe to the docs and nurses who cared for me. Even once I was coherent enough, when they began asking questions, I left Against Medical Advice and never looked back.

"How you been?" As I took a seat across from her in our usual booth, Blue sat as still as a statue on the floor beside Lauren.

"Good." Her cheeks caved with a smile and my sensors flared on high alert. "Seeing someone new."

"Who?"

"Her name's Jade."

Jade. Something about the name. Reminded me of *jaded*, being depressed and taking drugs. Three things I didn't want Lauren to experience, after she'd already lost everything and everyone around her. We both shared a bond in that respect—the night I lost my family, she lost her mom and older brother in the same sweep.

Somehow, she'd bounced back from it better than I had, had worked harder than most kids her age to make a better life for herself, and planned to go to college.

"What's her story?" The nice thing about Lauren's gay preference was that I didn't have to think about some misogynistic asshole pushing her around, though some of the chicks she dated could be ruthless in their own way. The last had left her crushed, starving herself for three straight days, before I finally had to whip her ass out of bed and convince her to keep going.

Me. I could hardly whip my own ass out of bed, yet there I was, dragging her across her apartment, shoveling food down her throat.

Hannah, the short, busty waitress who'd worked at Esteam's for years, set a new cup in front of me and poured in coffee before petting Blue. "How ya been, Nick?"

I buried my groan in the cup of coffee, taking a sip, and before I'd set it down, Hannah had already left. Nothing personal. She'd asked me out two Wednesdays ago, and I just didn't do the dating shit. Not even the *fucking* shit she'd offered in the same breath.

"Why you gotta be all … *mean*?" Lauren said. "Not like she asked you for a kidney."

"I'd have given her a kidney to not ask me on a date." I ushered her to continue. "So, Jade?"

"She's cool." A wily grin stretched her lips. "Different. Fun. She makes me laugh."

The kicker. *Find someone who makes you laugh*, I'd once said to her, like I had any fucking business giving relationship advice to a teenage girl.

"Using my words as weapons, now, huh?"

Laughter spilled from her mouth, and I couldn't help but smile back. The next five minutes were about to kill me as much as I knew they'd kill her, so I took a moment to enjoy the sound.

"Hey …." Goddamn the queasy feeling in my stomach. "Lauren …"

"Uh-oh. That's not good." She leaned back into the

booth, kicking up a knee between her and the table. "Any time you start with *Lauren*"—she attempted to mock my deep voice, lightening my somber thoughts—"I know it's bad."

"Something came up." My jaw shifted, making it hard to form the words I'd practiced in my head so many times before. "I'm not gonna be around."

Her face twisted to a frown, muscles twitching like she couldn't formulate the right words either. We had a code, Lauren and me. Not a lot of questions. No ties.

"Already?" Like her eyes had gone into spasm, she couldn't seem to stop blinking.

I couldn't look at her, so instead I stared down at my traitorous face in the reflection of the coffee. I'd promised to take care of her, to protect her, and what I couldn't tell her was that cutting off ties with her was the only way I could ensure she'd be safe. "I've got some stuff to take care of."

"So … when you say you're not going to be around, what exactly do you mean? Not around, like out of the country? Out of Detroit? Dead? How far away are we talking?"

She'd already broken the first rule, and I couldn't blame her. We'd made the pact early on, when neither one of us had much invested in the other. Three years later, she was like a kid sister to me, one I tended to treat more like a daughter. A daughter I'd grown to love, assuming I was still capable of loving anything.

"You know the rules, Ren. I'll continue to look out for

you. But it's safer if you don't come around."

Tears formed in her eyes, but before they could steal her pride, she shot her gaze toward Blue. "What about him? Who's gonna take care of Blue?"

"Blue's along for the ride."

She triple, quadruple-blinked, kicking her head back toward the ceiling. "Well, your timing's shit, as usual, Nick. I tell you I'm happy, you tear it down."

"Hey, c'mon. Don't say that." I leaned to the side, trying to catch her attention. "Remember? We had a deal."

"Fuck the deal. Whatever you've got going, I want in on it. I want to be a part of it."

Hell, no. I shook my head. "Too dangerous."

"You think this is ... making this easier?" Her voice cracked and her eyebrows pinched. "What if you die? What if something happens to you, and I'll never know!"

I reached for the hands she'd balled into fists on the tabletop but hesitated, choosing to keep mine at a distance. "You got your shit together now. You're gonna go to college—"

"I don't know that!" She looked around as her voice bounced off the walls, drawing Hannah's attention. "What if I don't? What if I'm not accepted, huh?"

"You're gonna be accepted. You're fucking brilliant, Lauren." I huffed. "I told you, I'll be around. Who knows, maybe I'll pop in on you and your girlfriend sometime. But no coming around my place anymore, hear? No asking about me. Promise me."

That seemed to bring some relief, because she slumped

back into her seat and crossed her arms a moment before reaching out to pet Blue. "Will you bring him to see me?"

"We'll see." No promises. In fact, I wasn't sure I'd follow through to visit her. Why pick at the sting?

Her lip twisted like she chewed on the inside of her cheek, as she often did in thought. "Okay. I promise." She wiped tears from her cheek. "Damn, Nick, why you gotta make me cry in public?"

Only on occasions that I made her feel uncomfortable, or pissed her off, did she lose her usually articulate manner of talking.

"I'm sorry. I don't like seeing you cry at all. What d'you get outta this, anyway, meeting up every Wednesday? Old people do that shit."

As planned, my comment tugged a laugh from her. "Someone's gotta take care of your ass. Not like you found yourself a woman." Her lips kicked up to a half smile. "If I didn't know better, I'd think you were gay, too."

I raised a brow and sat back, throwing my arm across the seat, and goddamn if that wasn't the precise moment Hannah chose to walk up—as if the two of them had planned something.

"Hannah?" Lauren's eyes shot to mine and back to the waitress. "Nick's a good lookin' guy, right? Would you fuck him?"

I choked on my coffee, leaning forward to catch the fallen drops on the tabletop. "What the fu—"

As she filled our coffee cups, Hannah pursed her lips, then her gaze locked on mine. "Hell, yes, I would." She winked and sashayed back toward the kitchen, tossing another wily grin over her shoulder as she went.

"You see? It's not like it ain't practically falling in your lap. And by *it*, I mean clean, straight pussy. Lots of it."

I ignored her comment. "Few weeks, I'm going to transfer some cash into your account."

"You don't have to keep doing this."

"Someone's gotta look out for your ass." I took in the weight of her smile, the sadness, as if she couldn't let go. "Hey, who guards the flock?"

She rolled her eyes. "The shepherd."

"And who's the shepherd?"

"My brother."

"Don't forget that." I hooked a finger beneath her chin and lifted her gaze to mine. "No matter what shit I got going on, I will always watch out for you. Got it?"

She leaned forward and kissed me on the cheek. "For a sadistic, loveless bastard, you got a heart of gold, Nick."

CHAPTER 4
Nick

It wasn't hard to identify a trap house. Any joint on the block a bastard would've ordinarily stayed the fuck away from, and he'd have stumbled upon a crack whore's dream. Chipped bricks lay half tumbled from the front porch, where posts from what must've been a banister in its heyday stuck up from broken concrete steps.

The rancid smell of shit stung my nose as I climbed the steps. The porch was littered with liquor bottles, shitty diapers, bicycle tires, a shopping cart, a white bucket filled with a thick black liquid, garbage bags—the kind of random objects that didn't make sense when piled together.

Plywood coated in graffiti covered the front door and windows. I gave three knocks to the wood, and a voice inside told me to go to the alley.

Tugging my Glock from the holster and sliding it just inside my coat, I headed along the side of the house toward the back.

The door flung open and an emaciated-looking woman stumbled down the stairs with a cigarette dangling from her fingertips. Forty fucking degrees outside, and she wore nothing more than a tight, long-sleeved shirt and some jeans. Her fingernails were dirty, hair a stringy brown that looked like it hadn't seen a brush in months. Her thin, sallow cheeks dimpled as she took a long look at me, with my black ski mask tugged over my face.

"Da fuck you sposa be?" She slipped down one of the steps as I passed. "Hey!" An ice-cold hand gripped my free arm–Christ, like she was dead. "Wan fuck and do on flight?"

I wrenched my arm from her grip. Sad deal, a crack addict. The very thing that could've turned her life around was the one thing that would've destroyed her.

"I'mma give you the best fuckin' blow you ever had." She waved me over. "C'mere. I gotta secret." She took a drag of her cigarette. "Know what makes'm the bes cock sucka?" Her lips slid into a wide black gap of a smile. "No fron teeth!" Laughter threw her head back, nearly knocking her back on her ass. "No fron teeth!"

I spun back toward the side door.

"Fuck you, then," she said.

With my head bowed, masked face concealed by the shadows of the alley, I waited. The door swung open to two men, one of which was a white guy reaching beneath his oversized sweatshirt. I shot him first, square in the head, and as his body dropped to the floor, I gripped the throat of the second, pushing him against the wall, before he could pull his gun or make a sound.

My fingers dug into his fleshy throat, just itching to snap his neck. "Where is Marquise?"

His lip twitched into a snarl. "Fuck you."

Cocking the gun, I held the barrel at his forehead.

"Bedroom. Fuckin' bedroom. You'll be dead before you get there, bitch." His lips curved into a smile, and with the butt of the gun, I smashed his nose, his teeth, and hammered one more blow that made him deadweight against my grip. He slid along the wall to the floor in a slump.

Another man appeared in the doorway, gun pointed at me, and without so much as a thought, I put a bullet between his eyes. The gun fell from his hand as he hit the carpet.

Around the corner, the sound of a TV played an eerie white noise as I stepped over blackened crack pipes, condoms, paper and garbage ground into a dirty tan carpet that covered the living room floor.

A black man sat on the couch watching TV with earbuds inserted, bobbing his head to whatever music played from the iPod clutched loosely in his palm. Beside him, a white woman lay passed out, while obviously, high as hell, he pecked at the air like he saw something there seemed oblivious to my entrance.

Gunshots tightened my muscles, and I lowered to a crouch, pistol aimed at the head peeking around the corner. I nailed a shot to his face, and blood sprayed from the back of his head, spattering the wall behind him.

As I headed down a dark hallway, moans overpowered the R&B blasting through the thin walls, and I cracked the door open to where a muscled black man pounded away on a young, light-skinned girl, who couldn't have been more than seventeen. His fingers tangled in her hair as he upped his pace. The room stunk of sex and piss.

"Whose fuckin' pussy is this, bitch?" he asked.

"Yours!"

"Whose?"

"Yours, Marquise. This pussy's yours."

Exactly the confirmation I was looking for.

Without wasting another second, I crashed through the door, gun cocked.

Marquise fell backward onto the mattress, away from the girl. "Who the fuck?"

The woman's scream rattled inside my skull, and I thumped the heel of my hand against my temple, as blackness seeped into my mind, threatening to steal my focus.

He reached for what I presumed to be his gun, but a shot to his hand left him crying out. Two shadowed figures appeared at the door, and I fired without saying a word. Both dropped to the floor. *Boom*. Dead.

I spun back around to Marquise, who nursed his wounded hand, while his girl slid backward from the bed. I boot-slammed his face, throwing him backward onto the bed, and aimed my gun at the young girl, naked and curled up in the corner of the room. "You come here on your own?"

Lip downturned, she trembled with a sob, nodding her head.

"Get dressed and get the fuck out."

She made a slow rise, like a foal trying out shaky legs for the first time, and gathered her fallen clothes from the floor, eyes on me as she snuck past.

Marquise twisted in my grip, making slow movements like the little fucking birdies still swam around his head, and I held him down while I yanked a black blindfold from my pocket. Driving my fist into his face halted his squirming and allowed me to tie the blindfold around his head.

Dragging him through the house was no small feat with his legs hanging up on the crap that covered the floor. We arrived outside, and I tossed his passed out body into the passenger seat.

From the glove box, I nabbed a pair of cuffs and locked him to the passenger door. At gunshots whizzing past the right of me, I turned to find another dealer at the doorway, his gun slanted sideways. Ignoring his shitty aim, I rounded the vehicle and climbed into the driver's seat. The wheels squealed as I took off.

***

Strong gusts of wind beat against my face as I carried Marquise up the rusty, winding fire escape stairs of Book Tower. Almost twenty stories in the air, and we were only halfway to the top when I started feeling a little winded. Goddamn, I'd spent months training, working out, but somehow it didn't prepare a bastard for a mountainous climb with a drug dealer strapped to his back. The pungent smell of sulfur emanating from the manholes didn't help, either.

Peering over the railings showed the back alley to the building, which stood empty for the time being. The alley ran perpendicular to Grand River Avenue—it'd be bustling the following day, but right then, the ordinarily gated channel was quiet. No one guarded Book Tower, another one of Detroit's sleeping giants.

I set Marquise down on the corroded grates of a landing and smacked at his face, until he jerked his head back and forth.

"Oh, fuck! What's ... what the fuck's goin' on?" His hands were bound behind him, the black blindfold still covering his eyes, and he strained his neck as if it'd miraculously fall away. "'The fuck you take me?" He kicked at the gravelly platform, pressing up against the rickety iron spindles behind him.

"That's a long story, Marquise, and I'm not sure you have that kind of time."

"Who the fuck are you?" He wriggled against his binds. "I'll fucking kill you! I'll kill you, bitch!"

"How's the cuffs? Too tight? Not tight enough?" I gave a tug at his arm, laughing when he recoiled and tucked his elbow tight to his body.

"Do you know who I roll with? Mothafucka, you ain't walking away from this shit. They'll find you and smoke you."

"Smoke? Is that a play on words?" Sneering, I pulled a black leather case from my coat pocket. "You like getting high?"

"I ain't sayin' shit. Corrupt fuckin' police. Can't trust nobody."

"I'm not the police." Unzipping the leather revealed seven syringes inside, strapped like a set of valuable pens. Five of the seven happened to be filled with twenty cc's each of potassium chloride—the same shit used in lethal injections.

Another gust of wind blew past as a horn blared from somewhere in the direction of Washington Boulevard, and Marquise perked up. "Help! Hey! Someone help!"

It didn't matter. No one would hear him. Even if they did, no one would save him. For kicks, though, I nabbed a white kerchief from my coat pocket, stuffed it in his mouth until he gagged, and yanked two knives, one from each boot.

I preferred to work in silence, anyway.

Waiting for him to calm down took longer than expected, so I grabbed his thigh and stabbed him in the kneecap.

He planked, trembling beneath my hand, though his muffled 'fuck!' hardly carried over the wind. I heard it though, and, somehow, it took me back to that night.

The open door leaves a sinking feeling in my gut, and, as if by instinct, my pulse hastens along with my pace, when I climb the stairs to enter my house. The first floor is dark and quiet, but somewhere above there's scuffling and laughter. My heart is beating fast in my chest, as I drop my computer bag along with my keys and wallet then race up the stairs.

The door to Jay's room is closed, and I tip toe past to where the noise leaves me feeling increasingly uneasy. Sounds of taunting and misery have my heart about ready to go AWOL.

There's a steady slapping noise when I approach my bedroom door. Peeking inside robs every bit of breath in my lungs as I take in the four men standing around the edge of my bed while one of them pounds into my wife, her muffled cries hardly carrying over their laughter.

Adrenaline surges in my veins. My hands ball into fists at my side. Without thinking or arming myself, I kick open the door, and all four men turn to me.

The one keeps going at my wife, tipping his head back. "Aww, shit, this pussy is tight! So fuckin' tight! I'm gonna fuck you 'til you pass out, bitch!"

I dart toward them, taking a fist to the face that kicks me back a step. Punches pummel my stomach, pistons of pain cracking against my abdomen, but my eyes are fixed on the motherfucker raping Lena. I twist to the right and drill my fist into one cocksucker's face, then turn to the other, hammering my fist into his cheek. Another kicks my feet out from under me, and suddenly I'm on the floor, scrambling to get back to my feet. A boot knocks my head back, sending jagged flashes of light exploding inside my skull, and I'm seeing double. Three more kicks damn near crack my ribs. Flames explode inside my chest, so hot it feels cold, as numbness coats the pain. Two of them hold my arms while *one continues to snap my bones.*

Lena screams as the rotten prick slips a belt over her throat, riding her like a fucking horse. Acid curls inside my veins until my skin is hot with anger, throat tight as a bellow builds in my chest and tears fill my eyes.

He falls forward, catching himself on the bed while still pumping behind her. "Scream if you want. Ain't nobody gonna save you."

Her scream, followed by a choking fit of sobbing, traipses along my spine, and by instinct, I attack again.

Shaking it off, I blinked back to the present. "I'm not going to lie, Marquise. You're going to die tonight. Painfully. Mercilessly. It doesn't matter what you say in the course of it all." I smoothed the gloves over my hands, stretched my fingers, and removed the cloth from his mouth, before tucking my arms behind my back and pacing. "I am a collector, and you're the first knickknack to grace my shelves."

"'The fuck did I do to you, man? What did I do?"

Coming to a stop in front of him, I bent in close until I felt his panting of breath against my cheek. "You stole everything from me." The glint of my blade caught the beams of moonlight. "Let's begin."

With both knives propped in the air, I made two quick slashes mouth to cheek, giving him an impressive Glasgow smile. His body trembled with his muffled scream. "Your smile's infectious." I chuckled, stepping back to get a look at his ridiculous clown face.

Rivulets of blood trickled from the slashes. With his

mouth slightly parted, he gave a stiff wail and his head fell forward. "F'ck ma'!"

"I read a medical record that said, the night you raped and tortured my wife, you got so high on crack that you underwent cardiac arrest and had to be resuscitated." I crouched in front of him. "Bet you were laughing in the reaper's face that night, eh, Marquise?"

I lifted the blindfold from his face, allowing his eyes to widen and adjust, while I tugged the first syringe from the leather. Removing my mask, I gave him a few seconds to study my face. "I know it's been a few years ... you remember who I am?"

His pupils dilated behind a shield of tears. "C'mon, man. We's just havin' fun that night. You know, we didn't mean nothin', man." Blood oozed from the wounds at his cheek, giving a wet clip to his words as he spoke. "Please. I'm sorry! I'm sorry, man."

"I've always wondered if it's true, that a person can survive battery acid injected directly into the vein." I tilted my head to the side and smiled when his body jerked with a sob. "Don't worry. If the experiment fails, I've got a backup. What's that law? What gets high, must crash down?" I peered over the edge of the staircase. "The Reaper's got your number tonight, Marquise." With a shake of my head, I directed my gaze back on him, boring right through his skull with my stare. "Scream if you want. Ain't nobody gonna save you."

His outcry echoed in the alley when I stabbed the first needle into his neck.

CHAPTER 5
Chief Cox

In the back alley adjacent to the Book Tower building off Grand River Avenue, Police Chief Richard Cox crouched beside the body that lay in a static pool of blood. Six syringes had been scattered on the ground, while one remained lodged in the victim's neck. Crime scene investigation wasn't one of his duties as Chief, but one of the biggest trap houses had been hit just prior to the murder, one that'd funded a good percent of his income.

His presence was a personal matter.

Fuck you had been etched in black on the casing of the single bullet that'd been shot into the victim's head.

"Marquise Boogeyman Carter. Dealer. Rolls with the Seven Mile Crew." Standing beside the police chief, Detective Matt Burke looked up toward the staircase then back down at the victim. "Shit, he'd have to have fallen a couple hundred feet, ya think?"

"Based on the damage upon impact, I'd say twenty stories." The coroner lifted the man's chin with a gloved hand, exposing where the needle punctures seemed to have festered. His assistant jotted notes beside him, while the EMS workers who'd confirmed his death looked on. "Shock likely killed him before anything. Whatever was pushed into his veins definitely did some damage. Suffered some necrosis at the injection sites. I'll have the fluid in the syringes analyzed." He huffed. "Whoever did this is one sadistic bastard."

Chief Cox straightened up from the body, stepping back to get a good look at the message painted in blood beside him.

Eye for an eye.

"Vengeful one, if you ask me." Cox stepped around, careful not to disturb the needles, blood, or fragments of bone lying about. "I've known this kid a long time. Pissed off a lot of folks." At the click of the forensic photographer's camera, Cox lifted his gaze and tipped his head, studying the victim from the new angle. Marquise's hands had twisted to a grotesque arc of his bone, and Cox eyed deep grooves just above the rope that bound his wrists, where he must've rubbed against something in an attempt to free himself. For hours, judging by the depth of the wounds and the tearing of surrounding flesh. "I think there's more than one on this. No one takes out an entire drug house, rampage style, then comes back and takes his fucking time killing. That's two completely different styles. This is psychopath shit here. Pre-meditated. Calculated. Torture. A rampage would drive a psychopath nuts with all the sloppy bullets flying."

The coroner lifted one of the needles, examining its contents. "You a criminal psychologist on the side, Cox?"

"This city's full of killers. I've done my share of investigations."

"Chief! Check this out!" Burke lifted a small folded paper from Marquise's jacket and, placing it in Cox's gloved palm, unfolded it to reveal a single typed number. "One? 'The hell is that?"

Cox stared down at the number, rolling his shoulders before looking back to Burke. "Sounds like the beginning, I'd say." He nodded toward the crowd lined on the other side of the caution tape, where four officers kept them from crossing over. "Let's finish and get this shit cleaned up."

CHAPTER 6
Aubree

"Mrs. Culling, your husband asked that I remind you of the hospital Masquerade Ball this evening." Carmen, the twenty-something maid, opened the drapes of my room to sunlight, blinding me as I turned over in bed. "I understand he's chosen something formal for you."

"I suppose he has." It was impossible to hide my lack of enthusiasm.

"Michael is a man that takes care of everything. You're a lucky lady!"

Carmen truly couldn't be blamed for her ignorance. She was present at the mansion for about two hours in the morning, mostly after Michael left for work, and knew nothing of my husband. Yet, it surprised me that the same woman I'd often heard bitching to the other maids, about how she'd never let a man rule her life, suddenly thought having one pick out clothes was a gesture of chivalry.

Of course, maybe she was just being nice. All the staff walked on eggshells around me. I knew what they said behind my back, though. The way they looked at me—the same pitiful way a gathering crowd might look upon a rat inside a snake's cage, anxious for the moment it'd finally strike and kill its prey.

"Yeah, lucky." I turned to the side, wincing at the low cramping inside my stomach, and pulled my knees into my chest, frightened that something might rupture. A quiet whimper escaped me.

The large phallus pushes deeper, burning at my entrance while he jostles the dildo around inside of me, as I hang from the hook to which I'd been tied. "You love this, don't you? How about you pretend its Achilleus fucking you, huh? I'm sure he's hung like a horse."

I flinched at the memory. After hours of torment, he'd finally abandoned his play, forcing me to damn near crawl back to my room without dropping a single bit of blood, lest he'd take a renewed interest in my pain.

"You okay, Mrs. Culling?" Carmen approached the bed, eyes wide. "Ay dios mio! Is that blood?"

"I'm okay, Carmen. Please, I'll be fine." Though enough splotches marred the sheets to rule out a paper cut, the worst of it was probably inside of me. He'd done it before, much more violently than the night before, so I knew I'd recover within a couple of hours. "Please, I'm okay. I ... just started my menstrual cycle." A lie, and as Carmen cleaned my personal bathroom, I was certain she had a pretty good memory that only less than a week ago, I'd finished my usual cycle.

"Should I call the hospital? Tell them you can't come in?"

"No!" I didn't mean for the word to come out quite as forcefully as it did, but I refused to miss the opportunity to leave the shithole for a few hours. The only thing that kept me sane happened to be hanging out with a bunch of broken and battered students—my reward. "No, I'll be okay. I just … had some residual bleeding."

"That's a lot of blood for residual." Her Hispanic accent almost made the comment laughable, if not for the air of concern behind it, but her gaze remained glued to the patch of blood on the sheet where my ass sat. "I'll start you a bath … or, I mean a warm shower, how's that?"

I'd once told Carmen I didn't particularly care for baths. In truth, I was downright terrified of them.

"And I'll get these sheets cleaned up for you, quickly."

"That sounds wonderful, Carmen. Thank you."

She headed toward the bathroom but paused, midstride. "Miss. You know, I have a friend who was in a really bad situation once." She'd lowered her tone, putting my *oh, shit* sensors on high alert, and didn't bother to turn and look at me. "She hired this guy …"

"Carmen—" I interrupted her for her own safety. "I said, I'm fine."

She nodded and continued on toward the bathroom.

I once took a psych class in college and struggled with the difference between psychopath and sociopath. To me, any 'path' was a path that I avoided in life, but truly, I should've paid more attention.

While the rush of water echoed from the bathroom, I glanced up at the camera in the corner of the room.

***

Renata, a cousin of Carmen's, who worked for the same family-owned cleaning agency, fixed the back of my dress, looking over my shoulder as we both stared in the mirror. A single strap of black satin crossed over my breasts to my right shoulder, and clung to my curves in a long, elegant gown, with a band of beads that clipped my small waist. A long slit exposed my thigh, and the strappy heels beneath added a delicate touch. While black gloves hid the scar on my wrist, a cluster of layered pearls at my neck concealed the mark where Michael had gotten carried away with his belt at my throat.

In truth, I hated the fancy dresses and expensive jewelry he made me wear, like his own personal Barbie doll. Having grown up with nothing, it went against my blood to flaunt something so flashy.

"Such a beauty!" Renata turned to a much smaller, meeker woman, who gathered the clothes I'd discarded for the dress. She never spoke. Couldn't. She had no tongue. "Isn't she pretty, Elise?" At her question, the woman gave a slight smile and nodded, but quickly returned to gathering up whatever mess she could scrounge in my otherwise meticulous bedroom. Renata smoothed her fingertips over my long, brunette locks that'd been curled at the ends. "What are you, Mrs. Culling? You got some European in your blood, yeah?"

"My father was French, and his mother was also Sicilian."

"And your mother?"

Instinctively, I rubbed the scar on my forearm and looked down at the tattoo of black cursive over my wrist. A quote by Charlotte Bronte:

> *There's little joy in life for me,*
> *And little terror in the grave;*
> *I've lived the parting hour to see*
> *Of one I would have died to save.*

God, the thought of her still stabbed me in the heart. I'd lost her at a time in my life when I probably needed her most. A time when my father had become so stricken with sadness, the mere mention of her name had him hiding away in his garage, his sanctuary, for hours. It'd only been later, in the letter he wrote to me the day I eloped with Michael, that I realized how much pain her death had brought him.

I'd never known anyone like my mother, so full on life, vibrant and free-spirited, it felt warm and right just to be near her. We could hardly survive on my father's meager income, and yet, I had everything I needed while she was alive.

"Beautiful," I said. "My mother was beautiful."

"Well, then, that's why you're so gorgeous. Mr. Culling's jaw is going to drop, when he sees you. Just hope he returns in time!"

"Michael left?" I shot my gaze to hers in the mirror's reflection. We were due to leave in twenty minutes, for the hospital charity he'd made a point to remind me of that morning. "How do you know, Renata? I thought he was working in his office?"

She shook her head. "Strangest thing. He normally keeps his office locked, but it was wide open when I arrived this afternoon."

The words were almost blasphemous. Michael never left his office door open. "This afternoon? It's been unlocked all afternoon?"

"I knocked, like I normally do before going in, and there was no answer." She slapped a hand to her face. "Oh, my! I hope he isn't …"

Dead? I tightened my face to keep my eyebrows from winging up into a happy little smile. "Did you go inside?"

"Oh, no. I would never go in unless he gave me the permission. He's very particular about that."

"Perhaps …" I cleared my throat and smoothed my hand down the front of my dress. "I should check it out. Make sure he didn't keel over on me!" I hoped my laughter didn't come off as fake as it sounded to my own ears.

"That would make me feel a whole lot better. I didn't even think that something could've happened to him!"

We can only hope. As much as I knew I'd be disappointed, the prospect of finding him lying on the floor, some vacant, lifeless expression amidst the blue of his skin that would surely pronounce his death, was *exciting?* Jesus, had I become just as psycho as the bastard?

"Thank you, Renata, that'll be all. I'll check on Michael. I'm certain he's only stepped away."

She nodded and smiled. "Enjoy your evening, Mrs.

Culling. Again, you look stunning."

"Gracias," I added, a little too jubilant for the morbid conversation we'd had two minutes ago.

Once she'd disappeared from the room, I made a beeline for Michael's office.

Please be dead. Please be dead.

"Shut up!" I whispered, chastising myself.

Why, it's not like he can hear your thoughts!

"He'd certainly try if he could," I muttered to myself.

Down the stairs, past the foyer and down another hall, I finally reached Michael's office. *What if he's in there?* I'd think of an excuse. Even snooping around the door of his office was enough to land myself in punishment, and after limping all afternoon, it was a wonder I'd even attempt something so dangerous.

I knocked on the door. Once, twice. At the third knock, I peeked my head inside. Damn, my heart felt like it might beat right the hell out of my chest!

"Michael?" I cringed at the normalcy in my voice, almost a plea, as if I needed him for something all of a sudden. When he didn't answer, I slipped inside.

The sight of his office spurred an urge to throw up, but I tucked it back. *Keep it in check.* The shit was monumental and I didn't intend to screw up the opportunity with a battle of nerves.

As expected, Michael was nowhere to be found. I rounded his desk and opened drawers. For months, I'd been anxious to find *something* on him—a photograph, a document, a goddamn severed head that might act as indisputable evidence in court. Though, knowing Michael, his connections would probably fabricate some outrageous story, like the headless victim fell on a guillotine, and Michael would be set free.

His desk was something out of a mental health magazine for OCD. Everything neatly spaced, stacked. Nothing appeared to be suspicious.

I lifted a document, knocking a flash drive to the floor, and ducked under his desk to retrieve it, setting the papers back in the drawer along the way. Chip in hand, I quickly backed out from under his desk and rose to a stand, gasping at the shadow in the doorway. *Oh, fuck. Oh, fuck.* My stomach could've fallen in a heap of bloody organs onto the floor at that very moment, while a blanket of ice slithered through my veins, crushing my chest with panic.

"What are you doing in here?" His voice carried the daunting calm that'd always acted as a red flag.

"Checking on you." The words tumbled from my mouth in all my stomach churning alarm. "Your door was open."

"My door is never open."

It would be futile to argue the point, and I wasn't interested in getting Renata killed—there'd be no convincing him that it was, in fact, unlocked. My stomach tightened as I dragged my finger across his desk, slipping into a necessary skin, but one I loathed, and came to a stand in front of it. "The truth is, Michael. I can't stop thinking about last night." The approach was tricky. I'd made it a point not to express any measure of enjoyment when it came to sex with him. "There's ... something about fucking on your desk. Ruining your perfect papers, with your cum dripping down my back. I like to destroy your important things that way." I had to stifle the urge to throw up in my mouth. Jesus Christ, the thought of his cum dripping off of me made my skin itch.

The short span of eternity that followed had goose bumps forming on my skin. *He's not buying it. He's not buying it.*

"Perhaps we'll revisit this conversation later this evening." I could almost feel his eyes scanning me for any degree of deviation from the truth. "We'll be late for the charity ball."

***

Detroit Riverside Hospital came into view. A cylindrical structure made of glass, sliced at an angle, extending from the brick building and stood lit with a soft, orangey glow.

"Darling, you look delectable." With his hand resting on my thigh, Michael sat beside me in the back of the limo.

I didn't bother to turn and face him. Fighting off the tremors in my hands had consumed me most of the ride, since, less than a half-hour earlier, he'd caught me inside his office. His office. In five years, I'd never ventured inside his office without invitation from him. Michael's office was off limits and, under normal circumstances, locked down during the day.

The night before was the first time we'd ever fucked in

his office, which allowed me the perfect opportunity to cover up the true reason I'd risked my life to venture where I'd been warned never to go. In his hasty and disheveled state, he'd forgotten to lock the door before *finishing me off* in my bed.

And with what I guessed was important information on that chip, I'd lied to his face, to my very soul, and told him I couldn't think of anything else but fucking him against his desk again.

It seemed he bought it, but I'd come to know a frightening realization about Michael—what seemed to be rarely ever was.

"Thank you, Michael," I said in the most robotic voice I could muster. My shoulder flinched at the wisp of breath against my neck, the desperation to push him away drumming at my muscles.

"I look forward to ripping this dress off of you later. Perhaps I'll make you come all over the executive summary I've been working on."

At that sickening thought, an urgency tugged at me— the same urgency I got on the rare occasions he took me out of the mansion to accompany him to some event.

Escape.

If I were to succeed, I'd be hunted.

If I failed, I'd be killed.

I knew, because it wasn't the first time I'd given thought to running. I'd actually acted on it, and each time I'd been caught, Michael had upped the punishment. I was confined to my bed for a week the last time, not as punishment, but as a medical recommendation for the wounds I'd suffered. Stupid move. *That's what you get when you don't have a game plan.* Didn't matter, though. The tight stretch of my dress confining my legs served as a reminder that I wouldn't get far. The dresses he chose for me were, themselves, a form of shackles.

Michael knew people and would pay a ridiculous amount of money to find me, so that he could kill me properly. He controlled the police department through his self-appointed, bastardly corrupt police chief. Between them, they could cover up my death with such finesse, it'd be like I never existed to begin.

Still, instincts had my stomach clenching, and my hand balled into a fist. If he found out I'd taken the chip, he'd know I rifled through his desk. No one ventured inside of Michael's office, aside from Renata.

Going back to the mansion meant punishment , the likes of which I'd probably never seen in my life. The charity was my one and only chance—that single moment I'd surely regret not taking advantage of. Who knew when he'd take me out of the mansion's confines again? He'd probably bury me alive in the cellar for taking that chip. I wouldn't pass up the opportunity. I would try to escape Michael, no matter how dangerous it might be.

The limo arrived to a stop at the front entrance, where valet approached. I tugged down the hem of my dress, and noticed the frantic bouncing of my knee, the dead cold stiffness of my fingers inside the gloves.

"Relax, it's just party. I'm right here." His clammy

hand covered mine.

I'd once told him that such affairs made me a nervous wreck, that I hated having to dress up and leave the mansion—a confession that'd secured my ability to accompany him on more occasions.

I mustered a fake smile, every bit of the exchange with him lending no insight into the thoughts running through his head. Did he suspect that I'd betrayed him? Would he take the opportunity later in the evening to investigate what I'd done? If he'd found the chip missing, I couldn't even say what fate would hold for me, because I'd never so blatantly defied Michael, aside from a few escape attempts. No doubt, it would all end in some grotesque death that would make *The Black Dahlia* look like a mercy kill. "I'll be fine."

I couldn't go back with him later. I had to find a way out, a means of escape. I didn't regret stealing the chip— after all, it had to end —but returning to the mansion with him could be the end of *me*. I'd seen him murder a man as casually as if he'd read the morning paper and tossed it afterward. No conscience. No remorse. I couldn't live a lifetime fearing that I'd be killed and discarded, though.

"That's my brave girl." He gave my thigh a squeeze and trailed his hand up my body, over my breasts, to the back of my neck. "In my sights at all times, is that clear?"

Gaze glued to my folded hands, trembling in my lap, I gave a sharp nod. *Fuck you.*

CHAPTER 7
Nick

I stood outside the dilapidated building that sat about five hundred yards from the brand new hospital. At one time, it'd housed the nursing students, who used the underground tunnels to move back and forth between the buildings.

I slipped the large duffle over my shoulder, pulled my hoodie over my head, and wedged the crowbar beneath the particleboard covering the window. With two sharp yanks, it pulled free. Grit and gravel hit the bottom of my boot as I climbed inside the broken window, and I flipped on the flashlight, cutting a wide circle of light through the dark.

A desk sat off to the right, a wall of mailboxes behind it. A sweep over the garbage and grime caked to the floor revealed a door to the left. I stepped over debris to reach it and with one good heave, it opened, and the distinct squeal of rats echoed from inside. Flights of stairs extended up and down, and I pointed the flashlight over the railing to peer below. A good two flights beneath was where it ended, and I descended the stairs quickly, jumping to round each landing, careful not to hit anything sharp that I couldn't see in the faint light.

At the bottom of the stairs, an old sign hung above a cracked door, rusted with faded letters that read *To The Hospital.* A kick of the door nearly threw it off its hinges, and I entered the mouth of the murky tunnel.

Upping my pace to a jog, I reached the end of it within minutes and clamped the butt of the flashlight between my teeth as I shrugged the duffle from my shoulder. Based on the blueprints I'd studied, I knew the door ahead of me had been welded shut—sealed tight. From inside the duffle, I pulled the portable plasma cutter and torch with a power pack. After donning a pair of welding gloves and plasma shades, I sliced a nice arc through the thick steel door. Sparks flew as the flame moved quickly over the metal, with little exertion on my part, and in a matter of minutes, I'd outlined a hole big enough to fit through. I kicked my boot through the center of the circle, knocking the loose steel, and climbed inside to about an eighteen-inch gap between the door and a steel cage that housed storage.

The cage butted up to the walls at each end of the alcove, with no other means of entry, except straight through. I directed the torch to the bars, cut away a good two-by-five feet, then slipped the torch back inside the duffle, exchanging it for a snap gun. Inside the cage, I cleared a path to the door exit, shoving aside an anesthesia cart, blood pressure monitors, small isolettes.

Lifting the padlock on the cage door, I snapped three clicks of the snap gun, until it opened, and removed the chain, leaving my bag at the entrance of it. Shrugging out of my coat exposed the logo of the housekeeping company the hospital had contracted, plastered to my shirt.

Thing about new hospitals? New faces weren't unusual—particularly the temporary contract workers. I'd learned that when I first scoped it out a couple weeks earlier—not a single staff member questioned me in my uniform.

After tossing the discarded clothes into the duffle, I grabbed my computer bag from inside and made another short jog past other storage cages, to a staircase. According to the blueprints, I sat one level below the Trabelsi Cancer Center, where the party was to be hosted in the elaborate Healing Arts Gallery.

Parking myself at the bottom of the staircase and setting my laptop across my lap, I proceeded to hack into the hospital's security camera program, based on some instruction Alec had given me. I'd already cased the place once and knew a camera sat at each landing, at which a door led to a new level. I glanced up at the camera mounted in the corner of the staircase, directed at the door one floor up. With a few keystrokes, it shifted upward and to the left, while on the screen, it appeared as if the viewer would only catch the outward swing of the door.

Peeling back my leather glove, I checked the time. Ten to eight. The mysterious distraction was set for eight fifteen, which meant I had only minutes to locate Aubree and secure my opportunity.

I'd watched them long enough to know I'd never have the golden opportunity of taking them out in some shitty area of Detroit, where no one would find them. Culling drove through the streets like the goddamn president of the country and only ever brought his wife along if there were cameras and big crowds. Aubree rarely left the mansion, and when she did, she was always accompanied by an entourage of bodyguards and police. A masquerade ball was the perfect opportunity.

Straightening my shirt along the way, I rounded the flight of stairs before casually slipping through the door of the first floor that opened up to an elaborate lobby. The building had a modern appeal, and I found it hard to believe that it once looked like the shithole connected at the other side of the tunnel.

Straight ahead stood a glass cylinder, inside of which were rocks and trees, with a small stream that circled the room and ended in a fountain smack in the center. The sign on the front said *Reflection Pond.* A second sign below it gave yoga hours. Adjacent to that was another glass enclosure, with walls that protruded at angles, and track lighting above the artwork on display within, perfectly centered on each small stretch of wall. Hanging precariously from cables connected to the high ceilings all throughout, odd twists of bronze offered a slight industrial look.

Conversation filled the room that looked less like a

hospital and more like an art gallery. The room was easily separated into invited guests and wait staff, based on the tux's and uniforms, though all of them wore elaborate masks on their faces, *mostly* concealing their identities. Women wore long gowns, and for a moment, I felt as if I'd crashed the movie set for *Eyes Wide Shut*, as risqué as some of the dresses were. A brush of my hands told me my Glock was ready at my hip in case shit went bad, as, from the table beside me, I donned a mask from the many set out in perfect rows.

"You with housekeeping?"

I turned only slightly to keep most of my face concealed and noticed blue slacks and tired, but shiny dress shoes. A clusterfuck of keys hung from his belt loop. Security. "Yeah."

"Got a problem in the men's bathroom. Need you to check it out, pronto." He cleared his throat in a way that reluctantly confessed he'd probably created the mess.

"I'm on it."

He paused for a moment then added, "Don't be too long. We've got important guests," before walking through a set of double doors.

Another glance at my watch showed twenty minutes until show time. Inside my pocket, I clutched the small vial containing the GHB. The drugs would need a good twenty minutes to kick in to the point of blackout.

Popping the top on the secreted vial, I scanned the crowd until my gaze landed on a tall brunette, standing beside Michael Culling in a clingy black number that had me momentarily stupefied. Yeah, Alec was right. Aubree Culling was beautiful with her long, chestnut-colored hair, skin so flawless it was painful to look at, and big, round golden eyes that seemed to sparkle under the orange-colored lights.

Claire Davenport, a young anchorwoman for Channel Six News, had the two of them cornered, with her cameraman close behind.

Sticking to the edges, staying inside the shadows, I rounded the room, making my way closer to where she stood. If I fucked it up, the plan was over. Done. Everything we'd plotted, out the window. I adjusted the mask on my face, making sure I'd covered most of my features.

On a pedestal table, a tray held one lone champagne glass, almost calling out to me. It seemed to call out to Aubree Culling, as well, with the way she tipped her head, eyeing it from beside Michael. Nabbing a rag I'd stuffed in my back pocket, I moved in, busying myself as I lifted the glass, wiped down the table, and emptied the vial into the champagne.

A bump to my arm tensed my muscles, as one of the servers lifted the tray from the table, and my stomach knotted as I watched him walk off. *Fuck.* I should've offered her the drink myself! My gaze trailed after the server, who'd only gotten two steps, before Aubree stepped away and grabbed the proffered champagne flute.

Shit, that was close.

As she tipped the glass to her lips, those golden eyes,

peering through the holes in the mask, connected with mine, and for a moment, a curl of heat swept through my body.

A stab of pain hit my skull and twitched my right eye in a seizure of tiny contractions. At a blip of Lena's face passing through my mind, the fury snaked back into my veins, and I snapped from whatever inexplicable enthrallment had enraptured me seconds before.

Lowering the glass, Aubree kept her gaze locked on mine. As if time had slowed to a stop, we stood across from each other, eyeing each other through the masks that hid our faces.

She chugged the champagne, set down the flute, and stepped toward me.

A little early, but my muscles coiled, prepared to strike if I had to, to do something fucking stupid in the middle of the event, like run off with the mayor's wife in plain sight.

Her determined walk clipped to a screeching halt when another tuxedo intercepted, lifting her hand to his lips for a kiss. Recoiling with a frown, her gaze flitted from me to the new guy, back and forth, as though there was some urgency. As if I might disappear.

I did. Though, peering from a darkened hallway that led to what I presumed were closed patient rooms, I kept her in my sights.

Culling approached her from behind, and unless my eyes mistook it, she bristled at the touch of his hand to her shoulder. He offered a smile to the man who'd kissed her hand. A few seconds passed before Culling shuffled Aubree toward a second dark hallway on the other side of the elevators.

Curious, I followed at a distance and ducked out into the adjacent ladies room, keeping the door cracked.

Caught by the throat, she flinched as Culling slammed her up against the wall and leaned in toward her ear. I couldn't tell what he said to her, but the pursing of her lips, almost to a snarl, told me it wasn't a bunch of sweet nothings. He dragged his hand all over her face, smearing the lipstick across her lips, as if he was angry, and I had to believe it was the kiss to her hand that must've set him off. His hand slid up the long slit of her gown, between her thighs in jolting movements, and I heard him growl, "Mine."

He motioned to her face, waved a dismissal, and walked away, leaving her as disheveled as he'd made her.

A sharp spasm struck my skull, and I screwed my eyes shut, mentally counting down the seconds it took to go away. Shifting my jaw back and forth worked out the lingering ache, until the blur to my vision shrank to clarity again.

I glanced down at my watch. Five minutes to show time, and fifteen since she'd chugged the champagne.

Michael returned to the other guests, while Aubree covered her face, ambling toward the ladies room.

The ladies room where I'd hidden.

Perfect. Almost too perfect.

Like a predator, I slid backward, closing myself inside the first of two stalls, and waited.

The restroom door flung open, and a distraught-looking Aubree, with her running mascara down wet, glistening cheeks, stormed toward the mirrors.

"Motherfucker," she whispered, peeling off her gloves and tossing them onto the counter. She dampened a wad of paper towel under the faucet, and used it to wipe away the smear of red and the smudged mascara from her face before reapplying her lipstick. "Don't let him see tears." Her words came off like a mantra running through her head.

At a knock to the door, Aubree startled. My own attention darted to entrance, waiting for a complication to come walking in.

Instead, a woman's voice called out from the other side.

"Mrs. Culling, your husband asked that I let you know, the president of the hospital is about to award the physician of the year. He'd like you at his side during the ceremony."

Two minutes.

"Thank you! I'll be right out." She leaned toward the sink, her eyes seeming to meet those in her reflection. "Please, God. Let me succeed this time. You can do this, Aubree. Time to ..." She stumbled back, catching herself on the edge of the sink. "Ditch this fucker."

One minute.

With brisk steps, she tiptoed toward the restroom door, opened it a small crack, and peered through. The way she wound the chain of her purse in one hand, the bracing stance of her body, she looked as though preparing for a mad dash, like the chick was about to bolt. She scarcely had time to move, though, before she took her second stumble in a matter of seconds, and I pushed out to her and tucked my arms beneath Aubree's, knocking her purse to her elbow.

A slight bit of tension stiffened her muscles when her head fell back, her eyes studying my face. Her brows drew together in a frown. "Who're ... what're you ..." Her drunken slur had the questions trailing off, until her movements softened and she stilled.

Hoisting her up into my arms, I stood at the door, ready. Waiting.

What sounded like an explosion rattled the walls, and suddenly the whole gathering seemed to gasp, before bodies broke into motion. Running. Screaming.

A perfect moment of chaos.

Now.

I slipped out of the bathroom, keeping to the wall, watching in awe as an SUV sat plowed through the art gallery with curls of smoke rising from the hood. Broken glass lay shattered all around it. The art that'd stood lined a moment ago lay in a heap of splintered canvases. The bronze artwork hanging above oscillated back and forth, until it broke free of the cable and fell, stabbing through the hood of the vehicle.

Another wave of gasps and screaming followed. Code triage was called over the PA system.

Kicking through the door to the staircase, I backed up

with Aubree and hoisted her over my shoulder. As the door closed, I caught sight of Michael spinning round, mouth parted in what I imagined was confusion and distress as his wide eyes swung toward the restroom. His head whipped back and forth between the there and the crowd, before he finally lurched toward the last place his wife had been seen.

I'd remember that image, savor it in the dark moments alone when I could imagine the events that would surely follow—the panic, desolation, never knowing what happened or who'd taken her.

I moved quickly down the staircase. A loud crack jolted my muscles, and at the echo of voices and the clang of keys, I hugged the wall, keeping away from the banister.

Security rushed through the first floor door, as I cut through the basement door. I carried Aubree's limp body until I reached the cage and slipped through, nabbing my duffle up from the floor. Fuck, between the two of them, my muscles burned. I tossed the bag inside the hole, dragged Aubree through the arc I'd cut in the door, and lifted her over my shoulder, before jogging through the long, dark tunnel, bag in hand.

No one followed. No one seemed to know that I'd just kidnapped the mayor's wife.

It was almost too fucking easy.

***

Back at the mansion, I carried Aubree's passed out body hoisted over my shoulder like a sack of potatoes. Gripping tight to the back of her thighs through her black dress, I climbed the staircase, her hands beating against my ass with each step.

To the left of the staircase, I kicked open the door to her room—one I'd chosen directly across the hall from my bedroom. Dark drapes decorated the one lone window, obscuring the security bars there, just like the ones I'd placed over all the windows throughout the mansion, and her bed had already been set up, equipped with leather restraints and a headboard that I'd tethered to the wall.

I deposited her limp body onto the bed and worked quickly to fasten her arms and legs, before securing a gag over her mouth, lifting her head as I tied it beneath.

For fun, I tugged the black ski mask over my face—the same one Alec wore in his infamous Achilleus X videos—and stepped back.

A quiet moan hit the air, and I backed away farther as she shifted on the bed, her dress hiking up to her thigh. As though suddenly aware, she gave one sharp tug of the binds, and her eyes flipped open. Wide.

Panicked whimpers laced a sharp exhale, and, lifting her head off the bed, she gave another pathetic tug.

I wanted to laugh. *So helpless.*

"Oh, Gah, I fil see." Her voice carried a slur behind the gag.

An awaiting bucket sat beside the bed, and I yanked the gag and lifted it in time to catch her vomit as she strained her head to the side. I'd anticipated it with the mixing of alcohol. Last thing I needed was to have the shit stinkin' up the place.

She caught her breath, her gaze searching the room. "W-where'm I? Are you … are you Achilleus X?"

I stared down at Aubree Culling's crinkled brows and mask of confusion. "Achilleus X wouldn't spare a minute on you."

What must've been an attempt at shaking her head looked like a bowling ball trying to stay propped on a piece of string. "'Cept tha …" Her eyes made a slow trail back to mine. "What d'you wan'? Money? I gah money. J'tell h'much."

"You think I'd kidnap you for something as insignificant as money?"

Another abrupt roll of her head looked like the heavy bastard might roll right onto the floor. "Did … di summin hire you?"

"Like who?"

She exhaled a sharp breath. "Oh, God, h'knows." Writhing on the bed hiked her dress higher up her thigh. "Lemme go. Never hear fr'me 'gain. Pr'mis." Huge, dilated pupils made her eyes look black, almost evil, and her lids fluttered shut with every uncontrollable roll of her head against the pillow.

I didn't answer her. She wouldn't remember anything I'd said, anyway. Besides, I wasn't there to put her at ease and fill her in. Instead, I remained in the shadows, quietly staring, waiting for realization to settle over her and the waves of panic that were sure to follow.

Her chest rose and fell more rapidly, as her eyes

wandered, from one side of the room to the other, then shuttered, her brows winging up like she fought to keep them open. A minute later, she lost the battle, her body falling flaccid and her mouth agape.

My gaze slid back to where the slit of her dress showed her splayed thigh, tan, tone and smooth, its sleek surface reflecting the dim light of the room.

Lena curls into a ball on the floor, her smooth legs coated in blood, burns and bruises. My hand hovers over the tender skin where they sliced her with a knife, and tears well in my eyes. She flinches at my touch, not bothering to look up at me, and I know why. She feels ruined. They ruined my girl. My beautiful Lena. Beaten and scarred.

Fury simmered through my veins, heating my blood. I rubbed my temples, numbing the sudden ache there, and paced like an animal in a cage, ready to tear into prey. Noticing Aubree's thigh brought an uncontrollable desire to bruise it, to dig my fingers into her flawless flesh and leave a mark of pain, just like they'd done to my wife. I wanted to put my gun to Aubree's temple and pull the trigger, take what was taken from me. An eye for an eye. Alec's words battled the images inside my head. *Don't do it. Don't fuck this up.*

I left the room before I could act on my urges and headed downstairs.

From the kitchen table, I swiped the bourbon and tipped it back, waiting for the cool to soothe the scorch in my throat. Before I knew it, half the bottle was gone. Slipping off the gloves, I ran my hands under the water and let the cold stream coat the heat that burned below my skin. The house originally hadn't come equipped with water, electricity, gas. I'd had to hook that up myself, tapping into electrical lines, gas lines, the water main. Damn near killed myself in the process.

I rubbed a hand down my face and pounded the heel of my hand against my head. Fucking headaches.

Having Aubree in the next room would take some hard hitting liquor—the kind that could drown out images of her thigh peeking out of the dress and all the things I wanted to do out of rage. I didn't know how long Alec wanted me to keep her. Had no idea why he'd added the kidnap onto what I'd considered a perfectly constructed plan that we'd gone over for months. What bad could come of killing her? Why did he need her? He'd told me to hang on to her during negotiations, but negotiations weren't part of the plan. I was to systematically kill each of the men who'd murdered my family, while Alec kept them on their toes, leaking information, keeping them occupied, off the trail. Culling wouldn't give a shit about a few missing thugs, if it meant his whole fucking operation was about to be exposed. In the end, Culling would get snuffed. No negotiations.

I didn't like that Alec had modified what we'd agreed on. The plan had changed and I had no choice but to go along. When I'd told him I'd do whatever he wanted, in exchange for the identities of the men who stole my life, I couldn't have guessed he'd task me with babysitting the only woman on the planet I could've happily stuffed with a bullet.

Thickness in the air tightened my chest and a familiar urge pulled inside my gut.

I needed to down some liquor and set fire to it.

CHAPTER 8
Nick

Lion's Den had two things going for it—half-naked women everywhere and the kind of hard liquor that could get a bastard shitfaced fast. It was also the only club in Detroit that served alcohol where the girls stripped nude. Illegal anywhere else, but hell if anyone bothered to report it.

I plopped down onto the barstool, gaze glued to the cop sitting beside Rev, the owner of the bar and somewhat of a neighborhood guard dog. Though he was no stranger to hustling deals himself, he kept an eye out for trouble. Rev didn't show much love for the Detroit Police—in fact, I'd heard stories about him beating the shit out of officers who'd attempted to raid the homes in his neighborhood.

For a Thursday night, the strip club remained pretty empty, so it didn't make sense why cops had been called. Aside from a small group seated alongside the stage, whose obnoxious laughter broadcasted that they seemed to be getting along just fine, the only other guys in the place were Jimmy and Sampson—two men who were probably approaching eighty.

I ordered a whisky, taking in the women up on stage, pounding against the pole, to the beat of *Adrenalize* by In This Moment.

Down in front, closest to the stage, a middle-aged man, amongst a bevy of drunken suits who must've met up unbeknownst to their wives, stood and thrusted his crotch in some kind of shitty cock dance the suburbanites were known for. Could always tell them apart from the Detroit folk. Like, once they crossed the borders, their dancing skills resembled that guy's fucking embarrassing display.

I'd hated when the dipshits came down to sow their wild oats at the bar where Lena had stripped. Always trying to touch her, or get her to meet them in the back. She never did. Not even when shit got bad and money was tight. She'd always said it was the one thing she could keep for me.

For others, she danced in darkness, concealing what she didn't want them to see. For me, she danced in the light.

Suit and tie jumped on stage, and, as if by instinct, my muscles tensed with the urge to go after him. His body flew through the air, hauled by three hundred pounds of muscle, known as Big John, the bouncer, who dragged him by the nape of his jacket, and escorted the group out of the bar.

I shook my head. *Dipshits.*

From across the bar, Rev laughed, slapping the cop on the back, and after what seemed like a good half hour, the stranger got up and left. As he exited the club, Talia, a long-time bartender and waitress at *Lion's Den* brought over another drink and set it on the table with a smile and a wink.

I pounded the fourth shot I'd had in thirty minutes and signaled to Talia for another, but at a punch to my shoulder, spinning spun toward the familiar face taking a seat next to me. "Reverend Lewis." I patted him on the back and faced the bar once more. "You come to make me confess my sins?"

"Shit." He shook his head. "I done heard enough mothafuckas sob stories for one night. Like I ain't got enough bullshit goin on in my own damn life."

"You got shit, Rev?"

He smirked. "You ain't been round these parts in a while, my man. How you been?"

"Livin' the good life. How's business?"

He huffed, twisting in the direction of the dancers. "Some shit goin' down on the streets. Had two girls gone missing last week." He leaned in close. "I'm no fucking saint, but I try to take care of these girls best I can. Get their asses off the strip and give 'em someplace safe. Some money. Word is, some gangs been picking 'em up. Promising 'em more than they make here. Ain't nobody seen 'em again."

For a while, drugs had been the big money makers, but selling sex had become the most lucrative source of steady income, without the same risks.

"Good ole' Culling, making the streets safe for e'erabody," Rev added before tipping back his drink. "That's the problem with folks coming up in here, trying to run this place. They still think this's just another shithole they can tear down with expensive cranes and build up some fancy buildings. What's inside remains. Detroit's a mindset." He tapped his temple. "And you can't kill what's in the mind. Nope. Burn it to the ground, and it comes right back. You can't kill it. You can't own it. All you can do, is make it *believe*."

Talia set down the shot, and I slammed it back, squinting as the burn slid down my throat.

"Some hard shit you hittin'. Men who drink whiskey's lookin' to fight." He belted a laugh, shoving a cigarillo into his mouth. "Or maybe that's just cause and effect."

Brushing my thumb across my nose, I sniffed and shook off the aftertaste coating my tongue. "Just lookin' for a good night sleep." I nodded toward the door the cop'd exited through. "Thought you weren't a fan of cops."

Rev sneered and nodded. "DeMarcus? DeMarcus Corley. Grew up with him. Probably the only straight shootin' mothafucka on the police force. Should've been made chief." He snorted then took a swig of his drink. "Got demoted for investigating some cases that pissed off the *appointed* police chief."

That piqued my interest. "Yeah?"

"DeMarcus don't take shit, and he sure as fuck don't

bow down to no threats. He's a good man, that DeMarcus. You ever in trouble? Ask for him. He got a heart a gold. Always willin' to help a brother out. Not like them corrupt mothafuckas always acting like they cool with you, then the second shit comes up, stab you in the back first chance they get. DeMarcus don't play that game."

"He looks out for you, then."

"Yeah, he looks out for me, I look out for him. We got a system, see? That's how it works. Cops and the people need to work together. We ain't perfect, but all of us is on the same team. Some just don't understand. Can't let those shady ass law men come through here, shootin' up the place like it's some kinda warzone in the middle east, know what I'm sayin'?"

I stared into the amber fluid, swirling my drink in the glass. "Yeah, I know."

Rev hiked an elbow up on the back of the chair and slouched in his seat. "Ain't you got a woman yet? Fuck's wrong with you, man? You got them bright blue eyes. Bitches love blue eyes." His laughter bounced off the walls of the mostly empty bar.

Burying my smile in the glass of liquor, I shook my head. "I'm not looking for a woman."

"You gay?"

I kicked back the last of my whiskey and slammed the glass on the bartop. "Nope. Don't have time for a woman."

"Man." He waved a dismissal. "You always got time for

a woman. Who else's gonna keep the bed warm?" Rev tipped his head. "Thought you smoked cigars. Or am I gettin' you mixed up with someone else?"

Yeah. He frequently mistook me for Alec, who also came into the bar on occasion.

"Nah, been known to smoke a blunt on occasion. No cigars, though."

"Ha!" He pointed and smiled. "Knew I liked you."

Rising up from the bar stool, he patted me on the back. "Good to see you. Take care, brother."

"Same to you, Rev."

I signaled another drink.

"Impressive."

The voice arrived from behind, and I twisted to the blonde Big John had saved from being suit-fucked. Her tits popped from the skimpy shirt she wore. Thankfully, she looked older than most of the girls up in the place, otherwise I'd have felt like shit for the sudden rush to my dick.

"I've had my eye on you since you walked up in here. Most of the assholes in this place would've been puking all over the bar by now."

"I heard holding your liquor is one of the seven virtues."

She laughed and swiveled on the stool, giving me a full view of both breasts, hardly hanging on inside her bra. "I wouldn't know anything about bein' virtuous." Her gaze fell to my arm, and, curling her fingers around my bicep, she licked her lips. "You wanna meet me in the back? Tell me more about these virtues?"

"Nah." I lifted my hand, softening the rejection with a half-cocked smile. "I'm all set."

"Listen," she whispered, leaning in. "You look like a nice guy."

"I wouldn't say that."

"I could use some extra cash tonight." Her body moved in tight to mine, fingers massaging my arm as she spoke. "My mom's sick and can't work. I take care of her. S'all on me, ya know?"

Don't do it. Somewhere in my subconscious I heard Alec's voice. A warning.

It wasn't that I had anything against strippers—hell I married one, and the ones looking for cash, most times, weren't looking for relationships. The few times I'd been with a woman for casual sex in the last three years didn't end well, though.

I'll be fine, I mentally battled back.

Of course, Alec'd been there the times I was drugged out, trying to piece together fragments of memory from the night before. Two weeks earlier, I'd brought two girls back to the mansion. What started out as a peep show, watching the two of them eat each other out, had ended with both girls huddled naked at the end of my bed, handcuffed to the post, shivering and scared shitless. I'd no idea what'd happened. Had blacked out halfway through their play.

"How much?"

Her brow lifted. "For you? Twenty bucks."

"And if we fuck?"

Her face lit with a smile. "Momma gets another week of medicine." She jumped up out of her seat, tugging my arm. "C'mon, babe. I can get you off quick."

The bit about her mom was a lie. Most of them conjured manipulative stories like that—ones that shadowed the fact that they probably had a drug addiction. Sex with the woman would be emotionless, though, guiltless. Nothing more than a transaction. Getting needs met. Having a woman strapped to the bed back home could very well incite some urges that I'd rather gouge my fucking eyeballs than act on. Might've been a good idea to fuck them right out of my system.

She led me to the back, where shelves stood stacked with boxes, cleaning supplies sat on the floor off to the side, and the lone dim light was about one flicker from shorting out. A storage room, from the looks of it.

"Rev lets me use the back." The equivalent of a rotating door for limp dicks falling for the same sorry sob story. She turned to face me, pushing herself against my body and stroking her hands along my shoulders. "So strong," she whispered. "You must look good enough to eat without all these clothes on." When she stroked my face, I flinched away, catching a twitch of her eye. She reached for my hand, pinching the tip of my finger as if to remove my glove.

I curled my hand into a fist to stop her. "They stay on."

"Am I so dirty?"

In truth, I hadn't touched a woman in three years. It was my penance. The price I'd opted to pay for feeding my craving. I wished I hadn't thought about sex as often as I had, that I didn't crave tangling my fist in the woman's hair, having her ride me with reckless abandon. I wished women with curves and big tits like hers didn't incite some primal urge inside of me.

I stroked a gloved finger down her cheek. She was a pretty girl, probably could've gotten into something slightly less dangerous, like modeling or television. With her porcelain skin and ruby lips, she reminded me of Scarlett Johannsen, or something; one of those classic beauties that belonged in some kind of noir film. "I wouldn't know. Are you a dirty girl?"

The flirtation put a smile back on her face. "You have no idea." Pushing up, she closed her eyes and gripped my nape, drawing me to her lips.

I turned my head to the side, resisting the pull.

I didn't kiss, either.

"Not one for much affection. I get it." Her jaw shifted, as she lowered herself from my face, and her hand slipped down the front of me, tugging with some haste as she unbuttoned my jeans. "You're about the sexiest thing I've seen in my whole life."

She reached down inside my briefs and her eyes widened when she grabbed my already-stiffened dick. After a couple of strokes that had my muscles tightening, she yanked down my pants and fell to her knees in front of me, like a sinner looking for forgiveness.

"Sweet Jesus, you've got a beautiful cock." One long lick up my shaft had my face pinching with the urge to slam myself into the back of her throat. She spat on her hand and grabbed hold, like a fucking pro, twisting up and down as she pumped me while her tongue swirled over the head.

My knees damn near buckled, and I braced a hand on the wall.

Two of her fingers dipped into her mouth before slipping between her thighs, where she shamelessly fingered her pussy, while jacking me off.

That was how it had to be for me to come. A dirty storage room that stank of mold and garbage, in the dim lights, with an eager hooker. Couldn't get hard any other way.

"I can't wait to have you inside of me. And just so there's no confusion, I love taking it in the ass."

Her words punched my skull, and I stiffened.

"You love this dick in your asshole, don't you, dirty little cunt?"

Lena screams into the mattress, while the masked man fucks her from behind.

"Richie, get my gun. Let's see if this bitch likes it from both ends."

Pain exploded inside my skull, swarming my mind with an inky blackness that I couldn't see past. Red splotches dripped into the black, like blood in water, and the cramping of my muscles subsided as the scene slowly sharpened into view through the oily red.

I had the blonde pinned by her throat against the wall. Mascara had smeared down her cheeks as if she'd been crying. Her body trembled in my grasp, and I released her, eyes scanning her for any blood or signs of attack.

She sniffled, rubbing her neck.

"Did I hurt you?"

She shook her head. "No."

I looked down to see my pants pulled up and fastened. The painful hard-on that'd bulged inside my briefs only moments before had gone slack.

I'd no idea what the fuck just happened.

Pulling my wallet, I removed three hundred dollars and placed them into the palm of her hand. "I'm ... sorry."

For what? I didn't even know. I didn't even want to know, because then the encounter would turn into the one thing I'd wanted to avoid—guilt. It couldn't have happened for long, and she didn't have any marks that indicated I'd put her through physical pain, aside from pinning her. Those tears, though. Tears told a story, and hers told me I'd said or done something despicable enough to smear her once-flawless face.

That was me. Mister fucking despicable.

Her lip quivered, and she looked away, nodding her head. "I promise ... to do as you said. I won't come back here."

Seriously, what the fuck did I say?

With some effort, I tried not to give away the barrelful of loose puzzle pieces swimming inside my head right then. I rushed toward the exit that opened up to the alley beside the bar. It was better that way, anyway. Shit seemed to get crazy the moment I whipped out my dick, like unleashing the goddamn Kraken every time I unzipped my pants.

Only one thing could wipe the last twenty minutes— more liquor and a bullet.

CHAPTER 9
Aubree

I clamped my eyes shut, for fear that opening them would have me seeing what I couldn't possibly fathom. The possibility that I'd gone from one shitty situation to another, just like that. Red bubbles floated behind my lids, and I cracked my eye open to a blurry darkness. A horrible taste flooded my mouth, metallic, reminding me of gasoline, and I swallowed it down to keep from tripping the vomit gates.

My throat was dry, my mouth like it'd been stuffed with cotton. I couldn't work enough saliva to coat the burn, and my voice wouldn't push past the dryness. I tried to remember anything from the evening, and the last visual I had was of putting on lipstick before the world faded to black.

The room expanded and shrank before my eyes. I could hardly take in what the hell I was looking at, and a steady thump beat inside my ears and sinuses, interrupting every observation. A window, covered in black drapes.

Thump. A door that must've been a closet. Thump. Walls that crawled with peeling paint and branching cracks. Thump.

I closed and opened my eyes until the room sharpened, though only slightly, the edges shrinking back into a wide but clearer view. Could've been five minutes or hours later.

I had no concept of time.

Resistance fought against my wrists when I attempted to move my limbs. I glanced up at the leather restraints binding my arms, and the chain that tethered them to the bed.

What the …

Pressure pulled at my chest, and I realized I hadn't taken a breath. In and out, I slowly sucked in the stagnant air, trying to make sense of what'd happened. Why was I there? *Where* was there? Who had taken me?

Images danced in and out of my head. *The party. Masks. Michael's stern grip on my thigh. Lipstick. Blackness.*

Panic shot through my veins, horror swimming in my blood, as realization settled over me, and my arms quaked, rattling my restraints, while tingles diffused beneath my skin.

I'd been taken. Kidnapped. By whom, I didn't know. And from the looks of my surroundings, it was someone who was all too content with ditching me in the middle of nowhere.

Michael's words surfaced.

And when you're on the brink of death, I'll dump you in

some cold and abandoned shithole, where you'll drown in your own blood before the rats can eat you to bone.

Oh, God. Was I dead already? I lifted my head off the bed, frantically searching for signs of torture, abuse. Perhaps I'd gone numb. Maybe the drug hadn't worn off and I was seeing myself through a dream or hallucination. Maybe the killer stood beside me, while I lay there comatose and numb from shock, mutilating my body.

Maybe he'd been hired by Michael to carry out the job of killing me. For what, though? My husband had made a few attempts to kill me over the years but never seemed to have the balls to carry through. Perhaps he'd found someone willing to do the job for him.

Or worse. Michael had made so many enemies over the years, perhaps I'd unwittingly fallen into the lap of one of them.

Warmth bloomed in my veins at the thought, a sensation that had no place where I was concerned. "Not now. Please not now." I wanted to stay in a state of terror, because that kept me sharp, alert. Kept me from doing something stupid. But hope. Goddamn hope. It spread through my body like a beam of sunlight at a Goth party. Unwelcome, but undeniably pleasant, just the same.

Whether my circumstances had gotten better or worse was yet to be seen, but maybe I'd *won.* Michael swore I'd never escape him, unless I was being carried out in a body bag, and there I was, chained and possibly facing a whole new slew of torture, but free from my sadistic husband.

The question was, who was my captor? Had I seen

him?

Think, Aubree. Goddamn it. Through a murky haze, I heard the faint sound of a voice, mumbled conversation, jumbled inside my head, like a TV playing behind a black screen. A memory.

Achilleus X wouldn't spare a minute on you.

Not Achilleus. I'd hoped his threat to Michael had somehow made me the object of his next attack. It hadn't. My fantasies of being set free by the mysterious masked man had been nothing but illusion, it seemed.

Not that I knew I'd be any safer with the infamous hacker, but at least he wasn't known for *hacking up* women and burying them riverside. Then again, neither was Michael, and yet, I suspected otherwise.

I had no idea who my captor was, what the hell he wanted, or worse, what the hell he planned to do with me.

If Michael'd hired him, I'd definitely need to find an escape, because no way in hell a hit man, hired by my political figure husband, would ever let me live. I'd need to get him to undo the binds, somehow. I'd come up with a good reason.

Somehow.

I should've been more frightened than I was, but getting handed off by psychopaths was a lot like a foster kid getting passed around, or playing a really messed up lottery, where the newbie might be less fucked up than the last guy.

I'd already been through hell and back and survived.

The charity ball should've been my chance for escape,

with all the important guests that could've kept Michael distracted. I could've kicked myself for failing, for falling into another complication. Another house of horror that I'd have to navigate for an escape door.

The guy could've been some insane, leather-faced serial killer who collected the skin of his victims, but I was married to the mayor of Detroit, and no one trumped *that* asshole when it came to crazy.

In a fit, I tugged all four binds at once and screamed in frustration. "Hey! Hello?"

Silence.

I blew an exasperated breath. "Are you shitting me?" Tendrils of fear climbed my spine, as the questions swirling inside my head narrowed to one singular thought: *what if he doesn't come back at all?*

CHAPTER 10
Nick

"Daddy?" In the black void, the voice whispers, and a slight shake wakes me. "Daddy, wake up."

I open my eyes to bright, almost blinding light. I feel as if I've fallen onto a blank page, and smack in the middle is my son, James, holding his ragged rabbit, Mister Tims. "Jay?" The urge to scoop him up into my arms burns in my muscles as I run toward him, but my body is heavy, weighed down by gravity, and he remains out of my reach. I stand still, arms outstretched, and smile. "Come here, Jay. Come see me."

His eyes study me from afar. Dubiously. Cautiously. "Did you do something bad, daddy? To that man?"

I bow my head, thinking of Marquise and the needle I'd stabbed in his throat. Only my son could incite the shame I'm suddenly feeling. "He hurt you and mommy, Jay. I had to hurt him. So he wouldn't hurt anyone else again." I frown when it occurs to me that one small detail is missing from all of this. "How did you know I hurt him?"

Jay tips his head and gives me a sidelong glance as he toys with a string hanging from Mister Tims. "Alec told me."

"Alec?" Anger stirs in my stomach, completely overshadowing the big question—how did he discuss anything with Alec?

"I have to go, Daddy."

"Jay! Wait!" I reach out for him, but I'm too far away to touch him. "Where? Where are you going? Let me come with you. Please." Tears form in my eyes. "Show me where to find you and mommy."

A smile stretches across his face. "That's cheating. You have to wake up." His voice morphs into the deep timbre of a man. He curls his lip and kicks me in the shin. "Wake up."

My lids flipped open, blinking hard as blazing sunlight streamed through my opened bedroom drapes and damn near fried my eyeballs. An obscure figure stood leaning against the doorframe, arms crossed, the smoky flavor of his cigar hitting my tongue at the same time a plume of smoke drifted upward from his mouth. I lowered my gaze to the surrounding floor, where I'd apparently spent the night with my boots on. "Fucking whiskey." A film of sweat coated my skin when I rubbed a hand down my face. "Does it to me every time."

"Fun night?" A sobering disappointment drifted on Alec's words.

I scratched the back of my head. "Your girlfriend's in the other room. D'you say hi?"

"Peeked inside. Sleeping like a baby." He blew another cloud of smoke. "I forgot to congratulate you on your first kill the other night. Potassium chloride. Nice finale."

"Thought you'd like that." I rose to the edge of the bed and swiped up a bottle from the nightstand, sucking down the last of the whiskey, before holding it up like a toast to Alec's stoic face. "Hair of the dog …"

"Speaking of which, perhaps you can train your mutt not to rub against my fucking two thousand dollar Armani suit."

"Courtesy of the good folks at DigiCoin International."

About six months earlier, Alec had hacked into DigiCoin, the world's leading digital currency exchange site, stole eleven million dollars that'd been carelessly stored in a hot wallet, and transferred the cash to offshore bank accounts. Completely untraceable. In the deep net, the exchange site was famously associated with some of the most sickening kiddie porn sites in existence. After hacking DigiCoin, Alec had proceeded to shut down a half dozen affiliated sites featuring children for sale.

"I think you'll agree, this is money well-spent, my friend," he said.

"I'm waiting for you to support a third world country somewhere and dispel any myths I may have developed, that you're a selfish prick."

"Why deny the truth?" The cigar hung from his clenched teeth as he grinned around it. "Thought I'd find you in bed with her. Which can only mean you went out trolling for prostitutes last night."

"Cap it. I never agreed to go celibate in this shit."

"Killing prostitutes in public places is not the best way to keep the authorities on the right trail."

"I never killed them," I said, pointing a finger. It was true. I never once killed the girls, though what happened in those moments of blackness, I honestly couldn't say.

"Yet." He tipped his head. "So, you innocently *fucked* a woman, and the two of you parted ways, all sated and happy with the world?"

I rubbed my hand across my skull. "I never hurt her."

"I've seen you, Nick. The blackouts. Gaps of memory you can't account for. The violence in your eyes. You're about a thread from losing control." He rolled his shoulders. "Are a few strokes to your dick worth fucking up the plan before it's begun?"

"I won't fuck it up! Trust me."

"Trust is all I've got, Brother. And if you fuck *that* up, I'll be running this show alone. I don't think either one of us wants that." Gaze fixed on me, he toyed with a cufflink and straightened the shirt beneath his jacket. "You got everything you need for tonight?"

"Yeah. All set."

"Staked the place?"

"Yeah."

"Good. Don't do anything stupid." His gray eyes drilled into mine, full of all kinds of serious that I just didn't have the fucking brainpower to appreciate through a monster hangover. "It's important that you keep yourself alive." He smirked then cocked his head toward Aubree's door. "Speaking of staying alive, she's probably starving. Try not to subject her to your eating schedule. And give the girl a bathroom break, for fucks sake."

CHAPTER 11
Aubree

Heat hit my face, and I was suddenly aware of a grotesque numbness in my hands. I opened my eyes to a room, lit only by the streaks of sunlight fighting their way past the god-awful paisley drapes. An upward glance spurred both nausea and relief at the sight of my hands chained to the bedpost—at least what I felt wasn't phantom limb from being hacked alive by a madman, but I was still bound to a bed in a room that looked like it'd jumped out of an Edgar Allen Poe Home and Gardening magazine. Dark gray walls and dark wood—aged-looking furniture—coupled with the peeling paint and cobwebs gave off a Halloween vibe.

The warm scent of a cigar filled my nose, notes of cedar over the delicious flavor of musk. Had my mouth not been bone dry, it might've watered at the scent.

Pumping my fingers did nothing to abate the numbness, and while I felt glad they moved at all, the dead sensation made my stomach queasy. Squirming definitely wasn't helping, but being able to move at all told me I wasn't completely paralyzed.

In one last futile attempt to break the chains, I kicked and screamed like a madwoman. The squeak and thump of the bed beat out the rhythm of my tantrum, until at last, my muscles sagged in defeat.

"Numb?" The deep, rich voice snapped my gaze to the dark figure across the room, propped against the wall with his arms crossed.

A zap of panic shot through my body, but crackled in my hot blood like ice cubes melting in boiling water. "Do you earn bonus points if I *feel* dead before you actually kill me?"

"I could untie you." Inflection gave his words an air of taunting.

Between his calm tone and casual posture, I didn't immediately peg him as a killer. "But that would make you a decent human being when clearly you're an—" *Asshole.*

Easy now. No sense pissing off the guy who kidnapped you and chained you to a bed.

Getting unchained was one step closer to getting the fuck out of there.

"A what?" He pushed himself off the wall, and the first features to come into view were his eyes—a striking cut of blue diamonds that sliced me open with his intense stare. Evocative, distracting eyes that didn't belong on the face of a kidnapper.

Not that I'd thought about kidnappers much, I

certainly didn't fantasize about them, but I'd imagined them with coal-black, almost demonic eyes—like Michael's. This man's powerful glare and calm vibe told me, without a doubt, he could probably slice me open while softly chanting a dirge like an angel.

The hood of his black leather jacket concealed his hair, but the white wife beater he wore beneath provided an eyeful of muscles. Deep ridges that looked like they'd been hand carved peeked over the top and disappeared behind the shirt where the outline of his pectorals and nipples punched through the fabric. The bronze tone of his skin left me wondering if he worked outside. Maybe a construction worker?

I glanced down to see if he sported any calluses on his hands, but black leather gloves covered them. People generally wore gloves indoors to hide fingerprints. While committing crimes.

His face was flawlessly chiseled and symmetrical, those eyes set beneath dark, broody eyebrows. The smirky shape of his lips, smooth and perfectly proportioned, left me resisting the urge to bite my own.

"My husband has connections. He'll find you. And he'll have you killed if he doesn't do it himself." It sickened me to give Michael's power any merit, but perhaps mention of the asshole might lead me to what this guy wanted with me.

Those eyes, as beautiful as they were, held a terrifying emptiness—a complete lack of empathy as he stared back with an evil glint, silently warning me that I'd said something stupid. "I'm not afraid of your husband."

I should've been scared. Why wasn't I scared?

Maybe I just couldn't feel fear anymore. Perhaps I'd stared into the depths of the devil's eyes for too many years. I knew the sting of a whip, the burn of a blade, and the uncertainty that I'd live beyond the next hour. I lived in a constant state of defense, and had taken enough punches in the dark that my body's reflexes were always wired, tense.

The guy wore an air of calm over the sizzling power that rolled off him in waves. His handsome features didn't match the faces of serial killers running through my head. Bundy. Gacy.

Don't be stupid, Aubree.

In my defense, his black hood and dark, enigmatic personality were reminiscent of Achilleus X—the man, or woman, I'd fantasized about for months.

The beauty I'd extrapolated from the stranger's face both confounded and pissed me off, that I'd notice it in the thick of a nightmare, like Red admiring the Big Bad Wolf's lovely teeth. The man staring back at me was a stranger in the literal sense—the kind mothers warned their children to stay away from at an early age. The kind that swiped young women and turned them into terrifying statistics found on crime television shows and forensic classes. He was also what the weird chicks probably fantasized about in their twisted rape fantasies, with his dark hoodie and deep voice—a far cry from the chubby, middle-aged guys with bad comb-overs and messed up teeth, who always played the perverted kidnapper in movies. Though, maybe he stole me *for* a chubby middle-aged guy with a bad comb-over, and he just happened to be the pretty precursor, meant to keep me calm, before I really lost my shit.

Still, I couldn't look away from those eyes, as much as every cell in my body screamed *retreat!* I'd seen them before. Behind a mask. "You … you were at the …" Realization hit me with a double dose of *fuck me* and a sudden case of indigestion. "I have to use the bathroom. Or would you prefer I go right here?"

He silently stared at me, his left eye twitching. I could only guess he might be fantasizing what it'd feel like to strangle me. As if confirming my thoughts, he smoothed his hands over his black leather gloves as though making sure they were nice and tight so they wouldn't bunch while his palms throttled my neck.

Something pulled at my body—an odd sensation that I wanted to push down and smother with good sense, but I couldn't. I hated what his unwavering stare had drudged from some primitive, animalistic part of my brain, and I was ashamed to admit that, for a kidnapper, he was gorgeous—a gorgeous *bastard* who'd tied me to a bed all night, while he skipped off to what I imagined was some kidnapper bar somewhere, getting drunk and bragging to all his kidnapper buddies.

I cleared my throat and shifted on the bed, my fingers turning to sausages while I waited.

After an eternity, he leaned forward and started

unshackling my ankles. My toes curled at the cold leather of his gloves against my skin.

"Any chance you could start with my hands? It's that … gravity thing, you know?"

The narrowing of his eyes alongside the slight twist of his lip said *shut the fuck up, I'm not here to make you comfortable*, but he went to work on my right hand, anyway. Even with his GQ face and pretty eyes, the guy radiated fiery waves of hostility like a swarm of sharks beneath a placid surface.

A line of tension ran down my spine as I watched while his black-leathered fingers unfastened the cuffs, anxious for the damage, the stomach-twisting sensation of dead weight. At once, my wrist was free, and my arm dropped.

Pins and needles, pins and needles. Ah, shit.

I shook out my wrist, pumping, pumping, pumping my fingers. Like trying to control a dead body. If the movies depicted their gaits right, the walking dead should've been less concerned with scouring for brains and more focused on getting the goddamn tingles to stop in that leg always dragging behind them and slowing them down. My hand pulsed with a heartbeat again by the time he loosened the other binds, and I was battling tingles in both, feeling like the green monster from *Yo Gabba Gabba*.

"Perhaps next time you might consider a more ergonomically correct kidnapping by installing retractable chains in the wall, instead of tethering to the bedpost." My comment was met by an unamused stare. "Just a suggestion." With a lingering thickness to my limbs, I flapped my arms one more time and rose up on the opposite side of the bed to where he stood.

He was huge, maybe six four or five, and if those muscles and ridges behind his shirt were any indication, he was probably pretty ripped, too. A fighter, if I had to guess. My best chance for escape would likely be outsmarting him.

"I don't know what you're scheming, lady. But if you think you can get past me, you're about two seconds from getting slapped down by reality." He had the accent of a man who'd grown up in Detroit. Hard to pick up on the night before, but clear as day, the more I listened to him talk—his clipping of hard consonants and slurring words. He probably needed money, which meant money might be a negotiating factor.

As if he could read my mind, he nabbed my purse from the nightstand, rifled through it contents, tossed it on the bed, and held up the chip I'd swiped from Michael's office. Perhaps he'd been paid to retrieve it. "I'll be keeping this." He stuffed it in his pocket, and crossed his arms like a bully on the playground after stealing lunch money.

Nice going, Aubree. Probably could've used it as a bargaining chip. Note to self: stuff important shit down the bra, not inside the purse. I didn't even know what was on it, but considering Michael and his Pentagon-secured office, any object holding information was probably important.

The stranger lifted a gloved hand, ushering me toward what I was certain was something else, entirely. My head snapped between him and the door. "I ... isn't that a closet?"

"Was."

My heart sank at the revelation, and with reluctant steps, I inched toward the door I'd been convinced had to be a closet. What the hell kind of bedroom didn't have a closet, after all?

I opened the door to find one of the *do-it-yourself* variety bathrooms, complete with a plywood floor and a pedestal sink. No mirror. The rack that extended to the back of the small room stood empty and useless. No window. No vent. And no possible chance for escape. I'd been certain the only place I'd be relieving myself would be out of my prison room, with a front door in my sights and freedom at my back.

"You look disappointed." The close proximity of his voice tightened my muscles.

"Do you plan to accompany me *into* the bathroom, or something?"

"Do your business. And hurry up."

I stepped inside, closing the door behind me, and, perhaps for the first time since I arrived there, reality began to penetrate my tightly woven cloak of denial. It wasn't a joke. I could very well die in the enclosing shithole with a psychotic Bob Vila wannabe and his mysterious black gloves that were clearly meant to hide fingerprints.

Battling the urge to fall into a heap and bawl my eyes out, I gripped the sink and flipped on the faucet, desperately filling my mouth with cold tap water that damn near sizzled over the dryness. "C'mon, Aubree," I whispered. "Time to make a Plan B. You're not a quitter. You're a survivor. You've survived worse than this." Maybe. Who the hell knew what the rest of the house had in store for me? I looked up, staring at the section of wall where a mirror would've been, and was kind of thankful I didn't have to look at myself right then. "You've become good at reading people." I blew out a breath , but a whimper of hopelessness echoed somewhere in the back of mind. I quickly batted it down with my uncanny skill for deceiving the logical side of my brain.

Quick analysis. He was tall, dark and broody. Wore his hood up over his head. Maybe he was hiding something? *Zero sense of humor. I mean, zero.* Could be pissed. At me?

Could be sexual frustration. *No, he's too good-looking.* "But his attitude is shit," I muttered in response to my thoughts.

I buried my face in my hands. Unless the guy was a total *torture-baby-animals* sort of mental case, the best bet would be to try appealing to his empathetic side. Did hitmen feel guilt? Was killer's remorse such a thing?

If that didn't work, there'd be only one thing left to try.

Seduce the bastard. *You've done it before and survived. You can do it again.*

I'd been held captive by the apex predator, in the

messed up jungle of dysfunction, and had gotten out. Not entirely *free*, but out. The guy on the other side of the door was nothing more than a temporary roadblock on my path to freedom. A peon, probably hired by the head *Tyrant*osaurus himself, my husband.

A quick sweep of the small room showed nothing that I could use as a weapon. The guy had stripped it down to the barest essentials, going so far as to remove the mirror that could've been cracked into jagged pieces for stabbing. *Shit.*

At two knocks on the door, I jumped back, nearly falling on my ass. "Just a sec!" I quickly hiked my dress, relieved myself, and scooped two more handfuls of water into my mouth.

When I exited, he was standing beside the door, arms crossed, practically *growling* as I snuck past him to the other side of the bed.

"Were you hired by my husband?" I asked.

His jaw shifted, as though he chewed on the question for a moment, before he spat back, "If I'd been hired to *kill* you, you'd already be dead."

True, and shame on me as the *kidnappee* for not having come up with that brilliant deduction myself.

"But that doesn't mean I don't intend to kill you ... eventually."

I'd heard that phrase before. Many times before. The delay resided in thinking smart and staying one step ahead in the game. After all, my father once told me the world was a hunting ground, and the only way to identify the predators was to set a bait pile.

Just as I'd learned to do on cue, I summoned tears in my eyes and fell to a sitting position at the edge of the bed. "Please. I don't ... I don't know if you have a family or ... someone you *care* about. If you do, then ... you know how devastating it would be to lose them."

I glanced back, expecting to find apathy at my pathetic ad-libbed performance. Instead, he looked furious, as if he might just tear my throat out and eat it in front of me.

A tremble beat through my body as I slowly rose from the bed.

Prepare to run.

CHAPTER 12
Nick

With nothing more than a bed between my hands and her throat, I stared at Aubree Culling in her flashy, expensive dress and three carat diamond ring, and tried to process her spewed bullshit about losing a loved one, as if she had any concept of giving a fuck about anything more than herself.

The rational side of my brain tried to convince me that she didn't know a single thing about my past, didn't know who I was, so how could she possibly be taunting me?

The irrational side urged me to use her comment as an excuse to cross her off the list. Maybe she did know. Maybe she and her husband sat in their hot tub, drinking champagne, toasting every life they'd stolen for their own personal greed. Maybe the two of them fucked to crime scene photos and the steady drip of coin in their wallets— their own personal pornography for the rich and remorseless.

"On the bed. Now." The words pushed through my

clenched teeth while a round of gunfire sat cocked at the back of my throat. Should she say one fucking word.

One word.

Her neck bobbed with a swallow, and she slid onto the bed.

Yeah, I knew all about losing loved ones. I'd lived the shit every day for three years, but I wasn't about to fall victim to her manipulation. Even I could see she'd become a master of two faces—the bright white smile for the camera concealing the forked tongue of a serpent.

Standing beside the bed, I bent over her, placing a hand firmly at either side of her head. Below me, she seemed to press her head back into the mattress, as if to get away. I'd have laughed, except that her knee smashed my groin and her head collided with my nose.

Jolts of electricity raced to my nuts and I cupped my nose with one hand. "Fuck!" Ignoring the pain, I smacked aside her flailing arms and random kicks to my side and nabbed both of her wrists, pinning them hard against the bed.

"Fucking let me go!" She writhed beneath me, her knee pounding into my side.

Holding both wrists captive with my right hand, I pushed her assaulting thigh flat, climbed onto the bed, and straddled her body, crazed with the desire to knock her out. Beneath me, she bucked and arched with more strength than I'd given her credit for, until I pressed into her, my forehead pushing against hers, and at last, she stilled.

With heaving breaths, I stared into her eyes, teeth grinding, breaths mingling. It was in that moment I became aware of the way her breast had popped from her dress in the struggle and pressed against my chest. The salty taste of blood coated my tongue as it trickled into my mouth. Lifting my head away from hers, I lowered my gaze to the perfectly rounded globe, set pert with her arms stretched above her head. I licked my lips and swallowed hard, taunted by her bare skin so close to my mouth.

She made a pathetic attempt to nudge me. "Don't you fucking dare," she growled, and I came to my senses.

"Don't worry, sweetheart. You don't do anything for me." I slipped her dress back over her breast and, still pinning her wrists, pushed off of her. "You want to live? Do exactly as I tell you. No fucking around."

Eyes wide, she trembled, nostrils flaring with rapid breaths, as if she expected me to inflict pain. The sight of her fear cast a ripple of adrenaline through my body, warming my muscles.

I tipped my head, leaned over her, inwardly laughing at the twitch of her eye. "Are you afraid of me, Aubree?"

Her answering snarl kicked my lips into a grin. The woman put on a good front, I'd give her that.

"You should be." Tugging her arm toward the headboard, I froze. One long scar stretched vertically down her forearm, the edges irregular, crooked. Across her wrist was a tattoo that, by the words, suggested the death of someone close to her. I hadn't noticed it the night before, when I'd tied her the first time. Didn't take a genius to recognize a suicide attempt.

My gaze shot to hers, and she narrowed her eyes, chin inclined in defiance like she had no intentions of explaining.

What did I care if she'd tried to kill herself? Except, the longer I stared, the more she seemed to get increasingly uncomfortable with the display, turning her head away from me.

"What's this?"

Her head snapped back in my direction. "What? Not as perfect when you peel the layers back?"

Evidently, she had something deeper going on, but I had neither the ambition, nor the interest, to give a shit. Aubree served a single purpose—revenge. So what that some fragment in her past didn't match the perfection of her present life?

"Everyone has scars. What makes yours special?"

"I never said they were special. In fact, they're my daily reminder that nothing is as special as people choose to believe."

All the alarms inside my head screamed at once—abort fucking mission. I didn't need Aubree Culling snaking her way beneath my skin, the way she had with the question about her husband hiring me to kill her, and then the scar, but something darker, deeper whispered below the noise in my head.

I quickly tied her hands to the bed, ignoring that nagging thought, but still, it persisted. Perhaps I'd missed something. All those hours logged, watching the Cullings, studying them day in and day out for over a year.

Maybe Aubree Culling wasn't who I'd thought she was.

Get the fuck out.

I hauled ass out of that room. Wouldn't let her shit infect me. She was the smiling face behind *The Culling* propaganda. The gentrification of inner city trash, and the driving force behind the brutal deaths of my wife and son.

A faithful, loving Stepford wife who served her husband's every morally corrupt whim. Scarred or not, she remained the enemy, for the same reason every soldier under Hitler's rule deserved to go down with the bastard dictator—they believed in the lies.

Alec and I had plotted for too long, to let some manipulative piece of work destroy it with her fake tears and pleas for sympathy. I'd lost the ability to sympathize long ago.

Still seething, I made my way to the kitchen and braced my hands on the countertop. *Reel it in.* A part of me'd never subscribed to the part of the plan that included kidnapping her. I had a feeling that spending too much time with Aubree was a bad idea. Didn't help that she was a natural beauty, with her long chestnut hair, honey-toned skin, golden eyes, and that dimple in her cheek that gave her a sort of playful, youthful appearance—something the cameras and news reports hadn't fully captured.

Throwing back the cupboard door, I nabbed the bottle of tequila, popped the cap, and tipped it back. After taking a long swill, I slammed the bottle onto the countertop and shook off the burn in my throat. From beside the sink, I grabbed a rag, flipped on the faucet, and soaked the corner of it before holding it to my nose, daubing away the drying blood where she'd gotten in a good punch.

"You play a nice game of bullshit, Mrs. Culling, but you're not going to bullshit me." Pinching the rag to my nose, I squeezed the remaining blood and, sniffing, I swiped up the bottle and tossed back another swig. I set the bottle down, glanced over in the direction of the staircase. *S'pose I should feed her something*. Much as I'd have liked to starve her, Alec would probably go apeshit.

It'd been a long time since I'd cooked a meal for a woman, though, and I had no idea what the hell they ate.

In a palette of color, I arranged cut strawberries, eggs, salsa, avocado, toast and sausage on a plate. All things Alec claimed he'd observed watching her eat. Back upstairs, I reentered her room, grabbing the chair propped against the wall on my way, and took a seat beside her.

The tracking of her eyeball from the corner of her eye had me inwardly chuckling. Only the liquor kept me cordial. With the fork, I stabbed a strawberry and placed it to her lips.

She snapped her head away from me. "I'm not hungry."

"I didn't ask you if you were hungry. Eat."

"Fuck you," she spat back.

My tongue raked across my teeth as my grin widened at her pathetic act of rebellion. "You'd love that, wouldn't you?"

She cut her gaze back to me, chin inclined again, and I knew something feisty was itching to fly from her mouth. "I'd rather walk a mile with a cucumber up my ass than fuck you."

"I can arrange that." Hell, I'd have paid to see that shit. "You're something else, Pistol Lips."

Her eye twitched. "What did you call me?"

"Pistol lips."

"What the hell does that mean?"

"Firing off at the mouth. Seems to be your signature trait. Should've grabbed a muzzle instead of the chains."

"I—"

As soon as her mouth opened, I shoved the strawberry inside.

Nostrils flared, she chewed and swallowed. "You're—" Another word, another strawberry slipped past her lips, and she growled, lifting her head up off the pillow, chewing all pissed off and gnashing her teeth.

The strawberry juice trickling out the corner of her mouth damn near broke me, had me choking back laughter, like I'd gotten a glimpse of some kind of rabid animal inside of her, ready to tear me apart. "Got something else to say?" I held up a forkful of eggs.

The corner of her lips lifted, eyes shooting daggers, and she nodded. "You're a fucking d—"

In went the eggs.

She remained silent while I fed her the remaining plate full of food, until the last bite, when she looked up. "Why me? Why am I here?"

I'd expected the question—was surprised she hadn't asked it sooner. Didn't mean I planned to answer her. "Open your mouth."

The groove of her brow deepened for only a moment before her eyes softened to sadness, and she opened her mouth wide, closing her lids. The sight was incredibly erotic, particularly when the tip of her tongue slid out ready to accept the last strawberry.

Mesmerized, I set it on her tongue, silently chiding myself for the hard-on pressing against my jeans. *What kind of sadistic bastard …* The kind of arousal I felt for her had nothing to do with feelings, or any level of attraction to the woman. I wanted the opportunity to take from Aubree Culling—something that would cut her as deep as I'd been cut. A hate fuck, where I'd leave her in pain and sobbing, drowning in her own self-loathing, the way I had that first year, before Alec had approached me with the idea of revenge.

I wanted her to feel small, vulnerable, *weak*.

She opened her eyes, and only then did I notice the way my hand trembled in front of her. I quickly lowered the fork and shot up from the chair.

I might've been a killer. A ruthless son of a bitch, but I wasn't a rapist. To keep from doing something stupid, I had to get away from her.

"I want to see it," she blurted.

"See what?" I couldn't hide the disgust in my voice, knowing she'd caught sight of my momentary weakness.

"Your scar. Earlier, you said, *we all have scars.*" She

lowered her head back onto the pillow. "Let's see yours."

The woman thought she'd softened me.

"Fuck off," I said, walking out the door.

CHAPTER 13
Nick

Aside from bringing her a plate full of lunch, I managed to keep my distance from Aubree for most of the day, locking myself away in my room, surfing the deep 'net. Nothing quite fucked up the day like a dose of the darkest bowels of web, and I'd hit the jackpot when I stumbled upon the Blue Orchid site, a copycat of the original child pornography site that'd been busted by the authorities a few years back. Only an idiot would assume the name of a high profile case, but then again, folk could get away with shit like that on the deep 'net.

It was there that I found my next victim via a naked twelve-year-old girl named Sapphire, presumably for her blue eyes.

The chip that I'd stolen from Aubree turned out to be a bonus as well, which had me questioning why it'd been given to her. On it, blue prints and contracts, approved by the city council president, for residential development of Brightmoor were listed alongside contact information for some of the city's most notorious criminals, including Angelo Donati, Capo of the Donati crime family. It seemed Brightmoor would be leveled out and some fancy condos built around a shopping complex. Only problem? Lot of old timers still called the shithole their home—some who'd been there for years and couldn't afford to just up and move.

It seemed I'd stumbled upon the plan for Devil's Night. Giving me more reason to be suspicious of the woman. Why would Culling entrust her with such vital information? Information I didn't suspect would be anywhere but that chip—portable enough to be tossed, if necessary.

In my room, I performed my usual weapons check: two Glocks strapped across my chest, dagger in my boot, hunting knife with a gut hook sheathed at my hip. After tucking the mask inside the pocket of my jeans, I made my way back to Aubree's room and set dinner down on a chair.

Her eyes roved me up and down. "Heading out?"

Ignoring her question, I unchained her arms and legs, watching with pointed interest as her eyes turned quizzical.

"You're leaving me untied?"

"Yeah." I glanced back at the plate of chicken, rice and vegetables. No fork or any utensils, meaning, she'd have to eat with her hands. "I don't have time to feed you."

With widened eyes, she stared up at me. "Fun night planned, huh?"

Twisting on my heel, I headed for the door. "You

could say that."

Upon exiting the room, I locked it and whistled for Blue, who obediently trotted up the stairs. Without a word, he sat beside the door, and smirking, I squatted in front of him. "Don't let her go anywhere. Got it?" A lick of his tongue across my cheek affirmed his understanding, and I pushed up from him, wiping the dog slime from my skin.

On my way down the stairs, I checked my texts. I'd sent the first about two hours earlier, requesting an hour with Sapphire.

I'd received a response: 'three hundred, anything I wanted'.

Vomit gurgled in my throat. Fucking twelve years old. It used to be drugs that ruled the streets, but with the DEA making so many busts, a lot of criminals had turned to sex trafficking. Unlike the one-time sale of crack cocaine, they could turn profits all night long on one girl alone. A gang-bang meant triple or quadruple the sales.

I stared down at the address lit up on my phone—a by-the-hour flophouse, where prostitution and drugs were known to be rampant, on the shit side of Cass Corridor. Sometimes, the rooms were rented out for months at a time.

"Be there in twenty," I said aloud as I texted back, then hopped into Shelby, my beloved '67 fully-restored black Mustang, and took off in the direction of The Pantheon motel.

The motherfuckers had no idea what kind of storm was about to hit.

***

I arrived within a half hour and parked my car in the small lot on the side of the building, wedged between two fire-gutted shitholes. From beside me, I lifted the files for Rick 'Grim Reaper' Harris, his brother, Jonathan 'Pyro' Harris, their shared girlfriend, Theresa Cruz, the recruiter for the trafficking ring, and Julius 'Casanova' Malone, whose brother ran the Seven Mile Crew. The texts I'd received had come from Rick, Jonathan's older brother.

As the Crew had become more renowned, operations had expanded, branched out into different avenues—prostitution, arms dealing, contract killing. For whatever reason, those four stooges had decided to stick together, which worked just fine for me. That'd be four more cocksuckers in the bag.

A surge of adrenaline spiked my veins, the way it did before every kill. There'd be no mercy. The three men were responsible for not only the rape and sodomy of girls and boys as young as ten, but they also partook in the acts, filmed it, tortured and ultimately mutilated the ones who ended up diseased or pregnant. The resulting babies were sold on the black market, and a percent of profits fattened Michael Culling's pockets, so long as he remained quiet and stayed out of their business.

I fitted the mask over my head and tugged my hoodie over it, exited the car, and strolled up to the front of the three level motel. Graffiti coated the chipped brick, and some of the windows had been painted black. Gave off an ominous warning that some bad shit went down behind those windows—the kind of place that'd make a parent clutch a child's hand just walking past. Three-three-five was at the top level and one of the bigger rooms in the joint—perhaps two rooms put together. I climbed the stairs to the top floor in less than a minute and knocked on the door.

Only a few seconds passed before a skinny white male I recognized from the files as Jonathan 'Pyro' stood in the doorway. Pale and smoking weed, he looked me up and down, twitching my trigger finger. "Nash?"

I'd given him a fake name. I'd also told him that I wanted complete anonymity, so the mask probably came as no surprise. Surely those places were no stranger to fucking weirdoes. The assholes who strolled up in gimp masks.

I nodded in response to his question, and he jerked his head, inviting me inside.

Like walking straight into the mouth of hell, I'd found the lowest depths of human depravity. Two cages lined the wall, inside of each was a young girl sat naked and hunched over her small bruised body. Neither of them could've been more than sixteen, seventeen, and my stomach coiled, a caustic knot of wrath burning inside of me.

Fuck. Keep it together.

I had to know how many of the pathetic cunts were in the place first. Third floor made for a tricky escape, and if there were others in the shithole who were in on the ring,

I'd have at least two girls to get past whatever roadblocks might get in my way—making the body count potentially much higher than I'd anticipated.

On the couch beside the cages, a brunette woman with dark eyes and light brown skin smoked a cigarette in front of TV, like nothing seemed remotely fucked up about any of the situation.

"Sapphire's just finishing up." Jonathan nudged his head toward a closed door in the hallway behind him. "Got the cash?"

I reached into my pocket, pulling out a wad of cash. When he flicked his hand, I caught sight of a tattoo that, with his hand curled in a fist, read 'fist fuck', and a memory drifted through my head, his voice echoing through the fog.

"Your husband ever fist you, baby?" The little prick licks his fist then shudders a breath. "Oh it ain't love if you haven't taken a fist in the ass."

I shook my head, choking back the fury, but I could sense the blackness settling over me, that dark, erratic monster wanting to take control and kill every one of them.

A tortured scream, followed by cries, broke my thoughts, and my head snapped up to the closed door.

Sapphire.

Before he could reach for his own, I pulled my Glock from inside my coat and propped it under his chin, aimed toward the top of his skull. Had I sneezed, the fucker's brains would've hit the ceiling. I slipped his own gun from the front of his pants, and, as the bitch on the couch slowly rose in my periphery, I used it to blow her feet out from under her. She screamed and fell to the floor, cradling her mutilated ankles.

I'd deal with her soon.

Thumps against the wall and the floor from the other rooms told me the gunshots had roused some alarm.

"How many of you fucks are here?"

Before Jonathan could answer, another male, Julius exited from the bathroom. I shot him in the thigh, screams of agony filling the hallway, as he collapsed to the floor. The objective was to wound them so I could draw out each death in the same agonizing measure that they'd brought to countless victims. Easier said than done, when all I could taste was the copper tang at the back of my throat and the voice inside my head telling me to fill every one of them with lead.

I moved one of the guns to Jonathan's nutsack. "How many?"

"Two. In the bedroom."

Two? Jesus fucking Christ.

The sound of a screaming child had me tapping the trigger of my gun, while rage taunted me to open fire.

Kill them slow, the voice chimed. *Painfully slow.*

I nudged him toward the door, using him as a human shield and kicked it open.

The sight that met my eyes damn near made me drop to my knees.

Black ink spread inside my narrowing field of vision

and the voice chimed again.

Kill them all.

***

I opened my eyes to Julius Malone screaming. His tipped back head had been strapped to a chair, and my palm squeezed his neck. A downward glance showed a bloody strip of flesh dangling from the gut hook of my knife.

The metallic scent of blood mixed with piss hit the back of my throat, and I lifted my gaze, catching sight of the macabre that filled the room. A gruesome display of dead bodies sat propped and posed like horrific sculptures. My attention landed on Jonathan, though, zeroing in on the glistening flesh where his other ear had been sliced away.

Had I done that? I didn't know. Had no idea how much time had passed.

Blacked out again.

Echoes of laughter rang inside my head as voices from the past and the memory of that night resurfaced.

Jonathan holds my son, who screams and kicks trying to get away from him. I spot a fallen knife on the floor in front of me. As I slice off Jonathan's ear, he drops Jay to the floor, and I revel in the sound of the bastard's screams —until the shot of gunfire steels my muscles.

I released Julius's throat, stuffed his mouth with a nearby rag, and walked out of the room, leaving him to sob. In the living room I'd first arrived through, all three young girls sat huddled and shivering in a corner by the cages. Probably scared shitless of me. Aside from the fact that they didn't have clothes, why hadn't they run? Why did they stay? I'd set up the perfect opportunity for escape, and yet, there they sat, trembling in the corner, perhaps waiting to see who won the fight and who would be their new slaver. Had I commanded them to stay there?

I searched the motel room and found a duffel bag filled with women's clothes—bras, panties, jeans, a couple of T-shirts. In another bag were men's clothes and I nabbed three of the sweatshirts packed inside.

Approaching carefully, I watched the young girls hide their faces in each other, and, keeping my distance, I crouched in front of them with the clothes I'd gathered for them held out, and cleared my throat. "I'm not going to hurt you." I nudged my head toward the bedroom door. "They're not going to hurt you, either. Ever."

A wave of sobbing filled the air, and the one called Sapphire finally pulled her face from the others.

I lifted my ski mask to my forehead, revealing my face, and offered her a sweatshirt to cover her naked, wounded body. I didn't want to look at her, but some of the injuries she'd suffered needed medical attention. I didn't have to be a fucking doctor to see that.

She carefully crawled toward me and slipped the garment over her head, her emaciated body swimming in the threads. Each of the other girls took sweatshirts I'd offered and slipped them on as well.

"My name's Nick. I'm going to get you out of here, okay?" I directed my gaze toward Sapphire. "You're going to need to get checked out. You need a doctor."

"Are …. a-a-are you g-g-going to call the p-p-police? P-p-please don't call them." Her chest quaked with a sob.

I didn't trust the police, and apparently, neither did she. But what else could I do? A thought popped in my head—a conversation I'd had with Rev.

He's a good man, that DeMarcus. You ever in trouble? Ask for him.

"I'm gonna call a good guy, okay? A friend." Christ, I hoped he was a good guy, otherwise I'd have to kill one of Rev's old friends. "And I promise he won't touch you."

Her face spasmed, as if a war against whether to trust me raged on inside her head. "You'll s-s-stay with us?"

"I'll be watching. But I can't be here when they come, okay? I hurt those men, really bad, and they'll be after me." I lurched forward at the panic in her wide eyes and set my palm on the floor for balance. "But I won't leave you alone until you're safe. You hear? I'll be watching."

She looked past me toward the door, maybe gauging her chances if she took off, and gave a shaky nod.

Setting my hand on my knee, I braced to push myself up, but the girl's body collided with my chest, almost knocking me back. She clutched me tight, shivering against me, and I wrapped my arms around her. "Hey, it's okay."

She broke down crying. A small, trembling little girl who'd suffered more hell than most girls her age, had built a measure of trust and felt safe with me. I wanted to hold her and tell her to hang in there, and not let the shit pull her under, but I knew better. I knew the days that'd follow would be filled with nightmares. I knew her hell had only just begun, and I wished I could take that from her, draw her pain into me and use it to punish them the way she herself couldn't.

"I want my mom." Her muffled voice vibrated against my chest, as she buried her face in my jacket.

The simple request reminded me how young and innocent she was, like a lamb ravaged by wolves. Flames roared inside my blood at the same time a metallic taste coated my tongue, where I'd bitten the inside of my cheek.

I nodded, gripping her tight. "You're going home. Don't worry. I'll make sure you get back to your mom."

She sat up from me, wiping tears from her sunken eyes. "I'm Danielle."

"Danielle." I looked her straight in the eye. "After what I did, those men will never hurt you again. I promise you that. They will never hurt you."

More tears slipped down her cheek, and I gripped her shoulders, bringing her to her feet.

"Do me a favor. I don't want you to go into that room. I want you to stay with your friends over there, okay? All of you stay together." I pointed behind me. "I won't let anyone come through this door unless it's *my* friend. Got it?" I didn't want to leave them there. Felt like I'd dropped them inside a shark cage after being attacked and abandoned ship. I couldn't risk being seen, though. Too much rested on staying anonymous.

Giving a sharp nod, Danielle backed herself beside the

other girls, taking the hand of the blonde to her right.

With quick strides, I made my way to the back bedroom and yanked the bedspread from the bed, gathering it up and tucking it under my arm. Theresa Cruz, the ring's recruiter, had been killed separately from the others, and from her bloody pocket, I nabbed the cellphone tucked inside, dialed the police station, and asked for officer DeMarcus Corley.

"This is Corley." His humorless voice carried through the line.

"I need an ambulance at The Pantheon Motel. Room three-three-five. Bring a coroner."

"Who is thi—"

I hung up the phone and tossed it onto Theresa's mangled body.

Returning to the living room, I draped the bedspread across the girls' bare legs where they'd settled in the corner. "You're going home," I assured them.

The sounds of Julius's suffering bled through the bedroom door. His pain had only just begun. After all, he was the one who'd shot my son in the back, having already taken his turn with my wife.

Slipping my mask back into place, I headed back to the bedroom where he and Jonathan had tortured Sapphire.

Julius lay bleeding out of small cuts all over his body, chunks of flesh I must've removed with the hunting knife I'd been holding when I came to. In all honesty, I couldn't recall, but his widened eyes and the way he kicked back in some pathetic effort to get away from me told me all I needed to know.

I crouched in front of him and the bastard probably would've gnawed his own arm to get away from me. "So, I thought I'd take you somewhere nice and intimate, where we can continue our play. It'll be quiet. No one around for—well, miles, to hear you scream. How does that sound?"

His lip quivered and a whimper escaped him, right before he broke into a gut-wrenching scream that probably would've touched some part of my black heart if he hadn't been a piece of shit child rapist.

"What? You don't want to play?" I tipped my head, smiling at his pathetic sniveling. "Is it because I'm not a helpless little girl?" I snarled and leaned in to his ear. "Is it because I can inflict more pain on you than you could ever imagine?"

I grabbed a roll of duct tape from the floor beside me—the same tape that held the other three in their somewhat artistic contortions.

His eyes widened, panicked. "Listen, I'm sorry. I didn't—"

Before he could spew his bullshit, I slapped a square of tape over his lips. Took everything inside of me not to pistol-whip the motherfucker right there. "I know you're sorry, Julius. And maybe, when you've lost more blood than you should and your organs are spilling out of the holes I slice in your body, maybe I'll feel sorry then, too. In the meantime, I'm just going to enjoy this."

He wriggled like a pathetic worm on a hook, as I bent

down and hoisted him over my shoulder. Glock in hand in case of trouble, I carried him out, past the girls, and down the stairs to the car. With a pop of the trunk, I tossed him inside, smiling at his saucer eyes and useless, muffled screams as I slammed the lid in his face.

After exiting the parking lot, I drove two buildings down, taking an obscure spot on the side of a fire-gutted bar across the street, from where I could see the lit hallway and the door to the room. With the barrel of my M-24 hanging out of the window, I aimed my scope, finger on the trigger. Should anyone besides an ambulance or DeMarcus Corley come to the door, their spinal column would be blown to shards all over the stairwell.

Nearly thirty minutes passed—no doubt, the girls up there must've been getting antsy—and then an ambulance and two police cars skidded to a stop in front of the motel. Through the scope, DeMarcus's face emerged from the first patrol car, and he jogged, gun pulled, to the top floor. After a few seconds' pause with his ear to the door, he signaled two officers who'd followed behind him and entered the room.

Two minutes passed. Five minutes. Ten minutes. I kept my sights set the entire time. Waiting. In truth, I didn't trust any of the bastards in the Detroit Police Department, but when Corley stepped out clutching his skull and shaking his head, I had a good idea the girls were in as good hands as they could've been.

A stretcher rolled out with two medics at each end, and Danielle lay strapped, head swiveling as though looking for something, *or someone*, while a female and male officer assisted the other girls down the stairs to the awaiting ambulance. Pulling a phone from his pocket, DeMarcus waved them on once they were loaded, and the siren signaled the ambulance's exit.

I puffed out my cheeks, exhaled a sharp breath, and slid the gun back inside the vehicle. Julius's muffled cries accompanied the pounding of his fists against the trunk, and a new wave of rage beat through my body.

I trailed the ambulance to Detroit Receiving, just to make sure I'd followed through on my promise. All three girls were rushed to the sliding doors, met by a doctor who stood bent over Danielle, as though asking her questions.

I hated the cold exit, wished I could've said something reassuring to the girls before I'd left. Killing those men was only the beginning of my war, though. There'd be more bloodshed. More pain. More retribution.

I couldn't risk the exposure before then. Particularly when I had one of the raping bastards in my trunk.

CHAPTER 14
Chief Cox

Against the desperate pull of air tugging at his lungs, Cox climbed the staircase to the third floor of the Pantheon Motel. He eyed a tall, slim blond, computer tablet in hand, standing just outside the room that spilled over with forensics and investigators.

Jim Riley represented the cybercrime unit at the FBI—one of those middle-aged hippie types who undoubtedly tucked a bowl under his pillow at night so he could light up first thing in the morning like a true fucking pothead. Unlike the stereotypical FBI agents, who wore suits and ties on TV, Riley wore a North Face coat, with his badges dangling from a lanyard around his neck, like the bastard was about to hit the slopes. What the hell he was doing at a murder investigation was beyond Cox.

Cox directed his gaze toward Burke. "Someone order a latte? The fuck is the geek squad doing here? You call him, Burke?"

"Nah, Chief." Coffee in hand, Burke stood opposite

Riley, staring into the open room. "I didn't call him."

Riley swung around, a fake smile plastered to his face. "Ah, what an honor, Chief. Must've heard there were dicks flying in this case, eh, Cox?"

Insolent little cocksucker.

Supposedly, the murder scene was the worst the department had seen in a while, and in a city where killings happened every damn day, that was saying something. The girls had already been transported to the hospital. Good thing, too. If one of them had happened to recognize Cox, shit would've taken a bad turn.

"Go fuck yourself, Riley. Why don't you leave the real cop shit to the boys who've actually handled a gun. This is local shit. A murder." Still winded as hell from his climb, Cox glanced around. "I don't see a computer, do you?"

"These sick sons of bitches have been running a copycat site in the deep 'net, selling young girls for years. 'Sides that, I was *invited* in an encrypted email."

Cox drew back. "Email?" What the fuck kind of killer sent an email?

Riley sipped his coffee, his finger slipping across the screen of his iPad. Goddamn hipsters. A peek over Riley's shoulder showed the mug shot of Julius Malone, who'd gone missing. "I have a feeling there's a link between Achilleus X and the Eye for an Eye killer."

"Ain't that some shit. You boys can't find the bastard tearing up the deep net, so you decide to overlap the two so the agency don't take away your Dungeons and Dragons membership." A raspy laugh tore from Cox's chest.

Riley's gaze lifted from the screen he'd been studying. "A denial of service hit the Detroit Police Department website for a full thirty minutes after the email was sent." He huffed and sipped his coffee, tucking the iPad beneath his arm. "So, now we know why I'm here. Why are you here? *Chief?*"

"I got a personal stake in keeping this city from going apeshit. Most murders here are gangs. Bad deals. Retribution kills. This shit's got the suburb folks worked up that he might cross the line between Detroit and Fashionable Fuckin' Ferndale." Cox's eyes narrowed on Riley. "Ain't that where you're from, Riley?"

"Southfield, actually."

Cox stepped past the two men to just inside the room that bustled with investigators.

"Chief," Burke said, following behind him. "Might wanna nab a barf bag on your way in. This shit's just … goddamn. The killer sure as fuck has something against pedophiles."

CHAPTER 15
Aubree

I squeezed the bobbypin I'd fished from my day-old updo, and lodged it into the keyhole, praying for purchase with the turn.

Growing up poor in Detroit meant learning shit the suburbanites never had to think about, with their fancy security systems and fast-acting police. My father, the survivalist hunter that he was, taught me a number of cool tricks like that, in case I ended up in some whack-job's basement. Bet he never dreamed I'd actually put that skill to work, or that I'd somehow manage to actually land myself in a psycho's abandoned mansion.

A click tightened my muscles, and I rose up from my knees to a standing position, slowly twisting the knob. Through the crack in the door, I could see the staircase ahead. To the left, another bedroom.

What an idiot. Who the hell left a house with their captive free to roam?

Although, I'd smelled the cigar smoke from earlier.

Maybe I wasn't alone, after all. I hadn't heard any movement outside my door, though. Widening the crack, I tiptoed out into the hallway, making light steps against the aged wood that just itched to croak under my weight. At the railing, I paused and listened for movement, searching my surroundings for some form of human life, but it seemed vacant. Artwork adorned the walls of the staircase, my hand smoothing over the banister crafted from well-kempt wood, as I descended the long staircase, toward freedom.

It always seemed in movies that, just when the chick was on the goddamn homestretch, leather face would come flying out with his chainsaw—so I took my time going down the stairs, testing out each step before committing my full weight.

I must've been halfway to the front door, when the first growl climbed my spine, raising hairs on the back of my neck.

My body froze. Paralyzed. I rotated toward the top of the stairs, where the most enormous, muscular beast I'd ever seen stood, baring its teeth.

Oh, my fucking God.

Swallowing a gulp, I licked my suddenly parched lips and carefully skated my attention toward the front door. I was about equidistance to freedom, as the dog was to me. If the front door happened to be locked, the seconds could cost me.

To my left, I noticed another opened door, a half bathroom, where a toilet and sink took up most of the room. If I didn't make it beyond the front entrance, that'd be my escape route.

I glanced back toward the dog and swallowed a gasp. The bastard stood two steps closer than I was to the door, and I hadn't even heard him move.

"Okay, Aubree," I whispered to myself. "On the count of three. One." I stepped down and the dog's growl intensified. "Hey … hey … boy." Hell, if I knew anything about dogs. I happened to think Michael would've flayed any animal we'd have owned. "Two."

The dog took another step, forcing me down one more. His lip curled up over teeth that looked more like tusks. I scanned my limited knowledge bank on dogs, trying to figure out what the hell kind of dog possessed tusks. A pitbull? He had to be a pitbull, maybe? I'd heard the breed were all muscle, and the dog in front of me could've won Mister Universe, hands down.

"Three." Spinning on the ball of my foot, I darted down the remaining half dozen stairs and grabbed hold of the knob on the front door.

Locked. *Goddamn it!* No time to piss and moan about that.

Barks and growls trailed my steps, as I high tailed it toward the bathroom, whirling around in time to slam the door on the dog's agape teeth.

A battle of strength ensued. I pressed into the door, against what felt like over one hundred pounds of muscle on the other side. The last meal I'd eaten rose from the pit of my stomach at the thought of being torn apart by a vicious beast that clearly hadn't eaten as recently as I had, judging by the way he snarled and tore away at the door.

Oh, what fun that'd be for my captor. He'd probably promised the bastard a T-bone if he happened to make me shit myself first.

Out of nowhere, the dog fell into a spasm of insanity, barking, shoving through the door.

I jumped to the left, in a pathetic attempt to get past the hulking dog leaping toward me, and exhaled the breath from my lungs as the floor smashed into my spine.

Those tusks closed in on me, and a stabbing pinch brought my hands to my throat. I dug my nails into its muzzle in an effort to dislodge the dog's teeth from my wind pipe. Futile. He wouldn't budge, and I screamed past the hoarseness in my throat, to which the dog responded by growling and jerking slightly. I flinched at the sting of my flesh, waiting for his teeth to sink in and rip out my esophagus, so he could wriggle it around like a prize—like that scene in *Predator* when the alien thing tore the spine from his victims.

It never came, though.

The dog never bit any harder than enough to keep me still, in spite of the incredible strength I could sense in his jaws as my artery pulsed against his teeth, pumping in the same tempo as my panicked breaths.

I wanted to cry, but didn't know the psychology of dogs enough to determine if he'd consider that a trait of weak prey and finish me off right there on the floor. Had he been trained for such shit?

Fear paralyzed my body, chaos pounded inside my head, and the room widened to a blur, then shrank into a small circle, until it disappeared to blackness.

After what seemed like only a few minutes, I opened my eyes.

My captor's impassive face stared down at me. "How long's he had you pinned like that?"

I forced a swallow past the pressure against my neck. "Time ... just sort of ... seems irrelevant ... when you're ... caught in the jaws ... of a ... *fucking* pitbull."

"Cane Corso." A half smile curved his lips before he whistled, and just like that, the dog released me.

I rolled over to my side, gasping for breath and coughing. Only a small streak of blood mixed with a whole lot of dog slobber returned on my fingers as I held them in front of me. "What did ... you say?"

"He's a Cane Corso."

With the hope that laser beams might miraculously shoot out of my eyeballs, I glared up at my captor. "Cool trick. You teach him that?"

He held out a hand toward me, but I batted him away and pushed myself to a stand. The dog sat at attention beside him, like a good soldier, and I couldn't help but snarl at the sight. As if what'd happened before had disappeared into some compartment of denial locked inside the dog's head.

"I have a feeling we're a lot alike, dog."

"His name's Blue."

"Blue?" For some reason, all I could summon was the

adorable face of the dog from *Blue's Clues*, and the bastard dog was the Incredible Hulk version of it.

"Yeah. Blue." My captor jerked his head, and I followed him back up the stairs.

Though the front door was tempting as I passed it, I didn't dare anything stupid with the dog trailing my steps—though, I was pretty sure that was what the whole psychotic lesson had been about in the first place.

Back in the room, I finally stopped rubbing my neck and turned around, realizing for the first time that my captor's hoodie was peeled back. Along the top of his left ear, a long white scar stretched up into his hairline, as if his skull had split open there at one time. Much as I wanted to ask him about it, I didn't want to be tied to the bed and shut out.

"Any chance you could answer one question?"

"What?" Exhaustion bled into his voice.

"Your name? I keep calling you *my kidnapper* in my head."

His jaw shifted with his blank stare, and goddamn, I had no idea what that meant. The man had more thoughtful expressions than a gaggle of nuns admiring the Statue of David. "My name is Nick."

"Nick," I echoed.

"Blue will be outside your door. I don't suggest you try to sneak out again."

CHAPTER 16
Chief Cox

Cox stared up at the wall-mounted screen across from Culling, on which Martha Baumgartner's head bobbed beside a small screen showing the Pantheon Motel behind anchorman, Will Thomas.

"We want to caution, the story we're about to report contains both graphic and disturbing material that some viewers may find difficult to watch.

"Detroit investigators are searching for a man believed to be responsible for taking down an entire sex trafficking ring, right here in Detroit. Our own Will Thomas is live on Cass Corridor, where police are on site at The Pantheon Motel. Will?"

"Yes, Martha, I'm standing in front of The Pantheon Motel. Once a landmark of the city, it's now falling in disrepair and rented by the hour for illegal activity, including prostitution and drug deals. It's here that witnesses say they heard gunshots and screaming, sometime around early evening, when a masked man entered the room on the top

floor, allegedly posing as a customer, and open fired. It's not known what went down in the two hours that followed, but police have stated this is the worst crime scene they've ever investigated."

"I understand three young girls, whose identities will remain anonymous, were rescued and brought to Detroit Receiving, is that correct?"

"That is correct, Martha. The girls described him as a soft-spoken man, likely in his late twenties, and an angel, as one of them referred to him. The girls were treated for severe cuts believed to have been made by knives, burns and bruises, and the youngest of the three is suffering from some pretty, uh, horrible injuries, which it appears she sustained prior to being rescued. Police will be conducting an investigation, but all three girls are expected to be reunited with their families, once they've been released."

"You said he was wearing a mask?"

"Yes, one witness in the motel described a black mask with red stitching across the lips."

"Red stitching, Will?"

"That's right Martha. Police Chief Cox is reluctant to call this man a hero, and says he may be armed and dangerous. Possibly associated with a terrorist group, known as Achilleus X, who is being sought by both federal and state authorities."

"I'd hardly call this an act of terrorism. He saved three girls who'd been reported missing from their suburban homes weeks ago."

"The labelling is due to the nature of the murders, which is, uh, quite similar to a recent murder that took place off of

Grand River downtown. Police, of course, declined comment on the details of the murder at this time, but did say that very sadistic methods were employed, *including the torture of these men and the one female, while the girls were in the other room."*

"In the case of the murder that took place downtown, wasn't that following the infiltration of a drug house?"

"Yes, that's correct. The murderer apparently stormed the drug house, taking out a number of the drug dealers inside, before kidnapping the head dealer, Marquise Carter."

"Hmmm. It seems this masked vigilante is something of a mystery. All right, thank you, Will.

"Yep, Will Thomas, reporting live from Cass Corridor in Detroit."

The small screen disappeared and the camera zoomed in on Martha. *"We're receiving a flood of comments about this case, which is still under investigation at this time."*

Cox entwined his fingers, sinking into the leather chair across from Culling in the mayor's home office. "Asshole brings new meaning to getting fucked. Ole Richie was found with his brother's severed dick in his mouth and tied to a fucking machine, with a gun up his ass. Now Julius seems to have gone missing. His brother's gonna go balls out to find him, I'm sure." He scratched his chin. "Discovered another number on Jonathan. We got one and zero so far. Not sure yet what it means."

"I don't give a fuck about some masked crusader saving the world. I want you. To find. My. Wife." Culling's round, black eyes could've spun a hole right through Cox's head, the way they drilled into him.

"We might have a serial killer on our hands here. Could be related to Achilleus X. These men ... they're part of the Crew, ya know."

"That's ... wonderful. Great. I'm glad you've wasted ten fucking minutes of my life, talking to me about two worthless bastards in the world." The crack of Culling's fist slamming into his desktop had Cox's muscles flinching. "Find my wife! Find my fucking wife, you fat piece of shit! Do you understand me? Find my fucking wife!" Nostrils flared, he adjusted his collar, straightened his tie, and smoothed his hair. "Not a single fucking camera in that shithole hospital caught one goddamn glimpse of this cocksucker. Not one!" Rubbing his temples, he closed his eyes and, in a moment of awkwardness, took deep, yoga-style breaths. "She has information. Information that, if found, could destroy our plans. Could destroy *us*."

"Yeah. Yes, sir."

"Whoever has her ... I don't want you to kill them." Elbow propped on the desk, Culling's hand balled into a tight fist. "I want them brought back to me. Alive. Is that clear?"

"Crystal."

"Good. As for these three, good riddance." Culling waved in dismissal toward the TV. "They were erratic. Sloppy. It was only a matter of time before somebody took them down, and I'm just glad it wasn't some nosy fucking FBI agent with a hard-on for some deeper investigation."

"The FBI are going to be involved, sir." Clearing his throat, Cox straightened in his seat, preparing for another round of fire from the mayor. He'd long threatened that if the FBI got involved, he'd send Cox fishing for air at the bottom of the river. "There seems to be a link between this guy and Achilleus X."

"I *personally* appointed you to keep the FBI off my ass, Cox. Do your fucking job."

Not easy when the murderer seemed to make a goddamn spectacle out of every kill. The butcher clearly had it in for the Crew, but finding each of the bastards in the city before they got snuffed was damn near impossible. "Yes, sir."

"In the meantime, not a word about Aubree's disappearance." Arm still propped, he flexed his fingers. "As far as the media's concerned, she took some time to get away. A vacation. I don't want to draw attention to this, do you understand?"

A fucking vacation. As if the asshole ever let the poor bitch out of his sight. "Yes."

"Get the fuck out of my office. And don't come back until you have something good to report."

CHAPTER 17
Nick

I fell back onto my bed, cupping my face in my hands. Shit got to me tonight. It was one thing to see those kids propped in ads on the internet, done in a way that'd make some sick fucking pig think they wanted it. It was another to see it in person, to hear their screams. A barbed wrecking ball crashing into my head, ripping through every other thought.

That dark shit ruined a bastard.

I'd never get Danielle's scream out of my head. It would continue to haunt me—a reminder that there were kids out there, scared, feeling hopeless and no one would ever hear their screams.

I heard them. And I hoped, for her sake, she felt free tonight.

No doubt, she'd have a long road ahead of her, but maybe she'd be okay at the end. Kids were resilient. Maybe she'd let that shit roll off of her in time, and feel a sense of power, knowing she'd brought down an entire trafficking ring through a man who wanted to bring pain and suffering to everyone of them on her behalf.

I could feel the blackness building inside of me again, curls of fire slithering through my veins. Anger. So much anger and that black poison crawling up my arm like razor blades, cutting me from the inside. Tugging the knife from my boot, I slid my legs over the edge of the bed and pulled back my sleeve. Had to purge it.

My arm trembled beneath the blade as I sliced across my forearm, relief trailing the line of blood that made a slow drip into my palm. "Fuck!" Felt so good. I groaned, tipping my head back, and closed my eyes.

I glanced along to where Aubree's closed door stood in plain sight. For a moment, I wondered what made me different from those men. Granted, I never planned to touch Aubree, wouldn't pawn her off as some cash dispenser, but was I just as bad as them for what I'd done?

No, my head battled back. She was one of the leeches, getting some benefit from the suffering of girls like Danielle.

Was she, though? If Aubree had seen what I'd seen tonight, could I have imagined any level of apathy from her? I'd only known the woman a couple days, but it just didn't seem like she could watch impassively, like that cunt Theresa, collecting cash at the expense of a child. Could I picture her sitting on a couch with that shit going on in the next room?

Of course not. Just like most people wouldn't watch a pig getting slaughtered for morning bacon. Didn't mean she wouldn't take the cash in the end, though.

The scent of cigar smoke hit me before I noticed Alec standing in the doorway.

"How the hell do you sneak up on me all the time?"

He chuckled, falling into the seat across the room. "Something's troubling you."

I pulled my sleeve back down over the wound. "What makes you say that?"

Leaning forward, he rested his elbows on his thighs. "You're pouting in your room, playing with knives, when you should be out chasing prostitutes or getting drunk."

I shook my head. "Saw some bad shit tonight. Fucked with my head."

"You saved three girls' lives, Nick. It's all over the news. They're calling you a hero."

"I'm no hero. Shit I did … can't even remember half of it. I don't know if those girls saw, but …" Screwing my eyes shut couldn't dislodge the images that would haunt me later. "I got darkness inside of me, Alec. A whole lot of darkness inside."

"We've all got darkness inside. It's what brings it to the surface that separates the psychopaths from everyone else."

"The one girl … Danielle. You know, she made me think of Lauren when she was just sixteen, on the streets." My lip curled in disgust. "I don't even remember half of what I did to those men. I blacked out through most of it."

"You did what you had to do, yeah?" He blew an upward curl of smoke. "You couldn't have punished them enough. It's too bad they died quickly."

"It's becoming increasingly difficult to figure out who the bad guy is."

"Ah." He glanced back toward Aubree's room. "You feel guilt."

"Why did I kidnap her again?"

"She is a means to an end, Nick. She may ultimately die, but others will no longer suffer in exchange." He tipped his head, his raised fedora showing more of his face. "C'mon. Come have a drink with me. We'll get shit faced and try to erase what happened tonight. You gotta keep strong. Keep it together. We're not done with this yet." He eased back onto the chair, cocking his elbow over the back of it. "Play it smart, Nick. They're going to catch on that you're systematically killing off members of their crew. They'll be expecting you. Keep that in mind."

"Yeah." Blood had soaked into the sleeve of my shirt, worked into a noticeable crimson patch. I sat up from the bed, kicking my legs over the edge, and rubbed my skull. "Hey, she asked about you the first night. Achilleus X. Thought I was you." I sneered at that. "Probably every woman's wet fantasy."

His mouth stretched to a wicked grin. "I'm running against some stiff competition as of late. What did you say to her?"

"I didn't say anything. She doesn't need to know who's involved in this." Steepling my fingers, I stared at him for any sign of disagreement. Finding none, I shrugged. "The beauty of being kidnapped."

He nodded. "Which is why I'm going to keep myself low key in this one. Now, quit stalling. Get your ass out of bed." His lip curled, and I followed his downward gaze to my palm where blood still trickled down my wrist. "Wish you'd stop doing that. Fucking go to church, if this shit bothers you that much."

"I don't need church," I said, wiping my palm on my jeans. "I bleed my sins."

CHAPTER 18
Aubree

Standing inside the poor excuse of a bathroom, I tore the bottom hem of my dress to mid-thigh, where it'd been shredded in my scuffle with Nick two days before and had begun to fray, catching on everything I passed.

Nick.

I hadn't expected him to give me his name. I'd expected him to storm out of my room, telling me to fuck off, like he had a couple times before. Perhaps I'd caught him in a vulnerable moment, because kidnappers didn't often get personal like that.

Could've been a fake name, Aubree.

Probably was, but at least I didn't have '*my kidnapper*' running through my head every time I'd thought about him. I had no idea what the man had planned for me, but just as he'd said before, if he'd wanted me dead, he'd have already killed me.

After shortening a good six inches from my dress and tossing the extra fabric into the trash, I slid my panties off and threw them in the sink I'd filled with water and hand soap. Decorum be damned.

What the hell kind of OCD kidnapper set out hand soap, anyway? Like he couldn't stand the thought of me not washing my hands after peeing.

Scrubbing the small bit of fabric, I felt strangely exposed, not wearing panties. I'd spent most of my time living with Michael not wearing any—a very specific request of his, which often resulted in humiliation.

In Michael's home library, I'm sitting across from the stranger, who can't seem to stop staring at my legs, and when I look away, I catch a glimpse of Michael's gaze, flitting between the man and my thighs.

My stomach sinks.

"Tell me something, Patrick." Michael shifts in his chair beside me, crossing his legs. "Do you prefer bare pussy, or do you like hair?"

The stranger clears his throat, and my muscles tense. "Excuse me?"

"Pussy. Bare or hair?" Michael chuckles.

The stranger's stare falls on me then back to Michael. "Bare, I guess."

Michael's arm clutches me at the same time he begins yanking my dress up.

I place a hand over his, snapping my head in his direction. "What are you doing?"

"Move your hands, darling, or I'll remove them all together." The glint in his eyes is as evil as his words.

Embarrassment has my cheeks burning while my dress rests

across my stomach, revealing that I'm not wearing panties. I want to crawl out of my skin.

"What do you think of her pussy, Pat?"

The stranger's Adam's apple bobs with a swallow and he licks his lips. "It's lovely. Perfect. You're a lucky man."

"I am." He squeezes me and kisses my temple. "Lick her."

"Pardon?" The stranger's voice cracks at the question.

"I want you to lick her pussy. Right here. Right now."

Panic slams into my chest, closing off my airways, the waves of heat pulsing beneath my skin as embarrassment twists my stomach into tight coils. "Michael, please. Don't do this." My begging is worthless. Michael does as he pleases, and somewhere in this, a dangerous outcome waits to unfold.

"The man just called your pussy perfect, darling. Don't be rude." He waves Patrick over. "C'mon. She tastes as divine as she looks."

"I ... I'd rather not."

"Oh, don't be a pussy yourself! I'm offering you my beautiful wife and her delicious pussy." Michael lowers his voice to a whisper. "It's just the three of us. It'll be fun."

Patrick's gaze slides back to mine, as if to question if I'm okay with it. I keep my expression as stoic as I can muster, knowing something bad is about to happen. I can feel the electricity in Michael's grip, can sense the tension in his voice, in spite of the feigned pleasantry.

Without making eye contact, the man rises up from his chair and crosses the small space separating us before lowering to his knees in front of me. My thighs tremble, muscles taut. I've never had another man's tongue there. Michael licked me once, when we dated, and hasn't touched me since.

"Michael, you—" I give one more effort to halt this embarrassment, the flush of heat burning my cheeks, as I remain splayed in front of the man below me.

"Hush, Kitten." Michael's nails dig into my arm. "Patrick has been dying to see your pussy all night. Haven't you, Patrick?"

"I'm … sorry?"

"You've been staring at my wife's thighs all night long." Michael shrugs, and a sense of doom washes over me. I had a feeling he'd noticed. He always noticed. "I'm assuming you imagined your tongue buried between them."

"I apologize—"

"No apology. I'm happy to share her. Now, please, have a taste."

The stranger can't seem to look at me again. His gaze only lifts to the level of my stomach and refuses to meet my eyes.

He leans forward, and the kiss to my inner thigh feels like an apology. A ball of tension curls inside my stomach, and I push back, halted by Michael's arm, locking me to the chair.

When the man's tongue glides along my cleft, invading me against my will, I cry out. "No! Stop!"

"That's it," Michael coos beside me.

Patrick continues his assault, massaging the stiff muscles in my thighs, as every corner of my soul screams in protest. I'm numb there, so lost to the horror that his tongue doesn't feel like pleasure to me but a wet irritation that leaves me wanting to curl into myself and push away.

His movements turn fervent, and he grips my thigh,

sucking, perhaps lost to the act, mistaking my agonized whimpers for moans.

Stop! Stop!

"Didn't I tell you, friend?"

A flash of silver strikes the corner of my eye, and at once the licking stops. Patrick lifts away from my sex, falling back on his heels. Blood pours from his throat in pulses that likely mirror the waves of shock beating out the last seconds of his life. Eyes wide, mouth agape, he gasps for air.

Michael leans forward, his mouth to Patrick's ear. "Her pussy is to die for."

I cringed at the memory. After watching the man bleed out his neck, Michael had simply rolled him up in the carpet and burned his body. Poof! Gone. It was the first time I'd seen how easily my husband could kill and get away with it. No one asked about Patrick. No one cared.

As a result, I learned to become charming in the face of horror. To wear a mask of indifference and carry the same wicked undercurrent behind my smile. I'd come to understand one very important survival mechanism: Do not blink when looking the devil in the eye. So, I'd taught myself to make him believe he was staring at his own reflection.

I would eventually become Michael's protégé in an effort to survive him. Bend just enough to please him, but keep my spine intact to challenge him. Build compartments on top of compartments, to protect the soft parts inside me that I'd never allow him to touch again.

Lock it up. Not here. Not now. Put it away.

I'd grown accustomed to smoothing over those images, tucking them away into the darkness burrowed in a place inside of me that I tried not to visit. Still, they haunted me sometimes. Drudged themselves from the black swamp of my soul, and left me feeling weak, dirty.

I wrung the panties out and hung them on the rack above the toilet.

Two days had passed in my new prison, and aside from tying me to the bedpost the first night, my captor hadn't laid so much as a hand on me. Not my captor— Nick. Nick hadn't touched me. Hadn't hit me, even when I thought I'd broken his nose and kicked him in the nuts.

Sure, his eyes had gone wild, and perhaps he wanted to string me up and knock me senseless. He didn't, though. Had that been Michael, I'd have been punished for nearly ruining his perfect face.

I rubbed the back of my neck as I made my way out of the bathroom, noticing, for the first time, that the string of constant tension I'd become accustomed to, that kept me on my toes and helped me stay alert, had dissipated. The knots I'd worked out night after night had dissolved, loosened into soft muscles.

Yeah, not knowing what was going to happen to me still weighed heavy on me, but I'd felt the same thing with Michael every day for years, all while enduring his abuses.

I sat down on the bed facing the prison window, its thick black bars mocking my freedom, and traced the scar on my inner thigh. That had been my punishment for Patrick's staring. For *allowing him to put his tongue inside* of me, as Michael had accused. I tipped my head back as the small rays of sunlight hit my face. So warm. When I opened my eyes, a speck of green at the corner of the window caught my attention, and I stood to check it out.

From the exterior rotted wood, a small sprout of the fern climbed and had worked its way through a tiny gap in the frame. As if it'd peeked inside to see me. I smiled, rubbing my finger over the tiny leaves. Even through destruction, life could continue to bloom in the oddest places.

The perfect metaphor for my life.

At the click of the door, I spun around to find Nick standing in the doorway, wearing a white tank and jeans, holding a plate of fruit and what looked like orange juice. Broad shoulders, pared down to a slim waistline, gave some indication that he had a nice package going on beneath all the concealing clothes he'd worn every time I'd seen him.

"Are you hungry?"

Call me a masochist, but the question left me wishing I could cross my thighs. With a nod, I rounded the bed, taking a seat at the edge.

Cords of muscle covered each of his arms, and ink decorated them in skulls and script. Not overdone or trashy, but tastefully and artistically etched in a way that gave him the ultimate bad boy appearance. A black tribal, pissed-off looking scorpion with red eyes covered his shoulder, over the ripple of muscle, its stinger snaking up the right side of his neck. I couldn't help but think of the way a scorpion stunned its prey before consuming it, reminding me of those striking eyes of his. Poisonous venom in one glance. As he approached, small white scars could be seen beneath the ink, as if he'd tried to cover them up.

Damn he looked *good*. Really good.

What was wrong with me? This guy had kidnapped me, tied me to a bed, and sicced his crazy, hulking dog on me.

At the same time, in an ass-backward universe, one could also say he *saved* me from my psychopathic husband, fed me with his own hands, and told me his name. Whether it was his or not didn't seem to matter in my mind. He also hadn't tied me to the bed in two days, not that I'd been keeping track of pros and cons, or anything.

Beyond him, Blue lay down just outside my door, as though an imaginary threshold existed between us. Good. I hoped he suffered some kind of seizure if he happened to cross over.

Nick handed me the plate, slipped inside the closet-slash bathroom, and the faucet turned on. Once it'd turned off, he appeared at the door a few moments later, drying his hands, and he threw the towel over his shoulder. Good God. He leaned against the doorframe, and I did cross my legs for fear I might stand up to a telling wet spot on the bed. The man defied any previous standards I'd ever conjured inside my head for what a beautiful male specimen might look like.

Arms crossed, he glanced over his shoulder and back to me. "Am I to assume you're not wearing anything beneath that dress?"

Seriously, what the hell was wrong with me that my nipples popped like a set of turkey timers at his question? "I refuse to wear dirty underwear. Captive, or not, I've got standards." Boom. Argue that, mister. The new me refused to take anyone's shit.

His head jerked forward. "You tore your dress?"

"It was getting in my way."

He tugged the towel from his shoulder and tossed it somewhere inside the bathroom. "You don't need to be walking around here without panties."

"Making you nervous?" *Bold, Aubree. Bold.*

Those icy blue eyes shot to me. "If you think tempting me is your ticket to freedom, lady, you're wrong."

"Aubree. My name is Aubree. *Lady* is reserved for women over the age of sixty. *Nick.*" I tipped my head. "Is that your real name, or the name you offer up all your victims, to make them feel special for a minute before you slit their throats?"

With a slight lift his chin, just enough to assert his dominance, he stared down at me, his tongue making a slow sweep across his teeth, and sweet Lord, the man had my pelvic muscles in a frenzy. "You think I want to slit your throat?"

I shrugged at that. "Just a guess, unless you're the sensitive quiet type under all that ink and muscle." In the moments that his eyes narrowed on me and he seemed to study my face, I stole the opportunity to avert a potentially abrupt exit and cleared my throat. "I could use a shower. I tried to take a bath in the sink, but it's a little cramped."

The twitch of his cheek told me he wanted to smile. "A shower."

"Yeah. I don't suppose you've got an extra razor." I had a feeling he didn't, but the comment allowed me to focus on the sexy scruff of his face. Some guys just couldn't pull that look off. Either too much hair or uneven lines that just made them look homeless. Nick had me cataloguing new features of sexy by the minute.

Stop. He's a kidnapper. For Christ's sake, stop.

His eyebrow winged up and his gaze landed on my arm, where the scar practically screamed from my wrist.

"N … not for that. I typically wax, but in a few days, I'll be looking like Sasquatch. Should you decide to kill me, I'd like to keep my dignity intact."

His jaw shifted back and forth.

For crying out loud, man. Laugh!

"Anything else?" He didn't ask as though he genuinely cared to jot a list, more like he was irritated that he suddenly had to entertain a shower and a razor.

Yeah, a new pair of underwear, a fluffier pillow, some socks to walk around in, a bottle of wine—what the hell is asking too much? "Paper and pencil for sketching. Maybe a book?"

"Book?" he echoed.

I held both palms up, butterflying them in mocking. "You know, like reading. Words on a page. Some semblance of a plot. A book."

"What kind of book? One of those romance books with a vampire and wolves?"

His laughter, whether fake or not, took me by surprise, and for the first time I noticed that, beyond those perfectly smirky-looking lips, he had a set of beautiful teeth that made up an adorable smile, complete with dimples.

Dimples. Hardly the vision of a dark and disgusting kidnapper.

"I'm not picky. I'm a pretty voracious reader. As long as it captures my attention. Classics are good, too."

He paused, eyes tracking slightly to the side, and without a word, left the room.

Blue's head perked up as he passed, as though even the dog didn't understand the sudden exit.

Brow furrowed, I stared after him, replaying the last few seconds of conversation through my mind, wondering if I'd said something wrong.

Within minutes, he returned, carrying a book whose jacket looked dusty. Worn down. He handed it to me and stepped back, crossing his arms again.

The Grapes of Wrath. "Oh, my God, this is a first edition!" I turned it over in my hands, marveling the relic. "It was one of my favorites in school."

"You like old books?"

"Yes," I said, cracking it open, inhaling the aged pages.

"You always smell your books?" At my nod, he nudged his head in my direction. "What's this one about?"

"You never had to read *The Grapes of Wrath* in school?"

Arms still crossed, he leaned against the doorframe. "I didn't go to school for long. Dropped out when I was sixteen."

"You dropped out? Why?"

He shrugged. "Wasn't my thing."

"Kidnapping just seemed like a more promising future for you, huh?" I clutched the book to my chest, waiting for his response.

"I liked computers. Games. Piecing puzzles. I worked on graphics and storylines for a game."

"That sounds ..." *Weird.* "... *incredible.*" He didn't strike me as a black turtleneck, computer geek type. "What happened? Why didn't you pursue it?"

"Shit happened." He straightened his spine as if I'd dipped into sacred territory again.

Rather than risk his silence, I dropped my gaze to the book. "It's about a family, the Joads, who lose everything and trek from Oklahoma to California, in search of a better life. Along the way, they face challenges, loss, suffering, pain. They find that what they'd hoped would be a better life, isn't. Tom Joad ends up killing two police officers, who killed his friend, and goes into hiding. Bad things continue to happen to this family, and through it all, they fight to survive."

Scratching the scruff on his cheek brought his chiseled jawline to my attention. He crossed his arms again, snapping me out of my musings. "Sounds depressing."

"It's about maintaining dignity in the face of tragedy and prejudice."

"So, that's what you believe?" He pushed himself off the wall and, with his boots set apart, took on a clearly defensive stance. "Those who suffer and face prejudice are supposed to prove themselves worthy and maintain their dignity in the presence of people like you who continue to oppress?"

I reared back at his words. *Where the hell did that come from?* "No ... wait, what? People like *me*?" I frowned at the accusation. "Contrary to whatever preconceived ideas you may have about me, we're on the same side, Nick."

"No. We're definitely not on the same side, Aubree. We're so opposite of each other, it's not even funny. You may have scars, but that doesn't mean you know the kind of pain and loss that could make you give two shits about dignity and earning anyone's approval." Just like that, he strode out of the room, slamming the door behind him.

Numbness crept over my body, threatening to penetrate my shield. Fuck him. Fuck him and whatever he *thought* he knew about me. He knew nothing. The *stranger* hadn't walked in my shoes, had no idea what I'd been through and survived. My scars were the markers of my pain and loss.

I rubbed my finger across the scar on my wrist, pushing back the tears forming in my eyes. I'd been to the bottom. Been broken. Stomped on. I got back up. Scraped what little self-respect I had left inside of me, and picked myself up. He didn't know that. And I didn't have to tell him— the guy meant nothing to me.

He was right—I didn't need his approval.

CHAPTER 19
Nick

Flashlight in hand, I descended the staircase into the bowels of the abandoned Michigan Central Train Station. While I should've been preparing myself for the next round of horror, images of Aubree's naked ass under that dress had me about one thread from losing my mind.

The woman did things to my head. If not for the fact that I was forced to bring her meals, I should've stayed away from her room. I was certain I'd be plagued with nightmares after the trafficking bust, and yet, a drunken night with Alec had ended in dreams of Aubree waking me up and riding me in my bed as I lay half passed out.

The fuck was wrong with me? Two days ago, I'd wanted to tear the woman apart, and suddenly all I could think about was hiking up that dress and burying my dick inside her panty-less ass.

With the heel of my palm, I knocked my temple. "Get her out of your head," I muttered, rounding the last flight of stairs. I had to focus. I had a job to do. The last thing I needed was images of her tight body and firm breasts jockeying for my attention.

Faint, almost ghostly screams echoed down the hall, as I trudged through water stagnant enough to leave a putrid sting in my nose. I followed the sounds that, to any other trespasser, might've been mistaken for the horrific cries of a ghost.

In time, he would be.

Brown and black stains coated the tunnel walls. The brick had been chipped away, crumbled in some parts, not only with age, but from scrappers who'd cased the place for all the copper.

Light bled beneath a door from inside, where I'd placed a lantern two nights before, when I'd imprisoned Julius after abducting him. As I reached there, muffled screams came into sharp clarity. The raspy quality of his voice told me the asshole must've screamed for two days straight.

In the center of the room, Julius sat blindfolded and strapped to a chair. "Who's there? Please! Someone help me!" At his ankles, large wounds glistened where rats had obviously chewed. Fuckin' room stank like shit, and I choked back the urge to upchuck right there on the floor. "Man, if that's you. Please. I'm … I'm sorry … for what I did to that little girl."

Those images, as much as I wanted to forget them, gave me the fuel I craved. The motivation to do what needed to be done.

According to Rev, word on the street was that Julius's

big brother Brandon had put out a manhunt for him. He wanted any information on the masked vigilante, as I'd been referred to in the news.

"I'll do anything … you want. Anything, please." His shoulders juddered with a sob. "Just get me the fuck out of here! Please! There's voices at night, man! And fucking rats!" His skin had grown pale, mottled, as if he'd become sick from his wounds.

"I understand there's an abandoned factory somewhere in the city where women and kids are housed before getting distributed to various pimps." Arms crossed behind my back, I circled him, sloshing the shallow water pooled on the floor. "Is that true?"

"I …" He gulped a swallow. "I don't know anything about that."

"It's my understanding that they're drugged. Raped. Beaten. Tortured. Kept in cages. Like animals."

His tongue swept over his lips, and he trembled as if he might cry again. "The girls we get are … they're kept at motels. Not abandoned buildings."

"According to your criminal records, you lured the girls to this abandoned shithole. Sweet talked them." Julius had a reputation of being a sweet talker. "I'm just giving you a taste of how it feels to be taken out of your element. Scared shitless. Willing to do whatever it takes to get free." I came to a halt in front of him. "Are you willing to do whatever it takes to be free?"

"Yes, yes, man. You want me to suck you off? I'll do it. I don't give a shit. Let me go, and I won't tell a single mothafucka what happened here."

"I don't want you to suck me off, Julius. I want you to help me with something."

"Anything!"

"So eager." I smiled at his pathetic stupidity. "No wonder you don't feel guilty raping little girls. I almost don't feel guilty for what I'm about to do, either."

His blindfolded face lifted, vacillating back and forth as he seemed to search the air for me. "What do you want from me, man?"

"I was sent by Culling to kill you," I lied. "Your little crew is getting far too powerful, and he wants to take you down. Unfortunately, Culling has too many connections for me to take on by myself." I crouched in front of him, and my nose crinkled at the stench of piss emanating from his body. "See, I don't want to kill you, Julius. I think, deep down, you want to be good, don't you?"

"Yeah. I don't … I want out. I don't want to do this shit anymore."

"Okay. Here's what we can do. We need to get the FBI on our side. Culling's too powerful to take down alone. They need to know what's going down. So, I'm going to send a message to a contact I have. I think he can help, but he needs some evidence. Otherwise, I'm afraid I'll have to leave you here to die. Because I just can't bring myself to kill you. You understand?"

"Yeah, yeah." He shifted in his chair. He must've been delirious from lack of food and water if he bought that bullshit. "I'll do it."

"Good. I'm going to start the camera, and I want you to tell me everything. Your name, your crew, and how Culling is involved."

His lip quivered, head nodding frantically. "You'll set me free?"

"Of course. I'll have what I need against Culling. And, I promise, I'll set you free."

I flipped on the phone's camera and pressed record, careful not to say a word. After a ten second pause, Julius began talking. In the ten minutes that followed, he confessed to the abductions, the drug deals, The Culling sweeps, and Culling's own personal stake in the operation. All the missing pieces I couldn't have garnered, not even on the deep net, came spilling out of his mouth.

Until, at last, he finished.

"Thank you, Julius." I stuffed the small phone into a plastic bag, then into my pocket, and removed his blindfold, allowing him the opportunity to adjust to the light.

"Who ... who are you? You look *familiar*." His eyes squinted as he studied my face, until they widened, damn near popping out of his head. "You're ... I *know* you." Surprise quickly turned to sobs. "I know you," he said on a wail. "Please don't kill me, man. Please." He rocked as much as he could against the ropes. "This place. The voices. The ghosts. I'm fucking going crazy up in here!"

"Do you know how old my son was when you shot him in the back, Julius?" I hammered my fist into his face before he could answer, knocking a tooth free that splashed into the water. "Five. Five years old."

After slicing into the man's ear, my head is wrenched back, and a fist pounds into my cheek, until all I can do is drop to the floor, half conscious. The room spins out of control, and smack in the middle is red.

My son's red pajamas.

He backs himself away from the room filled with a view that will ruin him for the rest of his life. "Daddy?" He cries, and all I want to do is scoop him up. Tell him it'll be okay, hold him to make sure some small part of him hasn't been destroyed by what he's seen, but the blackness is filtering in quickly.

I crawl toward him. "Jay?" I reach out for him with a trembling hand.

Black boots block my view. "Hey … little man. I'll give you five seconds to run. Five. Four."

My screams reverberate inside my skull as the seconds tick quickly.

My son is silenced with a bullet.

"I'm … sorry." Julius's words carried a lisp and snapped me from memories. "We … we was told to …"

I hit him again, kicking his head to the side once more, and he spat blood. "His birthday was in two days. He'd been telling me all week how excited he was. How he couldn't wait to blow out six birthday candles on his cake." I choked back the tears at the memory, allowing the pain and fury to give me the crazed rush of adrenaline I craved. "But that never happened."

"Please don't kill me, man. Please."

I tugged the knife from my hip with one hand and gripped his jaw, reaching in with the other to take hold of his tongue. He bit down onto my finger, and I drilled another punch to his face, knocking out a front tooth. Against the screaming and kicking, I sliced his tongue clean from his mouth.

Choking fits and gurgles had my lip crimping.

"Not so much the sweet talker now, are you, Julius?" I waved his severed tongue in the air and tossed it into the water. Cramming the barrel of my gun into his mouth, I chewed on my lip for a moment, waiting for his bawling to die down. "Hey … little man. I'll give you five seconds to run. Five."

His scream brought a smile to my face.

"Four. Three. Two." I pulled back the hammer. "Are you ready to be set free?"

Blackness filtered in.

***

Peeling off the black leather gloves coated in sticky blood, I tossed them to the floor and nabbed a pair of tongs from inside a plastic bag. I had Alec to thank for all the sterile technique. He'd taught me all the ways that police processed evidence in the lab, how even the tiniest fibers could be analyzed. I'd had no idea an entire genetic code could be found at the root of a single human hair. Fascinating.

Alec was something of a *Jack of all trades*. While I probably would've been inclined to throw caution to the wind, sending the recording to DeMarcus Corley without a single thought for the possibility that they could identify me, Alec insisted on taking great care in eliminating the possibility.

Keeping to his demands, I set the envelope on a plastic square I'd laid on the front seat of my car and addressed the package to the only cop who'd earned my trust so far.

Perhaps he'd find some use out of Julius's confession.

CHAPTER 20
Nick

With a plate of food in one hand, I entered Aubree's room, finding her sprawled on her stomach, reading. "Still working on that book?"

She rolled to her side and propped her head on her palm, looking like some fucking Flintstones pinup with her torn, ragged dress, and a sudden rush of heat shot through my body. "It's the only one I have, so I'm taking my time with it."

She went back to her reading, undeterred, when I set the plate down.

I tossed her a T-shirt and a pair of my sweats, almost hating to make her change, but goddamn it, I didn't need to think about her that way whenever she decided to wash her panties. I had bigger shit going down. Besides, she was the enemy for chrissakes—an argument that seemed to be losing steam with each passing day.

It wasn't until I'd already gotten halfway to the door that I heard her shift on the bed, and something soft hit the back of my head.

I spun around and found my clothes in a heap on the floor.

"Thanks. But I'm not wearing your clothes." With a stubborn tilt of her chin, she perched on the edge of the bed, arms crossed.

"You'd prefer to walk around in a torn dress and no panties, that it?"

Her brows lifted. "Yeah. I would."

Damn her, and damn my traitorous dick for lurching at that. "Well, too bad. I'm not asking you to wear the clothes. I'm telling you."

"And I'm telling you that I refuse to wear your clothes. I'm not letting you stake some claim on me."

I exhaled a breath, shaking my head. "You don't want to test me right now, Aubree."

From behind, Blue perked up and whined.

"Go fuck yourself, Nick."

I swiped at my nose, brushing off the urge to paddle her ass for such insolence. "I forgot. If it's not fancy and bought with innocent human lives, it's not good enough for you, right?" It wasn't my style to say something totally stupid, off the top of my head, but shit happened.

"What the hell is that supposed to mean?" She pushed up and crossed her arms tighter. "I haven't bought anything with human lives! And if all of this is about my husband, I've no idea how he *wronged* you, but I had nothing to do—"

Lurching forward, I wrapped my fingers around her

throat and slammed her against the wall. My teeth ground so hard they could've cracked, while her pulse hammered beneath my palm. A vision of Danielle popped into my head, and I snapped.

Alec had suspected that Michael received a cut of the trafficking, and may have even had a more direct role, but proving it seemed to be the crux of his suspicions, and he lacked the concrete evidence to expose him. I couldn't help but imagine Aubree and Michael admiring their fine clothes, while innocent girls like Danielle paid the price— and Aubree's haughty fucking attitude only grated on my spine.

Like I'd caught some kind of hellcat by the tail, she thrashed and pushed, scratching, fighting against me. Her body tensed, and I blocked the anticipated kick to my nuts with a lifted leg.

Wild. Feral.

With my right hand, I pinned her flailing fist, then released her throat and seized the other. She stilled, flat against the wall, with my body pressed into hers.

"You had everything to do with it." I pushed harder, my muscles steeled. "He didn't just *wrong* me, he annihilated me. And there you were, stroking his cock, smiling beside him all the while."

"All you saw was a smile, then. You should've looked deeper. So what? I'm your revenge? Your ticket to hurting him?" She sneered. "Guess what? He doesn't give a shit about me. He never did. So, go ahead, Nick. Kill me." She lifted her head away from the wall, only inches from my face. "Snap my fucking throat, if that's what you plan to do. You'd be doing him *and* me a favor."

Her body pulsed with tension, the tremble beating against me, through me, inside of me. Anger. Hate.

So much hate.

With one quick twist of my hands, I could've snapped her neck, been done with the whole plan and exited my miserable fucking existence on the wings of a bullet to my skull.

Instead, I slammed my lips against hers. Loving the struggle of her body trying to push me away. Hating the fact that her lips tasted like sweet salvation, beckoning me to whatever web of deception she'd been weaving since I'd taken her. Her delicious smell pervaded my senses—water on the flames burning inside of me, steaming up my mind.

Three years.

The last time I'd devoured a woman's lips was three years ago, and that had been out of love. Kissing Aubree was something else entirely. Not gentle or tender. I kissed her violently, with all the fury locked inside of me, our frantic breaths clashing with one another.

Her moan vibrated inside my skull, as her hands clenched to fists, trying to break free from my grasp.

She opened her mouth wider, dragged my lip between her teeth, and bit me.

Aggression surged through my body and rattled the cage of something dark inside of me.

I wanted more. More pain. More rage. I wanted to tear into her while cursing her name. Purge myself of the hate until it was spent.

I broke the kiss, breaths heaving, as I glared down at her. "What do you know about Brightmoor?" I rasped.

"I don't know anything about Brightmoor," she gritted out.

Lies. "Yeah? Then, why did you have the fucking blueprints tucked in your purse? Devil's Night plans safe and sound, beside your goddamn lipstick and compact."

Her chest rose and fell as I kept her captive against the wall, her stare deadpan. "I didn't—"

"Don't lie to me." I pressed harder, lips to her ear. "I fucking hate liars," I whispered, inciting a shudder in her that brought a smile to my face. "Why did you have the chip?"

"I stole it."

"You stole it." I wanted to laugh at the stupidity of such a thought, but my voice lacked any ounce of humor or inflection. "I don't think you did, Pistol Lips. I think he gave it to you. His little pet."

"I fucking hate you." Venom laced her words as she stared back at me, those golden eyes blazing with vehemence.

I licked my lips and glanced down at her pert breasts, and smiled. Squeezing her captured wrists with one hand, I reached up under her dress, only grazing the patch of lace that kept my finger from being inside of her, knowing everything she was too stubborn to admit.

Her lids turned heavy, as drunken eyes riveted on my lips.

"Tell me how much you hate me."

"Don't," she warned, and I caught the scrape of her tongue across her teeth.

Grabbing a handful of hair, I tugged her head back until her neck stretched taut, and like a creature of night, I wanted to bite down into that supple flesh and rip her throat out. Dragging my tongue along her shoulder, I made my way to the base of her neck and bit her collarbone. She let out a gasp and I released her wrists. Lust blazed through my veins, when her fingers tangled in my hair and her leg curled around my hip, drawing me against her.

"You know what, Aubree? I fucking hate you, too, but goddamn … you taste so good."

Hell was having her skin against mine and craving her so badly I wanted to crawl out of my own body.

I needed more. Needed to twist her around, tear away her panties, and slam into her with the wrath of a thousand nights of pain. She needed to feel my rage and madness, what kept me teetering on the edge for three long years.

Yanking the front of her dress popped both revoltingly beautiful tits from their confines, and when my tongue found her nipple, her nails dug into my scalp. I reached up into her dress, rubbed a finger across her wet pussy, then bunched up the thin fabric of her panties and tore them away.

"You're a rotten bastard, Nick, but you … fuck!" She squirmed, as my finger curved higher, nailing the sweet spot.

Gripping tight to her ass, I pressed her against the front of my jeans, where my starving dick nearly blasted through the zipper to get to her.

With a quick spin, I had her facing away, cheek to wall, and without a word, she angled her ass high and smacked her palms flat on either side of her.

I dug my fingers into the soft, supple flesh of her hips, and buried my nose in her hair, inhaling the faint smell of her perfume.

Arched into me, ass grinding in a slow, hypnotic wave against my already-hardened dick, she released a seductive purr that hit my spine like a tuning fork. Her long brown hair spilled in fountains that would look beautiful caught in my fist.

She had no idea what she'd unleashed. No going back. I had one objective in mind, and I didn't think she realized I was already halfway there.

Knotting my fingers in her hair, I tugged her head back and put my mouth to her ear. "What do you want, Aubree? You want me to pin you to this wall and fuck you senseless?"

"I'm already senseless if I've let you go this far."

"An answer. Now. Do you want this?" I cinched her hair tighter. "Just know, if you choose to be fucked, there's no going back."

"Do it."

"Do it? You wanted this all along, didn't you? You wanted me damn near groveling for a piece of you, so you could dig your claws in like every other bastard you've manipulated, that it?" I licked the shell of her ear. "Guess what? I'm going to fuck you, Aubree. But this isn't about you besting me in your little game. In the end, I still walk away."

I lifted her dress and everything inside of me came to a screeching halt.

On the lower part of her back, just above her ass, a wide, angry scar spelled out one word. WHORE.

Through heaving breaths, I stared down at the ugliness that'd been branded on her for life. Repulsive, cruel branding, like fucking cattle. I'd almost hate-fucked a woman who'd clearly been a victim of hate herself, and my stomach sank at the thought. Because the reality stared back at me, in five sharply carved, maliciously-seared letters, completely crumbling the fantasy I'd conjured where Aubree Culling was as much a villain as her husband.

I brushed my thumb lightly across the raised flesh, and her body planked.

She flattened herself against the wall and pushed her dress down her hips, covering it. "Don't. Don't fucking touch me," she whispered on a shaky breath.

"He did this to you?"

"He did everything to me." Her arms lifted to either side of her face, and she buried her head between them. "Please leave me alone."

"Tell me the truth. How did you get that chip?"

"I told you the truth. I fucking stole it. Now leave me

alone!"

I believed her. Five fucking letters sliced into her back suddenly had me seeing the woman in a different light, and for the first time, I believed she stole that vital information from the man who'd obviously betrayed her.

My throat went dry, my field of vision narrowing with the blackness seeping in from the edges. Slamming the heel of my hand against my skull, I stumbled back, catching myself against the wall, before I strode from her room, closing the door behind me.

From the other side, I heard her quiet sobs, and it occurred to me, even after the kidnapping, chaining her to the bed, threatening to kill her, that was the first time I'd heard the woman cry at all. Real crying, not the fake shit she'd pulled to swindle sympathy from me.

The pain I could hear then was real.

Rubbing the back of my head, I dialed Alec's cell and made my way to the kitchen, where I rifled through cupboards for whiskey.

No answer.

I hurled the burner phone against the wall, where it crumbled to the floor in small pieces, and pounded my fist into the tiles.

The game was changing before my very eyes and I had no clue what to do next.

A switch had been flipped.

Scars came in different flavors. The selfish variety, like the one on her wrist, spoke of a different kind of struggle. Maybe she had problems, but everyone had problems.

The one on her back was something else entirely.

Every scar told a story, but it was the ones we didn't want others to see that told a truth. Aubree's truth had been etched into fine markings on her back, written with the clarity of someone who'd taken his time. Only a sadistic bastard could've done something like that.

In it, I saw something I didn't want to see. Something painful. Broken. Something I hadn't anticipated uncloaking when I'd lifted her dress. Something that no longer made her my toy. I saw Aubree Culling as a human being. A scarred, ravaged human being who probably needed more than what I'd offered her in silence when I walked out the door.

My stomach twisting in knots, I rifled through cupboards. Where the fuck was my whiskey?

In one blink, Aubree had turned from a vector for revenge, an object of hate, to a curiosity. What had she done to deserve the wrath of an evil man? No matter how much I tried to rearrange the variables in my head, the answer to that question made her proportionately good. The opposite of Michael Culling.

Three years. For three years, I'd watched her on TV, as I'd followed the Cullings from one event to the next, plotting, building my rationale for committing the ultimate act of revenge. In that time, how had I managed to overlook a very obvious truth? Aubree was a victim, too.

Not a monster. Not some Stepford bitch. A *victim*.

No. The label didn't sound right inside my head.

I found the fifth of whiskey, twisted the cap off, and

pounded a double to straighten the words clanging against my skull. Aubree Culling and victim didn't belong in the same sentence, any more than Michael Culling and saint gelled together. Yet, I'd witnessed that fact, seen firsthand how wrong I'd been. How could I kill a woman who'd clearly been abused? How could I inflict my pain and suffering on her, when she'd bled from similar wounds and carried as many scars?

With every argument, the visual of WHORE flashed through my head and smashed each pathetic excuse into a million pieces of bullshit.

Maybe she'd asked for it.

Bullshit.

Maybe she'd lied to my face, by admitting that he'd been the one to inflict that kind of torment.

Bullshit.

I didn't have to be a therapist to see the shame in her eyes. The hate and humiliation. The human being buried beneath some fucking twisted veneer, upon which, I hadn't even begun to scratch the surface.

I was wrong. Alec was wrong. We'd been so focused on Michael Culling that we'd failed to see the truth behind those fake smiles. The glaring, irrefutable fact—that Aubree wasn't some political princess.

She was the abused maiden, locked in the tower. And I'd made her out to be a monster.

Jesus, what had I become over the last three years?

I stand at the window, looking out at the city below as I hold my newborn son in my arms. I hate this apartment, but at night, with him, it's beautiful. It's home.

"That's the kind of sight that makes ovaries drop."

I turn to see Lena leaned against the doorframe, in one of my T-shirts that hangs down to her knees.

"You better stop, or before you know it, you'll be holding two."

I lift an arm, holding Jay in the crook of my elbow. "Plenty of room."

Crossing the floor, she nestles herself into my shoulder. "Just as long as you have a place for me."

"Always."

She glides a thumb down our son's temple. "I can't believe how much he sleeps. All those horror stories of sleepless nights."

"Think he takes after his mom." I laugh when she playfully slaps my ass.

Resting her head against my chest, she cradles his head in her palm and plants a kiss to his cheek. "I hope he takes after his dad." Her face lifts to mine. "Promise me, no matter what—through the struggles, the lows, the highs, pain and happiness that's ahead of us— whatever comes of these dreams we're building now, promise me you'll never change who you are inside, Nick." She grips my nape and kisses me. "You're a good man. And I couldn't have chosen a better father for our son."

I stared down at the swirling amber liquor before tipping it back. I hated what I'd become. Thief. Kidnapper. Killer. Bastard.

She'd have hated me, too.

What now? I couldn't let Aubree go. Not yet. I

wouldn't send her back to the butcher who'd carved her back, but I couldn't set her free, either. She played a role in it all, but the plan would need to be modified, because no way in hell I could hurt a woman who'd been victimized by the same bastard to whom I'd planned to feed a bullet.

I wouldn't be killing her in the end, but I'd sure as hell be killing her husband. Unfortunately, Aubree still had to play the pawn.

In the meantime, there was something I owed her.

CHAPTER 21
Aubree

I slid to the floor beside my bed and buried my face in the covers. As if a dam had broken inside of me, the tears flowed without restraint, without any signs of stopping, and I succumbed to the encroaching tide that demolished all the perfectly stacked compartments inside of me.

It was my fault. I knew the scar was there, and that the stature I'd been given the last five years would have been staring him in the face if he'd slammed into my body, taking from me what I'd have been perfectly willing to give, had it meant freedom in the end. Perhaps a part of me wanted to blow whatever Barbie Doll image he'd conjured in his head right out of the water. I wanted to give him the smallest glimpse of my secrets.

I hadn't counted on him attempting to breach my defenses. He'd made it clear in the last few days that he'd no intentions of knowing about me or trying to humanize me in any way. I was a caged animal—a stolen prize, from which he hoped to gain.

It was why he'd worn the gloves the first day. Touching skin meant touching the soul, connecting with another person in a way that couldn't be made pure and chaste again.

In truth, I'd wanted him in that moment. Not just for my freedom. His kiss had surged with passion and anger, fervor and fury, and I'd wanted to be trapped inside that violent storm of confusion. I'd wanted it to crash over me, consume me, and drag me to the depths of whatever darkness it'd recede, because at least in those moments of trying to catch my breath, I'd feel alive. For once, I'd feel a reason to fight my way back.

Michael must have hurt him, too, somehow. I could sense it, feel it seeping into my bones when his fingers had dug into my flesh. In that, we shared a connection. Perhaps Nick and I were opposites in life, as he said, but in pain, we were the same.

Two broken halves, with jagged edges that seemed to fit together in some messed up way.

To hell with the fact that I was a married woman. My husband broke his vows to honor and protect the moment he laid a hand on me, so fuck him. I'd spent seven years locked in a prison of pain, devoid of emotion, and for once, it felt good to feel *something*. I couldn't say it was entirely lust, because an undercurrent of ferocity had laced every action—mine and his. In that intensity, though, I'd felt a certain passion, a hunger that I'd never experienced with Michael—or any man, for that matter.

In one moment of weakness, of unabashed bliss, I'd

surrendered to the exquisite destruction of Nick's kiss. My fingers traced my lips, remembering the feel of his mouth on mine.

How easily I'd have given him more. A thought that scared the shit out of me.

After all, the man was like a finely crafted blade—lean, beautiful and dangerous enough to cut me to the bone, if I wasn't careful.

CHAPTER 22
Nick

Slipping on my coat, I reached inside the pocket and tossed Blue a treat on my way toward the staircase. While descending, I dialed Lauren's number, wishing I didn't have to ask her for a favor. I had to do something right, though. Something I should've done the first night.

I drove along East Grand Boulevard until I reached the old abandoned church-turned-hostel. Always hated the idea of Lauren living in such a shit place on the shit side of town, but she claimed she liked it, enjoyed being around other kids her age, and always made a point to remind me that it was better than living on the streets. My intent wasn't to preach, or try to control her—hell, at nineteen, she had her shit together better than I did at twenty-eight. Just didn't want her to become another statistic on the streets, and some of the kids she hung out with seemed to be well on their way to that life.

I knocked on the door, tensing at the sound of laughter on the other side. The door swung open to Lauren, hair in disarray, wearing pajama pants and a thin tank top. Behind her, a slightly older-looking Asian girl, in the same slumber party attire, stood holding a cigarette and looking me up and down.

"Nick!" Lauren's face bloomed with a smile, and she slammed into my chest with a hug. Christ, I hated coming to her after trying to cut ties, but maybe it could be the promised visit—even if I was the asshole who planned to task her with a favor.

"Mmm, who's he?" The Asian woman blew smoke to the side.

"Was just about to ask the same question." I sniffed, crossing my arms as Lauren pulled away.

"Jade, this is Nick, my brother from another mother. Nick, this is my girlfriend, Jade."

"Girlfriend." Something about the woman rubbed me wrong. She just seemed to have a bigger agenda beneath the surface, and I'd become an expert at reading that shit.

Lauren smiled and rolled her eyes. "For fucks sake, Nick, you're not my dad. C'mon in, I gotta grab some jeans. Take a seat. Jade, keep him entertained for a minute." She planted an intimate kiss on the woman's lips, and I turned my attention toward the window, only looking back once she'd headed into the bathroom.

Her apartment looked like a teenager's apartment. Tiny, cramped. Claustrophobic. I sat down on the one lone futon, propped in front of the TV—both bits of furniture I'd picked up for her.

Leaning against the wall, Jade continued staring at me,

smoking her cigarette. "You're a Scorpio, aren't you?"

"What makes you say that?"

"Intense, intelligent eyes. Strong, stubborn jaw. Dark and mysterious. You're probably a master in the sack. Dominant. In control at all times." She licked her lips and, with the cigarette dangling from her fingers, scratched her chin. "Sexy as fuck."

My gaze skated to the closed bathroom door and back. "Aren't you a lesbian?"

"Bi." A smile stretched her face before she took another drag. "Men bore me as of late. Lauren's a wildcat—"

I raised a hand. "I don't need ... to hear this." Easing back on the couch, I attempted to muster that intimidating, fatherly stare. Not that I wanted to act like Lauren's father, by any means, but I sure as hell felt wary toward anyone who might have Lauren spiraling into depression. "What do you do, Jade? Student?"

"Yes. Art major, with a minor in Women's, Gender & Sexuality Studies."

"Drugs?"

"No."

"Alcohol?" I sat forward, resting my elbows on my thighs.

"Occasionally." She shrugged, and blew rings of smoke. "I have an allergy to shitty beer."

"So, what do you drink?"

"Slovakian, mostly. Guinness on occasion."

"What do you get out of this?" Hands splayed to the sides, I nudged my head toward the bathroom door.

"What do you want from her?"

She tipped her head, brows knitted as though confused by the question. "Love. What else?"

Lauren exited the bathroom, her tightly wound curls pulled back into a ponytail, wearing a Wayne State sweatshirt that undoubtedly belonged to Jade. "Bad hair day," she said, smoothing her hands over her shiny face that looked like she'd just applied lotion. "Okay, so I'm supposed to go shopping for who now? Your girlfriend?" A wicked smile danced across her face. "Do I get to meet her?"

"She's not my girlfriend. She's a … someone I know who can't get around very well." I pushed off the couch, tugging my wallet from my back pocket, and removed five hundred in cash, which I handed to Lauren. I hated having to ask her, but fuck if I knew anything about women's clothes, and she happened to be the one I trusted to do it without too many questions. "Try to get three or four outfits. Something trendy, but not too fancy. Practical. Some shoes. Lingerie. Shampoo. Conditioner. Shaving shit for women. Keep the change."

"Wait. You want me picking out lingerie?" Her lips curled into her mouth as she smiled. "Do you get to *see* her in this lingerie?"

"You can get Fruit of the Looms for Women, for all I care. I told you, she's not my fucking girlfriend."

"Feisty, feisty." Lauren cocked her head to the side and glanced back at the other woman. "He seem feisty to you, Jade?"

Jade blew another plume into the air. "Feisty."

I squeezed my eyes shut in frustration. "I'll pick them up in a couple of days."

"Or I could bring them to you. No biggie."

"I'll pick them up." I pointed a finger at her. "Remember. Practical."

"Yeah, yeah, I get it. Probably hit up some vintage shops downtown. Sure you don't want me to stop at *Lover's Lane?*" Her waggling brows had me groaning and wishing I'd never asked the favor. "I could get those fur-lined handcuffs. A whip."

"Ooh! Fuck Fruit of the Looms. Edible panties!" Jade chimed in.

"That's enough." I stuffed my wallet back into my pocket and stroked my chin. "Look, if you don't want to do this—"

"Awww, I'm just playin'. Chill the fuck out. Damn, you're sensitive when it comes to pussy." She shook her head. "Hey, what size clothes am I supposed to get?"

Fuck. I'd forgotten about that. "I'll text you the size."

"Don't leave me hangin'."

I strode toward the door, just noticing a topless picture of Jade in black lace panties plastered to the wall. Glancing back, I threw a thumb toward it, but howls of laughter kept me from asking questions. I shook my head. "I'm out."

"Shit, I love fuckin' with him," I heard Lauren say, as I stepped out into the hallway.

Aubree suddenly came to mind—specifically, *her* black

lace panties hanging in the bathroom. I rubbed a hand down my face at the thought of her sitting on the edge of the bed, panty-less under that dress.

Stay away, the voice of reason chimed inside my head.

CHAPTER 23
Aubree

With his head resting on his paws, Blue lay outside of my room. In spite of the door being propped wide open, the dog didn't move, never once attempted to cross whatever invisible barrier kept him from wandering inside. Had I not seen him in action and gotten a taste firsthand of the speed and strength he possessed, I might've thought him lazy.

I approached the door, aware that his eyes were tracking every step, and stopped just short of the doorway.

His gaze shot away from me, like something had told him *don't look at her, and maybe she'll go away.*

I reached my hand beyond the doorframe, and a low, guttural growl erupted from his throat. When I retracted, it stopped. Naturally, I reached again, but quickly yanked my arm to my chest when the dog's head lifted from his paws.

"Okay, so as long as I'm in my room, we're on friendly terms. Is that it?"

He pushed himself to a sitting position, as though responding to my question.

"Tell me something, Blue. Is he an asshole to you, too? Because I'd be willing to treat you nicer for a little … *freedom*? I'm not talking … through the front door, or anything. Maybe just, you know, a shower? I'm dying here. Washing in the sink sucks."

The dog's mouth widened with a yawn, his gaping maw lined with sharp teeth, and I suddenly couldn't believe I'd survived getting trapped between those unholy weapons of destruction. Damn. Like that scene in *Jaws* when Roy Scheider turned his back while chumming, and the big ass shark surfaced.

"Okay, so, look. The other day … when I tried to escape. You know, it was nothing personal. I'd like to start over." I reached out a hand, careful to keep it inside of my room, wondering if he'd bite it off to the wrist. "Truce?"

The dog lifted his paw, placing it in my palm, and I shook it, chuckling. "So, you wanna come in and hang out?"

His head cocked to the side.

"It's okay. Come. Come in."

Head bowed, he took cautious steps into the room, as if I'd coaxed him into breaking the rules. Maybe I had.

Once inside, he slipped past me, sniffing around what must've been uncharted territory for him, judging by the way his tail wagged and he dragged his nose over every corner. Inching my way backward toward the hallway, I kept my eyes on the dog as he continued to explore the room, nudging my heels off on the way. He could have them for all I cared.

Taking a deep breath, I bolted for the door and slammed it behind me, before the beast could catch me.

Fuckin' A. Freedom. Ha! That was almost too easy!

Whimpers rose from the other side of the door. Literally, dog-crying. I'd never heard anything like it, as if he was heartbroken that I'd up and betrayed him, and like a crazy bitch, I suddenly felt bad.

Go! Go! My head told me to run.

Where, though? If I called a cab, the driver might recognize me, and then I'd be back at Michael's House of Hell. After three days away, he'd probably already covered the furniture in plastic, waiting for my return so he could hack me into a million pieces.

Besides that, I didn't have a phone. Didn't know where the hell I was. Perhaps thick in the center of a shitty Detroit neighborhood, which would make the hulking beast on the other side of the door less intimidating.

With a huff, I opened the door, and Blue sat back on his haunches with something that resembled a smile.

"I'm sorry. It won't happen again." Shoulders slouched, I strode across the room and sat down on the bed, resting my chin on the palm of my hand.

Blue trotted up to me and, licking my cheek, set a paw on my knee. The gesture brought a smile to my face.

"What the hell do you do for fun around here, anyway?"

I pet him for what seemed like a good fifteen minutes,

until he, eventually, lay on the floor beside my bed, while I picked up my book and continued reading.

Blue perked up, and the click of the door caught my attention.

A minute later, Nick stood in the doorway, carrying a brown paper bag, and goddamn, if my heart didn't kick up like a pile of leaves in a windstorm. With his hood pulled back, it was easy to catch his stern eyes.

Scratch that, the man looked downright pissed.

"Why's he in here?"

I shrugged at the question. "He was lying by my door, so I asked if he wanted to come in."

"You talked to my dog?"

"You *don't* talk to him? The silence in this place must drive you insane. Hell, even Tom Hanks had Wilson." I scratched behind Blue's ears, his stiffening neck and the way his paw clawed at the air telling me I'd hit the jackpot.

"Leave him alone from now on." Nick whistled, but the dog didn't move. "Stop petting him. Blue! Come!" Still the dog lay beside me, reveling in the sweet spot I'd found just beneath his collar.

A growl rumbled in Nick's throat as he stormed toward the bed and looped a finger beneath the dog's collar. Blue rose smoothly from the bed and trotted ahead of his master into the hallway, taking his place just outside the door.

"I'm sorry. I didn't know befriending the dog was breaking your rules."

Nick swung around, hands on his hips. "He's here to

guard and protect."

"Against what? Me?"

His jaw twitched, and I could see something bothered him. Our encounter the day before?

The way his gaze slid up and down my body had me feeling exposed, as if I'd stripped naked in front of him, and he could see every one of my scars.

Before he could storm out of the door, all pissed off and moody again, I stood up. "Hey ... if I ... promise to *wear* your ... clothes, will you let me take a shower?" Every word arrived sour. I hated giving in to anything, but honestly, his clothes smelled a damn sight better than mine, and to hell with stubbornness. Clothes were clothes.

He stared back in silence.

"I'm about ready to crawl right out of my skin." I lifted a chunk of grease-caked locks plastered to my face. "And my hair is turning ... damp."

He pulled out a bag he had clutched beneath his arm and tossed it onto the bed, the contents inside clattering on impact.

I hesitated a moment before lifting the corner of the bag. A sketchpad and pencils sat inside. "Thank you."

"C'mon."

I gathered up his T-shirt and sweats from where I'd tossed them onto the chair and followed him down the hall to what appeared to be his room.

The space was vast, mostly empty but neat, and smelled like his delicious cologne. The furniture inside was darker, the colors more masculine in browns and muted blues. Same dilapidated walls as my room, but somehow cozier.

I pointed to a door across from the bed. "Am I to assume that's an actual closet?"

"Yep," he said over his shoulder.

An expansive bathroom, with a frosted glass shower and Jacuzzi tub came into view when he pushed open another door.

Ugh, I'd stay away from the tub.

The small ones were okay, but I had a pretty intense fear of drowning—a weakness that'd always kept me on edge around large bodies of water. Michael had once tied my hands and legs and filled the tub to the level of my chin. When I'd hyperventilated and passed out, almost drowning, he'd realized exploiting that weakness wasn't worth losing his toy. On another occasion, when I'd tried to escape, he tethered my hands and legs and water-boarded me. I shivered at the memory.

The bathroom was clean and tidy, with a long sink that housed dual faucets, as well as mirrors. God, did I want to see myself?

From a skinny closet, he pulled towels, washcloths—the simple things I'd missed in the last few days.

Without a word, he left the room, closing the door behind him. I didn't like the haste and the undercurrent of edginess from him. The steady thrum of tension, telling me to keep my distance. Being ignored by Michael was a blessing, but with Nick, it felt like punishment. Only I hadn't done anything wrong. My gut told me something troubled him.

The way he looked at me had changed, his stare, more intense, as though he studied me at every opportunity. Those eyes made me feel like a specimen, an experiment that'd gone wrong for him. Perhaps my scars had disgusted him as much as they disgusted me.

For the first time in three days, I stood in front of the mirror. Good grief. Much as I wanted to cry, I couldn't help but laugh at myself. In my tattered dress, with my hair in disarray, and oily complexion, I looked like something straight out of the Stone Age.

I unzipped my dress but held it to my breasts for a moment. What if he had cameras installed in there? Though, really, did I care? If the guy had wanted to rape me, he'd had plenty of chances. My scars wouldn't have deterred a true rapist—I should've known, because they'd never deterred Michael.

Even so, I hesitated to drop my dress. Not out of fear of being seen, but fear of *what* I'd see. The exposed skin remained intact, flawless as it'd always been. Michael had always been very careful about the wounds he inflicted. Never in the 'hot zones' as he called them—the parts that would be visible even in a cocktail dress. The scar on my wrist was the only exception, and I often wore bracelets or other jewelry, keeping my hands crossed to cover it up at formal events—Michael's rule. It was a scar he hadn't inflicted, which I think had always bothered him more than the risk of exposure.

Beneath the clothes told the bleak story of my life.

I allowed the dress to fall and stared at the scars reflecting back at me. Two just inside my thighs, the burn marks at my stomach, the slash at my hip that'd had to be stitched. Turning around brought the word that stopped Nick in his tracks into view—carved just above my panty line below a smattering of tiny marks where I'd been whipped too long and too harshly. The dark purple bruises that typically covered my legs and back had faded to yellow. Healing. I wondered what they'd look like once they'd disappeared. Michael had always kept a constant stream of healing bruises. I didn't know what I looked like without them anymore.

Strange that my captor, the one who'd vowed to kill me the first night, hadn't laid a single hand on me. Tears welled in my eyes, blurring my vision, and for a brief moment, I couldn't see any of the scars, until once again, they came into sharp clarity as streams trickled down my cheeks. I'd only cried with the first scars. There, stood beneath the unforgiving lights, parts of me began to heal and my shields began to crumble.

If there was one thing I'd learned in the political game of masks, it was when to crack. Not while lights beat down on my face, or when the city's *finest* were asking me what wonderful plans my *generous* husband had in store. It was when alone in the dark.

I turned off the lights. The window to the left of the toilet faced the shower stall, letting in just enough light to see by while concealing what I wanted to hide.

There was a time I'd feared the dark, but I'd since

found comfort in it. Felt protected by it.

I flipped the shower on, and within seconds, steam hit my face, leaving a damp layer across my skin. Once inside, I let out a quiet moan as the warmth of the water beat like fists against my body. Hell, maybe I craved the abuse, because, goddamn, the water's violence felt good. My knees threatened to give out on me while the heat swarmed me like a blanket.

In the dark, I could crack and crumble, but no matter what, I'd never let the man beyond the door break me. As the spray lashed against my face, washing away the filth, I made a vow in that darkness.

I would never be a victim to anyone again.

CHAPTER 24
Nick

I had no business entering that bathroom. I'd wanted to give her some peace and time to herself. Unfortunately, there was no other way of finding out what size clothes she wore.

The plan had been simple—slip in, check her dress size, then slip out, and I set out to do just that. The darkness of the room came as a surprise, but in some ways, I understood why. I'd always felt at ease in the dark, too.

Slipping through a narrow crack, I closed the door behind me, hoping the light from the window kept her from noticing the momentary brightness.

I'd been a prick for earlier and wanted to do something nice, but there I stood, holding her dress while staring at her perfect curves through the obscure glass.

What'd happened to all the hate and disgust the woman incited? Since when did the sight of her suddenly have my body hardening, heat pumping through my veins while blood shot straight to my dick?

Somewhere in the blur of her body, the word WHORE was eternally etched in her skin. It'd made me see her differently, because the scar on her back was no different from the one on my head. Inflicted by the same man, fueled with the same hate.

Her soft moans carried across the room, and I froze, riveted, as her hands caressed her body through the moonbeams filtering in. Her hands smoothed over her arms, her breasts, her legs. The dips and peaks bowed and arced in perfect proportions, from her large, rounded breasts, her tiny waist and tight, curvy ass. When she arched back into the spray of the water, the first pull of desire tugged at my dick.

Keep away from her, Alec's voice chimed inside my mind, only that time it sounded more like a plea than a warning.

I couldn't argue against it. Following my desires in the past, with other women, hadn't ended well, and the last thing she needed was to suffer whatever messed up shit happened when the lights went out inside my head.

But fuck, that body of hers called out to me like a siren. I felt like a rotten bastard for what I wanted to do to it. How badly I needed to watch her writhe with the pleasure of being defiled by my cock, while her screams reverberated inside the small shower stall.

Leave. Now.

Dropping the dress back to the floor, I backed out of the bathroom, closing the door behind me, and texted her size to Lauren.

A half hour passed before Aubree emerged, swimming in my T-shirt and sweatpants, with long, wet locks of hair falling around her shoulders. *Fuck. Me.*

The familiar scent of my shampoo and soap permeated throughout the room, but mingled with her own natural smell and made for an intoxicating aroma that had my mouth watering and my predator alarms going off like a wolverine about to tear into an innocent rabbit.

She seemed uncomfortable in my clothes and fidgeted with the hem of my shirt. "I didn't want to go through your things, but I didn't see a brush … or anything." Her voice had suddenly become more timid than before. Shy.

I pushed off the bed, slid past her, and grabbed the comb from the top drawer of the sink, holding it outright as I returned to her. "This work?"

"Yeah, thanks." She nabbed the comb, and when her soft finger grazed mine, I dropped it. As we both crouched to pick it up, I gripped her shoulder to keep from knocking heads, and my finger brushed the smoothness of her throat. My muscles stiffened, and I rubbed my thumb back and forth against that same spot, staring at her.

"You don't have to wear my clothes if you don't want to."

"I do." She hardly lifted her gaze, staring somewhere in the neighborhood of my chest. "I like wearing them."

"You look uncomfortable."

"It's not the clothes making me uncomfortable, Nick. When you … look at me the way you're looking at me right now … you're … making me nervous. I don't know if you're ready to strangle me, or—"

I quickly gripped her arms and lifted her to her feet, taking in the feel of her skin against my fingertips. Warm silk glided beneath my thumb as I stole the opportunity to touch her, really touch her, every ridge, every goose bump that puckered under my caress. "It's been three years since I've touched someone. I don't want to give you pain with these hands. I just want to feel." I pushed a strand of wet hair away from her face and dragged my finger down her cheek. "You're so beautiful," I whispered.

With some hesitation, I leaned toward her, eyes studying hers for the first twinge of resistance.

I parted her lips with mine, more gentle than our first encounter, and simply explored her mouth. Warmth feathered my cheek as our exhales mingled in the tiny space that separated us, and I pressed my lips against hers in a kiss so deep, so penetrating, each moan left me one fine thread from losing control.

As I pulled back, a tear fell down her cheek, and the bastard inside of me surfaced once again when I released her and stepped back. "Why are you crying?"

She shook her head. "I'm not going to let you break me, Nick. Not with your kiss. Not with your touch. Too long, I've survived, to let you tear down my guard. I'll survive you, too." Her sad eyes stared up at me, before she turned and exited my room, Blue trotting behind her.

I couldn't blame her. It'd been stupid of me to toy with something I had no intentions of pursuing. I had a job to finish, and Aubree was a means to that end. With a few smart moves, I'd own Michael Culling, would have him groveling on his hands and knees like a little bitch, begging me for mercy. That was the ultimate goal, and I didn't need the distraction along the way. In between, my goal would be to keep myself occupied. Find something to occupy her.

Even if her touch had rattled something inside of me—confirmed with a downward glance.

Much as I'd have tried to deny it, I liked seeing her in my clothes.

Too much. I slipped inside the bathroom, closing the door behind me, and like some kind of perverted fucking hound dog, I inhaled her scent.

I had to get it out of my system. Had to get *her* out of my head, and banging a prostitute didn't seem to be an option for me.

Flipping on the shower, I decided to keep the lights off, as she had, and I stepped inside the steam-filled stall.

Water pounded in angry vibrations along my spine. One touch, and everything suddenly felt different, more sensitive. I hated what she was doing to me, the bittersweet torture of driving me mad with lust, all while I knew I shouldn't want Aubree Culling that way.

My enemy's wife. The one woman in the world I should've avoided like a sane man running from delirium.

Touching her skin. Kissing her. Wet hair. Tight ass. Perfect tits. I was unraveling, coming undone.

It'd become a battle between my mind and my dick.

One taste, one touch, one fuck, my dick proclaimed.

Keep to the plan. Revenge. No distractions. The same words Alec would say to me. Except, Alec wasn't around and he couldn't be reached. Which meant I'd been left to my own devices.

I rested my forehead against the tiles and rammed my skull against the unyielding wall, taking in the jagged jolts of pain racing through my bones. Tightly wound knots of confusion tugged inside my head, all of them tied to Aubree. Without the makeup. Without the fancy dresses and jewelry. The Aubree in my mind had been stripped down to her most basic self, making her more exquisite than ever.

Steam filled my lungs, the heat of the water leaving a thin layer of sweat on my face, and I pressed my forehead harder against the cool tiles and took a firm grip of my stiff dick. Long, torturous pulls coincided with the visual in my head—of Aubree, bound and blindfolded to my bed. I let the scenario play out as I pumped in and out of my slick palm.

She wears my shirt that bunches up to her waist, as she writhes in a slow struggle. Her hips circle against the bed in a languid tempo, taunting me, testing my restraint, and have my muscles tensing with visuals of slamming into her.

"Please." Her plea carries an air of desperation. "I want to."

To be set free? Fucked? I've no idea what she's begging me for.

"Nick, please." Her moans become more intense, and her breasts jut forward, nipples peaking through the thin white

cotton as she arches off the bed. "Help me."

From the footboard, I stare down at her as she struggles—for freedom, or from need, I can't decide, but both are rousing dangerous thoughts.

Her knees come together, and her ass grinds into the mattress. Soft moans escalate to mewling, and her head rolls impatiently against the pillow, her fingers pumping within the confines of her binds, as if she's frantic to get herself off but can't.

"Please!" The harsh bellow bounces off the wall, finally snapping that fine thread of control to which I've been clinging.

I climb onto the bed and pry her knees apart, and she thrusts her hips upward, offering her pussy to me like a feast. Gripping her ass, I dip my head between her thighs and drag my tongue along her glistening seam, smiling when she cries out.

"Please, Nick. Fuck me. Make me come. I'm in pain."

Rising to my knees, I position myself at her entrance and slide inside her. She lowers herself to the bed and releases a pained sigh that is both relief and agony. I know this because I feel it, too, as I rock in and out of her tight pussy with the realization that I don't want the torment to end. I want to stay inside of her, with her warm, silky body around my dick and her soft whisper droning inside my head, telling me how good it feels.

I hate myself for wanting her, craving her so badly, I'd kill to hear her scream my name.

I up the pace and her fingers curl around the binds. She

bites her lip, arching her back, and the 'O' she moans, coupled to her trembling, tells me she's close.

Falling on top of her, I drive her home.

Her screams echoed in my ear, and light exploded behind my eyes as hot semen pulsed into the swirling water slipping down the drain.

Aubree. I rode out the last of my orgasm, forehead pressed into my arm against the tiles, hand balled to a fist, while the light prickles radiated to every muscle in my body, weakening them.

Rubbing a hand down my face, I pushed upright, shaking off the momentary dizziness. For fucks sake. I'd just blown my load while fantasizing about Aubree Culling.

CHAPTER 25
Aubree

I flipped open the sketchpad to a stark white page that almost glowed in my dimly lit room. As always, I closed my eyes and took deep breaths, searching my thoughts for that strange, fairy-like female that'd plagued my mind the last couple of days, trapped in a cage far too small for her body, wings bent and bleeding. Lounging on the bed, I set to work, trying to get as many details out of my mind and onto the paper as I could.

Time passed in a blur, as it often did when I got in the zone. I focused on the lines in her face, the shadows that clouded her eyes, the pain that aged her. Details I saw in myself every time I looked in the mirror.

Fingers curled around the bars, she sat crouched, head lifted, staring toward something outside of the cage—something that called to her, telling her not to give up. To keep fighting for her freedom.

"I see you've made use of the supplies."

My hand jerked at the interruption of Nick's voice,

sending a line of lead up the female's back that resembled a scar.

I paused to examine it, exhaled a breath, and lifted my gaze to where he stood framed by the door. I'd never seen him, or any man for that matter, in black leathers, but damn the way they hung loose on his legs and stretched across his groin had my throat turning dry. Chains hung from his loops and the holster at his hip carried a gun. The black tank only stoked my burning curiosity to know what the hell the man looked like without a shirt. The muscles in his arms and chest gave me a pretty damn good idea he sported a set of washboard abs beneath.

The gun caught my attention a second time. If he typically carried weapons, they'd hadn't been visible prior to then. "You startled me."

A smirk teased the corner of his lips. "You're an artist."

My shoulder twitched with a half-hearted shrug. "When I'm feeling inspired, I suppose."

His gaze fell to my lap, where the sketchpad lay open across my legs. "So, what's this?"

"Personal?"

He crossed his arms, his muscles bulging in the folds, and that pissed off scorpion scowled back at me.

"It's an image that's appeared a few times in my head. I'm just trying to capture it."

The narrowing of his eyes told me he was studying the sketch, maybe picking up on the similarities between me and the female in the cage. My cheeks burned at the full, pert breasts I'd drawn on her, in likeness to my own.

"This is your cage, huh?" His rich voice had a way of tickling my senses, and a part of me yearned for him to say something totally off the wall, completely inappropriate, just to hear how it'd sound. "The wings are bent and bleeding. Not broken?"

"Not yet," I whispered.

"What's she staring at?"

I looked him straight in the eye, my gaze unflinching. "Hope."

"So, this is how you deal with captivity? Drawing yourself as a victim?"

Clearing my throat, I gripped tight to the pencil, swallowing back the urge to stab him in the eyeballs with it. "It helps to purge these images. Gives me a moment of focus." Flipping the page, I held up the sketchpad and the pencil. "You should try."

"No thanks. I'm not an artist."

"You don't have to be. That's the beauty of creating art. It's cathartic. Think of your past, your present, your future. Draw what troubles you. It can be a face, a place, a story inside of one single image." I set down the sketchpad and crossed my arms, eyes narrowed. "Wait a second, you're a game designer. I find it hard to believe you can't draw."

"I never said I couldn't draw. I design games. Not a bunch of useless ink blot pictures for some arrogant asshole with a string of acronyms to come along and study."

Swallowing a chuckle, I tapped the pencil to the

sketchpad. "Draw something from your game."

His jaw shifted.

C'mon, give me something. "No one's going to study it. You don't even have to show me what you've drawn. Keep it for yourself. Burn it afterward, if that makes you feel better."

The way his face ticced, the sliding of his jaw, the twitch of his eye, I couldn't tell if he wanted to punch me, or if he might've been considering the suggestion. He sniffed and unraveled his arms. "You keep drawing your pretty pictures. Keep the hope alive. As for me? I've had enough fucking quacks trying to crack open my head, I don't need you digging around in there." He turned and strode from the room.

CHAPTER 26
Nick

I spun a bullet, with the words *fuck you* etched into its broadside, against the wooden table as I sprawled in a chair across the room from a strung out, drunken black guy—Jalen Wallace—trying to pick up the waitress. The bar, one of those offbeat venues along Vernor Highway, had long been notorious as a hotspot for shootings and illegal dealings. Fuckin place stank like cheap beer and grease.

Hidden in the back of the bar, out of plain sight, I'd been staring at him for the last hour.

Jalen slapped the woman's ass, and she stumbled forward two steps, catching herself on the side of the table before breaking out in giggles. As his hand slid beneath the table, cleavage blocked my view, lots of it.

"Hey, darlin'." The way the busty redhead bent over my table and snapped her gum left me wanting to reach into her mouth and smash it into her painted-on face. "My, you look good enough to eat."

I didn't say anything. I'd found people got uncomfortable quicker by my staying quiet while holding a deadpan stare. Like a natural predatory response. Just as I suspected, she slithered back from the table, eyes cowering in submission.

Once she'd walked away, my attention swung back to Jalen.

Thing about street gangs was they had nothing to bind them together. No loyalties. No single mission that tied them to each other. They were fragile, easily broken. As the Seven Mile Crew had gained some traction, built up some power, they'd begun to crumble, break off into their own pursuits.

Jalen 'Babyface' Wallace was a fine example of that. Of all the Crew, he'd been the most difficult to track down. A few bad deals had landed him on a lot of shit lists, and many of his customers were the kind of gangs that did bind together for a reason. Religious. Political. They took any act of mistrust as a reason to kill, and Jalen had been forced to hit the underground as a result. His ties to the Seven Mile Crew were severed when he didn't deliver on a large order of semi-automatics to a few infamous crime bosses. The leader of the Crew, Brandon Malone, couldn't risk the chance he'd become the target of a larger fish in the ocean, so he'd distanced himself from Jalen, eliminating that cozy layer of protection Jalen once enjoyed.

At a tug on her wrist, the waitress bent forward, and Jalen put his lips to her ear. Sickening giggles followed.

With his arm draped over her shoulders, he shot up from his chair and guided her out of the bar.

And the hunt begins.

Why I smiled every fucking time I was about to rain hell on their little picnics, I'd never understand. I left some cash on the table before following the two outside.

Jalen led her to a rusted, early model Tahoe, parked in the far corner of the lot, where both climbed in the backseat. Once they'd closed the door behind them, dark tinted windows made it nearly impossible to see, aside from the occasional abrupt movement.

I took a moment to slip the black ski mask down over my face.

Within earshot of the vehicle, I heard a smack followed by the woman's outcry, and Jalen's shouts of, "Stupid bitch! Nasty ass whore!"

Tugging my hoodie over my head, I checked my weapons. The guy's bare ass might've been hanging out in the air, but that didn't mean he wasn't fucking her with a gun in his hands.

Without so much as a courtesy knock, I threw the door open, my lip curling at the sloshing sounds that ceased the second both of them caught sight of me.

The female screamed, as expected.

"What ... the ... fuck?" Jalen reached for his gun, but stopped the moment I lifted my blade in the air.

An exceptional blade, serrated on one side with a mean looking gut hook. Couldn't help but imagine the damage it'd do if it happened to get lodged beneath the skin—a thought that must've passed through Jalen's mind, because he settled back against the seat.

"Get out," I said to the woman quaking beneath him, my gaze shooting straight back to Jalen.

Without skipping a beat, she scrambled out from under him with her gathered clothes into her arms and, eyes on the blade, took off.

To Jalen, I said, "Get in the driver's seat."

In an asinine move, he tugged his gun loose from its holster, but I sliced the knife across the back of his calf, yanking the hook to dislodge a nice chunk of flesh from the wound.

"Motherfucker!" He grabbed for his mutilated leg, and I raised the blade again. "No! No! Okay, okay, okay!" Dragging himself between the two seats, he fell into the driver's chair.

I opened the passenger door and took a seat beside him, as Jalen's trembling, blood-coated hand turned the key and the vehicle fired up to a roar. "Old Boblo Dock." I propped the blade at his balls, smiling as Jalen pulled out of the parking spot.

Blondie ripped through the bar door, flanked by two burly men, and pointed at us as we passed. For good measure, I lifted the blade higher, sneering at the whimper that escaped Jalen.

It pained me to think that, if I'd only had the training, the conditioning, the sense of calm I'd come to possess— so many things I could've done with that. I stuffed the thought aside—plenty of time to ruin myself later. For then, it was a celebration—before moving on to bigger and better kills.

"Who are you?" He kept stealing glances as I half-heartedly propped the knife to his nuts.

"In time," was all I said, watching the city pass through the window.

"Y-y-you want money? Drugs? I-I-I got connections. Whatever you need."

"Your connections want to kill you as much as I do, Jalen." I tipped my head back and, smirking, directed my attention back his way. "Thought I'd put your dick in a jar to set on my mantle."

There was a quiver in his laugh, and out of the corner of my eye, I saw his head whip between me and the road. "You're a funny guy, eh? Jokester."

"No. Not a jokester."

Within minutes, we reached the dock, where I'd already taken care of the lock on the fence. He pulled in where I directed him, alongside the abandoned building. Much as the city had turned its shit around, Detroit still boasted a good share of abandonment.

"Park here." I pointed to a spot where grass had grown up through the cracks in the pavement, beside my Mustang. I'd walked from the dock to the bar, planning to switch out his sore thumb of a ride that would have assholes chasing us through the streets. "Get out. And don't bother to run."

He slid out of the driver's seat and yanked his loosened pants up as he hobbled along toward the fence in a pathetic break for it—exactly as I'd anticipated he would.

Idiot. Gun cocked, I shot him in the ankle, blowing bits of bone onto the pavement.

He collapsed, clutching his leg. "Fuck! Awww, fuck!"

"I told you." I shook my head as I approached him. "No running."

Gripping his collar, I dragged him back across the parking lot, against the kicking of his good foot and his screaming. No one could hear him. Even if they could, no one would care.

I opened the passenger door on my Mustang and tossed him into the seat, hating the idea that I'd have blood to clean later. After rounding the vehicle, I plopped in the driver's seat and drove the Mustang out of the parking lot.

His sobbing beside me, trembling as he clutched his mangled ankle, had me about two seconds from knocking the bastard out. "You wouldn't happen to be diabetic, would you? That wound looks like it's gonna be a nasty one."

"Fuck ... you." I couldn't help but smile at the shaky threat in his voice. More sobbing, and goddamn if my hands didn't instinctively ball into fists. "What ... did I do ... to you?"

I glanced across to see him hunched over his legs, hand supporting his head. "Funny you should ask."

He lifted his gaze to mine, and his brows pinched. "What?" He scanned the interior. "Do I know you, man?"

"I wouldn't say you know me. I wouldn't say any of

you fucks knew me. Or my wife. Or my son." Instinctively, my lip curled at the mention of them. "But it's better that way, isn't it? You can kill indiscriminately without care or conscience." I rested my elbow on the back of the seat, casually, as if we were having a normal conversation that wouldn't ultimately end in death. "Nasty thing, a conscience, isn't it? Keeps us aware of what's right and wrong." I patted his back, and he flinched. "Good thing I no longer have one."

He rocked in the seat beside me, rubbing his skull back and forth, back and forth, while Detroit's cityscape passed beside him in a blur. Didn't take long for him to contemplate his next predictable move. He grappled for the door handle, but it broke off in his hands. He whimpered when it tumbled out of his opened palm.

"Broken on the inside." I sighed. "I know the feeling."

He screamed. Like a bitch.

In what must've been a moment of insanity, he leapt across the console, fumbling at the holster hugging my hunting blade.

I gripped his wrist and elbowed him square in his cheekbone, knocking his nose along the way.

He fell backward into his seat. "You bwoke my fuckin' nose!"

"My apologies, if I've given you the impression that I *don't* plan to hurt you."

Within a couple of minutes, we arrived at the metal stamping factory. Taking my time, I dragged my finger across the hood of the car as I rounded the vehicle and opened the passenger door. "I have a surprise for you." Squeezing his nape, I yanked him from the seat, and he fell in a heap on the ground. Fuck if I was gonna carry him. Instead, I cocked the hammer back with a click and pointed the gun at his good ankle, smirking when he squirmed like a worm caught on a hook.

"C'mon, man! C'mon!"

"Get up. Or I'll make you crawl with two blown out ankles."

Wheezes of panic ended on a long sob, but he dropped forward and pushed, propping himself on his good foot. Once upright, he pogo'd in front of me, and I gripped his arm, guided him over the rubble with my gun pressed into his skull. With some effort, he climbed over the charred brick and debris piled outside of a back entrance, while I easily stepped behind him.

I'd already taken the liberty of setting up a chair beside the huge hydraulic press in the back of the factory, and with a nudge, he collapsed onto it. His bloodied hands trembled when I chained them behind his back, and he bucked as I wrestled secure a blindfold over his eyes.

"How does that bullet feel?" I knelt down and examined the hole in his tennis shoe, slapped his shin. I laughed when he curled his foot up under the chair.

"Don't touch it!"

"Hurts, doesn't it?" I pushed to a stand. "Man, wait till you see what one feels like lodged inside your skull."

His cheeks lifted, as if he cringed behind the blindfold. "Look, whatever ... whatever I did ..."

"If you think you're going to win me over with your useless, artificial apologies, you're wrong." I shrugged. "You're lucky. We're just here to … mutilate you mercilessly until you die. No talking."

He let out a long and drawn out scream that echoed into the surroundings, reverberating off of the cement walls.

Through a black haze, I hear Lena screaming, but I can't see her. I don't know if I'm passed out, blindfolded, or on the verge of death, with a ticket to hell where my suffering will be hearing her pain for eternity.

"God, please no!"

The crackle is followed by the smell of burning flesh.

Wake up, wake up! I can't move my limbs. Like being buried alive. Lena! Lena!

"Nick! Please!" She screams for me, and it's in those moments that shards of agony rake across my heart, threatening to pull me into madness.

"He can't hear you." A male's voice taunts. "Scream, little piggy, scream!"

Knuckles to my temples, I paced in front of Jalen, coming to a stop when the screaming finally ended. Flames of fury rocketed through my body, leaving a wake of adrenaline, a need for violence and pain. Jalen's pain.

"Scream, little piggy. Scream." I drove my fists into his face, cracking my knuckles against his cheekbone with a spray of blood, sending his head kicking to the side. Another hit snapped teeth from his mouth. Picking one up from the floor, I turned the yellowing tooth in my hand and flicked it at his face.

His muscles twitched with my every step.

"Are you scared?" I asked.

"Fuck … you."

Cartilage cracked beneath the fist I drove into his nose. "Are you scared?"

"Yes!" He spat blood toward my boot. "You sick fuck!" The nasally words brought a smile to my face.

I yanked his blindfold away from his eyes and tugged my mask up, revealing my face.

His gaze popped. Always amusing, that moment when realization finally kicked in. Sometimes, I wished I could've recorded the shit to play over and over for laughs.

"Y-y-you. I shot … we killed … and burned the house."

Against my better judgment and, likely, the advisement of my therapist, I asked, "Do you remember what you did to her?"

He sank into the chair and frantically shook his head, as if he was on the verge of sobbing. "I'm sorry, man. I'm … sorry."

"I didn't ask you what you're feeling *now*. Frankly, I couldn't give a flying fuck how sorry you are. I asked if you *remember* what you did to her."

Rolling his head against his shoulders, he whimpered. "It … wasn't what you … think. I didn't do … anything. She fuckin' taunted us, man. She was … a stripper, right? Took her robe … off. Offered to suck—"

Rage erupted in my veins like flaming bullets of fury,

and I hammered his face, over and over, until his eye swelled with my punches.

Stop. Stop. I could hear Alec's words as if he stood there beside me, and I had to coax myself to quit hitting the sorry bastard.

He's supposed to die slow. Mercilessly. In truth, I already knew what he'd done. I knew that Jalen raped her, not only with his dick, but with the barrel of his gun. I knew they burned her with cigars. Cut her. Beat her. Until, at last, they finally shot her. All while I lay bleeding, half-conscious, right there in the fucking room.

Those images alone had landed me in the hospital for overdosing. Had I not been a coward, I'd have injected my own veins with sulphuric acid to burn the memory right out of me from the inside. Except, that'd leave the asshole in front of me running free.

I still had a job to do.

Rocking my head side to side, I cracked my neck, and took deep breaths.

"I'm … I'm sorry. For what I did." His words arrived on a snort, as though the blood had backed up into his throat.

"I'm not your fucking priest. Everyone's sorry just before they die. How many times did she ask you for mercy? How many times did she apologize?"

His lip quivered. "I'm sorry, man."

Curls of anger tore through my body like a hurricane, and I gripped his face with a snarl and removed my blade. With a wave of adrenaline surging through my veins, I sliced his ear away, my muscles tight as he jerked and fought my grasp. I wished I could've said that the kills moved me somehow. That the tortures touched some part of my soul—however dark it may be. They didn't. I'd disconnected myself, watching the kills through the eyes of an impassive assassin. There was nothing but a hollow inside of me, and the sooner he was dead, the quicker I could fill that hollow with the alcohol I so desperately needed.

How quickly a man could be reduced to an animal. A psychopath, disconnecting all sense of morals.

With some wrangling, his ear came loose, and I held it up like a trophy, while his guttural cries reverberated throughout the building. "Perhaps you're not hearing me, Jalen. I don't give a fuck how sorry you are."

Coughing and choking broke his screams, and I tossed his bloody ear in his face. Three years ago, I'd have been appalled by such a crime. Sickened.

Right then, I felt nothing. Except raw.

I couldn't look at the guy without seeing my wife—the tears streaming down her face. Begging them to stop. The helplessness knotted my stomach, and my hands balled into fists at my sides.

I took deep breaths. *Tamp it down*. His death was supposed to be slow and merciless, like the many hours he'd tortured her.

Can't. I'd clamped my teeth so hard it felt as if they'd crumble in my mouth.

I unchained then lifted his hands, keeping the cuffs

attached to his wrists, and strung his arms across the flat surface, as I rounded the hydraulic press to the side opposite of where he sat. "Ever watch how bullets are made?"

My question was met by the increasing intensity of his whimpers.

"I always thought they *melted* the lead to mold a bullet." A good tug on the chain killed his pathetic mewling. "They don't! A heavy billet of lead is loaded into a press, and using a *shit* ton of pressure, they form it by compressing the metal together." I slapped my hands together, and as the chains rattled, he flinched, before his lips quivered then soured with his sobbing. "Interesting shit."

Returning to his side, I knelt to the floor. "So, you're an arms dealer, huh? Ever wonder what they'd call you if you didn't have arms?" At the reverberating pitch of his scream, I smiled, reveling in his obvious fear—the same horrific sound that had torn from my chest just moments before the bullet hit my wife and son. "The fucking irony, right? You might want to go by arms *broker* after this." My laughter bounced off the walls.

"Please don't … do this, man. Whatever you want … I'll give you whatever you want."

"The night you broke into my house, you had a choice. Of right and wrong." I gripped the lever of the press. "You chose wrong."

Closing my eyes summoned the blackness from the dark shadows of my mind. His screams jarred my muscles to flip the switch.

CHAPTER 27
Chief Cox

"So, who called on this one?" Cox circled the man strapped to a chair with his forehead pressed against the hydraulic machine. Like the first two crime scenes, *Eye for an Eye* had been painted near the victim, in this case, across the machine above him.

"First shift. One of the factory workers found him." Burke knelt beside him, as the coroner tipped the man's head back. "Looks like he was beaten pretty bad. His face is swelled up like a balloon. Ear's been cut clean off."

"He has swelling all throughout," the coroner said as he continued his exam. "Compartment syndrome. Often the case in crushing injuries."

Burke peered up at the bullet wound just above where the guy's ear used to be. "Gunshot to the head. What'd you say, that's a twenty-two, Chief?"

"Probably." Cox turned to the manager and owner of the building, both keeping their distance outside of the investigation circle. "Can we flip this on? We want to lift this press. See what we got under here."

"Yeah, there's a switch. On the side of it."

"You ready?" Cox directed the question to the coroner, still manipulating the man's face with gloved hands.

"Yes."

With that, Cox signaled for the manager to fire up the machine, and a burst of air preceded the lift of the press.

"Ah, fuck! Fuck!" Burke spun around, hand covering his mouth, as the gore beneath was revealed. "Who the fuck?"

"You throw up on my crime scene, and I'll have you filling out parking tickets until you fucking retire," Cox barked.

"Crushing injury to both arms and hands." The coroner continued with his assessment, dictating as he examined the victim. "Bones appear to be completely broken, comminuted fracture, I'd say no more than one inch fragments. Skin is split, exposing the fascia beneath. Joint capsules and ligaments appear to have ruptured, dislocating the joint altogether."

Blood coated the surface of the press, over the edges and onto the floor, but trapped in the crushed hand, beneath a sickly twisted, thick finger, Cox eyed a white scrap. "Gimme the tweezers, Burke." After donning a pair of gloves, he lifted the scrap like a game of Operation.

Unfolding it revealed the number three.

CHAPTER 28
Aubree

Shouts yanked me from dreams, and I shot upright, head whipping back and forth, my breaths rapid and muscles trembling. I took in the stillness of my room, the darkness that seemed undisturbed, aside from the flutter of drapes dancing in the breeze created by my cracked window.

Just a dream.

Laying back against the pillow, I settled into the warmth of my blanket —until another outcry, tortured and pained, echoed beyond my door.

Nick.

I shot out of bed and padded across the room, toward the door, placing my ear against the wooden panel.

"Lena! Lena! No! Fucking bastards! No! We'll kill you! We'll kill you all!"

We?

I opened the door to find Blue with his head perked, as if to say, *you hear what's going on?* His whine told me he worried for his master, and he didn't so much as snarl when I tiptoed past him to Nick's opened bedroom door.

Clutching his doorframe, I watched the way his thrashing body had the bed pounding into the wall. The sheets lay in a white tangle across him. He arched his back, creating a perfect arc of agony, muscles so tight they looked as if they'd snap beneath his skin. His kicks and grunts clutched my heart, as I observed his sufferance in dreams.

The yearning to go to him, soothe him, had me pushing against the door, widening the crack.

No. Don't do it.

"Don't do this! Jay!" His bellow bounced off the walls and halted my steps.

Who were those names he called out in his sleep? Why did he sound as if he'd been immersed in something real, truly enduring some kind of pain and torment?

A glisten of sweat coated his skin, discernible in the moon's light. His brows creased to a frown heavy with pain, and his body trembled, along with my own.

"Nick," I murmured. The draw to lie beside him, to calm him, pulled me further into the room, as instinct beckoned me to go to him and quiet his agony.

He planked on the bed as his curses filled the air.

Backing away toward the door, I slipped out of the room the moment his eyes flipped open. My heart slammed into my ribs, and I gasped at the near miss.

From the hallway, I peeked through the crack, watching him jolt upright, to the edge of the bed, where he held his head, rocking back and forth. His rapid breaths were broken by whimpers, and I caught a glint of something he snatched off the nightstand beside him.

His arm shook as he held it outright and sliced his skin with a long blade.

An empathetic voice called out from somewhere deep inside of me— I'd had it ingrained into me from an early age to heal others, thanks to my beautiful mother. It was that which'd led me to work as a therapist, the desire to help ease someone's pain. Staring at Nick, although he was my kidnapper, had me feeling no less compassion. An ache bloomed inside my heart as he cradled his carved arm.

As fierce and dominating as he seemed, the man was broken. Tortured by something. Wracked by some kind of pain.

What?

It was a question that plagued my mind as I padded back to my room.

***

I folded the book, laid it on the bed beside me, and sat up when Nick appeared in my bedroom doorway, nearly a dozen bags hanging from his grip. Entering, he set them down before returning to the hallway, from where he grabbed shoe boxes and a blue milk crate, arranging all the items in the center of the room.

Though it remained covered, I couldn't help but stare at his arm where I knew a scar had begun to take form.

I slid my legs over the side of the bed, still unsure of what the hell was going on, but curiosity got the best of me, and at a slight nudge of his head giving me approval, I crawled toward the bags.

Each one carried an assortment of dresses, shirts, jeans, tanks, panties, and toiletries. There were two shoe boxes—a pair of Chucks and combat boots, exactly the style I'd worn before meeting Michael. As if he'd somehow reached into my past.

"I didn't … pick those out," he said.

"No, it's … it's good." Gaze glued on the bags of clothes, I offered a half smile. "Thank you … for doing this. I missed simple clothes."

So badly, I wanted to ask him about the night before—the nightmare and cutting, the names he called out. Thanks to the concealment of his coat sleeve, I caught no more than a glimpse of where thin scars lined his forearm.

"You used to wear this kind of stuff?"

"Yeah, before I became a politician's wife, and my wardrobe changed to cashmere and linen. And pearls." I shook my head at the thought. "Twenty four years old, wearing pearls. The only woman in my life who wore pearls was my grandmother."

Stuffing his hands into the pocket of his jeans, Nick shrugged. "I don't know, seems fitting for the job of stuffy politician's wife."

I toyed with the laces on the Chucks. "It actually wasn't fitting at all for my job. Not exactly the kind of thing you wear to get down and dirty."

"What the fuck were you, a mud wrestler?"

Laughter burst from my chest, the sound so *strange* to

me. I hadn't laughed in a long time, and by the frowned surprise on Nick's face, it must've struck him strange, too. "No. I was a therapist. I only got to go once a week, and it was usually on one of Michael's off-site meetings. Every Wednesday, I was given precisely three full hours of bliss."

"What did you do there? Pass out pictures of your husband's face to young, impressionable future voters?"

I dropped my gaze and my smile faded. "Seems I fooled everyone into thinking I was nothing more than a puppet." Pulling my knees into my body, I wrapped my arms around them. "Good for me. It's how you survive that matters most. I like to think some days that perhaps, in those three hours, I did more good than I'd ever done in my whole life."

"So, what made you get into therapy?" He crossed his arms over his chest and leaned against the wall.

"Well …" A hiccup of laughter escaped me. "Inside every therapist is a patient." I shrugged, still toying with the shoestring. "I needed to cope with a few things myself, so I thought helping others would teach me how."

"That's why you cut yourself? Trying to cope?"

Why do you *cut yourself*, I wanted to ask. It'd been a week since he'd seen the scar on my wrist, and I'd have thought he'd forgotten it by then. "You first."

He shook his head. "No. Tell me. Why did you try to kill yourself?"

"What does it matter?" A couple of days earlier, he'd asked what made mine special. "Does that put a monkey wrench in your plans, or something? Why are you stressing over it? Does that make me damaged goods to whatever bald, fat bastard you'd planned to pawn me off on?"

The twitch in his cheek confessed that he wanted to laugh, but, wisely, he didn't, and my muscles bunched with the anger rolling through me. "I didn't say I was stressing." The flat, no-bullshit tone of his voice clawed at my patience. I wanted to know his secrets, not spill my own. "I said I want to know why you did it."

No. That was a box I'd been good at keeping locked shut, and I didn't intend to open it for anyone. Especially not him. As a therapist, vulnerability was something I'd learned to keep to myself. It was one thing to relate to a student, but another to spill a dark box of secrets. That was my box. He could have any other story, any other box inside my head, except for that. "Something else. I don't want to talk about that one."

"All right. How 'bout the one on your back?" Another deeply brutal wound, though one that caused more anger than pain.

"I snuck away to my father's funeral. Never told Michael."

His face rumpled to a brief frown. "He scarred you for going to your father's funeral?"

"No. He scarred me for breaking one of his rules. I failed to tell him where I was going, so he strung me up to a post in the basement and whipped me." Scooting backward on my butt, I leaned against the wall beside the bed, next to where he'd set the bags of clothes. "He left me down there for three days. The doctor made a house visit to check on my wounds and treat me for dehydration."

"A doctor visited you and never reported what Culling did to you?"

"To whom, Nick?" I mindlessly rubbed my thumb on the inside of my palm. "He owns the police. The doctor wouldn't tell a soul, or risk having his tongue severed with a chainsaw. There is nowhere to run. He has all kinds of connections." Living with Michael was like being trapped by a dictator in a foreign country, surrounded by people who didn't speak the same language.

"What the fuck made you fall in love with this asshole in the first place? Why'd you marry him?" he asked.

"People marry for different reasons. Mine had nothing to do with love. I've lost my faith in *romantic* love. I don't believe in it anymore."

Nick didn't say anything, just stared at me.

"Now you."

His gaze fell away from mine, and I expected him to avoid the question, to be a dick and leave me sitting there with my open wound as he walked away. Surprising me, he stroked a hand across his head, over his scar. "I took a bullet to the skull. Spent a year in physical therapy, mental therapy, bullshit therapies. Still have trouble with some words on occasion, and I can't really do shit with my right hand anymore. Had to learn to shoot a gun with my left." As if he could anticipate my next question, he shook his head. "'Sall I'm sayin' about that."

Small steps. In time, I might learn what plagued him in sleep, but at that point, I knew a little more about him.

He knew a bit more about me, which I'd hoped would help change whatever preconceived thoughts he'd developed from the fake persona he saw on TV. That woman wasn't me. Hell, I'd be disgusted with her, if I didn't know a decent person lay buried somewhere beneath.

Lowering my gaze, I peered into the milk crate and my eyes widened. Books lay stacked upon one another, and as I investigated each one, I couldn't help but smile. Faulkner. Shakespeare. Tennessee Williams. Harper Lee and, my favorite, Poe. Even a few romances thrown into the mix. I lifted my eyes once more. "You bought me books?"

"There's a place I used to go to a long time ago. Kingston's Books. They have a lot of old classics."

I reared back at that, crossing my arms. "You used to hang out at a bookstore? I'm shocked."

His eyes fell away from mine and dimples caved his cheeks. "I wasn't necessarily there for the books." The smile on his face shriveled to something more serious. "It's where I met my wife."

The horrible exercise of trying not to stare at his ring finger must've had my eyeballs bouncing like a crack addict. "You're ... *married?*"

He sniffed and cleared his throat. "She, uh ... she's dead."

Was that Lena? The name he'd called in his sleep? I'd never been good with words, so I locked my stare on the books in my lap, pressing my lips together, before I finally said, "Nick, I'm sorry."

"Anyway, the owner of the store said these were some of his favorites, so I grabbed all of them."

"I love them. Thank you." Once again, our stares collided, and I felt something different about Nick—a curiosity that burned inside my head. Dead wife? Shot in the head? The questions had begun to mount—which meant I'd begun the jigsaw puzzle inside my mind, piecing together the edges first, in hopes of eventually getting to the center. "You're keeping me for a while, then?"

"As long as it takes."

Of course, his cold and distant demeanor would make it one of the more challenging puzzles I'd had to work. "For what, exactly?"

His brow winged up. "If I told you, I'd have to kill you. Let's keep it on good terms."

CHAPTER 29
Aubree

Somehow, a week had slipped by, and aside from bringing me meals, Nick remained distant. Hadn't touched me since the episode after my shower, and didn't say much. I kept to myself while he was around, drawing in my sketchpad, or reading for the most part, and wandering the house as soon as he'd left. As long as I stayed away from the front door, Blue seemed content to let me explore a bit.

Wearing dark jeans and a white fitted T-shirt that hugged the bulging muscle in his arms and chest, Nick stood in the doorway, his leather jacket slung over his elbow. "I gotta run out. Something I have to pick up. Shouldn't be long."

Well, this is new. He'd never once informed me when he planned to leave. It was almost as if we were becoming more like roommates than kidnapper and kidnappee.

"Okay."

When he snapped his fingers, Blue shot to his feet, and

Nick ushered him into my room. "Just don't talk to him like a baby. Don't want him turning into a pussy."

Laughing, I patted the bed beside me for Blue to sit down. The dog took a stately pose next to me and licked my cheek. "Thank you," I said, scratching behind Blue's collar. "What made you change your mind?"

Nick rubbed his thumb across his nose. "Wish I knew," he said, and left the room.

I stared after him for a moment, still trying to wrap my head around the last three minutes. One week later and, still, I knew nothing about the man. The edges of the puzzle still sat waiting for more pieces to fall into place. It was what kept me there when I should've been devising an escape plan.

I'd always been planning escape, living with Michael. Always on the lookout for holes in the walls he built, or ways to break his rules. He'd have never left me alone in a house unsupervised while he freely came and went. I had a track record of escaping. A few times, I'd even come close to freedom. Yet, there I was, sitting alone with a dog that I'd befriended with the same charm I'd used on every predacious species that seemed to fall in my lap.

Still, something kept me from escaping. Something inside of me that made up excuses why I couldn't yet leave.

I had to know why. Call me a flippin' masochist, but I needed to know who Nick was and why he'd chosen to kidnap me. Why did he wake from nightmares? Did it have to do with the scar on his head? His dead wife? Who was the mysterious man that seemed to have bigger plans brewing outside of this dark sanctuary to which he came home in the early hours of morning? Like a creature of night, he stayed out, stumbling back alone, hiding in his room until the following afternoon. I'd studied him for a week and still knew as little about him then as I did a week before.

As if he practically begged me to try to escape, he'd kept a rather loose watch over me. Yeah, Blue might've tried to stop me, but I certainly didn't see the dog as the monster from a week ago.

As soon as the click of the door told me Nick had left, I got up out of bed and made my way into the hallway. Blue followed behind me, down the staircase, and when I reached the front door, he shot in front of me, as though in a standoff, and barked.

I threw my hands in the air. "Damn, dog. You're as touchy as he is." I stared through the skinny side-lite window adjacent to the door, trying to make out a street sign or some kind of landmark, but all I could see through the darkness out there was the silhouette of one other house and a few trees.

Some parts of Detroit were like ghost towns—not a single soul for miles. Running for help could be hit or miss with all the crack houses and drug dealers. I could very well end up in a worse situation, and I didn't even have a cellphone on me for if that occurred. Escape would take planning—starting with how to subdue the big fucking Cane Corso blocking my way. Unfortunately, I'd gone and made friends with him, so trying to hurt the dog was no longer an option, not that it ever had been.

With his shoulders bunched in warning, Blue watched me dance around the slim window, until, at last, I made my way back up the staircase, but I paused at the top of the stairs.

Only one place I hadn't yet explored. Like some unsaid case of *Beauty and the Beast* and the *don't go exploring the west wing* crap. Well, to hell with that. Answers lived behind that locked door, and damn it, I needed to know.

I crouched to the floor and slid the bobby pin from where I stored it in my bra strap. Though his bedroom door was the only one that remained locked, it didn't hurt to keep hold of my emergency skeleton key. With a click, the lock popped. As I stood and twisted the doorknob, a waft of Nick's cologne assaulted my senses like a delicious attack.

I'd been in his room a few times to shower, but only ever when he was present, and somehow the knowledge of him standing just outside the room while I stood naked, showering in his bathroom, struck me as slightly erotic. Yet, he never made a move. Never invaded my space. For the first time, I realized, in spite of being confined to an old, run down mansion, I'd been given more space than I ever had before.

I moved to beside his disheveled bed, imagining his body tangled in the blankets. I'd heard him some nights, yelling in his sleep. The nightmares.

He'd told me his wife had died, but I knew none of the

details. I couldn't quite pinpoint why I never asked him. It could've been that I didn't want to pry, but perhaps the true reason was that I knew he wouldn't have told me anyway. Both of us had our secrets, like vests of armor, keeping us insulated from the other. Exposing secrets made a person vulnerable, opened them up to questions, probing little inquiries that ultimately didn't mean anything. He'd given me a small taste of his past, by revealing he had a wife, yet, a week later, it hadn't made a damn bit of difference.

Still, the curiosity rapped at my brain. I couldn't let it go. I thought about him most of the day, had sketched his face in my notepad. Searched the house for evidence of who the man might be. All I'd found was a cupboard full of liquor and some weights for working out. It was as if he lived two separate lives, interacting with me here, sober, serious, but not cruel— then stumbling around the house, knocking into walls before the sun came up every morning.

Who was the man who called himself Nick? Why hadn't he killed me? Touched me? Asked anything about me, aside from what I tossed to him in brief conversation? It was as if he had all the information he needed.

I wandered his room and opened drawers, smiling at the copy of *The Grapes of Wrath* that'd been dog-eared. I set it back in the drawer and found a small scrap of paper, written in faded red crayon. James Nicholas Ryder, Ms. Waddell's class. *Nicholas*—for Nick? *Ryder*, the name echoed inside my head. The paper didn't look too aged to have been from his own childhood. A son? Though he hadn't mentioned a child. He couldn't have had a child somewhere as much as he came and went.

An image lay amongst the other items. I lifted it from the drawer, exchanging it for the note, and studied the subjects sitting on the front porch of a bungalow-style home. In it, a young-looking Nick sat with his arm around a beautiful brunette, while an adorable little boy with bright blue eyes sat on his lap. Beside them, a small puppy stood with his nose to the ground, sniffing, and I glanced down at Blue, who stared back at me, sat back on his haunches.

A pang of sadness stabbed my chest, and I closed the picture back inside the drawer, feeling as if I'd seen something I shouldn't have.

The corner of a manila envelope peeked from behind the book when I returned to that drawer, and I carefully slid it out. From inside, I pulled out a stack of photographs.

Stood with the blur of a building at his back, Michael held a cellphone to his ear in the first image. The sight of him twisting my stomach, I flipped to another picture, taken months ago, where the two of us had attended a ribbon-cutting ceremony at the new casino downtown. In yet another, the photographer had caught me exiting the cemetery on the day of my father's funeral.

My breath hitched. Realization struck my head in a dizzy jumble of thoughts, and I gripped the lip of the dresser to keep from stumbling back.

Nick had been watching me for months. As far back as a year, from what I could determine from the remaining images. My kidnapping wasn't some haphazard attempt to steal the mayor's wife. He'd followed me—or, at least, *someone* had, and for a long time.

Another image had been taken through the window of my art studio at the hospital, where I stood before a classroom of students. I remembered the day. Vividly. One of my students had forgotten his medication and threatened to stab me with a pencil, until a distraction outside the window had thwarted his attack long enough to call security, to escort him back to the psych ward.

What did he want with me? To barter? Had Michael taken his son? Murdered his wife? Was I to be used to negotiate a deal of some sort?

Nick's words from the first night slammed at the forefront of my thoughts: *You think I'd kidnap you for something as insignificant as money?*

No fucking way. No way I'd go back to Michael. I had to get the hell out of there. It wasn't that I thought Nick would *hurt* me, but the possibility of sending me back to Michael would *kill* me, and I was too close to freedom to piss it away.

I had to find a weapon. A woman didn't just roam the streets of Detroit without some form of protection. I had to find a gun, a knife, something. I'd already cased the kitchen, but, surprisingly, Nick didn't decorate his countertops with a Ginsu block.

I turned to the closet, and as I crossed the room, Blue

came to a stand beside me. Placing my hand on the knob prompted a bark from the dog, like he'd been trained to keep people out of it.

Which only made me want to know what was inside.

Testing the dog's patience, I slowly turned the knob again.

Blue whined and paced, antsy—until he snapped out of it in a way that had the hairs standing across my arms.

Stiff as a board, he stood at attention, his eyes focused on the doorway. *Oh, shit.* Nick'd said he wouldn't be long.

I released the knob, closing Nick's door behind us, but instead of following me, Blue trotted down the stairs. A deep growl rumbled in his chest, freaking me the hell out.

"It's Nick," I whispered, but the dog kept on, stalking toward the front door.

It's Nick, I told myself. When had Blue ever reacted that way to *Nick*, though? It was like the dog knew his master's routine, the sound of his footsteps, and something didn't seem right to him. Which meant, it didn't seem right to me, either.

The pounding inside my chest beat a steady rhythm in my ears, and I rushed to the window in my bedroom, peering through the bars. Beyond the adjacent trees, in what I estimated to be the neighboring mansion, lights flickered to darkness, as though a set of headlights had been turned off.

Downstairs, Blue's constant low growl filled the otherwise quiet house.

As seconds ticked by, his growling grew louder, more

intense, peaking into the edges of a bark. I couldn't take my eyes of the vehicle outside, though. A vehicle meant a means of escape.

My stomach churned with the indecision swirling in my head. Should I take a chance and approach a complete stranger, or stay where I could land back in the arms of a psycho, one who'd surely kill me? At that point, Michael had to have figured out I'd stolen that chip from his desk.

I'd vowed never to be a victim again. I'd never be broken again. Not knowing Nick's intentions made him an enemy.

A quick glimpse outside the window showed the lights hadn't yet flipped back on. *Do it, Aubree. Go now.*

A bark tightened my muscles, and I tiptoed to the bedroom door, peering down into the dilapidated foyer. Blue's barks turned frantic, and he jumped at the door, scratching the wood like he tried to claw his way to whatever stood on the other side. He sounded like a starving lion ready to break from its cage.

With Blue occupied, it was then or never. Dashing into the bathroom-slash-closet, I nabbed my coat, slung over the rack, and slipped it on. Not the warmest thing to wear in October, but it'd have to do.

Holy hell, my heart hammered so hard I thought the damn thing might leap out of my chest, and my easy breaths turned to shallow pants of fear.

All at once, Blue stopped barking.

My body continued to tremble, though, as Blue remained by the door, frozen stiff one minute, whimpering and pacing the next. He lowered his head, as though sniffing through the door, then sat back on his haunches.

Padding down the stairs earned a quick glimpse from the dog, but as though he was too occupied to care what I did, he turned his attention back toward the door.

Inside the dark kitchen, I searched for something I could use as a weapon. Anything. Rifling through mostly empty drawers produced nothing more than spatulas and a can opener. I twisted around and zeroed in on the kitchen chair.

Blue's distant bark stiffened my spine, and I lurched forward, grabbed the back of the chair, and slammed it into the countertop. Once. Twice. The leg finally splintered into a sharp spike of wood, a pathetic little jabbing tool.

Better than nothing, though.

Through the kitchen, into an adjacent mudroom, I made my way toward the back door. The slamming of the chair hadn't interrupted Blue's incessant barking, and another glance over my shoulder showed the dog hadn't bothered to follow me.

I slipped through the door, shutting myself outside, where brisk winds whipped through my opened jacket. I hadn't had time to change and wore nothing more than a T-shirt and jeans beneath the coat.

Scampering across the lawn brought me to the edge of the shallow grove that separated the two properties. Christ, I didn't even have a flashlight.

Voices erupted from a distance away. Two? Three? Blood pounding through my ears made it difficult to distinguish, but each one definitely sounded deep, masculine.

The trembles wracked my body, and each breath arrived shaky. Who were those people? Drug dealers? Nick's neighbors?

Twigs crackled beneath my boots as I rounded trees and snuck through the narrow forest, until I arrived on the edge of the adjacent estate.

Perhaps more dilapidated than the one I'd just escaped, the mansion had more of a gothic look. Sounds from inside echoed across the yard. Glass breaking. Slamming, thumping. Crumbling, like whoever was inside had taken a sledge hammer to the walls. Laughter.

Thieves.

Across the unkempt lawn, an older model red truck sat parked, the bed of it filled with metal and furniture—objects that backed my suspicions. The closer I stalked toward the truck, the louder the noises became, like a stampede moving through the house with speed. Behind a lower level window of the house, flashlights flickered about, and in one of the rooms on the upper level. Crouching low, I rounded the vehicle and, finding it empty, opened the door and climbed inside.

My father, in his determination to protect me and teach me to get out of sticky situations, had shown me how to hotwire a vehicle once. That'd been years ago, though, and dread twisted my gut as I bent forward and searched the glove box for something I could use to remove the panel on the steering column. Depending on the age of the truck, a screwdriver could be used like a key to start it, too , but I found nothing. Still clutching the wooden spike, I flicked the sharp tine, testing its strength. Maybe I could use the tip as a key. Or lodge it into the panel to pop it off. Was worth a try, anyway.

As I sat up, breath trapped in my throat.

Through the windshield, a kid, maybe fourteen or fifteen, stared back at me. Dirt coated his pale face, and his clothes were no more than rags hanging off his skinny frame, like he'd been living on the streets. He glanced over his shoulder, toward the mansion behind him, then back at me.

Breaths arriving fast enough to make me dizzy, I slid my hand across my lap, patted along the door for the handle, and gripped tight.

Before I could bolt, he opened his mouth and screamed. Loud, piercing. It wasn't until it reverberated back that I realized he'd yelled, "Thief!"

I jumped out of the driver's seat, and the second my boots hit the grass, I dashed toward the woods. A backward glance showed three men exiting the mansion and trailing after me. I kept on, pounding as much speed as I could from the clunky boots I wore, ignoring how they thumped as I leapt over fallen branches and brush.

Oh, shit, oh shit!

"Stay on her, Trey!" I heard one of them call out.

"To the right!" Another masculine voice followed the

first. "She went to the right!"

The sound of their voices put them in their early twenties, maybe. Street kids.

All I had was a makeshift weapon from the chair leg.

One, I could probably fight off, just out of sheer adrenaline. Two, would be tricky. I didn't stand a chance against three, so the best thing was to run as fast as my fucking legs could hammer out.

"We catch her, she's mine! You hear? Mine!"

"Here, kitty, kitty." One of them laughed, and I choked back a whimper.

My mouth dried of all moisture at the nearing footfalls. I could just make out the edge of the trees when my legs flipped out from beneath me. The earth crashed into my face, and a shooting sting rushed through my nose, as branches bit through the thin fabric of my T-shirt.

Palms squeezed my thigh, pulling me backward, and a man's face appeared, dark, evil eyes above the wide grin stretching his lips. "Ha! Found the bitch!"

I let out a scream, stabbing him in the arm with the wooden spear. "Get the fuck away from me! I'll fucking kill you!"

"Bitch!"

Gripping my hair, he tugged hard. A slap across my face jarred my vision, sent a flash of light bursting behind my eyelids.

Teeth gritted, I attacked with everything inside of me as the cold forest bed tore through the jacket, to the skin on my back. Kicking. Scratching. I swung, and my knuckles drove hard against bone. Blood sprayed in my face.

"Fuck!" The one I'd struck covered his nose with one hand, while a flash of white hit my periphery.

Pain exploded in my left cheek, rattling bones and teeth. My jaw felt unhinged. Another blow numbed the first as lightning struck my skull.

"Bitch broke my fuckin' nose!" Fingers dug into my jaw. "Cunt!"

A thunderous crack against my cheek knocked my face to the right again. The surrounding forest tilted on itself while the men scrambled to hold me down. A black hole was closing in on my view, threatening to steal my vision. *No! Fight it!* I double blinked and concentrated. *Don't pass out. Don't pass out.*

Two dirty-faced, pale skin men stared down at me with missing teeth, their rancid breath like something had died in their mouths. Hands spread eagled my legs, and at tearing, my gaze snapped down toward the guy who'd wedged himself there.

"Oh, fuck, she's beautiful. Hold her down, Trey."

"Look at those scars!" The one closest to me leaned in. "You like bein' cut? Huh?" His wet tongue dragged across my face. "You get off on pain? Is that why you're fighting?"

I tried to move my arms, but they'd been pinned above my head by the third man.

The treetops beyond them came into view, a dark shroud looming over me.

A hand groped my breast.

"Hurry the fuck up! I'm about to blow my shit any second."

"Bitch has three holes!"

Their laughter pierced my ear like nails punching through my eardrum.

My stomach sank, twisted and turned in on itself as the one below lifted up to his knees and his cock sprung loose from his boxers. Both of my legs were held down, one by the man at my side, the other by the one positioning himself at my core.

The attacker beside my head unzipped his pants and beat his tip against my chin.

"No! No!" I strained my muscles to kick, tugged at my limbs, but a palm hit my forehead, slamming my skull into the ground. My breaths arrived faster, panicked.

"Choke on this, whore."

Deep menacing growls arrived out of the darkness to the right of me, and I caught a flash of black before Blue took down the man at my side.

"Oh, shit!" The one between my thighs pressed into me, squeezing the bones in my legs as he shifted about. "Get your fuckin' gun! Shoot the fucker!"

A thunderclap bang echoed through the trees. Blue's growls and barks followed. Three more bangs. More barking. Four bangs. A yelp. Each noise had my muscles jerking, and I kicked at the attacker below, knocking him back on his ass.

Fire ripped through my scalp as the other one tugged

my hair, and a sharp sting burst across my cheek with a slap.

The one I'd kicked scrambled up onto my thighs, digging his fingers into my flesh. "Hold the fuck still, bitch!"

I pushed past the dryness in my throat, and screamed. "Help! Someone, help!"

Terror curled through my veins in a rush at the reality that the men intended to *and would* tear into me.

"You try to steal from us? Huh, cunt? Try to take our fuckin' truck?"

I didn't even know which of them spoke, but the voice sliced through my skull, robbing me of the blackness that clung to the fringes of my consciousness. My head spun, the world tilt-a-whirling before my eyes, and all I could make out was the stench of their breath and the digging of their nails into my skin.

More weight pressed into my body, and I turned to find the man Blue had attacked had returned, his jacket torn and bloodied. Blue? Where did Blue go?

As their awkward hands fumbled with my shirt, hope slipped away. How fucking stupid! Why had I run?

I could see the mansion from where I lay, mocking me—my sanctuary from Michael, from the men ravaging my body, standing off in the distance like an impenetrable fortress. On the cold ground, in the woods between abandoned houses, where no one would hear my screams, I could die, ravaged, beaten and alone. The thought crushed down on me, pounding terror through my body.

A hard slap stung my thighs. "Stop fucking moving!"

I didn't even realize I'd continued to struggle against them. My body had gone numb, my mind disconnecting, falling into darkness. That same hopeless pit of doom that'd prompted me to run in the first place, to keep from getting sent back to a monster, just like the ones tearing into my clothes.

My thighs jostled with the wrenching of my jeans. I stared up at the man above me, and like a nightmare, his features contorted until they'd morphed into the sickening familiar face of Michael. "You love this, don't ya? You get what you come for? This is what you was looking for when you tried to steal our shit, yeah?"

Tears blurred his smile, and a sob ripped from my chest. "Please," I begged. "Don't do this."

A shot rang out. Warm spray hit my face, followed by a tortured outcry. Another blast of fluid hit my stomach, and a mass of weight fell on top of me, knocking wind from my lungs, as warmth oozed down my belly.

Like an answered prayer, my arms were released. A scuffle at my head knocked my ear, yanking my hair.

As a single gunshot blasted the air, the man above me stopped screaming. His body slumped to the side, crackling the leaves with his fall.

It happened so fast I couldn't keep up with what was happening. My gaze darted toward the right, and I didn't know whether to plead harder or whimper with relief.

Nick's silhouette stood for only seconds, before he charged headfirst into the guy beside me, knocking him to his back.

Trapped beneath the lifeless body of a man who'd almost raped me, I screamed and heaved until I'd thrown the deadweight off me, scrambling backward until my head hit a solid surface. I startled to the left, relieved to find it was only the trunk of a tree, and tugged my jeans back up onto my hips.

Straddling the stranger's body, lip peeled back in a snarl, Nick pounded his fist into the bastard's face. The sickening crunch of busted cartilage turned my stomach. When at last the man stilled beneath him, Nick pushed up from the savage devil, aimed his gun at the man's face, and shot a bullet square at his forehead.

My muscles flinched, breath trapped in my chest as I sat in complete shock. Through parted lips, a scream yearned to tear out of me, but I couldn't speak. Couldn't do more than stare in disbelief at the macabre that surrounded me.

I caught Nick's gaze and drew in a breath. His enlarged pupils merged into the blue, giving him a crazed, rabid appearance. Burning with wrath and rage. For a split second, my heart hammered, as he glared at me like he'd attack me next, but the echoing crackle of branches diverted his attention, and he took off, presumably after one of the men. Perhaps one I hadn't accounted for.

Every muscle in my body shook. On the forest floor in front of me, all three of my attackers lay unmoving and face down in a converging pool of blood that seeped into the thirsty ground.

"Trey!" At the sound of another foreign voice, I scrambled for one of the fallen guns and aimed it at the source.

The young boy who'd alerted the men back at the truck stood a couple yards off. Eyes wide, mouth agape, he stared at the gore, but as his gaze fell on me, he twisted away and darted off into the dark woods.

Lowering the gun, I curled my knees into my body and sobbed.

Minutes passed before the thump of boots had me lifting the gun again. I found myself aiming at Nick.

He rushed to my side and pushed back strands of hair. "Fuck, Aubree."

My body trembled with relief at the sight of him, another round of tears filling my eyes.

With a growl in his chest, he lifted me into his arms, as if I weighed nothing. Through the darkness and chaos inside my head, I heard him whisper, "I've got you," as he carried me across the lawn, toward the mansion.

Those three simple words blanketed the aftershock still quaking through my body, and the world around me stilled. *I've got you.*

Caught in his arms, all I could do was stare in awe at the raw intensity of his features—the tightness of his jaw, the furious pulse of the veins in his neck, the flare of his nostrils.

As he kicked open the door and carried me up the staircase, I felt numb.

He killed those men. For *me.* So easily, and with such

lethal grace, I didn't know whether to wrap my arms around him or fear him. In either case, Nick had instantly become something more than my kidnapper. He'd become my rescuer, my savior. A dark angel, with blood on his hands and fire in his eyes.

No one had ever fought for me, killed for me. Not even my own father. I'd always taken care of myself, faced my own battles, and part of me wanted to curl up into a ball of shame for being so weak.

Onto shaky legs that I swore would give out any moment, he set me down in his bathroom, still holding me up as he flipped on the faucet for the bath.

I clutched his jacket. "No!" Burying my face into his neck, my body planked, my jaw so stiff and sore from being punched, I could hardly form a word. "N-not the d-d-deep water."

Without argument, he walked me to the shower instead and flipped on the spray. "Let's get his fucking blood off you."

I nodded, tears streaming down my face. His spicy scent penetrated my senses, calming the tension wound so tight in my gut I thought I'd snap. With a lift of my arms, he stripped off my shirt and bra, tossing them to the floor, never once staring at my scarred body. At the yank of my pants that jostled my body, I gripped his shoulder to steady myself. He helped me inside, and while I stood shivering in the spray, he remained outside of the shower and sponged me down with soap, creating a pool of reddened water at my feet.

I stared at him, the blood spattered all over his white shirt and arms as he worked. A killer, who'd shot all three men without hesitation, murdered without remorse, was worried about the blood on *me*.

His strokes were gentle, careful, as he meticulously wiped every trace of those bastards from my skin while avoiding the new bruises on my legs and the cuts on my back. I should've been afraid of him, at the way he'd so deftly wielded a gun, the way he'd proven to be just as dangerous, perhaps more so, than Michael—because Michael would've weighed the risks to himself first.

Nick was impulsive, unpredictable, fearless and intimidating all at the same time. As I stood in awe of his kindness, gentleness of his hands caressing my body, for the first time in my life, I felt safe.

Once he'd gotten the blood off of me, he flipped the shower off and toweled me dry, before carrying me to his bed, where he wrapped me in the warm blankets. Shame tore at my heart and I cursed myself for what I'd done, trying to get away. I cringed at the thought that I'd betrayed him. He'd given me freedom, trusted me, and I'd exploited it.

"Stay here for a minute, all right?" He spun away from me, but I clutched his arm, not wanting to admit that I'd been shaken to the core.

"Who … were they?"

"Scrappers, I think. Saw their truck, full of steel and copper." He leaned forward and stroked my hair, giving me a good look at the way his dilated pupils had begun to soften, to shrink from the wild intensity of before, into a calmer blue. "They won't hurt you now, okay? Just stay here." His face pinched to a somber frown. "I have to find Blue."

CHAPTER 30
Nick

I searched the perimeter of the mansion, all the way to the back, where I finally found Blue, lying in a pool of blood. He didn't breathe. Didn't move. The wounds at his skull oozed blood around his head.

So many bullet wounds. As if he refused to fall.

My knees gave out, and I dropped to his side, lifted his head into my lap. "No, no, no. Blue, c'mon. No, buddy. C'mon."

His closed eyes didn't flinch. His head lolled with every shake of him, every attempt to wake him. Nothing.

I bent over him, listened for a heartbeat, confirming what I already suspected.

Silence.

Lifting him higher into my lap, I stroked his face, his expression as peaceful as if he slept in my arms, and an old memory struck.

Jay sits in a strip of sunlight that shone onto the floor through the window. The tiny puppy is stretched across his small legs. "Daddy? Can I name him?"

I reach out to stroke the puppy's ear. "Whatcha got, little man?"

"Blue."

"Blue, huh? How'd you come up with that one?"

Tipping his head, Jay toys with the puppy's tail, not even that disturbing the sleeping dog. "His eyes are blue."

I smile. "All puppies' eyes are blue when they're first born."

He looks thoughtful for a moment but shrugs. "I just like Blue."

"Blue it is."

"He's my best friend in the whole world." Jay plants a kiss on top of the pup's head. "I love him."

I pat my son's head, my smile fading to something more serious. "He'll protect you from the bad guys while I'm at work."

"But he's just a puppy." Jay frowns. "How can he protect me?"

"Well, he can't right now. But some day, he's going to be the best guard dog on the block."

He nods, holding Blue's tiny paws in his. "Because he loves us, too."

"That's right."

While the memory broke, I paced back and forth, stroking my skull. "Fuck!" Tears welled in my eyes, and I stopped moving, pinched the bridge of my nose to keep them from surfacing. "Fuck!" I kicked an empty flowerpot, sending it crashing into the brick wall of the house.

Once again, I fell to my knees beside him and lifted his head, rocking him as I stroked his ear. "You did good, Blue. You're a good dog." I sniffed and cleared my throat, desperate to hold back the agony itching to escape, and buried my face at his ear. "Do me a favor, huh?" Arms tight around his neck, I squeezed my eyes shut, my voice faltering. "Watch out for them for me."

Just like that, the last thread slipped through my hands. If not for Blue, I could've easily swallowed a bullet a while back. I owed him my life. He'd followed me out of the burning house the night of the attack, keeping at my heels as I stumbled along. It'd been his bark that caught Lauren's attention, as he stayed at my side.

Sliding my hands beneath his body, I lifted him into my arms, carried him inside the house, and set him down in his bed. I'd bury him the next day.

In the meantime, I had to get rid of the bodies.

***

It was nearly midnight when I returned to the mansion. I'd driven the truck just a few blocks over and set it on fire with all of the men inside. No one would find them there. No one would give a shit about them.

I entered my bedroom, found Aubree sleeping, curled in my blankets, her body twitching. Staring down at her bruised face, I stroked a finger across her cheek, and she startled awake, backing herself against the headboard.

I turned to leave, but she struck out, gripping tight to

my wrist. "Wait! Please, stay. Please."

I hadn't meant to wake her, but I did as she asked, taking a seat beside her on the bed.

Her eyebrows lifted, in a worried expression. "Blue ... did he—?"

I shook my head, and she ran her hand through her hair, tears shimmering in her eyes.

She cupped her face in her hands, curling her fingers into fists as she sniffled. "It was my fault. He was just trying to protect me."

"He was doing his job. It's not your fault."

"What have I done?" Pulling her legs to her chest, she wrapped her arms around them and buried her face in her knees. "I'm sorry, Nick. I'm so sorry."

"No reason to be sorry." I caught a glimpse of the bruise on her face, and mentally put the focus back on her. Blue was dead. Apologies wouldn't change that fact, and she didn't need to torment herself over it. "You okay? That bruise looks pretty bad."

She ignored my question. "I shouldn't have ... I'm so sorry." Her eyes shifted back and forth, lip quivering, and I sensed another round of sobbing would follow.

Reaching out, I hesitated a moment before placing a hand over hers. "Hey, it's okay. You're safe now."

"It's not okay. It was selfish. I was selfish to run from you. And now Blue ... because of me ..."

"Stop beating yourself up. Blue didn't do it for you, okay? He did it because that's what he was trained to do. I trained him to guard you. It's my fault."

The gold of her eyes dulled, and her refusal to look at me told me shame plagued her mind. "I just … can't stop seeing their faces." She shook her head, eyes wet with tears. "And … I tried to fight them off, but …"

"They were three men with guns, Aubree. Anybody would've been afraid."

"Except you." Her eyes shot to mine, staring so intently I almost had to look away. "You seemed … different tonight. Almost like you snapped. I was scared … at first." Her gaze lowered to my bare chest, forcing me to shift on the bed. Running her hands through her hair, knees still pulled tight to her chest, she closed her eyes and drew in two long breaths. The tightness of her jaw and the painful-looking knit of her brows softened. When she opened her eyes again, they remained directed on my chest. "Dylan Thomas."

The name, completely out of context, caught me off guard. "What?"

"The quote on your chest. A poem from Dylan Thomas. My mother had a large book of poems that I must've read a thousand times as a child. I remember that one." Her eyes tracked back and forth to each side of my chest. "The tattoos … what do they mean?"

Two sets of sound waves inked on each pectoral were the beginning and end of my son's first newborn cry. I'd uploaded the recording into a computer sound wave generator and had it made into a tattoo design. Over my heart, were two stars, one outlined with my wife's initials, one with my son's. Both carried the date of October 30,

2012—the date of their death. Below the stars was Thomas's quote:

Do not go gentle into that good night.

Rage, rage against the dying of the light.

I'd had it tattooed when Jay was first born. Three months premature, he'd spent the first sixty-two days in the NICU, fighting for his life. As a result, I called him Jay Louis, after the famous boxer, Joe Louis—my little champ.

The very thought incited a sharp sting in my eyes and nose with the threat of tears. How could a child, who'd fought so hard to live early on, be taken away so young?

"The stars … they were … something I used to tell my son. When he was young, he'd asked me what happened to my wife's father, who'd passed away when Jay was three." The memory filled my head, no less vivid than if I still sat at the edge of my son's bed, talking with him before he fell asleep:

"Where's papa?"

"Well, he's no longer here. He's up in the sky, looking down on us." Jay's small chin peeks over the spaceship blanket as I tuck him in tight.

"How? Does he live in space?"

The question makes me smile, and I run my fingers through his soft, downy hair. "The stars in the sky are the souls of the people we love. They shine so bright, not even the night can hide them. And when we're lost, they guide us."

"Will you be a star someday, Daddy?"

"Someday. When you see one shooting across the sky?" A sweep of my hand over him illustrates the visual. "That'll be

me, saying hello. I'll watch over you on the darkest nights. And just before the sun rises, when it's time for me to sleep, I'll whisper in your ear, see you in the night."

A tear slips down his cheek, and he tucks his face in the pillow as though hiding himself.

"Hey, why the tears, buddy?"

"I don't want you to die. I don't ever want you or mommy to die." He sniffles. "I'm going to pray every night that you don't ever become a star."

His comment brings a contradiction of laughter and sadness at the thought of ever leaving him alone someday. I wipe his cheek and kiss his head, letting him pull me in for a tight hug, when he wraps his arms around my neck. "Everyone becomes a star eventually, Jay. But no matter what happens, or where I am, part of me will always be here,"—I rest my hand against his heart—"with you."

"How?"

"Your heart was made from mine."

He glances down at his chest and then to mine. "Am I in your heart, too, Daddy?"

"Always."

"Nick … what happened to your wife?"

Aubree's question ripped me from the memory, and I could feel the beating against my chest—the punching on the outside from someone trying to get past the armor and steel that caged me in.

I'd only been asked the question once before, by a therapist, and I never returned after. Alec never asked. Lauren never asked. I'd never talked about the murder to anyone. I couldn't. That was a box best kept locked and stored away. I had no idea what unleashing those memories into the open might do to me. Like Pandora's Box, it contained my greatest pain in the world and my deepest, most intense love. My firstborn son would always hold a prominent place in my heart, and his mother, my first love, was the only woman in my life who had the power to destroy me. Losing the two of them took me to depths of pain I couldn't even remember, places so dark I feared them myself. I drowned myself in memories of their voices, their touch, the feel of them in my arms. And when those sensations had begun to fade, I replaced that soul-crushing misery and despair with anger. Anger so venomous and lethal, I'd become more beast than man. I dreamed of blood on my hands and tortuous screaming, not from my wife and son, but *my* victims—the men who hurt my family. I wanted a pound of flesh for every year that I'd miss watching my son grow up.

Opening that box was dangerous. Talking about them, without the protective coating of wrath to keep my insides insulated from the pain, could've left me blacking out and waking up to bloodstained sheets, and Aubree's lifeless eyes staring back at me. It was bad enough that she knew anything at all about my family, that she had some curiosity to explore and tease out when I might've let my guard down.

Shaking my head, I braced to leave, and felt a cold grip on my wrist.

"Please don't leave. I won't push."

My body relaxed and settled beside her once more.

Feather light, her fingers drifted across my neck, presumably tracing the scorpion tattoo. "Will you stay with me tonight?

I nodded. "I'll be right here. Get some sleep."

***

The screams. I can't get them out of my head. Blackness keeps me from seeing, from feeling. I could be alive. Or dead. This would be my hell if I were dead. Those screams rattling my bones, pushing me over the edge. Hurt. Kill. What made me a good man has turned me into a killer. Love. My muscles tighten as the screams intensify, and through the dark, I feel around, searching for the source.

Lena! Jay! Their names echo and fade beneath the undercurrent. I have to find them. I know what comes after this. I know the pain that will follow if I don't find them. Frantically, I pat around the walls, the floor. The dark room seems to shrink, squeezing me into this box where the screams become louder.

A cold, sticky substance glides beneath my fingertips as I crawl along the surface—up, down, I have no sense of direction. I rub my fingers together, and somehow, the biting tang of copper hits the back of my throat, as the smell penetrates my nose. Whose blood?

The screams drone on, kicking up my heartbeat, driving me mad with the desire to find the source. They need me. The desperation in the voice tells me they need me to find them. Help them. Save them.

A warm but stiff body hits the palm of my hand, and I explore the surface, anxious, searching. "It's all right, I'm here," I whisper to her.

The screaming subsides. A sharp blow knocks my jaw, kicking my head to the side. A hand grips my wrist, and on instinct, I draw back a fist.

A light flips on.

Movement in my periphery snaps my attention to the left. A streak bleeds into the darkness, swinging like a pendulum, back and forth, back and forth. I focus on it, concentrating.

Aubree's wide eyes stared up at me, her hand off to the side, waving back and forth, back and forth. Beneath me? A sweep of the room showed the light of the nightstand flipped on. I'd straddled her body, pinning her down. Her arm was drawn back beside her head, frantically vying for my attention, the other gripping my wrist at her throat. My arm was drawn back, too, as if the two of us were frozen in a standoff.

Fuck. Scrambling backward from her body, I fell to the floor and backed myself to the wall. "I'm sorry." I cradled my face in my hands and rubbed my skull back and forth. "Fuck, I'm so sorry, Aubree." With both hands planted at either side of my head, I rocked, wishing I could crawl out of my own skin to get away from myself. What the fuck was I doing? What would I have done? Hit her?

I could've hurt her! The agony of that thought left a caustic burn in my gut.

Warm hands across my skin set my muscles flinching, and my palms flattened against the floor, my spine pressed into the wall, as her sad eyes searched mine while she gently stroked my arm.

I shook my head— *please don't ask why*—but then she took my hand and kissed my knuckles.

"I'm sorry." Drawing my hand to her chest, she held it tight to her. "Please don't go."

Sorry? What the fuck was she sorry about?

She bowed her head, and I caught a glistening stream of tears down her cheek. "I woke from a nightmare. I thought ... I thought you were one of them. I didn't mean to hit you."

My brows came together. "*Your* nightmare?"

Wiping the tears from her cheek, she nodded. "You tried to calm me down. And I ... I hit you. I'm sorry." She sniffed, lifting her gaze. "I didn't mean to hit you, Nick."

Quiet followed as I attempted to process what the hell just happened.

Her eyes flitted to the side. "You called me Lena."

Jesus Christ. Drawing in long, easy breaths, I slowed the apeshit pounding of my heart. "I thought she ... *you* were hurt. I heard screams and ... blood." My gaze fell to my hands, and I opened them, studying the marks where I'd tightened my fists so hard, my nails had gouged the shit out of my palms. Puffing my cheeks, I blew a sharp breath and double-blinked. "What was the waving about?"

"A trick I learned. Helps break nightmares." Her eyes shied away, then flicked back to mine. "Who's Lena, Nick?"

What's your wife's name? Do you remember? What's your name? The therapist's voice rolls through my head.

A sting hit the back of my neck, and I suddenly realized I'd scratched the hell out of it.

Aubree's gaze fell from mine, a faint blush to her cheeks, as if she was embarrassed for having asked. Perhaps she thought it was another woman. A girlfriend.

"My wife. Lena was my wife." I couldn't explain why or how the next few words flew from my mouth. "She and my son were … murdered." I waited for the fury, the blackness to crash over and send me into rage. My stomach tightened as a tingle moved through my body and heat warmed my muscles.

It dissipated.

Along with it vanished the urge to thrash Aubree's body against a wall. To pummel her with my fists for trying to pummel my shield. All I felt was sadness. Like saying the words aloud meant, somewhere inside, I'd accepted that they were gone. I didn't. I refused, because with acceptance came contentment, and I would never dishonor them with such a passive state of mind.

"How?" she asked.

How? Telling her how might have given me a renewed dose of anger that I needed. It could also be dangerous for Aubree. God help her if she tried to convince me that my anger was irrational and unwarranted.

Could I trust her? Or, more importantly, could I trust myself?

An upward glance faced me with softened eyes that spoke of pain and understanding. They told me she knew something about holding back those demons and the uncertainty of trusting someone with those haunting secrets.

"It's okay if you can't, Nick."

Like she could read my goddamn mind! I cleared my throat, the maddening rub of my thumb back and forth over my trigger finger pulling my attention away from her sad, golden eyes. I'd stolen the woman's dark secret when I lifted her dress, discovered a very vulnerable piece of her.

I'd given her nothing in return.

Alarms blared inside my head, warning me not to peel back the armor I'd spent years casting and molding to protect the weak, soft bones beneath my skin. Bones so frail they could snap. *I don't owe her!* A dark corner of my brain battled. I didn't owe her a damn thing.

Tamping that inner voice down, I clamped my eyes shut, my mind searching for silence, preparing myself to peel back the scab of my most painful wound.

"I, uh … I had a meeting." I didn't recognize my own voice as I spoke, as if I'd climbed out of my skin and let the empty shell tell its story, while I watched from a safe distance. "With a game publisher who wanted to buy my design. Things were going well, so when he invited me to meet up with him for drinks, I did." Every muscle in my body yearned to twitch and fidget, a series of alarms, warning me not to go any further. Yet, I did. "My wife, Lena, had to pick up our son from daycare and it kind of forced her to rush. I normally picked him up. She, um, called me later in the night. Jay had forgotten his rabbit." Rubbing the back of my neck, I cleared my throat, as my muscles bunched and tension wound inside my gut. "He always slept with it, and wouldn't go to sleep, so Lena ended up staying up late with him. I swung by the daycare to pick it up after my meeting."

Eyes screwed tight, fingers digging into my palms, I swallowed back the unsaid confession—that if I hadn't been so selfish, so self-absorbed, so desperate to succeed and make a better life, I would've been the one to pick Jay up. I'd have held my son one more time, felt the weight of him in my arms. Lena would've been at work, like every other night. Our fate might've been different.

"I'm guessing maybe they saw the lights on in the house, or something. There were six of them." Ire pounded through my muscles, winding the tightly coiled ball of anxiety inside my gut, as I thought of all those men having their way with my wife, all at once. I stretched my fingers, uncurling my fists to keep from striking out at the wall—or worse, at Aubree. "All members of the Seven Mile Crew. When I ... arrived home, I noticed the door was unlocked. Wasn't like Lena. She never left the doors unlocked. Had OCD with that and checking burners. I heard noises coming from upstairs. Kinda muffled."

Rolling my head against my shoulders didn't lesson the tight pull in my neck and shoulders, and my fingers continued to stretch, my eyes twitching in one last- ditch effort to make me abort the story. To back away before shit got painful. The ball of rage burned inside my stomach, so fucking hot, my hands trembled. Poison. It pulsed through my body, leaving a black sludge in its wake that I yearned to cut out of me. I rubbed my forearm, licked my parched lips.

With tears in her eyes, Aubree stared back at me. "They hurt her, didn't they?"

My lip twisted as my nostrils flared, coils winding tight, so tight in my stomach. "Yeah. Two ... two of the men were raping her at the same time. The others held her down and ... watched." Dryness climbed my throat, as I remembered the sounds of skin smacking, the laughter over her agonizing cries. "I fought them off of her. Killed one of them. Sliced the ear off another." I smiled at that, the pain I was able to inflict. The pain I'd inflicted again just days before when I'd sliced off his other ear before killing the cocksucker. "All I had was a fallen knife I'd grabbed from the floor." My hand trembled as my thumb traced the inner lines of my palm. An ache throbbed inside my heart as a sharp pain struck my skull, and I tipped my head, pressing two fingers into the scar. "We never kept a gun in the house because of Jay. It's why we got Blue."

Her lips parted as she exhaled a breath, and the tear trapped inside her eye finally fell down her cheek.

At her silence, I kept going. I didn't know why. Maybe I did trust Aubree. Maybe a part of me needed to share everything with her because only she could understand what it felt like to have a life destroyed by that bastard fuck, Culling. it almost felt like I was purging the poison without cutting into myself. I still yearned for the pain, but Aubree's sad eyes, her silence and attention as I told my story, somehow kept me grounded. "They got the upper hand, knocked me out cold with the butt of a gun. I woke up hours later." Rubbing my hand across my forehead, I rocked to hold back the tears welling in my eyes. "They were still raping her. Torturing her." I pounded my fist into my head, then knuckled my temples, but still, tears fell. I couldn't keep them in, not at the thought of my helpless wife and the pain she'd suffered. Pain I couldn't stop. "My beautiful Lena."

Keep it together. Lock it in. A new surge of anger swelled inside of me, choking back the tears. "I snuck up on them, beat the one guy's face, and he shot me in the leg. My son woke up from the gunshot. He was ..." *Fuck.* Fuck. I widened my eyes and sucked in a breath as I battled a frown and more tears.

Why was I doing it to myself? Why was I telling her everything?

I slapped my palms to the floor, preparing to get up, to find my knife and cut the shit out of me, but a visual of Jay collapsing to the floor with the sound of a gun had me collapsing into myself. "He was murdered in front of me."

My throat tugged, and my elbow slammed into the wall behind me, crashing through the brittle drywall. I raised trembling hands to either side of my head, desperate for breath, but my lungs locked up and mouth open to a silent scream that I finally let go.

A string of curses bounced off the walls. I wanted to punch someone. Something. My entire body shook with rage.

My son. My beautiful boy, who'd fought to come into

the world, had been violently ripped out of it.

"Sometimes ... I still feel him in my arms, you know? Swaddled up. Safe. Protected." My voice cracked, and I dug my fingers into the wound above my ear that'd forever mock me. "I failed him. Failed to protect him, like I said I always would."

The bellows of pain that burst from my chest reverberated inside my skull.

When they quieted, the only sound that remained was the steady thud of blood beating inside my ears. Deep breaths blew back at my face as I sat with my head tucked between my knees. Sitting there, with my chest ripped open, heart exposed for the first time in years, it occurred to me how torn apart I was inside, hemorrhaging with pain. Pain that needed release. What else could explain the sudden dull ache that felt like wounds sealing themselves?

I'd never told anyone what'd happened. Not even Alec.

"Michael ... did this to you, didn't he? His men murdered your family?" Aubree's soft voice broke through the white noise inside my skull.

"I awoke to hear one of them take a call. He told the others that Culling had given the order to get rid of us. Burn it down." I lifted my head and dragged my face against my bicep to wipe the tears. "So they did. They burned it all. Including my wife and son."

"Ah, God! Why?" Agony carries on Lena's voice, overpowering the constant high-pitched ringing inside my head.

The taste of metal coats my tongue and smoke stings my

nose— so much smoke, it fills my lungs, as though a fire burns somewhere inside the house. I lift my head from the blood pooled beneath me. Mine? I don't know. I can't remember anything. So many blackouts dot the nightmare still playing out before my eyes.

The room is painted in blood, and I zero in on a long trail that leads to the hallway, where my wife has somehow crawled toward our son and curled her body around his, clutching him tightly. Her leg flinches, and that's all it takes for me to push up onto my elbows and drag myself toward the two of them. I can't even keep my head upright and there's that fucking ringing in my ear that won't go away, but I claw at the blood stained wood to reach them. I have no other choice.

Except for the surrounding pool of blood, they seem peaceful. As though sleeping curled into one another. Motionless. Tears have streamed down Lena's cheek, the glisten reflecting the light in the room, as she buried her face in our son's hair in a permanent kiss.

My heart bellows inside my chest, but as I lay beside them, the fear disappears. I'm not afraid to burn alive together, because I'll never survive this.

With my head resting on my son's back, I concentrate through the ringing for a heartbeat. Any sign that he might still be alive. Angry tears fill my eyes as his body remains still, so still, beneath me. My body trembles with the fury trapped deep inside my bones, fury I want to unleash on the world, on those rotten cocksuckers.

With an unsteady, heavy hand, I stroke his back and catch

the wetness that slides between my finger and the fuzz of his pajamas. Lifting my hand reveals a thick coating of blood dripping down my fingertips. A sob rips through my chest, and I close my hand to a fist, wanting to pound the walls, the floor where his blood lies pooled, the faces of the men who did this to him. Every fucking one of them.

Across from me, Lena's eyes almost seem to shift with the tears flooding them, but they're vacant. Unfocused. She looks like she's trapped inside a nightmare and can't break free.

I watch the last spark of life slip from her eyes. The beautiful brightness I've loved for so long fading into a dull permanence of emptiness. Like a home once filled with mirth and childhood suddenly abandoned and left to decay.

I drag my hand across our son and clutch her wrist, and when she doesn't so much as flinch, a howl of sorrow crushes my chest.

Closing my eyes, I kiss my son on the cheek, squeeze Lena's hand in mine, and wait for the flames to pull me into eternal sleep alongside them.

Laughter—evil, wicked laughter—echoes from somewhere below. It reaches me in the blackness, over my sobs and the ringing in my ears. It pokes holes behind my eyelids and scrapes along my spine like a knife chipping at my bones.

My eyes flip open. They're still inside the house. From across the room, I eye the fallen knife.

An urgency pulls at my muscles, and before my mind catches up, I'm already halfway across the floor, pulling myself along toward it. I don't know how many there are, but I'll die trying to take as many as I can with me. The knife fumbles in *my hand that feels too heavy, too big for my wrists. I drop it and pick it up again. Bracing my palm on the wall beside me, I push while drawing my weakened legs to a stand, stumbling across the floor towards the door.*

The room is blurry, out of focus. The ringing intensifies. I'm on autopilot, sliding across the walls to the staircase.

Over crackles and pops, the mumbling of voices precedes the echo of laughter.

I know now. I heard her voice. She stayed with our son and brought me to life for one reason—to avenge them.

"I'm haunted by fire." As the memory faded away, I stared off, watching the beams of moonlight through the window cut across the darkness of the room. "Couldn't watch a flame without feeling the scorching heat on my face and tasting the blood on my tongue, without the smell of burning flesh suffocating my lungs."

Tears fell down Aubree's cheeks. Lifting up onto her knees, she shot straight for my chest without saying a word and wrapped her arms around my neck.

Part of me wanted to throw her across the room. To push her away. To claw at her skin that touched mine. Instead, I wrapped my arms around her and dragged her into my body. I took in the feel of her warmth, the pulse of her breath at my neck, the tremble in her muscles that coincided with my own, like two bolts of electricity joining in one powerful surge.

My muscles tightened around her, as though I could squeeze the very life right out of her, as the shadowed side of my brain grasped an urge to snap her into the thousand tiny broken fragments that made up my insides. Forcing those thoughts away, I merely held her. Gently. Quietly. Selfishly. Burying my face in her hair filled my senses with her sweet, clean scent, until, at last, I calmed. Through long easy breaths, the tension in my muscles softened. The rage slipped back into its dark corner of my mind.

I finally breathed.

Aubree pulled away, and immediately my body cried out for her, craved the warmth once more. I wanted to grab her and take her to my bed, stealing every ounce of heat inside her body for my own—but I didn't.

"I'm your retribution," she said, in a solemn voice.

"Yes."

"Are you planning to kill me for revenge?"

"No." It was the truth. I couldn't kill such an angel of mercy. She'd given me the power to control the one thing that made me lose control.

Her head tipped to the side. "Then, why are you keeping me?"

I stared down at the smeared blood that'd dried over the palm of my hand. "Because I can't let you go yet."

I couldn't even say why, and thankfully she didn't ask. An urgency tugged at me to keep her, like a voice inside my head, telling me that the woman needed my help, whether she'd asked for it or not. That to let her go would ruin everything.

The same inner voice that uttered two words to change everything.

Save her.

CHAPTER 31
Nick

Rain tapped against the Mustang's windshield, as I pulled up to the empty lot where my house had once stood. Wasn't even five in the morning, which meant the block was quiet, dark, just as it'd always been each time I'd visited my wife and son.

I slid out of the driver's seat and strolled up to the charred remains of my home. Rotted, blackened wood lay piled over crumbled bricks and cinder blocks. Because no one had called the fire station, it'd burned right down to the ground and took the abandoned house next door along with it. Scrappers, no doubt, had stolen all the pipes and metal. One of the toilets had been propped in the center of the destruction with 'shithole' written around the rim of it.

What was once my entire world had been reduced to rubble and ruin. Nothing more than a joke for trespassers.

Aubree sat in the car, as I rounded the Mustang. From the trunk, I grabbed the shovel before making my way beyond the wreckage to the Willow tree in back. It'd been little more than a sapling when we bought the house almost eight years before, and had grown into a majestic tree that stood what must've been thirty feet tall. Jay had loved to hang out beneath its drooping branches, and often hid away there most of the day with Blue, playing in its fragile, swaying limbs. I slammed the shovel at the base of the tree, digging up the grass that'd grown there. The October rain was cold as fuck and my hands numbed as I toiled.

A shine caught my eye in the moon's light.

Crouching to the ground, I sifted through loose dirt. Lifting the small truck, one of Jay's I'd unearthed, I squeezed my eyes shut to hold back the tears.

Get it together. He's not here.

I returned to the car and opened the back, sliding Blue into my arms. As I carried him to the gravesite, the door slammed behind me, and I turned to see Aubree jogging over, her hair already wet with rain.

She stopped just short of us. "I'm sorry, if you need to be alone I can …"

"You'll be soaking wet."

"I'm fine."

We reached the gravesite, which had turned soppy with mud. Lowering down on one knee, I set Blue inside the hole I'd dug and stroked his damp coat. "Catch you on the other side, buddy."

Aubree knelt down beside me, petting him behind his collar. "Thank you," she whispered, and stood beside the grave as I pushed the dirt over with the shovel.

As soaked by the rain as I was, Aubree stood shivering, teeth chattering, while I finished burying Blue, but she never once complained of cold or my reluctant pace. Back inside the Mustang, I cranked the heat up and my gaze landed on the goose bumps broken out across her legs as I fired up the vehicle and headed back toward the mansion.

Little was said along the way, until we'd finally arrived home. The rain had intensified, and we jogged to the overhang at the front of the house. I opened the door, and once we'd stepped inside, she removed her coat.

Like I was a goddamn lion fixated on my next meal, my mouth watered at the sight of her—wet and shivering inside the darkened house.

Her boots glistened with water, the dress she'd worn so saturated, it clung to her body, giving a good peek at her lace bra beneath. The sight made me ravenous, thirsty for the water dripping from her neck to between her breasts.

Christ, she wasn't even trying to be sexy, and I somehow couldn't shake the urge to touch her, to have those wet thighs straddling me while I fucked her against the wall, right there in the foyer.

I slipped past her before I risked doing something stupid and made my way toward the kitchen, desperate for a drink. Nabbing the whiskey on the counter, I took a long swig, and when I set it down, caught sight of Aubree standing in the doorway.

"Can I have some of that?" She sauntered across the room until standing at arm's length from me.

In spite of the bruise on her cheek, I stood mesmerized by her wet hair, the shine of her skin, those pert breasts peeking through her dress.

For fucks sake, I silently chastised myself. She'd almost been *raped*.

Squinting, I handed her the bottle of whiskey, and when she tipped it back, I studied the bobbing of her neck as the fluids slipped down her throat. My eyes trailed down to her dress and the silhouette of her curves that showed even in the dim light of the room.

She handed the bottle back to me, licking her lips, eyes selling her intent, and I'd have offered up my soul at her request. Her step toward me kicked my pulse rate into the red zone. Alarms blared inside my head, like the cavalry of sanity had come to beat some sense into my brain.

The palm of her hand slid beneath my coat, not even touching my skin, and had my chest rising and falling, as if I'd never been stroked by a woman's hands. "Aubree … we …" My body rebelled by choking the words I should've said, and though her head remained bowed, her cheeks bubbled with a smile.

"I know." She shook her head. "God, you must think I'm … some kind of freak. Almost raped, and I'm coming on to the man who …" Her face lifted. "Saved my life. I guess I've been the target of pain long enough to know the difference between a man who'd hurt me without remorse, and one who'd sooner hurt himself than lay a hand on me."

Her gaze fell from mine, and I followed its descent to

my hands, where blood trickled from my palms as I dug my fingernails into them. "You must be a fucking masochist to want anything to do with me."

Her hand slipped beneath my shirt, making my stomach muscles clench on contact, and her eyes locked with mine. "Or maybe I see something deeper than the darkness you wear on the surface, Nick."

What overcame me, I couldn't say exactly, but I pushed her back, up against the counter. Perhaps by instinct, her fists lifted between us, but I hoisted her onto the island countertop, putting her level with my thighs, and pinned her wrists behind her, against the cold, gray tiles, before pressing my lips to hers. Soft and slick, they glided beneath mine and tasted like the sweet whiskey that coated them.

A moan purred inside her throat and the tension in her arms subsided, as she surrendered to me.

With both her wrists gathered in one of my hands, I yanked the front of her dress down so hard it tore the seam. One of her large, pert breasts popped free as I peeled back her bra. Fucking perfect, just as I'd fantasized. Her cold nipple piqued and hardened when I circled it with my tongue, and I groaned at the ease of conquering her. Her delicious sugar scent, like caramel and vanilla, filled my nose as I sucked her breast and flicked my tongue against her stiffened little nub.

Another soft moan escaped her, and she slid against the countertop as if she couldn't keep herself upright. Her brow creased in a pained expression that I couldn't read at first, until her half-hooded eyes lifted and her tongue swept lazily across her lips in a way that damn near screamed *fuck me*.

"Do you want me to?" The husky tone of my voice mirrored the tight thread of control I grappled to hang on to. I felt like a raging storm of lust ready to annihilate her as my thumb played against her nipple. "Do you want me to fuck you?"

Bottom lip caught between her teeth, she nodded, and I could damn near feel the sting of that fragile thread snapping inside of me. Like a beast set free from its confines, I lowered my hand between her thighs, nudged them apart, and wrenched her tiny panties to the side, nearly tearing the damn things right off of her.

Slow down. In long, agonizing strokes, I worked my thumb inside her silky seam, eyes locked on hers all the while. The soft flutter of her lashes accompanied the warm flush that colored her cheeks. *Beautiful.* I slid my index finger down over her pubic bone, to her slick entrance. *Fucking hell.* So goddamn tight and wet, my dick twitched at the thought of being inside her.

She cried out and jerked against me, like pleasure and morality battled inside her head.

There was no room for morals between us. We'd breached the line of decency and fallen into dark depravity. She'd become my willing victim, my muse, my toy to act out my most twisted carnal desires. No going back.

I glided my finger along her cleft and caught the slight

tremble in her thighs. With my teeth, I tore the fabric from her other breast and imparted the same attention there.

"Oh, God," she whispered. "Please!"

Lifting, I pressed my forehead to hers, squeezed my eyes shut. "Are you certain about this, Aubree? Because, fuck, I can't go back. I can't stop myself." I just hoped to hell it wouldn't end how it'd always ended with other women. I wanted to get lost in that scent, her sounds. Fall into that shadowy world of pain and pleasure, never to resurface again.

"I'm certain," she whispered.

With hands that longed to roam every inch of her skin, I caressed her breasts with furious movements, tugging both nipples to hardened pebbles, before I yanked the dress over her head, leaving her body exposed. Ready for me to feast upon right there in kitchen.

Like fine, imported silk, her skin passed beneath my fingertips as I dragged my hands down her shoulders, to her arms. Nudging her jaw tipped her head to the side, allowing me access to her throat, where her pulse hammered against my tracing tongue. Her neck rippled with a swallow. Broken breaths hit my lips when I captured her mouth in a kiss. "You smell so good, Aubree. I could devour you right here."

"Do it."

A yank of her legs pulled her to the edge of the countertop, and I gave a gentle push against her chest, until she lay back on the surface, and draped her legs over my shoulders. So close to her bare pussy and the pink bud of her clit, saliva pooled on my tongue, and like a God-fearing man in prayer, I damn near fell to my knees, admiring the absolute perfection spread out before me. I kissed her navel and dragged my tongue down, down, to just above the sweet spot. The clean, fragrant scent of her arousal shot tingles to my jaw and struck some primitive part of my brain that coaxed me to ravage the woman like some kind of wild animal.

Slow. Take it slow.

She pushed upward and, balancing on her palms, circled her hips against the countertop in a slow, teasing motion. Gripping her hip with one hand, I used the other to spread her pink seam open and licked upward, smiling at her curses. Tongue buried in her soft folds, I curved my finger up inside of her, a slow finger fuck that complimented each long lick across her swollen clit. A moan rumbled at the back of my throat at her sweet taste. Wetness coated the finger I pumped in and out of her while I feasted on her like a starving man. I stopped only long enough to suck it off before inserting a second finger alongside the first.

I could've spent all night savoring Aubree's body, learning all of her darkest desires, but the urgency burning inside of me told me to enjoy the moment while it lasted, before the blackness settled in and stole it away.

Her hands threaded through my hair, tightening as I tipped my head and sucked her clit with fervor, as though it'd all end any second. "Oh, fuck! Fuck!"

Her squirming beneath me did nothing to interrupt my focus—I couldn't get enough of the woman. A growing need to hear her scream my name had me upping the pace of my fingers while spreading her folds to explore every inch of her beautiful pussy. With her thigh draped over my shoulder, I grabbed her ass to hold her in place, and felt her muscles contract in the palm of my hand while her body jerked in time to my pumping. Our movements were mad, furious, craving. With steady thrusts, I finger-fucked her while suckling her, licking her, bringing her to climax. I'd forgotten the taste of a woman, forgotten the smell of arousal beating through my senses, like a war drum begging for her to be debauched. I needed to feel her shatter around my tongue, to feel her milk my finger with orgasm, and hear her screams fracture inside my head.

I needed her to come. I'd hold out for that sweet sound, would push away the blackness just long enough to know I'd sated her.

Her breaths turned to panting. Her fingers dug, scraping into my skull. Soft moans turned urgent pleas of, "Don't stop. Please don't stop."

As if I could. As if I had any measure of control right then that could keep me from what I needed, what she begged me for.

I paused only long enough to see her hands roving her tits, shamelessly feeling herself up while I went down, and I sank into something foreign, the undertow so strong, I feared I'd never surface from it. It'd been a long time since

I'd given pleasure, and I wanted to give everything I had inside of me, all the fury and pain and desire—soul-stripping desire that left me a hungry and insatiable bastard. I wanted to give it all to her, watch her brows come together in an agonizing string of curses before she fell back, so glutted with satisfaction she couldn't move.

Her muscles tensed, and the pleas faded, until all that filled the empty kitchen were her broken breaths and small squeaks that ruptured into full-blown screams.

Her fists thumped the countertop on either side of me before unfurling and gripping the edge. "Nick! Oh, God! Nick!"

Tiny contractions beat against my fingers as her orgasm crashed over her. She slid over the edge, and I caught her, lifting her into my arms. Cradling her like a child, I kissed her with the same desperation that hammered through my body.

I needed to bury myself inside of her, so deep it'd have her clawing at my back, caught between begging me for mercy and praying I'd keep going.

Lips locked, I blindly carried her up the stairs, to my bedroom, my body strung the fuck out, with her arms wrapped around my neck, her fingers digging into my nape. I could hardly breathe after the long trek up, but I didn't care. I was so frantic to have her in my bed, I'd have crawled on my goddamn knees with her in my arms to get there.

Once inside, I lay her back against the mattress. With her dark hair fanned across the sheets, her eyes hooded, cheeks flushed, lips full and swollen with kisses, she damn near stole my breath.

Dread struck the pit of my stomach and spread to my head. That same dread stole the enticing image of her sprawled across my mattress, blackening it to darker visuals of her chained to my bed, trembling at my approach. It wouldn't end well. Sex in the last three years hadn't.

The thought was enough to make me pause. Because I didn't want to hurt her, didn't even want to take a chance. *Pleasuring her* might've kept the blackness at bay , but if I took her, if I selfishly fucked her to sate myself, was there a chance I could kill her? The injury to my head had fucked with my brain. I didn't know what I was capable of anymore.

"Stay here. I'll be back," I said.

Her brows came together in what I could only surmise as confusion, but still, I slipped into the adjacent bathroom and turned on the water.

From my holster, I nabbed the long blade and set it to my skin. *Purge it. Get the poison out before the shit consumes you.* I made three small slices on my forearm, a hiss escaping me as the crimson venom slid down my arm, and my cock painfully hardened inside my briefs.

Quickly undoing my belt, I pushed my jeans to the floor and reached down, gripping my dick as I braced a hand on the edge of the sink.

I had to make the moment about her. Not me. If I fucked her, things would end up the way they always had.

My expression in the mirror carried pain—the pain of needing release so bad it had me bent over myself. Pain of knowing there was something dark inside of me, capable of hurting her.

Long strokes along my shaft left me wanting more, wanting to be buried inside of Aubree, with her ass high, screams muffled into the pillow.

I closed my eyes and pictured the scene, so vivid in my head. "Fuck yes," I whispered, imagining myself sliding into that slick pussy, until I became lost, so lost.

Hands drifted down my stomach, and I jerked back when she grabbed hold of my dick. "Shit!"

"Shhhh." Her grip tightened, and she kissed my arm, ignoring the wounds there. "Turn around."

"I can't do this." Through deep breaths, I fought the urge to stroke myself in front of her.

"Because of me? Because I'm married?"

Shit, there was that, too. Not that I gave a fuck about Michael Culling. "Because I can't." I attempted to stuff my dick back into my briefs, but she batted my hand out of the way.

"I have to tell you something. Please."

With some reluctance, I turned to face her.

"Nick ..." Her gaze fell from mine, as if she suddenly couldn't look at me. "I'm so used to men taking from me. Using me. From an early age, sex has always been about getting them off and enduring their pain."

The thought had my stomach clenching, and, like a crazy bastard, I wanted to punch every motherfucker who'd ever laid a hand on her.

She shook her head. "I've never felt what you made me feel downstairs. No one has ever ... left me wanting so much more, the way you did. Please." She fell to her knees, looking up at me while her tongue circled the head of my dick in a way that shot hot bullets of lust straight through my veins like a drug. Those crazy fucking pistol lips of hers, slipping along my shaft in slow torment, left me weak in the knees. "Let me do this. I want to. I *need* to."

Everything inside of me roared a warning. *Don't do it.* Except, her tongue ... that fucking tongue licking and sucking my head had me messed up like a bastard on a monster dose of E.

When she took me all the way to the base, while cupping my balls, I had to grab the edge of the sink again. Up and down, up and down, she bobbed, twisting and circling, like a goddamn pro.

I tangled my fingers in her hair and tipped my head back. Fuck, yeah.

My breaths arrived hard and fast, and I gripped tight to her hair, damn near staggering with each intense suck. The light graze of her teeth along my shaft added twinge of pain to the pleasure.

She upped the pace and made me nearly whimper like a bitch when she popped off, until those lips found my balls, sucking them as if I'd laced them with crack.

Massaging her skull, I followed each pull of my cock with a thrust of my hips, gnawing the inside of my mouth to keep from slamming into her throat.

"Goddamn it, Aubree." My voice rasped with the tension curling through my muscles. "You've got me one stroke from losing my mind."

All sense of right and wrong went to shit, and I lifted her from the floor, suddenly ravenous when her tits jostled with the movement. I rolled her nipples between my fingers, claiming her mouth with a kiss, then spun her around to face the mirror.

Long, brunette locks framed her beautiful face as her half-hooded eyes lit with arousal, and she bit her lip. Her body writhed, ass grinding against my dick, waiting, patiently waiting.

I dragged a finger down her spine, trailing it with a kiss. Reaching her scar, I kissed her there before I shoved her panties aside and pushed my finger inside of her.

The groan that escaped me bounced off the walls. "So fucking wet." Curling over her, I bit her shoulder.

She jerked with an, "Ah!" and curved her ass higher, like a horned-up kitten.

Slow and steady, I pumped in and out, teasing, high on the look of sheer ecstasy plastered to her face, the half-shuttered eyes.

"Mmmm, you feel so good. Please, I need more. Give me more, Nick."

The request was enough to break me. I caught both of her arms behind her back, holding them captive with one hand, while I pumped my fingers into her with the other.

A quick sweep of her tongue along her bottom lip, and

her mouth gaped again, as moans ripped out of her. She stared back at me in the mirror, eyes locked on mine, brows drawn as in a silent plea.

Faster , I slammed into her like a piston, reveling in the feel of her wetness dripping down her leg as I nudged her thighs further apart. Sensing the blackness seeping in from my periphery, I slowed it down, taking long strokes in and out. *Can't risk the blackout.* Didn't want to lose the moment to it. Just a little longer. *Please.*

The warm vanilla scent, as I buried my nose in her hair, sent waves of calm through my muscles and battled the rolling clouds of doom.

She tipped her head back, her skin carrying a sheen. "Nick, fuck me. Please. I want you inside of me."

"You want more?" I gritted out in a rasp.

"Yes!"

"Say it."

"Please, give me more."

"Say my name."

"Nick, please. Give it to me. I need it."

I gripped her head and leaned forward. "What are you doing to me?" I whispered, my entire body quaking with tension.

She stared at me in the mirror. "Make me come."

I curved my finger up inside of her, and as a scream ripped from her chest, blackness leaked into my periphery like ink spreading across a white page.

I grabbed her throat.

CHAPTER 32
Aubree

Arms pinned behind my back, palm squeezing my throat, I ground my ass against Nick's cock, as he stood unmoving, staring at me through the bathroom mirror while his tongue swept across those smirky lips of his.

Teasing? The sweet torture. How long would he keep me like that?

He spun me around to face him, setting my ass up onto the cold tiles. His teeth grazed my earlobe, fingers wrapped around my throat, but not tight, just enough to say, *you belong to me.*

And, God, I did. The bastard owned me, which was saying something because nobody owned me. Not anymore.

Those eyes of his overpowered everything—my willpower, my patience, my sanity. Dark. Mysterious. Dangerous. They did things to the body, silent little commands, assuring that, one way or another, I was fucked.

I stared into his crisp blue irises, so bright they appeared to be powered by tiny electrical storms of lightning. An icy chill climbed my spine. He was the only one who could take me to a place where no one else could. A place where I was free. My salvation rested in the hands of a cold-blooded killer.

The tension that'd been building between us for days had finally pulled taut, ready to snap at any second. A quiver of anticipation ran through my body as I waited, my muscles burning, heart hammering a steady cadence of excitement inside my chest.

I wanted the man before me. A beautiful, dangerous and mysterious man, who reduced me to nothing more than a giddy schoolgirl under the weight of his intense stare. I wanted to get lost in those eyes, drown inside of them, never to surface again. Forget about my world, my past.

"I'm tired of always having to be in a state of constant control. Control of myself. What I say. My actions, for fear that what I do or say will result in punishment." My words arrived fast, tumbling from my mouth before I had the chance to stop them. "I want to lose control." I leaned forward, against the pressure at my neck that eventually fell away, and brushed my open mouth against his throat, trembling at the sensation of being so close to heaven I could almost touch it. "Help me. I want to lose myself with you, Nick."

Pulling back, I studied him, the carved-out perfect cheekbones, a chiseled jaw that ticced as he stared back, and the scruff that'd set my world on fire mere minutes ago. His pupils seemed dilated, eyes bigger, wider. Excited.

Like a predator's.

Grabbing my left ankle, he lifted my leg, the awkward contortion forcing me to scoot back when he set my foot flat on the countertop. At his grip of my right ankle, I raised my other foot atop the counter. I sat completely spread before him, exposed, and when his gaze fell from mine, my stomach clenched. The wetness probably glistened like a goddamn disco ball in front of his eyes.

"Touch yourself, Aubree."

His demeanor had changed from the kitchen. Before he'd seemed rushed, uncontrolled, *hungry*. He was suddenly calm, much more calculated in his movements.

The rebel inside me wanted to lash out, tell him to fuck off, because no one told me what to do anymore. His command was different to Michael's, though—his voice holding a fascination that lacked the sadistic undercurrent of unexpected pain.

Touching myself in front of a man was nothing new, but a tickle in my stomach brought forth the realization that Nick made me nervous, like I didn't want to disappoint him. He'd brought new sensations to the fore, and I desperately wanted more, was willing to become a slave to it, so I slid my finger over my swollen mound and confirmed what I already suspected as I teased the tiny knot there. Soaking wet.

His eyes remained fixed on me, while I skimmed my fingers up and down my cleft, and he grabbed hold of his undeniably proud cock, stroking himself as he watched me. Fucking hell, the sight of him could make a woman do the unthinkable, like come on demand, with his dark, menacing tattoos, the angry shift of his jaw and the controlled glide of his hand along his shaft that had his biceps flexing with each pull. He wasn't doing it to get himself off. It was probably written all over my face—I wanted him. I wanted that beautiful cock inside of me, and the man was teasing me with it.

Well, two could play at that game.

I closed my eyes, tilting my head back against the mirror, and plunging two fingers inside myself, I moaned. "You do things to me, Nick. Things I've never felt before." A heavy basting of lust dripped from every word, and when I fondled my nipple, his grunt had me opening my eyes and brought a smile to my face.

Tongue raking across his teeth, he cupped my jaw, looking down at me with intensity, so much intensity. His chest expanded and contracted, nostrils flaring with each heavy breath. His hand skated down my stomach, across my clit, and I jerked as his finger danced along my seam. He gripped my throat again with the other hand, not hard or violent, almost in reverence.

At the nudge of my palm, I slid my fingers from between my thighs, tensing, as his curled around my wrist and lifted my hand to his face. His gaze flicked to my captured fingers then back to me, before he inserted them into his mouth, and *goddamn*, my pussy twitched, as he licked them clean.

The moment with him felt incredibly erotic, intimate, as if we'd stripped ourselves out of skin and connected on a level I'd never reached with anyone before him.

Even though his eyes appeared feral and capable of violence, I trusted him. I wanted him in all his dangerous potential. Craved the dark glint in his eyes that warned he could fuck me in more ways than one.

He leaned forward, the skimming of his teeth along the shell of my ear sending a jolt of anticipation running through my body. "I need this, Aubree. Give this to me." His deep voice tickled my ear, more commanding than before, but not in a way that put me on edge. Moving his hand to my nape, his kiss landed at the base of my throat.

I wanted his dominance, craved his demands. I didn't have the best track record with men, but something inside of me told me he was different. Just as much a killer as any I'd been with before, but different. Passionate. "Take me."

Something flickered in his eyes. Confusion? Fear?

"Nick?" I stroked a hand down his cheek, and he blinked, pupils shrinking, revealing more of the blue.

He yanked me to the edge of the sink, wrapped my legs around his hips, and slid inside me, jackhammering, violent, needy. He filled me completely, so deep, I had to lift my ass to keep him from plowing through me. A throaty, almost animalistic sound ripped from my chest as, like animals, we fucked. His fingers laced through my hair, alternating between squeezing and releasing. My breasts bounced with each hard slam into my body, not cruel or mean, but ravenous. Urgent, as if the world might come crashing in on us at any second, and all we had was right then.

Without so much as a flinch of warning, he pulled out of me, and my body went cold, desperate to be filled again, neither of us having reached climax.

Sliding his hands under my ass, he lifted me off the sink, carried me to the bed, and pushed inside of me once more. "Aubree." His husky voice gushed like a dark, wicked chocolate inside my mind. "Can't get enough of you. You've got my head so fucked up right now."

I loved that I made him that way. As he pounded into me, I felt unbreakable, fluid and relaxed. Beautiful, too. Like a blind man watching the sun rise for the first time, he never took his eyes off me. From the bliss of never wanting it to end, to the pain of needing climax, he seemed to read my expressions like an opened book, and shifted with them, keeping me on edge, keeping himself from release. His abrupt changes—the slow, easy glides, to spurts of railing into me so deep, he damn near touched my womb, the pull of my hair and gentle strokes along my face—told me chaos swirled inside his body. As if he yearned for something darker, but fought to rein it in. I'd seen it in the bathroom, a flicker of confusion before he took me hard and fast. The man was an enigma. A torn mind. One I yearned to lose myself in.

"Please," I begged, clawing at the edge of pure ecstasy, a steady vibration running through my muscles, so desperate for release, I could've cried. What felt like an hour must've passed. "Oh, God please."

He slowed his hips, rolling them against me. "Not yet. A little longer."

I wasn't used to such control. So different. Not cruel, or painful in the way to which I'd become accustomed. His demands were laced with a promise—of pleasure for us both.

Pausing, he flipped me onto my stomach and drove into me, faster, harder. Powerful thighs beat out a cadence of pleasure with each smacking of our skin, never once faltering in pace, while the sounds of his cock gliding inside of me left me wanting to be ravished.

"When you come, Aubree, I want you to come apart," he told me. "Explode into a million pieces. Scream my name so loud, this whole goddamn city will know who's fucking you."

A sharp sting to my ass accompanied the echo of a smack, and I cried out. Tighter, I wound into myself, every muscle trembling, stomach flexing and relaxing with each slam, slam, slam from behind. I reached down and pinched my clit, head rolling against the pillow. *Yeah, yeah, yeah*. A moan droned inside my mind.

His grunts and groans excited me as they rippled through my body, titillating my beaten muscles. I felt like a ball of livewires bouncing against the mattress, looking to ground itself. Every touch, every caress exacerbated by the tension so taut, I could've snapped. My stomach coiled, my pussy clenching him, milking him. Sweat covered both of us, a slick coating of toil and exhaustion.

I prepared myself for the pain of another missed

climax, gripping the bars of the bed, burying my face in the pillows, but still he kept on. Desperation pulled at my stomach, and I lifted my ass to meet his thrusts, wondering if I'd regret the expense of energy.

A string of curses was all my parched throat could form. How the hell could he hold out so long? He hadn't come yet.

Higher, I climbed, clinging to the edge. *Oh, Jesus, yes! Please!*

He yanked my hair, and that was all it took to shatter around his cock. Heat blazed through my muscles and cooled to a wash of tingles. He pulled out and warm seed pooled in the small of my back.

"Fuck, Aubree, you little pistol. Motherfu—!" Spurt after spurt, it shot out of him

He released my hair, and my head fell to the pillow. Languid. Exhausted. A slow, morphine drip of satisfaction swam through my veins, making my heart pound. I tried to catch my breath as my hips fell to the bed.

Drawing me into him, he kissed my shoulder. No pain. Only pleasure. Intense pleasure that would take hours to recover from.

I couldn't move. Could scarcely breathe.

As though two men with their own level of stamina lived inside of him, Nick had kept me tense, wired, and ready to snap, before delivering a series of the most powerful, world-rockin' orgasms I'd ever experienced. No other man had ever brought me to the pinnacle of pleasure the way Nick had, and I feared, none ever would.

In my captor's arms, I drifted asleep. Sated. Warm. Safe.

***

I glanced at the clock on the nightstand. Three in the morning. We lay in a tangle, his arm draped over my side, cupping my breast. Nick's body twitched, his tip pressed against my ass, and suddenly I missed the feel of him inside me, needed him filling me. I squirmed in his grasp, hoping to rouse him again.

He groaned, his long deep breaths turning to a sharp inhale, and his grip tightened, rolling my nipple between his fingers. From behind, he wedged his knee beneath my thigh, lifting it enough to spread my legs, and pushed two fingers inside me.

"How'd I know you'd be wet?" His deep voice tickled my ear, penetrating despite its drowsy slur.

I laughed and reached behind, gripping the back of his head, as he pumped his fingers from behind. Withdrawing, he smeared the wetness between my ass cheeks and over my hole. He did it again, lubricating the entrance, before pressing the tip of his cock there.

I exhaled a captive breath. "Wait." Anal had been forced on me once, an experience that'd left me wary of anyone coming close to touching me there. "Nick, I don't …"

"Fuck. I'm still half asleep—I'm sorry, Aubree. I don't know what I was thinking."

"I just …" I squeezed the top of his thigh. "I just don't

want to bring any bad memories into this. With you." Craning my head brought my gaze toward the ceiling, the cracks and peeling paint there somehow matching the way I saw myself— not quite as I used to be. "I still want you, though."

He slid his tip down to a more comfortable entrance, and as he pushed inside of me, his cock grew, pressing against my walls. He didn't move at first, just held himself there for a moment, but a shuddered breath told me he couldn't remain still for long.

Reaching back, I gripped his thigh and ground against him in slow, erotic circles, digging my nails into his tightening leg muscles. He kissed my shoulder and, with his leg wrapped around mine, rocked into me. Calm, gentle, lazy. No pain, only pleasure as we lay side by side.

His draped arm moved from my breast to the juncture between my thighs, and those magical, strong fingers slid, feather light across my clit. The slow rocking relaxed me, put me in some erogenous trance, and I found myself meeting each thrust like a well-timed machine—a perfect machine that matched each push and pull, like waves crashing against a shore. Bringing his hand to my face, he inserted his fingers into my mouth, allowing me to taste myself. As I sucked, his thrusts hastened. Faster. He held tight to my jaw, fingers still lodged inside my mouth, before he his hand fell back down to my cleft and rubbed my clit.

Closing my eyes, I accepted the easy glides that filled me with each slam from behind, while my mind painted a vivid picture of what we must've looked like from a birds-eye view: his body curled into mine, rutting against me, my body arched, paralyzed in his grasp. Heat scorched my muscles, my head tipped back until his chin hit my shoulder, lips brushing the ridge of my ear.

"You'll be the death of me, Aubree." He whispered my name with an air of power that crumbled my defenses. "I want more of you. Can't stop. I want to stay buried inside of you forever."

"Nick. Don't stop. Please don't stop." My walls gripped him with each deep drive, and I reveled in the muscle control. His scent penetrated my nose, the warm spicy cologne mixed with the thick aroma of sex that had my muscles burning with tension as I clung to the edge. My stomach clenched. Heat flared, a wildfire of lust spreading through my veins.

Light exploded behind my eyes, rippling through my body like an aftershock. Blinding pleasure trailed it, coating my hot muscles with a cool tingle that left me numb, weakened. I called out his name, and when he pulled out of me, his body shuddered, breaths broken by moans and curses.

We lay breathing, just breathing.

"I feel so warm. So good. No one has ever made me feel so good in my whole life." I wanted to laugh and cry at the confession, at the sadness and pathetic truth that a stranger, a man I'd only known a couple of weeks, had shown me more reverence than any other man I'd ever been with. I'd been used for so long, I'd forgotten how pleasurable sex could be.

"I will obliterate any motherfucker who lays a hand on you again." His sleepy voice carried almost a drunken slur, as his arm tightened around my body, as if claiming what was his. "I'd kill for you."

In his bed, amid the darkness, the destruction, the ruin, he fixed me. His gentle hands delicately fastened together the pieces of me that'd become so broken and scattered with no hope for convergence. As I lay beside him, the soothing tap of rain against the window, I felt whole.

CHAPTER 33
Nick

The heady scent of sex and the sweetness of sugar filled the bedroom, when I opened my eyes to faint rays of sunlight trying to peek beyond the dark drapes. Sweat coated my body, made more apparent every time a wisp of October air drifted through the window that must've been opened sometime in the night. Brushing across my skin, it cooled the heat that burned inside of me.

I hadn't slept so goddamn good in ages, and even then, every muscle sagged with exhaustion, as if I'd gone to battle and lay in the aftermath of war. The sweet floral scent intensified, long, silky locks of hair tickling my face, and soft skin passed beneath my fingertips as I dragged my palm along the smooth contours of the woman lying next to me. I had to lift my head from the pillow to believe that it was Aubree Culling.

Aubree.

What the hell?

I hadn't finished sex inside of a woman in years.

She stirred against me, arching as she stretched, and I caressed the curves of her body, needing to touch her just to be sure it wasn't another dream. I'd had so many of her in the last week.

"Mmmm, good morning," she purred.

I pushed the hair away from her ear and whispered, "Shower with me."

With a smile and nod, she rolled onto her back, mid-stretch. "I feel amazing."

I made her feel amazing? I rubbed a hand down my face and rose up from the bed, heading toward the bathroom. Flipping on the shower, I turned to find her standing naked and perfect in the doorway.

She tipped her head. "Who's Alec?"

A jolt of electricity shot up my spine. "What?"

"You were … talking in your sleep last night. You said Alec is going to kill you."

"Alec is no one." I spun back around and stepped inside the stall, hoping I wouldn't have to say something regrettable to drop the subject as I beckoned her inside.

She placed a hand on my chest, not looking me in the eye. "You're an enigma, Nick. I feel like I'll never fully know anything about you." Her eyes met mine. "And that's okay. The way you make me feel …" She smiled and nodded. "That's okay."

Knots unfurling inside my stomach, I dragged my fingertip along her temple then pulled her inside with me. I wished I could tell her everything, because she made me want to get fuckin' spill-happy, the way she spoke with such understanding. She seemed to know all about shields and secrets and keeping my cards hidden. That only came courtesy of her own pain and suffering—her own demons I was certain I'd never know about.

That was the thing about pain, it came with a universal understanding for those who survived it—don't ask, don't tell.

Hot sprays of water pulsed against my back, and I leaned forward, seizing her lips in a kiss to say *I'm done talking*. Rising up on her tiptoes, she wrapped her arms around my neck and kissed me back, as if to reply *I agree, let's get back to sex*.

I'd screwed shit up royally, because after last night, having Aubree so much as glance in my direction would make her tackle bait. I turned her around and pulled her into me, resting my head in the crook of her neck, kissing the side of her throat, down to the base, and across her shoulders. She felt small and right, her curves pressed into my body in all the right places. Together, our bodies melded perfectly, like two halves of a whole. Paired with her words from moments ago, a realization struck me. We fit the only way two fucked up people could possibly fit together.

I saw darkness in her beauty, and she saw beauty in my darkness. Yin and yang. Black and white. Beauty and scars; fury and forgiveness. She should've been my nemesis, but in her, I found something I didn't know I was looking for. I shouldn't have wanted her. Sex with her was forbidden, after all, as I was the loveless villain, and she the prized possession of a man who'd taken everything from me. Every instinct screamed inside of me to kill her. Destroy her. Break her, the same way I'd been broken. By the law of the streets, she was my retribution.

An eye for an eye.

Laws meant shit when it came to love, though. Could I love her in time?

From what I knew of love, it was a wild flame that would consume me with no apology. I'd lived it once, felt it. Knew the duality of love's seductive and destructive natures. The tranquil glow with a deadly burn. Yet, somewhere in that fire was my salvation.

A moment of bliss in a dark world of pain.

A beacon of light on a shadowy horizon.

Love was the only thing stronger than hate. Fuck, if I didn't already try hating her once. Something deep inside of me had awakened in the last few days. The moment we joined the same side, as I'd peered down at her brutal scar, was the moment an odd sensation clicked inside of me. I wanted to save her in a way that I couldn't save myself. I'd found a reason strengthening my determination to follow through with my revenge. For her. For me. For my family.

The lingering question remained, though. What would happen in the end?

A blackness lived on the other side of my revenge—a future I'd never planned to live. Aubree couldn't change that. I'd planned it for far too long, and with the grand finale of my vengeance, police, gangs, everyone who'd be looking for restitution for the deaths would be out to hunt me down if I happened to survive. I'd never endanger Aubree by putting her in the middle, making her an enticing object for retribution.

Her thumb traced the tattoo on my forearm. "I've had to wake up on guard for the last five years, always playing the game. Always watching that what I say doesn't give away something that I'd be stabbed with later. Here, in this old, abandoned wreckage, I feel so calm and relaxed with you. For the first time in years, I'm genuinely content in my own skin."

I nabbed the shampoo beside me and squeezed some into the palm of my hand before massaging it into her head. I didn't know what to say to her. I'd made a promise, one I intended to keep. I didn't know what that meant for Aubree and me. I certainly couldn't promise her a happy home and white picket fences. That world had passed me by years ago.

"I love your hands on me." She tilted her head back into the water, washing the lathered soap away, then twisted to face me again.

Her body felt almost weightless in my arms as I lifted her up and pressed her back against the wall, slanting my mouth over hers. Water trickling between our lips made for a wet kiss. I positioned myself inside of her, reveling in the sounds of our slick bodies beating against each other, her breasts bouncing. Her moans echoed inside my head, as I took her again like the selfish fucking bastard that I was.

I couldn't help it.

I'd become ravenous for her. Fucking her wasn't enough. I wanted to tear Aubree apart and claim all the pieces of her as my own. Even if the future was nothing more than a black splotch of ink on an unwritten page, in that moment, she belonged to me.

CHAPTER 34
Aubree

Staring up at the bedroom ceiling, I lay in Nick's arms, unable to move, scarcely able to breathe. We'd had sex so many times, in so many positions, it was as if I'd opened the cage to a lust-hungry beast that lived trapped inside me. In spite of my scars, my bruises, I felt beautiful with him. Alive. Strong.

In return, I wanted to heal the broken, beautiful man within him. His pain surged through me with every passionate kiss that spoke of loneliness and desolation. The anger and fury beat through me in the same tempo as his thrusts. I wanted all of it. I'd take all those hours, minutes, seconds of his suffering and let them swirl and simmer inside of my body until I could give him the exquisite fusillade of release that he craved.

Somewhere in between our tangling, we'd eaten, showered again. Exhausted from climaxing so many times in a matter of hours, I should have had nothing left, but as he pushed inside me from behind, I found I needed him again. Despite my dry throat, aching muscles, and spasms trembling my thighs, he simply felt too damn good to deny. I'd never felt so sated, deliciously weak, yet craving more.

He remained unmoving inside me, as though reminding me of the potential in his rock hard cock while he kissed behind my ear. "You're tired and hungry. I'll get you some food and let you rest."

"No," I moaned, but my stomach answered with a growl.

Laughing, he pulled out of me, and suddenly my body screamed for him again. "Sleep now. I'm not done with you, yet." As he pulled the covers over me and stood, the dampness of the sheets caught the cool draft that blanketed my battered muscles.

My mouth watered at the sight of his cock beside my face, and again when he turned to reveal a tight, muscled ass disappearing behind his briefs. With lids so heavy I could hardly keep them open, I closed my eyes.

I could've sworn only minutes had passed when he returned, but I awoke, lying on my stomach, to his fingertips gliding down my spine. When the sheet lowered, I instinctively flipped to my side.

"I've seen your scar." His kiss landed on my exposed hip. "Many times now."

"I know." His touch right then had felt too intimate, though, and I didn't want to feel like he was examining it.

His fingertips drifted upward, and when he circled the right side of my back, I knew he'd found the yellowing bruise from Michael's abuse. "Men who do this are weak. Cowards. A woman should never carry scars of pain and suffering." His soft lips caressed the bruise before he left another kiss there. "You were with him a long time, yeah?"

I nodded, hating the confession, dreading the next question, one I'd ignorantly issued to so many women who'd come to me, desperate for healing after suffering similar pain.

So why did you stay?

All those women had had their own crippling reasons for staying with abusive men—children, money fears, lack of confidence in their own survival.

In my case, it was lack of options. My husband happened to own the police, the judicial system, and the government. On top of that, he had connections that would assure I'd never get far—connections that could find me in the farthest corners and darkest shadows. Still, I hated myself for being so weak.

I also hated that Nick, a man who'd shown me how fierceness could co-exist with gentleness, might've seen me the same way I once saw those women.

"You're a strong woman, Aubree."

His words stole my defense parked at the back of my throat, and the look on my face must've been more of an accusation than what was really spinning through my mind. I hadn't been expecting him to say that. I'd expected him to tell me I was an idiot—that I should've fought harder.

He shook his head. "Years of bruises and scars. You

must be exhausted."

I'd fought every day of my life—even the days it seemed futile—and I'd been tempted to piss Michael off enough for him to kill me. "Thank you." Lifting the sheets higher, I smiled, though I wanted to bury my face in the pillows and cry. Not for myself. Not for the scars. Not even for what Nick'd said so much as from relief that someone finally understood, finally saw the real me behind the mask I'd been forced to wear. Such a cathartic realization, it made me want to crawl inside of him and stay there forever. "Surely, strong women aren't wrecked with bruises and scars."

"You're a fighter. Your scars aren't about the rounds you've lost. They're about the ones you walked away from. The ones you survived."

At his pat to my ass, I twisted into myself to get a look at him as he stood, earning myself a view of the sexy happy trail and the top of the delicious 'V' that disappeared into his jeans. "C'mon. Get up."

"What's going on?"

Bending forward, he planted a kiss to my temple and whispered, "No questions."

"And if I don't want to get out of bed?" My confusion turned to a wily smile.

The raising of his brow coupled with the intensity of his eyes said, *I didn't ask you, I'm telling you.* He reached out a hand to me, beckoning me with a flick of his fingers, and I took the bait. After all, how could I deny those beautiful instruments that'd pushed me over the edge more times in one night than I'd ever experienced in my whole life? I rose to meet him, and he dragged me into his body. "Wear something warm." He kissed me and left the room.

A pair of ripped jeans, a thick, black cable sweater, and the black combat boots made for what I hoped would constitute *warm*. When I ventured downstairs, Nick jerked his head for me to follow him out back.

Blood still coated the pavement where Blue must've been shot. Nick didn't so much as spare a glance, like he'd told himself not to look at it, as he made his way down the stairs to the back yard. Though abandoned houses could be seen off in the distance, the house sat on a pretty good chunk of property, with a small copse of trees, the sight of which brought a rush of bile to my throat.

He slid a pistol out of a holster at his hip that I hadn't noticed on the way out. Eyes squinted, he peered down the barrel of the Sig Sauer and pointed it toward a mound of dirt a couple of hundred yards off. "Ever shoot someone?"

"No. Last I checked, hunting people is considered *murder*."

His lip kicked up into a smile. "I think you need to learn."

"Why would I do that?"

Lowering the gun, he glanced over his shoulder at me. "All women should know how to protect themselves." He motioned for me to stand in front of him and held out a gun to me.

I caught a quick glimpse of his stoic face, then glanced back down to the gun before lifting it from his opened palm. *This could be fun.*

"How's it feel?"

I shrugged. "Like a gun in my hand."

He moved behind me and pointed toward a mound of dirt. "Aim there."

With my finger half-heartedly curled at the trigger, I lifted the gun and, tilting it sideways like I'd seen gang members do, I aimed it at the mound.

"No, no. Hold it level and keep it upright. Not cocked to the side." His hands covered mine, and he turned the gun upright. "Gangstas do that shit because it's a fast way to deliver a bullet, but you want to steady your hand and aim at your target. Grip with both hands. Click the safety off, here." He pushed my thumb against the hammer and pulled it back. "Ready?"

Oh, yes. The whole experience had me swimming in excitement.

At my nod, his fingers curled around mine. The gun kicked back at the same time a thunderous crack hit my ears. The lingering ring had me working my jaw, as a plume of dust kicked up from the mound of dirt.

"That's good. Let's do it again. This time, aim a little higher. You might've hit a set of nuts with that one, but nothing that would kill a bastard."

"What makes you think I didn't aim there?" I laughed at the roll of his eyes and raised the gun once more. It wasn't the exhilaration of the weapon itself in my hands that had me excited right then. As he gently guided my aim, I realized it was the excitement of the man putting that power in my hands, adding another layer of appreciation for Nick.

My father was the only man in my life who'd ever made any attempt to empower me like that.

Nick's chest pressed into my back and his arms wrapped around mine. I wanted to focus on the lesson, but being enveloped in his stiff muscles and his delicious scent left me distracted, burning with a desire that shot through my veins like lust bullets.

Just as before, he squeezed my fingers and the bullet bounced off the dirt. "That's a little better. Might've hit a kidney that time." He chuckled at my ear.

Smiling, I turned around and held the pistol out to him. "Aren't you afraid I'll turn the gun on you?"

He hooked my chin with his finger and glided his thumb across my lips, staring at them intently. "I'm more afraid that you wouldn't," he said, kissing me. "We'll try again then set up some targets."

"And if I hit them?"

His brow kicked up. "Perhaps I'll keep you tied to my bed and administer your reward over the next few days."

A shiver hit my spine at the thought.

CHAPTER 35
Chief Cox

Cox sat in his office, his finger hovering over the mouse, before reluctantly opening the email that'd been sent to his personal account. The sender's name stuck out from all the other shit mail he still had to weed through, written in bold caps, encrypted.

From: **ANONYMOUS**
Subject: EX

I'd like to discuss a transaction, as I have information you may find useful.
One week ago, a girl was rescued from traffickers at the Pantheon Motel. I'd like to know her name. Should you choose to provide that information to me, I've been made privy to E4E's next victim.
Perhaps you might decide that a surprise is in order.

Not a single identifying clue existed anywhere in the

email. Odd that the mysterious sender would inquire about the girl, whose name had been withheld by the media, as a victim of a sex crime, but what did Cox care? He himself had been the one to make the drop at the eastside Palms Motel, when he'd picked up the runaway from the streets a couple weeks back. In fact, he'd been her first customer, broke her in right on the spot, before threatening that if she ever told anyone, he'd kill her family. When she surfaced in the media, Cox just about had a goddamn heart attack.

Fortunately for him, she'd suffered some traumatic amnesia bullshit tied to her torment, leaving her unable to recall how she'd been picked up, let alone most of her abuses thereafter. If some bastard was ambitious enough to kill her off, so be it. Cox had alibis and connections. Her 'stage name' was all that most of the involved parties had, anyway.

Cox hit 'reply' and typed a single response: *Sapphire*. Dragging the mouse to the top of the screen, he prepared to exit the account, when a completely new email bounced back.

He clicked on the second ANONYMOUS in bold and frowned.

From: **ANONYMOUS**
Subject: EX

The Palms Motel.
Room 313
You'll find the next victim.

A sharp pain struck Cox's chest like a vice grip closing in on his ribcage. He slapped a hand to his heart and attempted deep breaths through the short pants. *Fucking angina.* Knocking papers to the floor, he rifled through the drawer beside him and grabbed his Nitro tabs, popping two pills beneath his tongue.

The pressure gradually dissolved with the tabs, and Cox sucked in deep breaths through his nose.

Room 313 had been rented out by Jonathan and his girlfriend, Theresa, as a second location to sell the girls.

With trembling hands, Cox replied.

Who are you?

An eternity passed before it became clear that the sender had no intentions of identifying himself. Cox slammed his fist against the desk before grabbing his jacket.

***

With cautious steps, Cox approached the room of the old, rundown shithole he'd frequented a few times. His hand instinctively rested on his gun holster, and as the door with the faded numbers came into view, he slipped the weapon out, trigger finger at the ready.

After a quick glance at the surrounding shuttered rooms, Cox placed an ear to the door, jumping back when it clicked open. He lifted his gun and pushed it in farther, giving way to darkness inside, as if the room stood empty.

Every nerve in his body flared like a livewire. He took long, easy breaths, having already popped his pills, and flipped on the lights.

Eyes wide, he fell back on a chair behind him with a gasp. Strung around the walls and ceilings like ghosts were large photographs—black and whites that showed him talking to the girl, her getting into his vehicle, him walking her to the room of the motel, the subtle stroke of his hand against her hair as he ushered her into the room.

She'd been scared at first, but he'd assured her he was leaving her with a good friend who'd help her find some odd jobs and make some cash, rather than send her back home. Theresa had convinced her to stay by promising to look out for her. After a few drinks laced with roofies, she'd passed out and woke up a prisoner.

Cox thought he'd seen the last of her.

Gun held level, he swung around the empty room. Rubbing the tightness in his chest, he headed for the bathroom, kicked in the door, and flipped on the lights.

A message screamed from the mirror, red like it'd been written in lipstick:

Her name is Danielle.

You're Next.

Cox clutched his chest and exited the bathroom, ripping down pictures from the ceiling and walls. With images spilling over in his arms, he darted back down the staircase to his car. He'd burn them. Every single one of them. And the fucking bastard who'd pulled the stunt would die a slow, merciless death, he promised.

A shudder ran down his spine as he wiped the sweat from his brow and ignored the tightening behind his ribs.

He pulled his cellphone and scrolled through the names, shaking his head when he stopped at the last cocksucker he wanted to talk to in his current state. Unfortunately, the asshole was the only one he knew who could answer the burning question inside his head.

At the greeting on the other end, Cox cleared his throat. "Riley, this is, uh ... Cox."

"Something come up?" No doubt, a polite version of *what the fuck are you calling me for?*

"Nah, I got a question. Encrypted emails." He raised a trembling hand to his face and pinched the bridge of his nose. "Any way to find out who sent them?"

"Depends on the sender. For the most part, they're not easy, no." A pregnant pause followed his comment. "Is this related to our Eye for Eye dude?"

"No. This ... this is a completely different case." Back up. Abort mission. He needed to get off the phone before the guy asked questions that'd have him slipping up. "I thought you might say that. Thanks. I gotta go. Have a good night."

"Yep."

Cox clicked the phone off, kicking himself for what he could've gathered on his own. He'd been stupid to loop Riley into his mess, but, hopefully, the bastard'd been so fucking stoned, he'd forget they'd had the conversation.

CHAPTER 36
Aubree

I walked into the bathroom, Nick following behind. Candles had been placed along the tiles. Petals drifted across the top of the steaming water. Warm jasmine pervaded my senses, the calm scent attempting to overpower the tremor in my muscles.

The ambience should've been beautiful and perfect. Instead, I stood trembling, my heart beating like a hummingbird, as I stared into the depths of the tub. It was huge, the size of an outdoor hot tub that could've easily fit three, and probably about three feet deep.

My fingers curled into Nick's, and my gaze flitted from the tub to his. "I ... I can't." I took a step back, and his grip tightened, inciting a panic that had me twisting my wrist free from his grasp.

I'd feared deep water since I was twelve years old.

"Talk to me?" he asked.

I couldn't help the frantic shake of my head. "I ... I don't ..." I'd always had a hard time admitting a fear—

particularly one that made me feel truly vulnerable. Weak. Ice crawled up my spine, a wake of shivers following its path.

His finger hooked beneath my chin, and he tore my focus away from the mesmerizing placid water. "I'm not going to force you, but I promise I won't hurt you."

My gaze trailed down to the irregular jagged skin climbing my wrist.

"Something happened to you. It's why you cut yourself." It wasn't a question.

I nodded, not wanting to elaborate, for fear I'd break down in front of him. Yet, at the same time, I couldn't stop the words. "Um. When I ... When I was about twelve years old, I ventured down to the river with some kids from the neighborhood." I cleared my throat. Instinct had me swinging my attention back toward the door, in the event I had to run. "River Rouge is where I grew up, and we often played and swam down by the bridge. Some bigger, older boys showed up and jumped in the river. They were horsing around. They .... They pushed my friend and me underwater. I hadn't taken enough air. I panicked." Dryness crept up my throat at the memory, and I had to suck in a breath as I recalled the terror of seeing sunlight blur the water's surface. It'd seemed too far from reach. "And that's when my mother showed up. Looking for me." I smiled at the memory of my beautiful savior. "She raised some hell with those boys and told them if she ever saw them down at the river again, she'd cut their balls off and feed it to them." Laughter hummed in my chest, wanting to escape, but in the next breath, I frowned. "I developed a fear of water from that day forward. Had nightmares, imagining what would've happened if my mother hadn't shown up. Three years later, my family and I were staying with my grandmother, who lived on the water." Fidgeting with the hem of my shirt, I drew in a breath against the crushing of my chest, which always preceded the next part of my story. "My mother decided to swim out to a small island in the middle of the lake, like she'd done when she was young. She got tired on the way back and slipped beneath the surface. By the time my father reached her, she'd drowned." The puffy line of my scar passed beneath my fingertips as I rubbed over it, back and forth. "I remember wanting to jump in after her, but I was paralyzed. Too frightened to go into the water. I couldn't save her. She was a great swimmer, taken by my greatest fear in the world." Wiping a tear from my cheek, I sniffed, staring down at the red halo surrounding my scar where I'd rubbed too hard. "I felt useless. Worthless. A coward."

"You're not a coward." His palm cradled my cheek, the warmth of his skin penetrating my bones, and I squeezed my eyes shut to hold back the tears.

"My mother was ... amazing. I so desperately wanted to be like her." I glanced up, comforted by the silent sympathy in his eyes. "But, beauty isn't meant to be coveted. It's only to be admired."

He seemed to study my face for a moment.

"What?" I asked.

"In that case, I'm in complete awe." The pad of his thumb brushed across my lips. "I don't like to see fear on your face. You don't have to do anything you don't want to, Aubree. But I want to prove to you that you can trust me."

Unable to hold his gaze, I looked away. He could probably convince me to do just about anything with those intense eyes—even something that terrified the shit out of me. "I can't get in the water, Nick."

"Will you get in with me?"

My muscles tensed, and I frantically shook my head. "I can't."

"I won't force you." He removed his briefs and stepped down into the bath, patting the edge of the tub. "Just sit with me."

Reluctantly, I walked over to the edge, staring at my reflection on the surface for a moment before taking a seat beside him. Even there, so close to the water, my hands turned cold and clammy, the nausea gurgled in my stomach, itching to eject the last meal I'd eaten. I choked it back, in my best attempt to hide the fact that he'd stumbled upon a weakness so crippling, it'd nearly killed me.

Legs dangling over the edge of the tub, away from the water, I sat beside him. "So, what about you? What was your childhood like? Anything traumatic?" A hiccup of nervous laughter flew from me.

His lips curved into a half smile. "Not really traumatic."

A few seconds passed, and I raised my brow, tipped my head forward, nausea still churning in my gut. "You gonna tell me?"

He scratched his chin, the smile on his face shriveling. "My parents ignored me, mostly. It's why I got into gaming. Lot of time by myself." Lifting his knees up onto whatever invisible ledge I couldn't see down inside the water, he wrapped his arms around them. "I grew up in a trailer in Highland Park. My dad worked a lot. Mom drank a lot. So, I stayed away from home a lot. I wasn't a bad kid, you know, I was just doing what kids do." He scooped water up onto his arms, and I zeroed in on the glisten it created across his skin. "My mom, she ditched us when I was about ten or eleven. 'Nother dude. My dad always blamed me for it." Shaking his head, he clasped and submerged both hands in the water, swishing them around, like he needed the distraction to keep telling his story. "So, at sixteen, I hit the streets and didn't look back. Got into some bad shit with kids who rolled with gangs." He bowed his head, and his lips tightened with a smile. "And that's about when I met Lena."

"She kept you out of trouble." An air of amusement hung on my words, mirroring my thoughts of a young girl whipping the troubled boy into line.

He nodded. "She did. Her dad hated me at first. Thought I'd corrupt his baby girl."

"Did you?"

A shrug of his shoulders brought a smile to my face. "Maybe." He twisted until facing me and set his warm hands on my thigh, making my muscles tighten at the sudden fear that he might pull me in. "Tell me more about you."

The tension eased, my body sagging with relief.

We talked for what must've been a half hour, mostly about my childhood, growing up with my mother, and he never once coaxed me inside, though every bone in my body wished I could be in that water with him. The longer I sat beside him, the more at ease I felt being so close to my greatest fear, to the extent I almost dared to submerge my foot inside.

He pushed up from the tub, as though preparing to get out.

"What are you doing?"

"There's no reason to stay in here if you're not joining me."

I didn't know why I suddenly felt the need to prove I could trust him, the same way he'd proved to me he wouldn't betray my trust. It was a beautiful juxtaposition—what I wanted submerged in what I feared.

Something overpowered me, and I gripped his arm. "Wait." I couldn't look at him, in case I changed my mind. "I want to try."

"I promise I won't hurt you, Aubree. I won't let you go." He reached out a hand to me.

It must've taken a good five minutes to slip out of my clothes, while he patiently waited, never rushing me.

Naked, I stood at the edge of the water, staring down at the space he'd made for me to sit down beside him.

From the depths of my stomach, a sickness churned, a betrayal to my mother. How could I so easily slip into the water with him, when I hadn't brought myself to save my own mother from drowning?

"Why'd you try to kill yourself?" Nick's question was a faint sound to the noise beating inside my head.

"Because I was tired of feeling helpless. And of the endless nightmares."

The words of my father drifted through my head, and bless him, he'd tried to spare me of my self-loathing. He'd tried to ease my guilt and teach me to face my fears in a different way.

I'd have never let you in the water, Bree. I couldn't have lost both of you that day.

In my heart, I knew I couldn't have saved my mother, but that was the shit thing about feeling helpless—the mind searched for blame. Irrational blame that could possibly justify the weakness of feeling unable to do anything, and perhaps erase the horror of what I'd seen that day. My father, as strong a swimmer as he was, brought her lifeless body back to shore, and not even *he* could save her.

I hated her for dying. Hated her for enjoying something I feared, something I couldn't save her from. Something I couldn't save myself from. The more I thought about it, the more furious I became that something had such a fierce hold over me for so many years. It'd given Michael something to use against me.

Taking Nick's hand, I stepped down into the warm

water, cringing at the surface line against my shins as it separated the warmth from the cold. My heart beat against my ribs, and I realized, when the room spun, that I'd been panting.

He rose up from the water until towering over me and pulled me into his body. Hot, slick hands wandered my skin, down my sides and back up my spine, until he gripped me tight and pressed his lips to mine.

The dizziness of before kicked up, and I gripped his arms to steady myself in his embrace. When I closed my eyes, the room spun out of control, as his hand gripped my nape and his kiss turned fierce, demanding. The sudden violence and passion consumed me, stole away my preoccupation of standing in the tub. Against my stomach, his erection told me what he wanted, and as the heat of his body spread into mine, my muscles softened, melting into him.

I opened my eyes.

The water level sat at my breasts as I straddled Nick's body. Sucking in a breath, I wrapped both arms around his neck, holding him for dear life, and his arms enveloped me, clutching me to him. My muscles shuddered, locking my lungs. Cold blanketed my chest, and I drew in short bursts of air, crawling higher onto his lap.

"Shhh." His hand stroked my hair, and he kissed my ear. "Relax, Aubree. I'm right here. I've got you."

Those three words again. *I've got you.*

Clamping my eyes shut, I tensed, batting away images of my mother's blue skin, her lifeless brown eyes, and her gaping mouth, into which my father had attempted to restore her soul with part of his. I saw the sunlight reflecting off the water's surface and my small hand reaching for it, fighting against the pressure at the top of my head. I hated the vulnerability—the place inside someone could reach me.

So, I let go.

I opened my eyes to a calm blue staring back at me. Nick stroked my temple with his thumb as he held my face in his palms. Exhaling a shaky breath, I relaxed my muscles, taking long, easy breaths, just letting him hold me.

"That's it. Just breathe." His whisper echoed in the vastness of the room.

Submerged in the water, pressed into his body, I stilled. Just breathing.

His lips skated down my throat to my collarbone, distracting my intense concentration until all I could feel was want. I desired him so strongly, needed to feel his calm inside of me.

He shifted beneath me and slid into my body.

I eased myself over him, knees against the seat of the tub, and slowly ground myself until he glided to the hilt. My quiet moan echoed off the walls, and I rocked my hips, circling, before slamming down on him with each thrust.

His mouth claimed my nipple, and I cried out when his teeth pinched the sensitive nub. Tingles shot beneath my skin with each slick glide of his body against mine.

The tension of before, wound so tight inside of me, unraveled, transforming into a new kind of pressure that built toward battling my fears.

His moans bounced off the walls in a sound so beautiful, I craved it while he was silent. I needed to hear those small confirmations of his pleasure. Nick's moans, grunts and growls brought forth a primal need to sate him. Please him. Upping my pace, I rode him fiercely, wantonly, while the water splashed around us in an exhilarating celebration of passion.

His tug of my hair tipped my head back, and he continued to torment my swollen nipples. My body came alive in the water, and in spite of my exertion, each movement felt like slow motion. The euphoria of conquering my fear, alongside Nick's touch, his voice, sent me to the edge.

I dug my nails into his scalp, my body tensing, easing, tensing, tensing, holding onto fringes, until I opened my mouth to a scream ripping through my chest and his name reverberating inside my head.

His mouth slammed against mine, and he pulled me into him. Deeper, deeper, I fell into silence and came to a distant awareness that I'd gone below the surface. As I slid against his body, riding out the last of my orgasm, with his kiss staking its claim, I didn't need air. I didn't fear the silence. My desire for him transcended my needs and what terrified me more than anything. I could've stayed underwater with him forever, straight into certain death, safe and comforted by his arms while we fell into eternal sleep.

When we breached the surface, I felt his smile against my mouth, and I opened my eyes to those beautiful blue irises pulling away from me.

He captured my face in the palm of his hands once more.

"That was fucking amazing." A chuckle escaped my heaving breaths, and I wrapped my arms tight around his neck, kissing him as if I'd devour him right there.

"You're amazing," he murmured at my ear, before his teeth grazed my jawline. The smile in his eyes withered to something serious, pained. "You make me dream things I shouldn't dream. Crave things I shouldn't crave. My weakness." His lips slanted over mine in a kiss that stole my breath. "You'll destroy me, Aubree. And I won't stop you."

I felt the same, like we'd breached a dark place, from which there was no return. I was trapped in the arms of a killer, as vulnerable as a kitten to a lion and, yet, stronger than I'd ever felt in my life. Nick didn't take from me, he infused me, showed me the woman I could be—the one I wanted to be.

Sexy. Fierce. Shameless.

One who took what she wanted without apology.

Without fear.

He may have found a weakness in me, but in him, I found strength.

The experience didn't *cure* me of my fear. In fact, even then, my body trembled as the water level bobbed at my chest. It merely proved that I wouldn't let my anxieties stand in the way of what I wanted.

CHAPTER 37
Chief Cox

Tucked inside his office, Cox read through the file for Julius 'Casanova' Malone. He'd known the kid from the time he could walk. Julius happened to be the baby brother of the most ruthless drug lord in the city, with connections all over the world, so whoever it was that'd fucked with him could pretty much kiss their ass goodbye.

A man Cox had known for years had raised both boys. He'd been at the center of an investigation a while back, involving a missing girl from their neighborhood. Christ, it was no surprise that Julius would grow up prostituting them. The shit his father had been into, it was a wonder he didn't eat them afterward.

Julius had gone missing after the shakedown at the Pantheon, and Cox had a pretty good idea that another murder was about happen. Big brother, Brandon, had threatened to have every cock-sucking gangbanger in the state track down the bastard who'd kidnapped him—just what the city needed in the thick of a serial-killing spree.

At a knock at the door, Cox scrambled to deposit the file in the drawer beside him. "Yeah!"

Burke peeked in. "Corley got a tip. Found Julius."

"Corley? Where the fuck did Corley get a tip?"

"He's connected to all the homeless bastards. Apparently, one of them was drunk, going on about a dead dude he found in the sub-basement of the old train station. He'd taken some kids from the suburbs urban exploring for cash. Found the poor bastard."

"Poor bastard?" Cox crossed his arms. "I take it he's not among the living anymore?"

"No. I'm on my way to check it out."

Pushing up from the desk, Cox slid the drawer beside him the rest of the way closed. "I'm coming along on this one."

"Sure, Chief? I'll get ya the report."

"No, I want to be personally involved in these cases." His thinning hair slid between his fingers, as Cox rubbed the top of his head. "The city is going nuts over these murders—I don't need to be the dipshit reading about it, like everyone else."

***

A growl rumbled in Cox's throat, when they arrived in the sub-basement below the old Michigan Train Station, to where the tip on Julius had led. Forensics, the District Attorney, Deputy DA, the coroner and his assistant, FBI agents, including Jim Riley, and Corley had already arrived. The flurry of bodies danced around the bloodied remains of Julius Malone, who'd been propped on a chair in the center of the room. The pungent scent of piss and rotting flesh overpowered the mold and stagnant air of the aging building.

No doubt, Corley had been the one who'd gotten in touch with Riley, and anger simmered in Cox's bones, as the two of them chatted with a forensics specialist scouring the crime scene that'd been lit like a goddamn football stadium.

"Looks like a fuckin' party in here." Water sloshed beneath Cox's boots as he made his way across the room.

"Chief Cox. Just found another number." Riley nabbed a plastic baggie sitting beside a forensics duffel, on what looked like a card table. "This one's printed on the back of a napkin for a bar on the west side. Has some apartments up top. Gonna need a search warrant."

Cox eyed the napkin through the plastic. On it, blood red letters in bold font read *Devil's Pointe Bar and Grille,* and he inwardly groaned. *Jesus Christ.* Two Polish brothers, who made the mafia look like a bunch of saints, owned the place. A search warrant wasn't going to be enough. Cox would need a goddamn Black Ops team to deal with Bojanskis.

"Looks like we've got ten-thirty. Might be an apartment number," Riley said.

"Or a date."

"I'm sorry?"

"October thirtieth. Devil's Night," Cox clarified.

Setting the bag of evidence back atop of the table, Riley

nodded. "Ah, right. Never thought of that."

Cox stroked his chin, and glanced back to Burke and Corley, who stood off to the side, while the forensics investigator pulled a purple, fleshy-looking object from the water. With a crimped lip, Cox turned to Riley and lowered his voice, "I need to run something by you. Wanna take a walk?"

***

Cox stared at the sign inside the skinny stairwell to the apartment above Devil's Pointe Bar. *Apartment For Rent* had been scribbled in large black letters onto a poster, nailed over the chipped and peeling paint of the wall.

"Empty apartment." Cox shook his head, the irritation simmering inside of him flexing his fingers with the urge to punch something. "This asshole better not be leading us on some goddamn goose chase, or someone's head'll fuckin' roll."

"Want me to grab the owner, Chief?"

Burke's ignorance had Cox rubbing a hand down his face, as he began his ascent up the stairs. "No. I don't want you to get the fuckin' owner."

Newbie cops often made the mistake of thinking police could tread anywhere they wanted in the city. A rookie mistake. Some communities had their own laws, their own ways of dealing with law enforcement, and the neighborhoods that bordered Hamtramck happened to be a few of those places. Made of up of mostly Polish, they were a tight community with long-standing roots, and the

Bojanskis were like the goddamn prom kings. Their connections could rival the mayor's, and busting into their property, even with a search warrant, was enough to get a man killed.

Waving a hand, Cox signaled Burke and Corley to follow him to the upper level. Like most bars of Poletown—as it was commonly referred to—Devil's Pointe was small, probably a maximum capacity of fifty people, if that, and something of a watering hole for the community. Only a single apartment stood above the bar, where it's previous owner probably lived. No way in hell the Bojanskis lived in the shithole. The two brothers made more money than the whole damn neighborhood, combined.

"Where's Riley? Thought this was his gig?" Burke asked, the heavy thud of his boots on each step toying with Cox's edgy nerves.

Christ, Cox would probably have to kill Burke and Corley, if they stumbled upon the same shit he had at The Palms.

"Said something came up." In truth, Cox had given him an ultimatum—stay back, or risk getting picked up on his way home from work some night and dropped off the end of a pier into the Detroit River. The eager bastard was still convinced that Achilleus X and the Eye for an Eye killer were connected, and Cox didn't need the nosey agent dipping his hands into shit and stumbling upon something Cox had every intention of keeping under wraps. Besides that, Michael Culling and all his political connections would back the Chief on the threat—which meant the mellow son of a bitch could easily lose his cozy pot-smoking job.

The growing need to identify the little prick behind the murders—the one who'd made it clear he was next—had consumed Cox to the extent that he didn't give a shit if Culling *didn't* back him up. He needed to find the killer before the killer found him. Any longer, and Cox'd be shitting sticks of dynamite, with as many Nitro pills as he'd taken. If it meant taking out an intrusive FBI agent along the way, so be it.

The numbers still remained a mystery, too. With each member of the Seven Mile Crew getting snuffed, it didn't take a genius to know it had something to do with The Cullings and Devil's Night. But what did that have to do with him?

All three men climbed higher up the stairs, the search warrant tucked inside Burke's back pocket.

"That's weird," Burke sneered, a wheeze of air confessing he was out of breath as they continued to climb. "Major case breaking here and the asshole ... what? Had a fucking hair appointment he couldn't miss?"

Cox kicked open the apartment door. "I didn't ask." Gun cocked, Cox made his way in first. Muscles tense, he prepared to blow away the first bastard that came into view.

Voices spoke from another room, and pausing, he straightened his stance and concentrated on the sound. Like laughter, maybe? He motioned Burke and Corley to keep quiet and padded across the room to the bedroom door. Muffled tones bled through the wood, and he kicked in the second door, gun aimed at a mostly empty room, aside from a table where a laptop had been set.

After a quick sweep of the vacant space, Cox approached the dark screen, where what sounded like a news report played over another video. He tugged a pair of gloves from his coat, donned them quickly, then swiped the mousepad. A box popped up, requesting a password.

"What d'you think his password is?" Cox stared down at the keys, mind swimming with what to type first.

"Ten thirty?" Burke's voice arrived from beside him.

Cox pecked the numbers slowly. Carefully. The box disappeared, and the screen opened to two videos playing simultaneously on loop. One showed a news report and Pulitzer Prize winning journalist-turned-drunk, Bill Warden, talking about a murder on Theodore Street. Another appeared to be some kind of home video, only about ten seconds long, with a boy and a woman talking to the camera. In it, she smiled, while whispering into the boy's ear, and the boy laughed, tipped his head back and said, "Go get 'em, Daddy!"

"Damn." Arms crossed, Burke shook his head as he watched the video. "Looks like the whole damn family was killed. I don't remember this one, do you, Chief?"

"Nah," Cox lied. "No idea who they are."

"I do." Hands on his hips, Corley sniffed, eyes glued to the screen before they flicked to Cox. "I remember them real well."

Anger bubbled in Cox's gut. Corley had been assigned to investigate the case a while back. The snooping bastard once tried to probe a little too deep into Cox's affairs, an act that got Corley subtly demoted. Cox would've fired the self-righteous little cocksucker, too, if he hadn't been second generation cop and son to the highly respected Chief who'd preceded Cox. Firing him would've sparked a mutiny, and worse, a visit from Internal Affairs.

Cox cocked his head toward where Corley stood. "What's this guy's name again?"

"Nick ... *Ryder*. That's his wife, Lena. The boy is his son, James," Corley added, stoking the ire burning in Cox's gut.

Pieces came together. Ryder. Theodore Street. Devil's Night. The Culling.

Hell, Cox could hardly remember the details, except that he'd given the green light to Julius Malone, who'd broken into a family's house, wreaking havoc. What the fuck made them do it, Cox didn't know. Could've been a primitive savagery ingrained in the little bastards, or they may have been pissed off for getting stiffed on the last deal they'd made with Culling, where two of their guys had gotten shot in a drug bust gone bad. A dead family would've sabotaged Culling's public support for more aggressive measures to curb the city's out-of-control crime rate. The deaths had to be covered up and brushed under the rug. That was the last time Culling tapped the Crew for a job, and over time, they eventually disbanded, hiding out from the enemies they'd made along the way.

"Can I help you, gentlemen?"

The raspy voice from behind jolted Cox's muscles, and he twisted to a group of three men in white shirts and black slacks. Standing in the doorway, all of them stared intently back.

"We've got a warrant," Burke said, stepping toward the men like he couldn't possibly be filled with lead in the next breath

The urge to roll his eyes tugged at the back of Cox's sockets. *Rookies.* Undermining the cop, Cox stepped in front. "Followed a tip. The guy who owns this place led us here."

"I own the fuckin' place." The heavier male stepped forward, rubbing his hands like he was itching for a fight. Cox recognized him as one of the Bojanskis. "And I sure as shit didn't lead you here."

Hand rested against the butt of his gun, Cox stood with his feet apart. "The tenant of this apartment."

"There is no tenant in this apartment, asshole. You see the sign out front?" A smile stretched across Bojanski's face. Whether he was Leon, or his infamous brother Frank, Cox didn't know. Both men carried a bad reputation on Detroit's west side, and most cops didn't fuck with them.

"Then, who the fuck left the computer?" Burke pointed over his shoulder.

Bojanski's eyes shot to Burke. "No idea."

Cox gave a nod toward Burke. "Meet you downstairs."

"I'm sorry ... what? We're leaving? We need to dust for

prints. Collect evidence. This is as much a crime scene—"

"You shut your fuckin' mouth, Burke," Cox barked back. "Downstairs. Now."

"The fuck?" Burke's lip twisted as he passed, and he waved to Corley beside Cox. "What about him?"

"Corley stays."

Corley had a relationship with just about every non-law-abiding bastard that roamed the streets, like a fucking pied piper of criminals. They respected him, which ordinarily grated on Cox's nerves, but right then, he'd make an exception.

Burke pushed past the group of men, storming off like a pissed off toddler.

"Now you're outnumbered." Bojanski tipped his head and smiled, like threatening a police Chief was as normal as changing his goddamn underwear.

"I want his name." A bold request, but Cox had been brought to the level of stupid moves since he'd been tagged the next victim.

"Go fuck yourself. Pig. I don't take orders from cops."

Cox snapped for Bojanski's throat, pinning him to the wall inside the bedroom.

Three guns clicked at once, two of them pointed at the Chief.

"Whoa! Hold up!" Corley's voice thundered above the blood swishing inside Cox's ears. "Just hold the fuck up! We're here to investigate a string of murders. We have reason to believe the killer lives here."

Bojanski snorted when Cox's grip fell from his throat.

"Killer. More like hero. Taking out all the shit that you cops are too fuckin' lazy to do."

"Look, this *person* is a bit unorthodox, and I can't deny that." The calm in Corley's tone made Cox want to punch the bastard. The cocksucker probably hoped Bojanski would snuff Cox right there so he could steal the throne and be crowned the next police chief. "Whoever it is, is targeting some major players, no doubt. But he's climbin' the food chain, and sooner or later, he's gonna hit one of the top dogs. These are psychopaths he's going after. Ain't like you and Rev, Leon."

"You know Rev?"

"Yeah, I know Rev. We go back a long ways." Just as Cox suspected, Corley knew all the shady bastards.

Bojanski sniffed. "All right. Name's Alec Vaughn. Skipped out six months ago. Ain't been back. Bastard stiffed me on half a year's rent."

"Alec Vaughn," Corley repeated. "What's he look like?"

"Looks like a fuckin' gangster, that's what he looks like. Like Al Cappone, or some shit. Likes pinstripe suits and fedoras."

"You know anything about him? Relations? Family? Interests?" Corley's line of questioning seemed worthless at that point. It was no mystery why the killer chose the Bojanskis. If Cox hadn't been so damn preoccupied with the possibility of stumbling upon something incriminating, he'd have called on the goddamn military to take out the asshole, if necessary.

"Look around. This ain't Trump Tower. The fuckin' tenants who've lived here came from the streets. I'm not courting the bastards, I'm their landlord, not their goddamn fairy godmother." He straightened the collar of his shirt. "You got the information you needed. Finish up and get the fuck out. And if I ever find you on my property without my knowing, search warrant or not, you'll be the next Jimmy Hoffa."

The three of them exited the apartment, sparing no fear that they'd just told off the Chief of Detroit Police.

Cox turned to Corley. "I want you to look into this Alec Vaughn. I want to know everything about this cocksucker—his favorite color, what time he shits, how he takes his goddamn coffee. And you report directly to me. No one else. Understood?"

"Yeah. I understand."

CHAPTER 38
Nick

Tipping back the bottle of whiskey, I kicked back a heavy swill, watching Aubree sip her beer while she cooked bacon on a griddle, with nothing more than a pair of panties peeking beneath my white borrowed shirt.

The whole scene felt out of place. Oddly *domestic*, after a marathon of sex inside the broken down, dilapidated surroundings. Like some fucked up version of June and Ward Cleaver in the ghetto.

"Bacon is for breakfast." I leaned into the countertop, crossing my arms.

Her cheek dimpled with a smile. "You've never had bacon and eggs for dinner?"

"Never. In fact, you're probably breaking a law in some country, somewhere."

"No, no, no." She lifted a small piece she'd already cooked from a nearby plate, and sauntered toward me. "Bacon is like sex. You can have it any time of the day." With the bacon caught between her teeth, she pressed into me, offering the food from her mouth, and as I bit down, I stole the meat *and* her kiss. "And it's so damn good."

"I can't argue that." I wrapped my arms around her, clutching both of her rounded ass cheeks, and bent forward for another kiss. Digging my fingers into her muscles had me appreciating the high lift and firmness of her ass. "Tight," I said through clenched teeth against her mouth. "You've got one hell of a Brazilian ass."

"French Canadian ass, thank you very much."

I could see she had some exotic blend, in the chestnut color of her hair and the golden tone of her eyes. "You're Canadian?"

"My father was. Anton Levesque. The first and only man I ever loved."

"He died."

She nodded. "Both my parents are gone now. My father, just about a year ago."

"You said he was the first and only man you ever loved. What made you marry, if not for love?"

Her nostrils flared with a deep breath, as though she braced herself for the explanation. "Michael was a student of mine, suffering from the loss of ... probably the only man in the world he ever respected. I suppose he thought love could fill that hole. And I was foolish enough to believe him."

"So ... you work with troubled adults? Thought it was kids."

"Kids, too. Most of my patients have been severely abused. A lot of them have developed disorders as a result of trauma." Sliding from my embrace, she stood beside me at the counter.

I crossed my empty arms. "What sparked that interest?"

Her eyes dipped away from mine, but only for a second. "When I was nine years old, we lived in a pretty quiet neighborhood of Detroit. It was actually River Rouge area. Lot of auto workers. Blue collar types. My dad was a factory worker." She sipped her beer. "We didn't have much. We were pretty poor." The corner of her lip crinkled, giving the impression that whatever existence she'd lived was well below her new standard. "A boy lived next door to me, a little older than I was." Gaze cast beyond me, she shook her head. "I'd never seen him in school, didn't know if he went to school at all. He was never allowed to leave his back yard, so we used to play at the fence, where I had a sandbox that my father built for me." As she talked, she toyed with the rim of the beer bottle, circling her index finger over the mouth of it, her eyes unfocused as though lost to the memory. "I'd make mud pies and pass them through the fence to him. I remember he always had bruises on his legs, during the summer when he wore shorts. As curious as I was, I never asked him about them, but I was mesmerized by the deep shades of purple and yellowing of the ones that'd begun to fade. I'd never been abused. Had no idea that an adult was capable of such cruelty."

Listening to the way she described him, I couldn't help but wonder how the kid had come to affect her life so profoundly.

"I … gave him a ring. Nothing expensive, just a plastic piece of junk I'd gotten from a cereal box, or something. Told him he was my best friend. My *boyfriend*, though I didn't know what that was at the time." Her brows pinched together. "He went missing two days later. For an entire week, I didn't see him. He never came out to play. I thought maybe he'd gone to his grandma's house for the week, as I sometimes did during the summer. At night, I'd hear noises that frightened me, like monsters outside my window. And then, one day, his backyard was full of people—police, cameras, news reporters. At the time, I didn't know why all those people had gathered. My mother told me I was too young to understand, and so it wasn't until later that I found out he'd been tied to a tractor in the shed and tortured." She cleared her throat, her gaze dropping away from mine. "I think what bothered me most was, the whole time I thought he was gone, he was merely a few yards away from me. I'd even called out his name to play, but he never answered. He must've been so scared that he wouldn't even answer me." She blew out a shaky breath. "I could've saved him. If I'd told someone about the bruises, I probably could've saved him. If I'd asked where they'd come from, given him the chance to ask for help … but I never did." Her gaze lifted to mine. "I vowed to listen from that point on. I promised to ask and never ignore the bruises and scars. I'd never ignore the signs again. So, that's what I do. I help interpret signs."

"What exactly do you do with your clients?"

"Art therapy. I used to have a class once a week." She smiled again, standing beside me at the counter. "Before I was *kidnapped*. Really hope they're not expecting a note to excuse my absence."

Her comment made me chuckle. "So, what does an art *therapist* do?"

"Create. In loss or suffering, there can be joy in creating something that didn't exist before. Creation and healing are born of the same thread. Bringing something to life can sometimes heal the soul, while still honoring what a person has lost."

I frowned. "You can't replace what's lost with inanimate objects."

"No. You can never replace what's lost through art. In fact, a number of pieces I've created were made out of rage and frustration, for that very point you just made. I'd give anything to have my mother back." Her head tipped back, and she smiled. "I remember she had the smoothest skin and the thickest hair. I could barely get my little fingers around it when she'd let me gather it into my hands. And her smell." Her lids fluttered shut, nostrils flared as she sucked in a breath. "No painting could ever capture such a wonderful smell. Like home. But it wasn't until I first painted her face that I was forced to remember all the things I loved about her."

Elbows rested on the countertop, Aubree balanced her chin on her palm, and as she talked, and I tried to recall what my home had smelled like. The laundry my wife insisted on hanging out on the line during summer. The dinners she cooked in the evenings, so rich they filled every room. Lena's perfume. The soap in my son's hair after she'd bathed him. If I concentrated, I could almost remember.

"For so many years, I was haunted by the thoughts that I'd soon forget what she looked like. It's the truly amazing things in life that we remember most vividly, in the most vibrant colors. Everything else is simply a white canvas." She let out a huff. "And some are painted so black, you'll never see the colors. With Michael, I always thought, if I could just get out, get away from him, I could paint this blackness into a world of vibrant colors again. As it once was." She shook her head, her gaze directed beyond me, and her eyebrows lowered in an expression of hopelessness that made me want to lift her up into my arms. "Nothing can be painted over black, though. No matter how many layers of color you paint, the blackness beneath it will always bleed through."

She finally lifted herself from the counter, crossing her arms over her chest. That beautiful smile lit her face again as her gaze fell from mine. "Anyway, that's my lesson for today. Please come back tomorrow for another riveting half hour of Aubree's mostly incoherent ramblings."

I took another swig of whiskey, letting the burn coat my throat, staring at the incredibly complex woman I didn't think I'd ever fully understand. "There's sweetness to your poison, Aubree—as intoxicating and beautiful as it's deadly. The more I know about you, the more I want to know."

Before she could respond, my phone buzzed from the holster at my hip. I lifted it, eyeing the familiar number across the screen, and stepped out of the kitchen into the foyer before answering. "Yeah."

Bojanski's raspy Polish voice spoke low on the other end. "Cops were here."

"Only cops, or FBI, too?"

"Police Chief, I guess. Didn't think the bastard worked cases."

I wanted to laugh at that. "He has a personal interest."

"Gave 'em the name, Alec Vaughn, just like you said, right?"

Alec's idea. A way to throw them off my trail. "Good. Was DeMarcus Corley there?"

"Yep. Good thing, too. Almost had a dead fuckin' Chief, and I'm sure the natives would've gone apeshit over that." He'd coughed like his lungs might pop through the receiver at any moment, and I tugged the phone from my ear until he'd finished. "Anyway, the ball is in motion now. Good luck, my friend."

"Thanks. For everything." My wife had grown up with the Bojanskis. Leon, and his brother Frank, had always looked out for Lena, like the big brothers she never had. And since police stayed away from the notorious brothers who were known for some of the most brutal murders in the city, they didn't hesitate to help when I came to them.

That was the thing about Detroit. Had to be careful who you fucked with, because everybody had connections.

"Anytime. You make 'em pay for what they did. You make 'em pay big time, hear?"

"I will. I promise you that."

When I returned to the kitchen, Aubree sat on the countertop, beer bottle set between her splayed thighs, and my throat went dry. She raised a fork with eggs and bacon piled on it from the plate beside her.

With a much bigger appetite than her proffered food, I strode across the room, setting my hands flat on either side of her, and opened my mouth to take the bite.

Her hand jerked back. "Wait. I have a question." The sweep of her tongue across her lips seized my attention. "So, we never got to you. You told me you were a video game designer. What kind of games?" She smiled. "Kidnapping unwitting damsels in distress?"

I grinned, and she shoveled the food into my mouth, the smoky bacon coating my tongue as I chewed before swallowing. "Not quite. A mafia crime game called *Ladder of the Gods.* Players take out major figures on behalf of the notorious Gabrielli crime family to climb the ranks. The ultimate goal is to take out the Capo of the Gabrielli family. It's a game of revenge."

"Ah. And who is the hero of the game?"

"Someone I spent years creating. Long before I designed the game. He's the ultimate hero."

"And why does he want revenge?" Her brow winged up.

"I never really fully developed that part of the game. He had a backstory, but … I just sort of kept it obscure. It made him something of a mysterious madman. An anti-hero, of sorts. He had a pretty brutal means of delivering punishment, and throughout the game, players battle their conscience. All they're given is snapshots of memory. They create their own backstory to justify the cruelty, as they play."

"That sounds like it'd be a hit." She stuffed another piece of bacon into her mouth, chomping as she talked. "No pun intended. I'm not much of a gamer. Was it pretty popular?"

"Never made it to production. I had a meeting with the publisher the night—" I cleared my throat, choking back the guilty confession that'd always stung the back of my thoughts. "Just didn't happen."

"Nick? I don't want to pry, but ... that night ... how did you *survive*?"

It was a question I'd asked myself over and over. I didn't know how I'd survived. Physically or mentally. "I somehow got to my feet, ready to go after those bastards. Somewhere along the way, I collapsed. No idea where. But a young girl found me. Girl from the streets." My cheek twitched with an urge to smile, as I thought of Lauren so young. "She called an ambulance. Took my dog while I was in the hospital. I owe her my life."

"You have such an amazing sense of loyalty, Nick. It must be a wonderful feeling for a young girl to have earned your respect like that."

I sipped the last of my whiskey and set it atop the counter. "Lauren's not so young anymore. Nineteen."

"She's something of a daughter to you, then."

A dull ache throbbed in my heart at the thought of cutting ties with her. "Was. She's pretty much grown up now. Has her own place. Goes to school."

"You've cut yourself out of her life, then?"

"We have a rule, Lauren and me. No ties."

"Ties make you vulnerable." Her gaze fell from mine. "So, tell me … what will you do after you've won your vengeance?"

"I haven't gotten that far."

"Because you don't know what's on the other side?" She kept her eyes cast downward. "Are you afraid you won't have a purpose once you kill him? Is that why you avoid making ties?" When she finally looked up, my muscles tensed at the knowing look in her eyes, the way they seemed to look right down into my soul. "They keep you connected to the world? To life?"

"I can't lie to you, Aubree. I'm not the man you think I am." I battled her gaze, keeping my stare locked on hers, but goddamn she could crumble a man's defenses. "I know you've had some fucked up shit in your life. But it doesn't get any more fucked up than me. I want to be the white knight who chases away all of your nightmares." Finally breaking our stare down, I hung my head. "I used to be. Now, there's so much darkness inside of me, and I'm afraid …" Hell, I couldn't even say the words that'd tormented me the last couple of days.

"You're not afraid of anything, Nick."

"I'm afraid of causing you pain." I nodded, resigning

myself to confessing what would ultimately be less heartache for her in the end. "You're right. There is nothing left for me after this."

In my periphery, I could see her arms cross over one another. "So this ... this is about you biding your time. One last hurrah before you ride off into the blazing gun show, right?"

I couldn't look at her, let alone answer the question.

"I'm not the woman you think I am, either. I'm not looking for a *white knight*, Nick. I gave up on white knights a long time ago." At my persistent silence, she huffed. "Why keep me? Why not let me go, or better yet, why don't *you* kill me?"

Smirking, I shook my head at what had grown to be a ridiculous thought. Strange, how the mind could change from one state to another. "I might be fucked up, Aubree. But I couldn't kill you if I tried. Not now."

"Then, why keep me here? Why not set me free?"

"I can't yet."

"Why? Dammit, tell me why!" Her fist pounded against the countertop, and my gaze shot up. No doubt, she probably felt the same state of limbo that had me suspended, drifting along in a plan that didn't make sense to me either. "I'm tired of hearing you can't. I want to know *why* you can't! I saw ..." She cleared her throat. "In your room. You had pictures of me. From as far back as a year."

I frowned at the intrusion, wondering how much of my life she'd gleaned while rifling. "You went through my things?"

"I need answers. I need to know what part I play in this, Nick."

"Alec wants to keep you." *I want to keep you.* I felt like a selfish bastard, crueler than any of the men I'd killed over the last two weeks. Before me, I had a beautiful, wounded creature, trapped in my small, dark cage, begging me for freedom. Freedom that I refused to grant because I selfishly craved something more. More than her.

"For what? Do you even know? I'm worthless to Michael. If you think you're going to snag some deal of a lifetime by offering me up as a trade, you're wrong! He doesn't give a shit if you kill me. The only regret he'll feel is from not having done it himself! And if he does come to you for vengeance, it's only because you beat him to it." She lifted my phone from the countertop and banged it against my chest. "You call Alec. You ask him what he wants with me."

"You don't understand, Aubree."

"Call him."

"I can't—"

Her chin inclined in the defiant pose that I'd somehow come to enjoy from her. With those golden eyes full of fire, hell if I didn't feel a rush move through my body. A burn that snaked beneath my skin, and left me one delicate wire from detonating into a raging bomb of lust. "Try to stop me from leaving, then." She spun around, long locks of hair dancing around her shoulders, and ran straight for the doorway out of the kitchen.

I charged forward, knocking her back against wall, dick pressed into her core until she could feel my need for her. Cupping her jaw with my right hand, I seethed when her mouth clamped shut. Goddamn the little pistol could work me right into a massive explosion.

I slanted my lips over hers and stole whatever fiery canon of bullshit she was about to spew.

Her palms slammed into my chest in an effort to break the kiss. Futile.

Grinding against her in slow, imagined thrusts quieted the muffled debate vibrating against my lips. Gripping her crown made sure she couldn't slip out of my grasp, and she surrendered, arching her body into mine.

"The truth?" I asked. "Yeah, the plan was to kill you alongside Culling, if he didn't negotiate. I'm not going to kill you though, and I won't send you back to your piece of shit husband. But I can't … let you go yet." Gritting my teeth, I tightened my fist around a handful of her hair. "Do you understand? I can't."

The plea in my eyes must've shown through, loud and clear.

Behind a watery shield of tears, her eyes softened to defeat. "Yeah. I understand. And that probably makes me as fucked up as you are."

CHAPTER 39
Chief Cox

Cox pulled into the circle drive of Brandon Malone's newly renovated mansion. It chapped his ass, the way drug lords lived better than the goddamn Chief of Police. He hobbled up the stairs to the front door, cringing at the guttural growls that seeped through as a warning. Malone owned three Great Danes, and Cox had wanted to shoot the horny fucking leg-bangers the first time he met them.

The doorbell chimed, exciting the dogs into a frenzy of barking, until the butler came to the door, holding one of the devils by the collar while it lurched and bared its teeth.

"Here to see Brandon."

"Certainly, Chief Cox. Right this way." The butler barked a command at the dogs, and all three of them retreated to the wall of the foyer, where they sat stiff and statuesque.

Once inside, Cox followed the butler toward the back of the mansion, admiring crystal chandeliers, expensive paintings, imported tapestries, marble staircases, all the shit Cox couldn't afford on his salary. The scenery morphed into framed Pistons jerseys, signed Tigers baseballs and Red Wings pucks, held in glass curio cabinets—a variety of sports paraphernalia that made up Brandon's game room.

Brandon sat amongst a bevy of black males around a sectional couch—some drinking, some smoking, some snorting—and Cox took a seat beside them. Football played on the theater-sized television screen, and women, clad in clothes so tight he could see their nipples through the fabric, lounged around and between them.

"Chief Cox. I hope you have something to share about my brother," Brandon said, taking a hit of his cigarillo.

With a stoic expression, Cox responded, "Your brother was found this morning at the old train station. He'd been cut multiple times and left to bleed out. Rats consumed most of his entrails."

Brandon shot forward in his seat, knocking the woman draped across his lap onto the floor. His nostrils flared as he brought both fists to his temples, pounding there. "Who is this mothafucka?" His voice bellowed, drowning out the commentator on screen. "He just messed with the wrong fucking family!"

While Brandon sat rocking, damn near sucking his thumb, in a tantrum, Cox leaned forward in his chair. He'd have to choose his words carefully. Though Brandon answered to Cox, and was paid through Cox, losing his brother could've sent him on a tailspin into madness. Enough to do something stupid like shoot the messenger.

"We got a tip we're following. In the meantime, I need to know something. Three years ago, your crew at the time broke into a house on Theodore Street. Burned it down. You remember that?"

Frowning, Brandon threw his hands out to the side. "Yeah, so fucking what?"

"The man who lived in that house. Nick Ryder. Did you kill him?"

"Shot the mothafucka in the skull. Yeah, we killed him. He burned with that house."

"You're certain?"

"I'm certain." He straightened, throwing his arms out again. "'The fuck does this have to do with my brother?"

"Because I think your brother was killed in retaliation for what you did that night, by someone who knew this Nick."

"Who is it? I want his name."

"I don't have a name yet," Cox lied, pushing off the couch. "But I will tell you this. If you're lying to me, if he's not dead , I will take you down, and what happened to your brother will be a mercy kill for what is done to you."

Springing to his feet, Brandon drew a pistol from his hip. "You think you can talk to me like that? I'll smoke your fuckin white ass right here!"

"Whoa!" One of his cronies laughed, their eyes rolling back, obviously high, to the point Cox was surprised the fucker had even caught what was going on.

"And you'll be taking it up the ass in your prison cell

for the rest of your life, you fucking thug piece of shit." Cox pointed, despite the gun still cocked in Brandon's grip. "Don't forget who signs your fuckin' paycheck."

Brandon sniffed, his jaw shifting as he swiped the back of his hand across his nose and lowered the gun.

"You ever pull a gun on me again, and the last thing you'll see will be the tip of my bullet before your skull is split in half." Bending, Cox grabbed a rolled up bill sitting on the glass coffee table and snorted the line of coke one of the assholes beside him had set before heading for the door. "You cocksuckers have yourself a nice day."

CHAPTER 40
Aubree

Lying on a bed of pillows alongside where flames crackled in the old brick fireplace of Nick's bedroom, my eyelids grew heavy as his naked body pressed into mine. "So, this place ... have you lived here long?"

"Only a couple months."

"Did it always have heat, water and electrical, or did you rig that yourself?"

He kissed the sensitive skin behind my ear, and I twitched at the tickle of his scruff. "Rigged it myself."

"You went through all this trouble just to kidnap me? I'm flattered."

"Nothing but the best for you." With his lips dragging along the edge of my neck, he cast an exhilarating prickle against the tautness of my skin, while his palm smoothed over the curve of my hip.

"Your hands are like nothing I've ever known before, Nick. Both pain and pleasure in your touch."

"Pain?" His words vibrated against my throat.

Exhaling a long, easy breath, I closed my eyes and rolled onto my back, where he stared down at me, propped on one elbow. "Pain of knowing it doesn't belong to me. That this is all temporary."

Those blue eyes cut away from mine. "Being with you has only strengthened my reasons for going after Culling. Not just for what happened to my family." His stare lifted, drilling into me with intensity as his brows furrowed and his lip twisted in disgust. "For what he did to you. How he hurt you. Tortured you." His fingertip drifted along my shoulder. "This touch does belong to you, Aubree. And I promise these same hands that seek to bring you pleasure, will bring pain to those who hurt you. I will destroy the nightmares that haunt you, and deliver Culling's fucking head on a platter for all he's done to you. All he's stolen from you. I promise you this."

His face blurred behind the tears filling my eyes. "What if I told you that I don't want that from you? Fuck Michael." My blood thickened with ire. Was vengeance so important that he'd risk dying? Michael had too many connections to make him an easy kill. "I want *you*, Nick. Don't you understand? If you die, even having killed Michael, in the end he's won. He will have taken the last shred of hope." I placed my palm against his cheek. "I can't lose this. I can't lose *you*."

Frowning, he rolled over my body and cupped my face in his palms. "If ever a woman was capable of owning my heart again, you are. No matter what happens, Aubree, I will take care of you." His lips brushed mine in what felt like a shushing of my thoughts, and when his mouth closed over mine, tongue dipping past my teeth, his kiss penetrated the wintry shroud of despair that kept us at a safe distance. It somehow broke through the suffocating uncertainty that loomed like a black cloud on the verge of destroying both of us.

I yearned to know his secrets. Not the ones he'd given me, but the ones he refused to share. The ones buried in some locked chamber inside his head where I couldn't reach. The ones that didn't answer the burning question swimming inside my own head—why me? What did I have to offer in his grand scheme? A ransom? A vendetta?

If only I could somehow unlock the secret door inside his heart, where I sensed something darker burrowed, protected by an ominous lie that hung on the air, perhaps then he'd trust me enough with his truths. I could heal him and perhaps he'd see something beyond the vengeance.

He'd see me.

CHAPTER 41
Chief Cox

Cox slouched in the chair across from Culling, who ignored him while talking on his cellphone. Not a single black hair on the mayor's head stood out of place, and the slicked back style glistened under the office lights. Must've been in his thirties, Cox guessed, but the lack of wrinkles and the smooth surface of his skin, lacking any sort of texture, swiped ten years off his guess. Clearly, the asshole put too much time into his beauty regimen. No man should look like he caked on a bunch of fuckin' makeup before coming to work, yet, the patch of red at Culling's cheeks almost looked like the bastard'd blushed 'em.

"I'll figure it out. I'll come up with something and call you back." Culling rubbed his forehead in what seemed like distress. "Thanks for calling." He flipped off the phone and, tossing it onto his desktop, cupped his face with both hands and let out a string of muffled curses.

Christ. Cox had come to him with the developments on the case—a task he never looked forward to, as it seemed his efforts were never enough for the asshole— yet, he had a feeling he was about to get roped into whatever shit-storm had just stolen the first half hour of their meeting.

Culling's hands slid down his smooth face, and for the first time, Cox had a good look at his eyes, dark and bloodshot. "Please tell me you're here because you've found my fucking wife."

Cox had known the bastard long enough to recognize the daunting calm to his voice as the placid moment before the fucker snapped into a hurricane of rage. Straightening in his chair, he sniffed and cleared his throat, muscles tense. "We, uh … got reason to believe there's a connection between this Eye for an Eye killer and Mrs. Culling."

"*Reason to believe.*" The articulation of every word set Cox's spine tingling, like the instincts animals had when preparing themselves to flee. "And what, pray tell, *brilliant* sleuthing brought you to this conclusion?"

"Found a video of the Theodore Street massacre from three years ago. Looks like someone connected to that family might be out for revenge."

"Theodore massacre. Would this be the same fucking video that just hit a major news station about an hour ago?"

Cox frowned. "I'm sorry, sir. What?"

"That call was my Chief of Staff, telling me that the city is going ballistic over a story that, apparently, went viral on social media earlier today and ended up on the evening news. There are rumblings of a massive protest planned for Devil's Night. They've come up with an endearing name for it—The Culling Conspiracy." The pounding of his fist against the desktop had Cox flinching. "I, somehow, have to answer to thousands of residents wanting to know how I could overlook and suppress such *an atrocity.* They're questioning my methods of crime reduction in this city, and when they begin to question, they begin to dig. And when they dig, they begin to rebel. And when they rebel, you have a fucking anarchy and the Detroit Riot of 'sixty-seven knocking at your door! I have every king pin in this city ready to help me take down some of these hellhole neighborhoods that suck the life right out of this goddamn shit stain on the fucking map, and now I have to find something shiny enough to distract the restless flock of jobless hippies who have nothing better to do than save humanity between tokes of their fucking peace pipes! This has Achilleus X written all over it. Now, perhaps you might explain how a dormant video managed to go viral on the same day you happened to discover it?"

Like a thunderclap inside Cox's head, Culling's words jolted the clues that'd been swimming around his mind the last couple of days. Vaughn. Achilleus X. Could there have been a connection? "We got a tip from the guy who owns the apartment where we found the video. Some Alec Vaughn. I don't yet know how he's linked to Theodore Street, or why, but this Vaughn ... he's one sick son of a bitch. Might be tight with Achilleus X. Like some kinda faction, or something."

"Then, I suggest you pull your finger out of your asshole and make sure you find him first. Does anyone else know about this Vaughn?"

"Another cop. DeMarcus Corley." A twinge of fury licked Cox's spine at the mention of Corley.

"Make sure he keeps his fucking mouth shut. You're going to need an element of surprise in order to catch this one, if he's as slick as Achilleus X."

"I'll make sure DeMarcus doesn't say a word."

"In the meantime, I have to find a way to distract an entire city."

Cox leveled his gaze on Culling. "How can I help?"

"Devil's Night is coming up. They're going to see me as much a victim as any one of them. I'm going to tell them, in my most gut-wrenching performance, that my wife was kidnapped and may have been murdered by their *hero*, their *beloved* Achilleus X. After all, he did threaten that I should watch what I value most. And I'm going to offer a reward to anyone who has information on her whereabouts. You are going to find her. And when you do, I want both of them brought to me alive."

"I'll find them."

"Good." Culling straightened his cuffs and sniffed. "Because if you don't, the city will soon be looking to fill a spot for their Chief of Police, who met his unfortunate and untimely demise while sleeping peacefully in his cozy little bed."

CHAPTER 42
Nick

Dawn broke across the city, casting light on dark spires that I could see from the observation deck of the Penobscot building. Staring down at the city from five hundred and sixty-eight feet in the sky, I waited for Alec to arrive at our old haunt, accessible via the staircase that lead out onto the parapet, where the famous red beacon blinked behind me. All the major landmarks of the city stood beautiful and proud around me, the graffiti and broken windows invisible from that height.

My whole life, I'd never had anything against the place where I'd grown up. Detroit pumped through my veins, infected my blood. No matter where I lived, it'd always be home.

The Penobscot building was the perfect place for our meets, and Alec and I often sat plotting over beers while balanced on the narrow wall of the parapet. The view reminded us why revenge wasn't just about what happened to my family. It was about being a voice to the voiceless.

Unusually, as I stood there, the height made me queasy.

"Still think you have the balls to jump?"

I turned to find Alec standing behind me, his cigar hanging out of his mouth, but snapped my attention back to the edge of the building and peered down at the rooftops below me. I probably wouldn't even hit the streets. "Maybe."

"I don't like the sound of that."

"Does it matter? Unless Culling does the honors first, you're going kill me anyway. That's the deal, remember?"

"How could I forget?" he said, but I caught the flinch of his eye.

"Of course, if you've come to throw me over the edge of the building, at least let me pick the side first." I glanced over the railing. "The east end looks like a messy fall."

"Then, you still wish to go through with this? To the end."

I twisted to face him. "I have to."

"Am I to assume you've spent two weeks with a woman and never once fucked her?"

His question brought a smile to my face, despite the sobering expression on his furrowing his brow. "You assume wrong."

With the cigar caught between his lips, he crossed his arms behind his back and paced. "And this fucking you gave her, how was it?"

Scratching my cheek couldn't hide the widening of my smile, and I turned away from him, facing the magnificent view of the city. "Good. Real good." I entwined my fingers, resting them atop the wall.

"And yet, you have no desire to explore her body? To see how dark and depraved she's willing to become at your command? You'd prefer death instead."

"At my command? She might act all sweet and obedient, but that woman does what she wants." Cocking my head to the side brought Alec's stiff form into my periphery, and the smile on my face shriveled. "She's the wife of my enemy, Alec. Her husband destroyed everything that meant something to me. He destroyed the man who might've been capable of loving a woman like her. There's nothing left. Why do you keep probing about this? What the hell do you want from me?"

"The truth, Nick. No one knows you better than I do. And I happen to believe you've fallen in love with her."

His bold statement had me rolling my head against my shoulders. "Love is a bit too strong for what I feel. She's been a good distraction, I'll give you that. But that's—"

Pain exploded in the back of my head as I hit the wall behind me, and I caught my balance, while Alec stood, cigar in mouth, his fingers curled around my throat.

"'The hell?"

"Stubborn fuck! I'm losing patience." He released me, and my knees damn near buckled as I drew in a breath, desperate for air.

I rubbed the back of my head, a growl brewing inside

my chest alongside the urge to punch him. "We've got bigger topics on this meeting's agenda, don't you think? Like a plan to take out the goddamn mayor of the city? Who gives a shit about the woman?"

He leapt on top of me, gripping the neck of my T-shirt, his fist drawn back, but I flipped him over, and both of us pushed to a stand.

I swung, but he ducked, and my fist drove through the window of the door behind him. "Fuck!" The glass had sliced the delicate skin, leaving a lick of flames dancing across my flesh.

My feet kicked out from under me, and gravel smashed into my spine, knocking my field of vision left then right, wide and blurry, before it shrank back to normal. Alec straddled me, that fucking cigar hanging on like a champ from his mouth.

I caught his returning punch midair and held firm to his wrist, ready to volley the next strike. "What the fuck has gotten into you? What does it matter?" At his silence, I continued, "Here, I thought you'd be pissed that I'd developed feelings for her, and you act like you're ready to kill me if I didn't."

"Then you *do* have feelings for her."

"Yeah. I do." I puffed a breath. "She makes me fucking crazy and has my body all strung the hell out. But my feelings won't get in the way of the plan, so chill the fuck out."

He lowered his fist and released my shirt like I'd satisfied him.

"Tell me something, Alec. Kidnapping Aubree Culling was never part of the original plan. What made you change your mind?"

With a push off the gravel, he rose to his feet and wiped the dirt from his pant legs. "It's not important." He reached a hand out to me. "Let's discuss the end of this plan."

CHAPTER 43
Chief Cox

Cox put the paper cup to his lips, but when cold coffee slid across his tongue, his nose crinkled. Setting the coffee back into the cup holder beside his seat, he refocused his attention on the entrance to Bojanski's apartment building. Probably a waste of fucking time, staking out the place from his car, but Cox wasn't in the mood to get hit with any more death threats from Culling.

Through a staircase window, he had a good view of Alec Vaughn's apartment. It seemed the asshole was a complete mystery—not a single record of him anywhere—and since Bojanski didn't exactly have his tenants submit applications, Cox couldn't even be sure the asshole landlord had given him a legit name.

Ah, fuck it. He'd been sitting on the corner, a block away from the building, for most of the day. Aside from some drunk piece of shit, who must've passed out somewhere along the staircase, he hadn't seen a single person come or go.

Cox fired up his Buick, ready to take off, but paused when a young woman, or teenager perhaps, strolled up the sidewalk toward the stairwell. Tight black curls had been pulled back into a ponytail, and she wore a vest over a sweatshirt, with jeans torn at the knees and black combat boots, which made her look more like a student than a street rat. Pretty, too, from what he could see, with her honey brown skin and slender frame. Had Julius still been around, Cox could've made some coin off her ass.

She climbed the stairs, and through the window of the stairwell, Cox damn near choked when she stopped in front of apartment one-oh-three.

"Well, well. What the fuck do we have here?" he muttered, grabbing his binoculars beside him.

She withdrew a hand from one of her pockets and knocked on the door. Once. Twice. Placed her ear to the wood and knocked again.

A minute passed, and she skipped back down the stairs, looking over her shoulder like she'd been trained to watch her back, and kept on down the sidewalk.

Cox crept forward, maintaining a good distance, watching while she slipped on a helmet, hopped onto a motor scooter, and took off.

He followed her through the streets, about a dozen car lengths behind, until she arrived at what appeared to be an old church. She hopped off the bike, swinging the helmet from her hand, and when she reached the door, she disappeared inside.

The sign hanging from the building had *Sanctum*

written in large, old English letters and *Youth Hostel* below it. A smile slid across Cox's face, and he lifted the cellphone beside him and dialed.

"What d'you want?" The twinge of contempt in Brandon's voice told Cox he still harbored hard feelings after their last meeting.

"A favor."

"I know you didn't just ask me for no mothafuckin' favor."

"Then, perhaps you're not interested in identifying the man who killed your brother."

A long pause followed, before Brandon finally said, "I'm listening."

"I need you to retrieve a girl. Looks mixed. Light skin. Student, maybe. She's somehow connected to him. She's at Sanctum. I don't know if she lives here alone, or with someone. Get rid of any others. Bring her to me. Alive."

"Consider it done," Brandon answered without the slightest hesitation.

"Oh, and just for shits and giggles, have someone film it. Perhaps we'll send a message of our own to this cocksucker."

Cox smiled at Brandon's sneering laugh.

"Fuck, yeah," Brandon said.

CHAPTER 44
Aubree

"*My people of Detroit …*" Onscreen, Michael's lips formed a hard line, and the camera zoomed in on a slight quiver to his chin. "*It is with a heavy heart and …*" He cleared his throat. "*… so much pain, that I …*" Covering his face behind his hand, he shook his head in a way that had me shaking my own. "*I've lost someone so … dear to me. My wife, Aubree Culling, was kidnapped, and is believed to be …*" The asshole's voice shook as he spoke. The theatrics must've exhausted him. "*Dead. I'm offering a large sum of money to anyone who might have information on her kidnapper, believed to be Achilleus X. In a prior video, he threatened to take what I value most. And well …*" Culling broke into a laugh-worthy sob. "*… he did. And I want justice. My wife did not die in vain. She has brought so much to this city, and I'm asking you, my wonderful people, to help me find her killer. Help bring her the justice she deserves.*"

"What a fucking fruitloop," I said, lying beside Nick on the bed, as we watched the news report on his laptop.

"As if he gave two shits about me!" Set against Nick's chest, my hand balled into a fist. "Ooh! If I had a gun …" I drilled his stomach, but slapped my hand to my mouth when I realized what I'd done. "I'm sorry."

"Easy, Pistol Lips." His cheeks dimpled with a grin, eyes sparkling with humor. "I like when you're pissed off. It's like foreplay."

I smiled. "You like aggression, huh?" I asked, stealing the opportunity to dig inside his head. "Want me to tie you up and beat your ass?"

He shivered, though whether fake or not, I couldn't tell. "Don't tease me."

"Nick … when we were together the other day, I wanted to ask you. There was a point when …" My stomach coiled when his gaze fell away from mine. "… you seemed different. Like … something *else* … something darker was inside of you and you were … trying to keep it hidden from me." Still, his eyes shied away from mine. "I sense there is something more to you." Unfurling my tight fist, I clutched his arm. "I want you to know, Nick. I like what I saw. I'm not afraid of it."

"What exactly did you see?" The interest in his voice told me I was on the right track, and the innocent sweep of his tongue across his lips had my predator sensors on high alert. I wanted to take those sweet lips into my mouth and bite down.

"I saw a tormented mind. Conflicted. I know a part of you wants to hurt me. Punish me for what happened. The other part of you … the calm, humane side wants to stuff those thoughts away and touch me with gentle hands." I lifted his knuckles to my lips, closing my eyes as I kissed them. "I want both." Perhaps bringing the two desires together might heal his torn mind.

"I told you, Aubree. You're no longer my retribution. I don't want to hurt you."

"I'm not saying you consciously want to hurt me. But I think, deep down, something inside of you craves an end to your pain."

His chest heaved, and he cast his eyes away from mine as if the request made him nervous. "What are you saying?"

"I'm saying, I don't want you to hide from me. If this is what keeps you at a distance. If it's why you wore the gloves when you first touched me. Why you hold back when you're inside of me. I want both sides to come together—the hate and the gentle. I want to show you that … I understand both sides." I chewed on the inside of my lip for a moment, in an effort to choose my words carefully. "Whatever happens at the end of this … I gave you all of me. My fears. My desires. It's all yours. And now I want all of you."

He pushed me onto my back and straddled my body. Arms at each side of me, he caged me beneath his massive body, pinning me between his powerful thighs.

I didn't fight him. Didn't want to. Instead, I waited for him—whether he'd tell me to fuck off, or not, I waited for one shred of evidence that I was right. That he was holding back.

"I do have a darker side to me, Aubree. I'm not sure you want inside that shit."

"But I do."

Whether it was ingrained in me from the start, or the result of my fucked up life with Michael, a part of me was drawn to darkness. Craved the kind of sex that spiked my adrenaline. I wanted both of us to come undone, unravel, until we lay completely exposed. I wanted to breach the uncertainty with him, and fall into the intensity of his rough hands on my flesh. Sex with him was perfect, but I wanted his chaos. A moment of entropy. For him to abuse me with passion, unleash his wrath and let go. Not rough and cruel, as it was with Michael, or those men with their dirty hands all over me. I wanted raw sex. Primal. Powerful. Uninhibited. Beautiful, but gritty. I wanted to feel him deep inside of me.

His countering groan rumbled against my lips, growing louder when my hands drifted down his stomach. Pressing his chin into mine, he parted my lips, and for a moment, our breaths mingled. The anticipation of what was to come tightened my stomach. Gripping my crown, he traced my mouth with his tongue before pushing past my teeth to tango with mine, and waves of heat rushed straight to my core, as the man annihilated every bit of what I thought I knew of a kiss.

Buried beneath the armor, the steel that guarded his heart and caged his soul, was something deeper, darker. Painful. I wanted to tear him open and expose his secrets, stroke them so that I could lay them to rest.

The menace in his eyes exhilarated me. I had no idea what to expect. I'd opened a box with *Danger!* plastered all over it, and might've flipped the detonator switch, threatening to blow myself into a million pieces. Yet, whatever darkness lurked in his shadows, I wanted it. I'd caught a spark of it the night we'd first had sex. He'd bound my hands, then, as if something else battled inside of him, he released me, opting to have me touch myself, instead. I needed to know how far he'd go. How deep were his depths?

"Are you sure about this?" he asked.

Was the goddamn sky blue? Of course I was sure. I wanted him to see something more, something beyond the blurred edges of his future.

"Yes."

My tongue raked against my back teeth, as he leaned over to the nightstand and produced a black cloth from the drawer—perhaps the same black cloth he'd used to blindfold me the night he kidnapped me.

"This violence, though … it's in my blood. I don't want to hurt you, Aubree."

"I think we've proven you're incapable of hurting me, Nick."

His chest heaved with each breath, the intervals of inhalations growing shorter, his pupils dilating as if he'd somehow gotten high off the thought. My God, what kind of tormented and abused woman did it make me, for thrilling in what would come? I might've had confidence the man wouldn't hurt me, but that was the only card he'd shown me so far. What twisted pleasures hid behind that smile, those intense blue eyes, was yet to be seen, and I couldn't wait to make myself his willing victim.

I'd never given the reins to a man before, never allowed one to take total control over me. That came with trust, something I didn't toss out like candy. It was hard earned, and after the experience in the bathtub, I'd decided Nick was the only man on the planet that I would follow into the water the way I had.

It'd troubled me that he'd kept his desires on a short leash—that he felt he couldn't let go entirely with me. That was something I could give back to him.

I wasn't a fragile woman. I'd been hardened. Trained to withstand even the darkest desires. A small part of me was ashamed to admit that I found solace in that darkness. That I craved depravity and pain. Not deep, penetrating pain, like the cuts I endured from Michael's knives, or the whips he used across my backside , but the animalistic desire to claw, bite, smack, tear him apart, unable to stand the thought of not having him inside of me. That was how I felt about Nick.

Unless I'd read him wrong, he craved it, too.

He opened the drawer beside me once more, and the clunk at my ear had me turning to see the long blade he set atop the night stand. The serrated edge caught the light, mocking me as I stared back at it. I forced a swallow, my heart kicking up in my chest, blood cooling to panic. Perhaps he misunderstood.

I wanted passionate pain. Not mutilation.

From the edge of the bed, the heat of his stare burned holes in the side of my face, while I studied the sharp teeth of the knife, and I lifted my gaze to his. Those powerful, predacious eyes studied me, looking for any sign of fear, I suspected.

I didn't misread him. I was right about him, and I planned to prove it. Even if he thought for a moment he *could* hurt me, in my heart, I knew he couldn't. That darkness beneath the surface was the rage of his pain, and I intended to give him release—the same release he'd shown me in the bathtub. The elation of conquering a fear, the ghosts that kept us at a distance. I wanted him to breach the darkness, the way I'd breached the waters.

I eased back onto the pillow in surrender and gave a nod.

The intense pinch of his brow was the last image I carried into the darkness of the blindfold.

Only the sound of tearing, the cold hilt sliding along my chest, and a slight chill against my breasts gave brief warning, before he trapped my arms behind my back, using the sleeves of the shirt I'd borrowed.

"I like slicing clothes off of you. I want to buy you a whole fucking wardrobe of shirts and panties that I can rip to shit whenever I feel like it." He bit my bottom lip, dragging it into his mouth, before letting go.

"Or I can keep borrowing your clothes."

With the shirt holding me captive, he peeled back my bra, and his teeth gently grazed my nipple to a hard peak before he bit me.

Moaning at the exhilaration of having my arms bound while he toyed with my breast, I tipped my head back, both peaks jutting forward, and allowed him to do the same to the other side.

"Look at the way your body responds to me. As if it was made especially for my play." The gravelly tone of his voice, the sound so deep and rich and full of menace, had my thigh muscles working overtime. It'd morphed from before, calm but commanding.

His warm hand slid along my thigh and inside the loose boxers, until he found my wet slit. The boxers slid down to my ankles, shackling my legs as he tightened the fabric around them, and squirming atop my arms, I surrendered my knees to the side, giving him rein to play with my clit.

He kept me there, writhing, waiting for his touch.

"Please, Nick." Licking my lips, I lifted my ass up off the bed, grinding my hips against nothing, as pain tugged deep inside.

"Why, Aubree? Haven't you seen what I'm capable of? Why do you want to taunt this side of me?"

"Because," I said, "I want all of you. And if this is who you are, then this is what I crave." Through blackness, I imagined Nick's features—those eyes, jaw, face tight and hard, his body taut, as he railed into me with such intense concentration and curiosity. My legs scissored beneath him. "Please, touch me. Do something." Heat pulsed through my body, the need to feel his hands driving me mad. I'd have touched myself, if not for the binds at my wrists.

His skin feathered against my nipples as his lips caressed my throat, and I let out a long, droning moan that probably resembled that of a wounded animal. His fingers slid into me, pumping like two pistons in sync.

"Nick, give me more."

"You want more?"

"Yes, give me more."

Pressure hit my shoulder and the soft tickle of hair, like his head had rested there. "Okay. I'll do this. God forgive me if I hurt you."

He set my hands free from the shirtsleeves and stretched them above my head, where they were tethered to the bedpost, though he didn't remove the blindfold.

The warmth of his body left me, and the sound of the door clicking shut had me lifting me head up off the pillow.

"Nick?" I tugged at the binds, kicking against the mattress, as I lay naked. Exposed. Dying from the anticipation of needing to be filled.

At another click, I sucked my lip into my mouth. I tipped my head back and let out a pained sigh, grinding against the cool sheets on the bed. "Please, Nick."

A grip to the back of my head lifted my shoulders up off the pillow, and the scent of whiskey stung my nose.

"Drink this. Trust me, you'll need it."

My jaw tightened, as the whiskey coated my mouth, burning when it slipped down my throat.

Forehead pressed to mine, the sweet liquor on his

breath fanned against my face, and he tugged the hair at the back of my head. "How far do you want to go?"

"Until you feel free."

His grip tightened, the sharp sting across my scalp parting my lips. "How can you be the one thing I've craved this whole time?"

"Because I know how it feels to hide behind a mask." I blew out a shaky breath, neck stretched taut. "Now, show me what's behind yours."

A tickle hit my breast, shooting pleasure straight to my core. I lifted my hips in offering. What I estimated to be a feather drifted lower, to my bare feet, and I laughed, brows knitted in pain from both need and the tickle he incited there.

Up my calves, he dragged the feather, then across my thighs, and I cried out, arching my back. "Nick!" When it reached my ribs, I laughed aloud, twisting into the agonizing tingle.

Soft plumes danced across my skin, higher, until he reached my breast again, leaving my mouth agape as the sensation consumed me, pulled me into desperation. I wanted every inch of his body touching mine, his cock filling me, pushing me over the edge into the stratosphere. I needed to come so badly, an ache wound inside my stomach.

"If this … is your dark side … feel free … to pull me under … anytime," I said between pants of breath.

Grabbing my hips, he flipped me over, and my arms crossed over one another, pulled rigid by the chains, as I propped myself onto my knees.

Skin slid across my inner thighs, and a solid force hit the back of my knees. "Ride my face."

Oh, fuck, his words!

As he commanded, my hips undulated against the scruff of his jaw, and I took in the harsh tickle against my folds. "Jesus!" The wet probing along my seam dipped inside, and I arched my back as his tongue curved up like a pussy-licking master. Half laughing, half wanting to cry, I surrendered to the sensation, the knot pulling deep inside my stomach, itching to explode all over him.

Chains rattled against the headboard, the sound a cadence to the bouncing and squeaking of the bed. My muscles pulled, my hands growing numb from the tension, as I rode him faster, in complete abandon. The unrelenting dip of his tongue, the sucking, licking, blowing, vibrating groan against my sex had me galloping toward the finish line.

Fire blazed in my thighs, and my stomach drew up with the arch of my back. My mouth gaped in pain and pleasure, as I coiled into a tight ball of tension ready to burst.

His fingers dug into my thighs, and two dipped inside of me, fucking me as he licked and sucked.

From my toes, the flash of lightning climbed my legs to my spine, higher, and smashed into the back of my skull in a blinding wave of light.

Heat spread through my muscles, tingling as each shuddered breath pushed past my parted lips. "Oh, fuck!"

The crack of his hand against my ass echoed in the room, and I cried out a curse, lazily rolling my hips as he milked the last of my orgasm.

Sliding my knees out to the side, I lowered myself, resting my pubic bone against his chin, as I tried to catch my breath. "Goddamn." I could barely speak.

His body slipped out from beneath me, and he grabbed my hips, angling my ass into the air once more.

A hand cupped my breast and pinched, and I bucked against him. "Nick!"

"You asked for dark. I'm going to give it to you." His cock pushed inside of my ass, and my scream bounced off the walls. "You *are* the violence inside of me, Aubree. My most exquisite destruction."

CHAPTER 45
Nick

I lay beside Aubree on the bed, fingers entwined, bodies tangled in the sheets. Her left arm draped across my chest, as if she feared I might up and leave.

She'd begged for the depravity inside of me, and much as my conscience battled against me, I gave it to her. She took all of me, for hours, until both of us had collapsed. In ecstasy. No blackouts. No screams of fear. No pain. Only Aubree and me, lying in the blood and sweat of what we both had craved.

Two days had passed since the call from Bojanski, and Devil's Night had arrived. The final show. The one I hadn't planned to come back from.

My head swam in questions, to which I suddenly didn't have answers. Like, *What now?*

Should I pursue my vengeance? The final plan to destroy Michael Culling and all of the gangs at once? To blow them all to hell, and let Alec turn the gun back on me.

Or should I walk away?

What would Alec say, though? All the work. The planning. The surveillance. The years we'd invested into the final act of revenge—all of it—out the window for some woman?

Not some woman.

Aubree.

Her fingers gently clutched my jaw, and she guided my stare back to her. "You're somewhere else right now."

"Just thinking."

"What's troubling you?"

I shook my head, and rolling over her until I'd caged her beneath me, I kissed her, transported back to no more than an hour ago, when the chains had dissolved from my mind. I was free. Consumed by nothing but my dark craving for this woman. When I pulled away, her downward gaze told me something troubled her as well.

"Nick ... I know this isn't what either of us planned." Her eyes trailed back to mine. "I'm not going to trap you. But I can't let you run off into certain death, either. Not now. I'm too invested in you."

"Invested?" I huffed an exhale, and fell onto my back once more. "Aubree ..."

Christ, I felt like I'd just given the same speech to Lauren. I hated having to say the words again, but my life came with too many risks. Even if I decided not to go through with the plan, to run off into the sunset with her, I'd pissed off too many people who'd soon be on a warpath for revenge. Aubree would be the perfect target.

"I think it might be best for you to get as far away from me as you can," I finished.

"Why would I do that?" She rubbed both hands down her face. "You've got my head spinning right now. You hate me. You want to fuck me. You can't let me go, but now you think I should walk away?"

I couldn't blame her for the confusion. Christ, I didn't even know what the hell I wanted.

One minute I wanted to kill her, the next, I wanted to kill every cocksucker who'd ever laid a hand on her.

"Culling and Cox have to die. I have to finish this."

She shot up and planted her hands on either side of my body. "I'm with you on this, Nick, believe me. He's hurt so many people. Including me." Her fingertips drifted down my cheek. "You want revenge? Let's get out of here. Get the fuck out of here and never come back. We'll smile at him from a place where the sun shines and the world is right. Come with me."

If only I could. If I thought I'd never be hit with the remorse, remembering my wife and son in those final moments, I'd go with her. Attempt to put some semblance of a life back together and see what the fuck happened. Maybe I'd be happy again someday. With her, I probably could be.

I smirked and pulled her in for a kiss. "And what would we do with ourselves?"

A wily grin dimpled her cheeks. "Anything your heart desires. Your command is my wish." She nipped my earlobe and giggled when I gripped her sides and tickled.

"The hell it is. You're too feisty to be told what to do, Pistol Lips." I continued my assault, dodging kicks to my side, as she attempted to break free, and I rolled on top of her. Pinning her arms to the bed, I held her there, staring down into those beautiful, bright golden eyes that'd begun to sparkle. Slanting my lips over hers, I took in her struggle against my body, until she calmed and her moan purred in my mouth. "You make a man question his motives, that's for sure."

"Could you even imagine a place where we watch sunrises, have sex, eat, shower, have sex, lay in the sun, watch sunsets, sex."

"I'm picking up on a theme ..."

"I haven't watched the sun set in five years. Five years, I've been so focused on surviving. And now ..." Her smile wilted to a wistful sigh. "Make it stop."

"Make what stop?"

"Time. I want to stay here, in this place for eternity, with you."

I opened my mouth to speak, but the chime of my cellphone alerted me to a text. Lifting the phone, I clicked on a message from Leon.

I've got something for you. Pick it up at the drop.

"What is it?" Aubree asked, as my stomach curled into itself.

I hadn't planned a pick up from Leon. Had no idea what might await me there.

I set the phone back on the nightstand and looked down at Aubree. "I'm not sure I want to know."

***

The drop was the place in an abandoned office building off Mount Elliott, where the Bojanskis often left packages for me—drugs, guns, whatever I needed. For months, they'd let me rent out the apartment atop their bar, a place where a person could stay completely anonymous, since no one fucked with Leon Bojanski. That was like messing with the Capo of the Gambino family.

While I should've been mentally preparing myself for Cox's gruesome act of retribution, I, instead, wracked my brain, trying to imagine what Leon had left for me. A drop wasn't necessarily good. A drop meant he didn't want anyone tracking him.

Broken glass, decaying wood, and paper littered the floor beneath toppled furniture heavy with grime, and I trampled through them to the back room. Inside, a package lay propped against the wall behind the shelving unit with a typical note attached by a thin strip of tape: Nick.

I tore off the small piece of paper and opened the envelope. From within the dark depths of the packet, I carefully slid a cartridge out of the envelope and held it up to see what appeared to be an SD card inside.

A burning in my gut told me that whatever happened to be on the cartridge was bad, and part of me wanted to toss it, run from the building, and pretend I hadn't seen it.

The logical side of me tucked it away into my pocket and exited the building.

***

Sometimes, I had a sense about things.

A half hour had passed since I'd collected the SD card, and although I still hadn't checked out its contents, something told me that, at some point in the night, I'd find myself at a standoff between Aubree and whatever it'd call me to do.

Perhaps it was my own doubts about the future of our fucked up relationship, which shouldn't have come to be, or maybe it was disappointment in allowing myself to fall prey to her charms every night, to be pulled into bed with her, where the only thought, the simplest thought inside my head, was making the woman scream my name.

Either way, I had a sense I couldn't ignore, so instinct had me pouring a glass of wine from the bottle that I'd picked up on the way back to the mansion.

Aubree lay sprawled on her bed, reading Faulkner. As I approached with the glass of red, her eyes lit up. "Ooh! I've not had wine in so long. What's the occasion?"

I shrugged, the very gesture itself a lie, and set the glass on her nightstand. "I thought it might get you drunk faster. Let me take advantage of you."

Smiling, she lifted the glass from beside her and took a sip. "Mmmm. Piquant. I love a dry red."

"I'll leave the bottle here. I have to finish something, and I'll come back to make sure you're preheated." The corner of my lip kicked up in a smile, in spite of the knots twisting inside my gut, and I exited her room, pushing through my bedroom door.

Once inside the closet, I popped the disk into the computer.

The file had been labeled, *Collateral*, and the knots in my stomach coiled tighter as I clicked 'open'.

Screams spilled from a blackness onscreen that eventually opened up to an unfamiliar room. The camera panned down over the naked body of a woman, whose breasts bounced with the jostling of her body. It zoomed in on the cameraman's dick slamming into her then back up her body in a shaky quality. His rapid breaths overpowered her agonized screams, and the view angled to the right, revealing her arms tied behind her back.

I'd no idea who the woman was—until the camera lifted to her face.

Narrow, bright brown eyes.

Jet black hair, fallen around her face.

Pale skin with a slight pink tinge.

Jade.

My heart caught, not so much for the woman on the camera, but for the one not on camera at that moment.

"Who's Alec Vaughn?" the man asked, driving hard into her, so much that her features folded and she cried out in pain. "Huh? C'mon. Fuckin' slut. Little fuckin whore. Who's Alec Vaughn?"

"I don't know! I don't … know an Alec!"

The cameraman laughed, like her sobbing amused him, and twisted her nipple before gouging his dirty nails into her ass.

"Yeah ... that's it, whore. Scream. Scream loud. No one's gonna hear you."

"I'm ... a member of ... a dangerous group. They will find you. And they will kill you!" Her cries echoed inside the room, and the male's laughter chased it.

"You'll already be dead, sweetheart."

Her scream hit a bone chilling pitch, then splintered to silence.

The camera went black before opening up to a new scene.

In the center of what appeared to be a basement, with its high walls and stained cinderblocks, a figure sat facing away in a chair, their hands tied. A burlap sack had been tied over the head.

Lit only by the light of the camera, the basement looked to be mostly empty, with few shadows cast in the background. Abandoned, perhaps, but as the person recording rounded the victim, a tray of tools came into view—all coated in what must've been blood.

Deep raspy breaths, followed by a quiet chuckle, indicated some excitement on the part of the mysterious videographer, and I braced myself as a hand reached out from the camera and removed the sack.

Pain stabbed my chest. I could scarcely draw in air. My hands balled into fists at my side, itching to punch right through the wall.

Blood matted her hair to her face, and her cheekbone looked as if it'd been smashed then gouged with a pick. Her eye had puffed black and blue, glistening with pus.

Lauren.

Pulling the chair from beneath me, I slammed it into the wall, leaving a gaping hole of dust and crumbling drywall. Slam after slam, I smashed the wood to pieces, and throwing it to the floor, I paced, rubbing my skull.

"Who is she?"

The intruding voice tightened my muscles, and I slowly turned to find Aubree standing in the doorway.

"Lauren."

Her eyes closed, and I caught the slouch of her shoulders, the same defeat pulsing through me. "Michael has her, doesn't he?"

"I'm assuming his men, yes." I squeezed my eyes so tight a twinge of pain shot through my head, and I pressed my fists harder at my temples. "She saved my life."

"And now you intend to save hers."

Through deep breaths, I attempted to calm the storm raging through my veins, the fury ready to break free and kill something. "I have to."

"This ... this video. It's a trap. You realize that, right? She may already be dead. And when you—"

"It doesn't matter, Aubree." Lowering my hands, I opened my eyes and leveled my gaze on her. "I made a promise to her."

"Don't do it alone, is all I'm saying. I want to come with you. I can be the eyes to watch your back for you."

I shook my head. "No." I pushed a row of clothes aside and tugged open a hidden door embedded into the wall, where I stored my guns, and pulled out the M-24, Glocks, magazines.

"This is ... suicide, Nick." Desperation bled into her words, but not even Aubree and her dream world existence could stop me. "Listen to me. Right now, you're anonymous. They have no idea who you are. You plow through that place?"

"I have no choice. Lauren is going to die." The push to my chest kicked me back only a step, but a growl of frustration still rumbled in my chest.

"You might die! Dammit! Stop! Think!"

"I have to try to save her."

Tears filled her eyes, and I had to look away. Couldn't stand to see the hurt, the betrayal staring back at me. "And if ... something happens to you? What then?"

"All my promises seem to come down to killing this man. So I'll make this promise to you, too, Aubree." Twisting away from her, I packed the rest of my guns. "Tonight, I promise to set you free."

A click snapped my attention back.

Aubree had moved to the end of my bed and stood, pointing a barrel at me. "I swear to fucking God, Ryder, I will shoot you where you ..." She double blinked. Frowning, she rubbed the back of her hand across her forehead as she tripped a step back. "What the hell?"

I checked my watch. Fifteen minutes had passed since I'd fed her the drugs.

Her hands trembled against the grip when I stepped toward her. "What did you do?" She stumbled sideways, making my muscles tense, before she caught herself on the bed. "What?"

"I'm sorry, baby." Shaking my head, I watched the drugs take effect. "I won't let you get hurt."

"Nick!" The gun fell to the floor, and she tumbled onto the end of the bed. "Please listen ... please ... don't ... I lo—"

I lurched forward and captured her weak body in my arms before she hit the floor.

Her eyeballs rolled as she fought to stay conscious, and I kissed her while gently setting her down in my bed. "Ni ...ck. Plesayu ... don ... I neeyu. Loffustay. I nohashoogn." Her eyes fluttered shut and the rigidity in her body softened in my arms.

"Aubree," I whispered, stroking her cheek. "I have something to tell you." My thumb brushed over her shuttered eyes that didn't so much as flinch with my touch. "Crazy, beautiful girl." I kissed her slowly, tasting her lips one more time. "I would've run with you. If things had been different. You'd have been the one woman to make me give it all up."

I exhaled a weighted breath at the truth in my words. The small, seemingly meek woman had blasted through every bit of steel I'd forged inside to keep everyone out. She'd shown me a glimpse of a heart that could be healed. If only I didn't have so many promises to keep, including the one I'd made to her. Culling had to die. I couldn't let the motherfucker who'd branded her walk free. "Just not in the cards for me. Be free. Be happy. The one who hurt you will die tonight, and you can rise up from the ashes.

You can have whatever life you've dreamed of." Lowering her head to the pillow, I kissed her soft lips. "I love you."

After making a final check of my artillery, I exited my bedroom. Barely a step out the door, a wrecking ball slammed into my chest, sending jolts of electricity across my back. I hit the wall and slid to the floor, and my world tipped on its axis, teetering to one side, then righting itself.

I looked up to see Alec's obscure form standing over me, his hand curled into a fist.

"You're not going anywhere, Nick." His voice held no humor, no room for argument.

"They have Lauren. I have to save her."

"Lauren was never part of the plan. In case you've forgotten, I told you to say your goodbye's a long time ago."

Alarms went off inside my head, warning me that a fight was on the horizon, because I knew that deadpan stare of his was no bullshit. "I did. And I have no fucking idea how they found her, but I'm not going to stand by and watch her die. She saved my fucking life, Alec."

"Did she?"

My eyes narrowed on him. "You know damn well she did. Now get the hell out of my way, or I'll—"

"You'll what, exactly?" His lips stretched into a wicked grin. "Kill me? We both know you can't."

"I don't have time for this."

The wall smashed into my back again, and air exited my lungs.

He held me there, teeth gnashing in the kind of anger

I'd only seen on a few occasions. "It's over Nick. The fucking game changed. The plan to blow it all to hell is no longer an option. Too many innocents will die. Culling is offering up young girls for the night. He's keeping them there. You pull the detonator, and all of them will burn."

The game entailed blowing up the meeting place—the spot where the gangs would converge, to go over the evening's plan to wipe out another neighborhood. It would've been the perfect opportunity to obliterate them all to shit. To hit the city's most notorious kingpins, crime lords, plus the ringleader himself, Michael Culling.

"Then, I'll take them out. One by one."

"You won't walk out of there alive, which means neither will Lauren."

Eyes squinted, I pressed my hands against the throbbing ache either side of my skull as it threatened to pull me into another blackout. "What are you proposing, Alec? That I let her die?"

"I'll go in your place."

"Why would I do that? That solution is no better than mine. And there's no guarantee you'll save Lauren."

He released his grip of my throat and tugged a cigar from inside his pocket. "You need to stay alive. For her." His gaze lifted toward the bedroom where Aubree slept.

"She'll be fine."

"For a year, we've both watched her. You've always seen her through the eyes of a killer, whereas I saw her through the eyes of a savior. Someone I wanted to capture, possess, and protect." He lit the cigar, blew on the end of it to stoke the embers, and puffed twice, before pacing in front of me. "I fell in love with her, while you continued your crusade to destroy her. It's not your fault, Nick. You weren't privy to information that I had. Information that I kept from you, because I thought you'd feel betrayed." Exhaling a sharp breath, he paused his pacing and splayed his hands to the side. "And you don't exactly have the best track record for trying to keep yourself alive."

"Why have me watch over her, then? If you thought I might kill her?"

"Because you're not an evil bastard, in spite of what you think. I had faith that you'd see what I saw in her, and that your drive to kill her would disappear." Cigar caught between his lips, Alec shook his head, adjusting his cuff links. "I can't let you do this alone, Nick. It's a set up, and you won't come out of this alive. It's suicide. Aubree's fragile— she'll break if she loses you."

"She's stronger than you think, Alec."

He nodded. "She is. And she's in love with *you*. Could you put her through that pain you know so well? Could you take from her what had once been taken from you?"

"Motherfucker." I shook my head, anger pulsing through me in waves. "You brought her here, so I'd fall in love with her and give up on the notion of finishing this. To the end." I clamped my eyes shut and rubbed my hand down my face. "She was the only part of the plan that didn't fit. Never made sense to me and now ..." I nodded, wanting to kick myself for being so blind. Not that I wasn't in love with the woman, but had I known that was the plan all along, I'd have certainly tried to avoid the inevitable pain. "Now I understand. You hoped she'd make me change my mind."

"I did what I thought was right. What was good for all three of us. I can't let you kill yourself, Nick. I'd never planned to follow through on the deal." I could feel him studying me, looking for any indication that I could be swayed. "Think about Lena. What would she want for you? What would she tell you right now?"

An ache throbbed in my heart. My wife, the selfless woman she'd always been, would tell me to stop the madness. To call on others to help find Lauren, and lay the past to rest. Be happy again.

"But you're the one who loves her!" Rubbing my forehead somehow kept the blackness at bay. "You never tried to make yourself known to her because ... you were *giving* her to me."

"Yes."

A moment of clarity sliced through the thick fog of confusion clouding my brain, as I recalled his words from the day I'd watched the Cullings pass out care packages in the streets, when I'd asked him about moving on.

What makes you think I haven't?

"I guess there's only one thing left to do, then." Rising up from the floor, I reached out to shake his hand, pulling him in for a hug. "You deserved her more," I whispered.

Kicking back a step, I hammered my fist into Alec's face.

Blood sprayed to the side and his body slumped to the

floor. A sharp sting shot up my wrist, and I lifted my hand to bleeding knuckles and a throbbing ache in my bones. I shook out my hand, flexing my fingers to work out the ache, and crouched down beside Alec's passed out body.

"I'm sorry, old friend. I'm doing what I think is right, too. You're wrong, if you think I'm doing this for myself, though. I'm doing it for her. I'm saving her. You're not the only one who fell in love."

CHAPTER 46
Chief Cox

Cox rounded the perimeter of the old Ironworks building, checking out all of the possible hiding places where a savvy assassin might hide, pausing when his phone rang and Burke's number flashed across the screen.

Rolling his eyes, Cox answered the call.

"Chief, where are you?" The frantic tone of Burke's voice put Cox on edge.

"Out of the fuckin' office. Why?"

"Internal Affairs is here. Someone reported you for something." He lowered his voice. "They want to speak with you. What do you want me to tell 'em??"

Riley. The rat bastard. Probably turned him in for threatening the little cocksucker. Should've killed the motherfucker when he'd had the chance. "Just … keep 'em out of my office. I don't give a shit what you have to tell them, but don't let the bastards in there, got it?"

"They're asking about the E-for-E case."

Irritation battled the panic in his gut. "E-for-E? What

the fuck is that?"

"Eye for an Eye. It's the hashtag everyone's calling him on social media."

Fuckin social media. "We're investigating. We don't have shit on this guy. That's what you tell them."

"We did get a tip on Aubree Culling. Don't know if it's legit. Some kid, must've been thirteen, fourteen years old, said he was scrappin' with some guys he knows from the streets. Said he found her in the woods near an abandoned mansion on Brush Park."

"Brush Park?"

"Yeah. He was lookin' for the reward. Told him to come back when you were in."

"Fuck that kid. He comes back, tell him to get his ass in school. In the meantime, I'm going to check out this lead. See if it's legit."

CHAPTER 47
Nick

The SD card that held the gut-wrenching video of Lauren also carried the vital geolocation data that allowed me to trace where it'd been recorded.

Exactly as the sender hoped, I was sure.

The old Ironworks building had long been the most recognized machine shop, before it'd closed its doors in the early nineties. Located on Atwater, along the Detroit River, it was considered an eyesore, with its boarded up windows, broken glass and graffiti-colored walls, amid the businesses moving in there. Construction equipment stood rusted in the adjacent field, as if someone at some time had planned to do something with the shithole but then opted out. Perfect place to house a bunch of kidnapped girls to entertain the city's most notorious crime lords.

I crouched across the street, along the river, concealed by the trees and brush, aware that every minute ticking by meant one less breath for Lauren. I'd already staked two eastside thugs using the ramp entrance, but no saying how many might've been inside. No sign of Culling, either.

They'd all be expecting me, though. I'd had to have my gun re-barreled for the custom silencer I attached to it, in the hope of keeping my arrival as undiscovered as possible.

Keeping to the shadows, I slipped along Atwater, toward the side of the building where a copse of bushes concealed a broken out window. Peeking inside revealed two men, dressed in black, smoking cigarettes as the AK's in their hands dangled casually. They appeared to be alone in the small room off the larger machining area.

Through the scope of my M-24, I lined up my sights and shot twice. One bullet for each head. The men fell to the ground in a heap, and I climbed inside the building and lifted my gun, ready to shoot anything that moved.

As I passed the dropped men, I strapped one of their AK's to my back and kept on to the next room.

A wall of steel separated my position from the open floor of the machining section of the building. Rounding the corner brought me to a large block of equipment, set along a wall that met a staircase to the second floor.

At a table in the center of the open room, a dozen men played cards, smoking and drinking, like a fucking friendly gathering of the city's scum under one roof.

Pausing at the mouth of the stairs, cloaked behind the machines propped against the wall, I took a deep breath and swung the M-24 forward.

The first shot set the ball in motion. Like penetrating a mound of fire ants, the bastards would come scampering out of their hiding places, so as I ascended the stairs, I aimed for the men packing guns first—four casually standing about; three behind the men playing cards.

One.

Two.

Three.

Boom. Down.

And the game was on.

Bullets whizzed past my head like they'd just caught up with the program. I ducked behind the steel banister, scrambling up a few more stairs, before I stopped and shot again, taking out one more gunman.

The sound of gunshots bounced off the walls, as the dozen or so men below bolted out of their chairs and swarmed the open floor. I tugged the AK and bump-fired in rapid succession, blanketing the room from my vantage point, before they even had a chance.

At a flash of movement in my periphery, I aimed the gun toward the top of the staircase and took out two more men, keeping my pace as I went along, always moving. Had to keep moving.

Bullets pinged at my boots, bouncing off the steel. I targeted a male from the first floor, bleeding out his wounds as he crawled over gunned down bodies and tried to take me out. With one shot from the rifle, he fell back, a bullet in his head.

I kicked open a door, gun at the ready. On a dirty mattress butted against a concrete wall, a girl covered herself with a sheet. "Get dressed and get out. You're free to go."

At the next door, I kicked the wood open.

The whizz of a bullet grazed my ear, knocked me to the side. I leapt backward, striking two shots in the gunman's chest on the way. Sucking in a deep fucking breath, I sent up a silent hallelujah and signaled for the girl to leave.

Next room stood empty. Rounding the corner, I touched my ear, bringing back a small splotch of blood.

Fucker.

Another door separated me from whatever hell lay on the other side. I clutched the AK and kicked it in, jumping to the side as gunfire sprayed bullets through the entrance. At its pause, I crouched low, kept tight against the adjacent wall and peeked around the corner. Four men stood with guns aimed at the door. I showered the interior of the room with return fire and slipped just inside.

Two men lay dead. Two more ducked behind rusted metal benches.

I slid behind a large steel cabinet, directed the gun at the men through the scope of my twenty-four, and capped them.

Sticking to my hiding spot, I waited. Three more men, toting rifles, padded into the room from the adjoining hallway.

One. Two. Three. Boom. Down.

I kept on through the maze of empty, abandoned rooms that looked to be empty offices. It was on the first floor of the west side of the building that I heard Lauren's screams.

Muscles tense, I prepared myself for more fire, but

before I could draw my gun, a fist collided with my cheek, knocking my head to the side.

I shook it off and slid the guns from my shoulder to the ground. Stretching my jaw, which damn near felt unhinged, I dodged the next punch, coming back with a shoulder pop, followed by a counterpunch that knocked the asshole's head back.

On wavering feet, the brutish redhead with a beard to match, maybe six feet tall, stood with his fists up. Dodging two missed punches, I gripped the back of his head and took him to the ground with an upward elbow strike that left his head lolling.

I spat blood on him and continued on toward the sounds I'd heard.

Down a hall, through another door, Christ, did the fucking place ever end? I reached a much wider opening and, slowing my steps, stalked toward the entrance. Inside a break room, with empty vending machines lined against the wall, four males stood around a steel table.

Amid them, a further two took a girl who looked no older than eighteen.

Through the scope, I steadied my hand and systematically took each one of them out before any of them could do more than spin to me in surprise.

Lauren's screams reached my ears once again, kicking up my adrenaline. The girl the men had been on whimpered as she scrambled for scattered clothes on the floor, and passing her, I headed for a stairwell across the room.

Through another door, the loading dock of the building sat below, where they stored most of the machinery. A balcony connected the two walls of the vast staging area, with a short staircase at either end.

In the center of the room, a large man in an oversized white T-shirt and sagging jeans, stood with his back to me, blocking my view of what lay on the other side of him. Only black curls dangling over the edge of a long wooden workbench, and the familiar sound of her voice, gave any clue that I'd found Lauren.

My lip curled, and I shot a bullet in his ear. One more in his throat for good measure. I made my way down the staircase, and as he dropped, Lauren's bloodied body came into view.

Gunfire erupted from my right, and I slid the AK forward, taking out the man below the staircase. I leapt the remaining half dozen stairs and tugged the AK across my chest, capping two approaching men in leather vests with biker patches, the pair of them toting guns.

Swinging left then right, gun cocked and ready to fire, I backed myself toward the workbench, kicking the fucker who lay beside it, oozing blood from his ear and throat.

Seconds passed. No one else arrived.

I spun around and lifted my mask. Lauren's beautiful model-worthy face had been cut to shit, left bruised, swollen and seeping pus. I choked back tears.

"Nick." A sob thumped her chest as she lifted a trembling hand to my face. "Th-th-ey asked … me."

"Shh, it's okay, sweetheart. I came here for you. We're

gonna get you out of here."

"I'm ... sorry." The breath she sucked rattled behind her ribs. "I know ... you said don't come 'round ... I just ... wanted to tell you ... I got my letter." Her lip downturned and tears pooled beneath her head. "I got ... accepted ... full ride."

Fuck! Panic twisted in my gut. I couldn't let her die. Not there. Not like that. Her whole fucking life slipped behind my eyes, and I could see her one day in her graduation gown, accepting honors, because Lauren wouldn't allow herself to become anything less than the best. "I'm gonna get you out of here. Just hang on."

"I ... I ... I have to tell ... you something. P-P-Please."

I could barely see past the tears welling in my eyes, as thoughts of Culling burned holes in my head while my gaze roved Lauren's mutilated body. The cuts and gaping wounds told me she might not make the ride to the hospital. Seconds ticked inside my head, not knowing what to do. Let her talk, because I might not otherwise hear her last spoken words, or face the possibility that I wouldn't get far with her in the backseat of my car.

Steeling my muscles, I steadied my trembling hands and blinked away the tears. "You have to hurry, sweetheart. We don't have time." My gaze scanned downward and my blood froze. Her abuser had cut her abdomen open, spilling blood onto the floor. "Oh, fuck, Lauren. We have to go now!"

"Nick ... I didn't tell you something. I should've ... a long time ... ago. That night ... of the fire. I was with ...

my brother and his crew." She spoke through sobs that had my heart hanging on her words, anxious to get her away from that place, the hell she must've suffered. "Bunch of ... drug dealers. They set fire ... to some abandoned houses. Just havin' fun. And these men ... came from out of nowhere. They shot up ... all of them. Tried to ... rape me ... and kill me, too. I got away. I was screaming ... for help. Nobody answered. Whole damn 'hood shut me out ... like some criminal. Your wife ... let me inside. I hid in ... the basement, like ... she told me."

Numbness spread beneath my skin as the one missing puzzle piece finally came together, fitting perfectly into what I'd wondered for years. Why did they choose us? Why had they been there?

"She let me hide." Tears slipped down her cheek. "From them."

"It doesn't matter now, Lauren. None of that matters, you hear? Now, shut the fuck up. We're getting out of here."

"It was ... my fault. I'm so ... sorry Nick. I was stupid ... a kid on the streets. Had nothin'. You changed ... my life. I'm sorry ... for what I did. I ... love you ... Nick." Words flew from her mouth, as much as they could between each desperate bid for breath.

"Don't you fucking die on me, Lauren. You just hold on. I'm going to hoist you over my shoulder, okay? Just hang in there."

"Nick ... they did ... so many bad things." Tears streamed down her cheek, gathering in a small puddle beneath her head that mingled with the blood spilling from her wounds. "I'm so scared."

"I'm ... I'm lifting you up. Just ... I don't want to hurt you, but I gotta get you out of here."

Her weak clutch of my arm made me pause, and I stared down at her swollen, beaten eyes, flickering with the light's reflection in a stark contrast to her pallid complexion. "Who guards ... the flock?"

The sudden ease in her voice filled me with dread. I slumped my shoulders and bowed my head at the realization that I wouldn't be carrying her out of that place alive. "The shepherd," I whispered back.

"Who is ... the shepherd?"

"Your brother."

"My ... brother." Her eyes fluttered, before her muscles softened against my grip and she went limp in my arms.

I buried my face in her hair, muscles taut as a bow, and my curses bounced off the walls.

"How very precious." The voice arrived from behind.

I tugged my mask over my face and turned, with the AK pointed at Culling.

A dozen thugs stood behind him, some with their own AK's, all guns pointed at me.

Didn't matter how quick I was, they'd execute me like a fucking firing squad.

CHAPTER 48
Aubree

I opened my eyes to a blur, like looking too closely through a magnifying glass. I could make out details—the bathroom door, a light, the adjacent wall. Everything else remained too wide for my eyeballs, and I squinted, trying to blink it away. A dull ache throbbed in my head as I sat up from the bed. The bed. Nick's bed. Why couldn't I recall how I'd gotten there?

I remembered holding a gun at Nick. Why? Had he hurt me? I didn't feel pain, aside from a slight headache. Had he threatened me?

I wracked my brain, trying to recall the last few minutes. Screams bounced inside my skull, forcing me to slap both hands on either side of my head.

The video.

Pieces came together, retelling the story, just moments before I'd blacked out. *A girl. Torture. Nick went after her.*

Oh, God. He went after her!

He went after Michael.

I slammed the heel of my palm against my temples. "C'mon! Remember!" I'd caught him watching the video inside … inside … his closet!

Jumping up from the bed had me falling back down on the mattress. Wooziness overpowered my urgency to remember what the hell had happened. I stood up, catching my balance for a moment, before rushing toward the closet.

Hangers, perfectly spaced apart, carried two leather jackets, along with hoodies, white wife beaters, and a number of jeans and T-shirts, varying in shades. A shoe rack held four pairs of heavy black boots.

On the right side, at least a dozen suits—pressed and pristine—hanging from wooden hangers. Crocodile shoes filled a second rack, and fedoras lined the top shelf.

As if two different men shared the same space.

A desk had been set up at the back wall of the closet. I stepped inside and toward a laptop left opened. As I twisted, my sights caught on something, and I turned back toward the door, closing it just enough to catch the object hanging on the inside. A black poster with white lettering: 'Never Be Silenced.'

Achilleus X.

I pressed a key on the laptop, which brought up a password request.

The sound of breaking glass froze my limbs, and I rushed out of the closet.

On the nightstand, my gun lay atop of a large, sealed envelope with 'Aubree' written across the front.

For one brief moment, I forgot where I was, like time stood still, as my eyes focused on the cursive scrawled across the package. I traced it with my fingertips before tearing one end. Inside, was a key, a letter, a series of numbers jotted down on notepaper, and a black flash drive with '*If you want to know the truth*' written in silver across it.

Truth?

The first part of the letter detailed instructions, something about a bank account, a house. I couldn't do more than scan the words, as nothing so emotionless could possibly stick inside my head right then. I searched for *Nick's* words, his heartfelt words. I found those on the second page.

> *The door of opportunity has opened, Aubree. You hold the key, and I'll break your chains.*
>
> *You were exactly what I needed, but I'm selfish. I wanted more for both of us. More retribution. You gave me a glimpse of what life could've been, but this suffering is my curse.*
>
> *He can't win, or we both lose. I have to finish this.*
>
> *The ultimate revenge isn't the murder of my enemy. It's the whisper of truth on my last stolen breath.*
>
> *I love you, Pistol Lips. Never miss another sunset again.*
>
> *Nick*

A thump from below popped my attention back to the present and the breaking glass that'd brought me back to the bedroom to begin.

My muscles juddered, hands trembling as I shoved the letter back into the envelope. Searching for a place it wouldn't easily be found, I crossed the room to the old fireplace, slid it against the crumbling brick behind an old copper engraved fire-back, and buried it in the ash

Grabbing up the gun en route, I softly made my way toward the door that over looked the foyer.

Nothing.

No movement. Scrappers again? Maybe. There was that kid that'd gotten away. The one who'd screamed, alerting the men when I'd tried to steal their truck. Had he come back? Decided to seek revenge? He'd looked so young, though. Not much of a threat.

I lifted the gun, keeping it level with my eyes, and aimed at the staircase. Any motherfucker on his way up would get a dose of lead.

The sound of heavy footfalls on the lower level traipsed down my spine, spreading like ice crystals along my nerves. Closer, they advanced, and I backed into the shadows of Nick's room, crouching low to stay out of sight.

A bald head appeared in the foyer, twisting side to side. A gun swung ahead of the guy, and as his gaze flicked upward, toward where I hid, I crouched lower.

Cox.

I'd seen him on rare occasions that Michael opted for meetings in his office. Hadn't known his name until one of the house staff identified him as the Chief of Police—corrupt bastard. No doubt, he'd come to collect me on Michael's behalf. The two of them were tight.

I lowered my pistol and aimed square at Cox's cock, while he stood at the foot of the stairs. I'd never trusted the bastard from the moment I met him. He'd always come across as slimy and slick—one of those men you wouldn't dare leave a small child with. Somehow, killing him felt like I'd be doing the world a favor.

He ascended the stairs, one at a time, his gun leading the way. I had the upper hand. I could kill him right then. Or wound him. Staying within the shadows, I kept a steady hand on the trigger. *Aim Shoot Kill. Aim Shoot Kill.* The words repeated over and over in my mind.

Aim Shoot Kill.

I steadied my hand, fingers curling the grip. Dryness climbed my throat, but I swallowed it back.

I scarcely took a breath as he advanced toward me. When he reached the top of the staircase, he flanked left, in the direction of my room.

From Nick's room, I tracked the sounds of his footsteps, the slide of drawers, what sounded like rifling through the mostly empty nightstand beside the bed, where I kept my art supplies. The whoosh and crinkle of paper told me he flipped through my sketchpad.

Breathe in, breathe out. I'd never killed a man before.

I didn't like the link to Michael. Too close. Way too

close. It told me that the bastard and his cronies had more information than perhaps even Nick had anticipated, because no way he'd have left me passed out if he knew that asshole had been lurking around. The queasiness filled my stomach with dread at the thought that Nick might have walked straight into an ambush, and perhaps he wouldn't survive. Though, maybe that was what he'd planned all along.

The ultimate revenge isn't the murder of my enemy. It's the whisper of truth on my last stolen breath. Words from his letter.

Last stolen breath? My stomach flipped on itself, as hairs on the back of my neck stood on end. He never planned to come back at all.

That envelope probably contained answers to every question spinning through my head, including what the hell would've possessed him to go storming into certain death.

I glanced back to where I'd stuffed the envelope behind the fire-back, but at the sound of Cox's boots against the wood floors, my attention snapped back to my bedroom.

"Where are you, bitch? I find you, this fucking nightmare ends." His mutter could be heard in the quiet.

I peeked around the corner, then propped my knee beneath my wrist to steady my aim.

Aim Shoot Kill. Aim Shoot Kill.

He came into view. I had a clear shot of him.

I took it.

"Motherfuck!" Cox fell into the door of the adjacent

bedroom before crashing to the floor.

Within seconds, shots pinged off the wall beside me, forcing me to duck out of the way.

"I'll kill you, cunt! You fuckin' shot my leg!"

"I'm warning you, Cox. Get the hell out of here, or I'll kill you."

"I was ordered to bring you back alive, but I wasn't told I had to bring you back unharmed."

My hands trembled harder, and I pushed my muscles, straining them to keep steady, while keeping my gaze on the man whose stiffened leg was raised into the air. "This is your last chance. Leave now!"

"Fuck you!"

More gunfire, in a rapid burst.

I lay back on the floor and aimed my gun at his head. "One shot. One kill," I whispered.

He sneered, staring down at me, pistol aimed at my head in a standoff. "What are you, a fucking sniper now?"

"Don't do it. I'll blow your fucking head off, Cox. I swear to God, I will."

His eyes narrowed. "I have a question. You're all alone in this house. Why didn't you run? Call for help?"

At the lift of his lip, I shot his shoulder.

"Fuckin hell!" The pistol fell from his grip, and he slapped his good hand to the wound and lunged toward me.

Hands swiped out at me with no purchase, and I hammered a fist into his face, kicking his head to the side. I pushed myself to a stand, keeping him in my sights, and nabbed his cellphone clipped at his hip.

Scrolling through the numbers, I found Michael. "Call him."

A part of me couldn't believe I was about to do something so dangerous and stupid. Throw myself back into the asshole's lap. I probably wouldn't come out alive this time. I couldn't let Nick get killed, though. Not after he'd saved my life, cared for me, and set me free. I loved him. And for that reason, walking away wasn't an option.

There was something to be said about the heart's tenacity, it's refusal to accept defeat and give up on what it desired most. Maybe it was my restored faith in love that drove me to fight for what I wanted, when I knew the battle was so much bigger than me.

Or maybe I was just bat-shit crazy.

"Fuck you."

"Goddamn it, Cox. Don't make me shoot your other shoulder. It's a pretty sure bet I'll hit the mark from this distance."

His eye twitched, and he snatched the phone from my hand. "Your little *boyfriend's* probably been skinned alive by now."

I ignored his words and the urge to pummel his face.

"I want you to tell him you found me. And Achilleus X. Understood? Both of us." As he lay beneath me, I pressed the barrel of the gun to the top of his head. "You fuck this up and you'll be fishing for brains, fingers and toes across the floor."

CHAPTER 49
Nick

Dark. Cold. I opened my eyes through the fog clouding my brain, to a room that shifted in and out of focus. Tugging my hands brought me to the realization that I'd been tied up.

A sharp angle pressed into my back, and I blinked past the fog to see the drill above my head. Binds bit into my forehead when I attempted to look down. I'd been strapped.

To an industrial-sized, vertical milling machine.

Culling's face came into view, and that fucking smile I hated stretched his lips. "The infamous Eye for an Eye killer." He lifted the black ski mask, before tossing it over his shoulder. "Welcome! I've waited a very a long time for you. Tell me, how should I address you? E-for-E? Alec Vaughn? Which do you prefer?"

"Nick. Nick Ryder."

His eyes narrowed. "Nick Ryder is dead, my friend. A very trusted source assures me he was shot in the head."

"Well, your trusted source is for shit. That, or you can see dead people."

His lips pursed for a moment. "Whether you are, or not, your name is inconsequential to me. My police chief informs me you've been wreaking havoc on the Seven Mile Crew."

"Man, fuck that crew." The voice to the right of me told me there were more thugs in the room.

"My concern isn't the Crew," Michael continued. "My concern is that you've stolen my wife!" His lip curled into a snarl. "And I want her back!"

My mind made a mental rundown of any torture I'd been subjected to while I was out. No trouble breathing. Aside from a fading blur, I could see, so my eyes hadn't been gouged. No nausea or numbness or tingling anywhere. "I'm afraid you've got the wrong man. See, I don't plan to tell you shit."

His snarl popped to an evil grin—one that warned of pain. "You know ... the jig borer is said to have accuracy up to ten thousandths of an inch. I could essentially perform a lobotomy on you right here."

"Brilliant. I'm sure I'll have the wherewithal to remember where I stashed your wife after that."

Eyes clamped shut, Culling rolled his shoulders and his nostrils flared. "You know, my father was a machinist. In fact, he worked in this very factory when I was a child. A lowly blue collar worker."

"The hell kind of torture is this? Crucify me with a genealogical lesson on your goddamn family tree?"

I caught a flash of white, before pain rocketed through my jaw.

Culling flexed his fists and shook out his hand, as the dull ache throbbed in my teeth. "As I was *saying* ... my father worked in a factory for years. When he came home, he drank until he could hardly keep himself on two feet. Every. Fucking. Night. And when he was drunk, he liked to seek out my mother, or me, if I happened to be in his way. Any reason he could find to beat the ever-loving shit out of the two of us, he would." He paused for a moment, eyes narrowed. "On one occasion, I was given a gift. A ring from a young girl I'd befriended. Nothing particularly special, aside that I'd never received gifts. Never had a friend. Never understood the concept of friendship, until she came along. Even then, I struggled to see the benefit but found her ... a curiosity." Head bowed, he paced beside me. "My father, the bully that he was, found my ring and took it from me. When I fought to get it back, my mother stepped in. He murdered her in front of me. And for a week, he kept me tied to a machine in the shed, where he spent his drunken nights beating me. Torturing me. Doing whatever the fuck he wanted, because no one in that shithole neighborhood gave a fuck about another bastard child. They're all white noise to the dysfunction that thrives in hellhole cities like Detroit."

Realization hit my gut like a sledgehammer. "You're ... the boy. That Aubree told me about."

His brows winged up, lips stretched into a weak smile. "Ah, you've had intimate conversations with my wife about me. I'm flattered." He sniffed, licked his lips. "You know what the problem is with this city? It's not the crime. It's not lack of money. It's really not even about blacks or whites." Fingers curled into a fist, he stood beside me. "It's lack of ambition. An entire class of lazy, ambitionless fucks, who have nothing better to do than go to the same miserable fucking job day after day, then come home and drink, and beat the shit out of their families." With a sigh, he shook his head and went back to his pacing. "Eventually, I was found. After a week of hell, someone finally noticed I'd gone missing. I was taken away from my father and moved to the suburbs, raised by a stoic but successful man—a lawyer—and his wife. What a different life. I'd never dreamed of college before then. Never hoped to do more in life than become some fucking apprentice at a machine shop. And yet, look at me." Hands brushing down his side, he tipped his head and smiled. "I run this fucking place now. I *own* this city. How ironic is that? The shop that owned my father, who owned me, is mine!" The smile on his face withered to a serious expression. "In all that time, I never forgot Aubree, though. Never forgot the little bitch who'd claimed to be my best friend, and yet, never said a word when I'd gone missing." His stare, directed beyond me, told me he'd fallen into memories. "I came back for her. Found her. Stalked her night after night. Enrolled in one of her therapy classes. I decided to give back to her what I'd felt every night that my father came to mete out my punishment, while she'd lay cozy in her bed, sparing no thought to what happened to me at all." The devious twist of his lips had me wishing I could break the binds and pummel his fucking face. "That hopeless feeling, when you wish someone would just fucking kill you already."

He must've somehow manipulated her into feeling sorry for him. Guilt-tripping her into marrying him. No other reason could explain what the hell would make a woman like Aubree, as strong and bull-headed as she could be, fall for a psychotic asshole like Culling.

"The first job I took out of college was as an internist at my foster father's law firm. With the money I earned, I paid a man in prison to murder my father. It was one less blue collar worker in the world. One less miserable, drunken asshole. And it occurred to me then, how brilliant a plan it was—to eliminate the middle class all together." His finger pointed in the air, emphasizing his words. "Divide the city into rich and poor. And then have them kill themselves on the streets. Why have the good people pay to keep them locked up? Hand feed them in their prison cells. Survival of the fittest. Stop the breeding of complacency, and open the doors to prosperity and innovation."

"How very Hitler."

"Yes! Though I'll admit his execution was poor ... the idea was sheer brilliance!"

"I thought *I* was crazy." Much as I wanted to shake my head, I couldn't. "You're fucking insane."

"I am. That, I am." His eyes narrowed. "I understand that your wife and son were murdered on this day three

445

years ago." He glanced back to one of his men. "What were their names, Tony?"

"Lena and James."

"Ah, yes. Lena and James." His nod morphed into a shake of his head. "Now, if there's one thing a sadistic, rotten bastard like me understands, its vengeance. I have it in spades. I'm sorry for your loss, my friend, but with big ideas come small sacrifices."

Fury ignited in my veins and burned inside my muscles. Had to get loose. Needed to hear him howl with pain, watch his face twist with agony. Pain I yearned to inflict. I flexed against the binds holding me in place, the urgency to tear into the motherfucker dominating my senses, telling me to ignore the fire ripping through my wrists with every pull. "I'll kill you! I'll fucking kill you!"

His punch-worthy grin toyed with my last thread of sanity, and I yanked the rope, desperate to get loose—even if I'd have one less hand in the process.

"I'd like to make you a deal. I'd have loved to have a man with your talents and knack for evasion, but loyalty drives the engine and trust guides the ship." Slapping his hands together, he steepled his fingers. "I'm afraid I'd have neither with you. So, how about this? You tell me where to find my wife? I'll end your life with a bullet to the head. Quick. Painless. An act of mercy on my part, for all you've suffered."

"I've already been there, fuck-face. And, I can tell you, it's neither quick nor painless. So, why don't you take your act of mercy, shove it up your ass, and fuck yourself with it."

Another blow popped my lip, and the chasing burn told me he'd split it open.

"My, you have quite a tolerance for pain. Not so much as a grunt each time I've hit you."

"If you were hoping to hear someone scream, you should've strapped one of these pussies to the bench." I nudged my head against the stiff binds, toward whoever stood to the left of me. One of the men growled.

"It's not my nature to be kind, and I must say ... you make it fucking *impossible*." Culling signaled one of the men beyond my periphery, and a cart was pulled alongside the machine to which I was strapped. On it, sat a small grinder with a wire wheel on one side, an abrasive grinding wheel on the other. "You're lucky the lathe is completely out of order. I understand you have quite a sharp trigger finger."

My hand loosened from the straps, and I drove a fist into the side of the fat fuck who tried to hold me down. Grappling with the second thug, I swung two more times through the air, before my hand was pressed into the metal platform of the cart, the weight of both men crushing against my bones. I struggled in their grip, using all the strength in my arm, but with the rest of my body confined, I failed to move them.

"I'm going to ask you one more time. Nicely." Culling's fake, plastered smile taunted my fists, and had they not been strapped, I'd have knocked those perfect fucking teeth right out of his mouth. "Where is my wife?"

"Okay, okay." I took deep breaths. "If I had to guess … right now, your wife is … *basking* in the glow of ecstasy after my giving her what your small cock never could."

The grinder flipped on.

Fire and ice tore through my hand, the sharp bite of electricity stiffening my muscles before they turned cold with creeping numbness. My curses were drowned by the hum of the machine, and the smell of burning flesh stung my nose.

"Ah! One moment. Please." With a finger in the air, Culling lifted his cellphone to his ear.

The machine cut out, and the numbness crawled up into my wrists, my elbows, my chest, crushing each breath.

"Cox, how wonderful to hear from you. Where the fuck have you been?" Culling paused. "Aubree? Interesting. Bring her to me." He pulled the phone away from his face then placed it back, his smug grin turning to a frown. "Loading dock. The Ironworks building. Atwater." Tucking the phone into his jacket, his smile returned. "Well, that's out of the way. I'd hoped to torture you a bit, into telling me the whereabouts of Achilleus X, but it seems Cox has discovered that as well as found my wife, and they're on their way here. So, I'm afraid I've no use for you, my friend." He rounded the machine and put his mouth to my ear. "I do intend to punish Aubree for fucking you. I'd hoped she was nothing more than a victim, but I should've known better. Once a whore, always a whore."

I spat in his face. "This isn't over. I'm coming for you,

asshole."

"I believe the only one coming tonight will be me. Having fucked you." He kissed my forehead. "You put some excitement in my life, Nick. I'm truly going to miss you." He glanced down at his watch. "Now, if you'll excuse me, my wife should be here any minute."

He straightened and gestured toward the men still holding my hand captive. "I want you to take it slow with this one. And when you use the drill, take a video, so Aubree and I can fuck to it later." His gaze swung back to me. "Between her screams and your screams, I'm sure to get off."

Culling spun around, two men from beyond my periphery at his heels, and the grinder flipped on again.

Searing pain left my entire arm trembling. I clamped my mouth shut, a silent scream splitting my skull, while jagged flashes of light burst behind my eyelids. My stomach cramped with the tension, my muscles so stiff they ached. In those moments, I thought of Lena, Jay, Lauren, Aubree—all the people I'd let down. The victims of Culling, and I'd be just another statistic for the sadistic motherfucker. My teeth chattered, as the grinder hit my bone and the vibrations zipped up my hands.

A thunderous crash shook the building, and my nerves exploded, jerking my hand.

An aftershock rippled down my spine, dispersing tiny trembles throughout my muscles. The flare of pain fizzled to a dull burn, and the grinding stopped. Plumes of dust and smoke drifted over me as my eyeballs shifted back and forth, searching the ceiling for signs of caving.

A rainstorm of shattering glass and the explosive *thunk*s of crumbling brick sounded from behind. The two men beside me dropped to the floor like dead flies. On the fringes of my view, two other bodies smashed into one another in a flurry of movement.

What the fuck?

I couldn't move my head, but my hand had been released, and I raised it to my forehead in an attempt undo to the bindings there. A deep gash along my index finger exposed the bone, but I ignored it, and using my other working fingers, I pushed off the leather strap and went to work on untying my left hand.

Gunfire reverberated through the building. My body flinched with each thunderclap that bounced off the walls, as bullets pinged off the metal all around me. A clink hit the mill, and my muscles seized as the bullet deflected.

A gunfight had broken out, and I lay helplessly fucking strapped to the machine.

With a useless index finger, and the sprawling numbness, working the knot free with one hand proved difficult. I couldn't lift my head for fear of stabbing myself with the drill above me. Digging my fingers into the thick weave of the knot, I slipped, unable to slacken the loop.

"C'mon!" Frustration wound in my gut the longer I toyed with it, my hands still trembling from both the torture and the explosion a minute ago. Gasoline burned my nose and the smell of gun smoke filled the room, like firecrackers on the fourth of July.

Seconds ticked by, and the gunfire lessened, until two guns dueled back and forth with lengthy pauses in between.

One final shot, and the room fell to an eerie silence.

Abandoning my work at the knot, I rolled my head back, looking for signs of activity with the world turned upside down. A patrol car sat in the middle of the opened floor. It must've crashed through the rolling door of the loading dock. In the driver's seat, I could barely make out the figure of a man slumped over, a black mask covering his face. The same mask I wore.

Tinkering at my ankle had my head snapping downward.

Aubree stood, untying my binds, an AK-47 strapped to her arm—perhaps the sexiest fucking thing I've ever seen.

Relief and anger pounded through my body, as it occurred to me she was the only other person in the room with a pulse.

"What the fuck are you doing here?" I rolled my head around again, taking in the body count lying in pools of blood all around me. "And did you just take out four gangstas in a matter of minutes?"

A smile lifted the corner of her mouth as she freed my right leg and tossed the rope onto my body. "Did I forget to tell you? I know how to use a gun. My dad taught me. Shot a thirty aught six at five years old. At targets, mostly."

"You're a damn good shot." My attention turned back on my bound wrist. "Any chance you could work on my arm? It's that ... gravity thing."

The smirk turned into a full-blown smile, but it quickly disappeared when she lifted her gun, aiming like a goddamn ninja sniper, and shot at something behind me.

I craned my neck to see *yet another* body crumpled to the floor. "You, uh … want tell me what the fuck is going on here?"

"Later." Still toiling away at my binds, her brows pinched together, a whole lot of pain clouding her eyes. "I've never killed anyone before. I'm trying not to think too much about it right now."

Within minutes, all four of my limbs were freed, and I slid out from beneath the drill, cradling my mangled hand for a moment as she rounded the machine and strode up to me. A blow to my cheek knocked my head to the side. I turned back to her in complete and utter fucking confusion.

"That's for drugging me again." Gripping my nape, she pulled me to her face and crushed her lips to mine, her tongue darting into my mouth. "That's for leaving the gun on the nightstand."

"You wanna ditch this party and find a dark corner somewhere?"

"I want to find Michael."

A tearing sound drew my attention downward, to where she tore away part of my shirt and wrapped my hand tight. "If you're so good at being badass, how did you remain a prisoner all those years?"

"Asshole never gave me a gun." She made a final knot, pinching the flow of blood from the wound. "I'm not so hot with hand to hand fighting, so you're gonna have to watch my ass."

My brow kicked up at that.

"Let's go find this bastard and end him."

I gripped her arm. "Aubree, I can't let you get hurt in this. I'll find him. I'll end him."

She rolled her eyes, tugging her wrist. "Not happening."

"I'm serious." My grip tightened around her forearm. "No fucking around."

She twisted her wrist, wrenching her arm free. "I'll be fine."

No way I'd convince the woman to follow my command. She'd proven time and again how stubborn she could be. All I could do was protect her. "You stay behind me. If shit gets crazy, you bolt. Don't come back. Promise?"

"Promise." She kissed me again, and I stepped in front of her, taking the lead.

"So, that bullshit you pulled with me, the shooting lesson. That was—" I picked up my fallen rifle, awkwardly toting it in my non-mutilated hand.

"I thought it was sweet, you showing me how to use a gun."

A bullet sparked beside me, and both of us halted. Flanked by two burly men with beards, both wearing leather vests, Culling aimed his rifle from the center of the top balcony above us. Two seconds later, bullets sprayed over the open space, a beat after Aubree and I ducked behind equipment. Separated from me by a narrow walkway, she crouched low, keeping her gun tucked close.

A quick peek around the mill showed Culling, heading toward the stairwell, leaving his goons to fight for him.

With a wave, I caught Aubree's attention and swept my gun left and right, demonstrating that I planned to cover her and for her to run.

She nodded, but a strange, nauseating sensation hit my gut when the corner of her lip kicked up, like she planned to do something fucking crazy.

Sure enough, she bolted from her hiding spot, before I had the opportunity to shoot.

CHAPTER 50
Aubree

Bullets rained above me, and their shells clanged to the floor, as I kept low, shuffling across the open factory toward the staircase. I planned to go after Michael—he'd broken away from the other two men, heading for the door of a stairwell. Had I hinted at the plan, Nick probably would've shot me himself, because when he'd told me to run, I was pretty sure he meant the opposite direction.

Toward safety—not straight into the mouth of hell.

Then again, he'd have probably advised me not to have Cox drive a patrol car straight into the building, either, but that'd turned out just fine.

I dashed toward the staircase, and a hot jolt of pain struck my calf.

"Fuck!" Grabbing my leg, I fell forward and lifted my pant leg, where a bullet had hit my calf. A quick examination showed a long path of the bullet at the surface of my skin. A grazing. I ignored the pain and pushed to stand up.

"Aubree!" Nick's voice thundered from behind me, just before a shot struck one of the bikers.

I glanced back, to see the second biker had already descended the staircase at the opposite side of the room. About fifty yards behind, he made a dead run toward me, but Nick slammed his rifle into the guy's face, knocking him back.

I kept on, after Michael, not willing to let the bastard get away. Up the staircase, I hobbled after a flash of his black suit, as he entered the stairwell.

Shooting twice had bullets bouncing off the closing door, not even close to hitting their target. Legs burning, I pushed through the door.

Michael appeared one level below me, and I forced speed from my muscles, leaping three stairs at a time. I fired another shot into the black abyss below, and missed, as he rounded another landing. Bullets pinged as I blindly shot into the dark spiraling staircase.

The desperation to catch him kept me from caring that we headed straight for the basement of the building, until he disappeared and a cold chill swept across my skin.

Gun aimed, I twisted left to right, all the way around, looking for him.

The sudden stillness raised the hair on the back of my neck, and before I could spin to what had given me that eerie feeling, a blade lifted my chin at the same time arms enveloped me.

"Drop the gun." That bone-chilling voice I'd heard in

nightmares chimed inside my ear.

"Fuck you."

Flames licked the thin skin of my neck, where he sliced the blade, and I flinched. "In case I haven't made it clear to you before, I am perfectly capable of ending your life." He licked the side of my throat. "Almost as easy as I ended your father's."

Anger snaked through my gut, and I balled my hand into a fist. "I knew you killed him, you psychotic piece of shit."

"Why ... that's the sweetest thing you've ever said, darling. Walk." He wrenched the gun from my hand and held it level, jerking it to the side for me to take the lead. "Into the tunnel."

A long, dark tunnel stood before me, lit only by the opening at the end, about two hundred yards away, that appeared to lead outside the building. The shine of metal piping lined both sides of the brick walls. Sludge squished beneath my boot, and the scent of mold and stale air overwhelmed my nose, as I trudged along, in front of Michael.

"Steam tunnels. All over Detroit. It's a shame to see someone's brilliant ideas overrun by filth, destruction, graffiti." His words arrived on a sour tone. "Bunch of fucking animals in a zoo."

Something knocked into my arm, and I stumbled. My head jerked back with the tug of Michael's hand, yanking me back to a stand.

At the mouth of the tunnel, we reached a small

staircase that opened to dirt and machinery at ground level, like a construction site, closed off by a tall fence that'd been lined at the top with barbed wire. Hardhat signs had been plastered on all corners of the site, along with *Do Not Enter*.

The only way out appeared to be back through the building, from where we'd just come.

"Up those stairs." Michael nudged me forward.

A short distance from us, another staircase stood alongside a square concrete structure, only about eight or ten feet in the air—a vault, of some sort. Reluctantly, I climbed each step, eyeing a white square hatch at the top—large enough to squeeze a body through.

"Why?" I asked, as my shoulders violently twisted around to face him. "Why did you kill him?" Mouth set in a hard line, I clenched my jaw to hold back the furious words itching to escape, and took two deep breaths. "You swore that if I married you, he'd be safe. Left alone. So long as I stayed away from him. And I did," I gritted out.

His cheeks puffed before he blew out a sharp breath and reached for the handle on the oversized hatch. "About a year ago, your father came to me, begged me to see you. He'd grown lonely. On the streets. A drunk. Said he couldn't live without you in his life." A smile skated across Michael's face, and my heart sank at his words.

The last time I'd talked to my father, we'd met for coffee one week before Michael swiped me away to elope. He was well, working a lot, but healthy. I had no idea he'd sunk into such a low place.

"He threatened to … expose my business interests. So, I sent him to a watery grave. Thought the irony was appropriate—drowning in debt."

Michael's chuckle grated on my spine. I clenched my teeth as the anger rushed through my body, coaxing me to nail the bastard square in the face.

"And, of course, with your mother … it was kind of poetic."

I knocked the gun and drilled my fist into his nose, then kicked my knee up and struck his balls. Air pinched inside my throat, as his fingers dug into my neck. The solid force behind me smashed into my spine, and the air blasted from my lungs.

Squeezing his bloody nose, Michael pushed me upward until my body covered the hole of the large hatch on top of the vault. Clawing the edges offered no purchase, and I grabbed to his arm with one hand, his belt loop with the other, my fingertips grazing the hilt of his blade in the holster.

Through clenched teeth, he growled, his grip at my throat tightening. "I should've killed you five years ago when I found you. I was going to. I'd planned to. If you hadn't spread your legs like a fucking whore that night, taunting me with your pathetic apology, you'd be dead, and we'd all be in a better place."

Michael had enrolled in my class, surprising me. For years, I'd thought he was dead, and there he was, standing before me, a successful lawyer, mourning the loss of his foster father. He was charming, at first. And I was foolish.

"I knew you … came back … to kill me. You never … forgave me."

He leaned in, pupils dilated and crazed, like a shark before the attack. "It was because of you that he tied me up and tortured me. Because of you, no one came for days."

"Because of … my father … that anyone came for you … at all! I … told him of … monsters outside! He found you! And you … killed him! Bastard!"

In a battle of wills, our bodies trembled, his pushing into mine, and mine pushing into his.

His nose scrunched with the effort. "I have no use for you after another man's dick's been in your filthy cunt. You're nothing but trash. And I can do better."

"Burn … in … hell." I popped the knife from its holster, sliced the blade across his neck, though not deep enough, and felt weightless as my body slipped from his grasp.

A cold hard slam smashed into my spine, and I cried out, my voice echoing inside the dark room where I'd been thrown.

My legs numbed.

My muscles burned.

A long pole slid down through the hatch and a squeal bounced off the enclosed walls. The sound of running water washed me in panic, as an ice-cold seeped into my clothes.

Michael peered down at me from the hatch above. "It seems the Levesque name will come full circle and die with

460

you, Aubree. This is an oil retention vault. Your very *own* watery tomb."

Fear climbed my spine with the icy wetness soaking my coat.

Against the paralyzing pain shooting through my back, I rolled over to my stomach, and pushed myself to my knees. Water flowed from the open pipe quickly. No valve. No shut-off nozzle that I could discern in the faint light. Whatever pole he'd shoved down into the vault must've been a key.

In the haze of panic, my mind searched for a solution. Like the dread seeping into my thoughts, light slid into complete blackness, and I looked up to see the hatch had been closed. The air turned frigid, penetrating me down to my bones, crushing my lungs, as I sucked in a breath.

"No!" My voice bounced around the vault.

Water had climbed to my shins, and I patted around for the pipe. Bitter cold steel met my fingertips, and I followed it to the angry pulse of water pouring from the mouth of the pipe. Nothing. No way to stop it. Placing my hands over the mouth of it only succeeded in kicking me backward onto my ass.

My heart raced. Pulse pounded. My head felt light, and I struggled to suck in air between rapid, panicked breaths.

"Help me!" I stood from the water suddenly at my knees, and pounded at the walls. "Somebody! Help me!"

In a matter of minutes, the vault would be filled. Concrete scratched my fingertips as I patted the walls, and I whimpered a sound of relief on finding a bolted ladder.

Taking each step easy, in spite of my trembling limbs, I climbed to the top and pushed on the hatch. It wouldn't move. Wouldn't budge.

I thumped my fist against it. "Somebody help me!"

Screwing my eyes shut brought flashes of my past, the light at the surface, the struggle for breath, the pressure at the top of my head.

I pounded with both fists against the hatch. "Help me! Open the door! Open the door!"

Frantic thrashing of my limbs knocked me backward, and I slid down the ladder, my foot catching between the wall and the ladder. Reaching for the rungs above me, I pushed up on my good foot, but my leg merely twisted in painful contortion, as water splashed around my chest.

"Oh, God! Help me!" Branches of terror shot through my veins, threatened to pull me into blackness

Using every ounce of energy I had, I pushed upward and yanked on the rungs. As the water reached my chin, I reached out to the darkness above me, the echo of my scream falling into silence.

CHAPTER 51
Nick

Crouched in the darkness of the basement, I peered down the tunnel, where the figure moved through the shadows, getting closer. I already knew that the tunnel ended at the dead end construction site, where the adjacent building had been torn down. Only when he neared, did I notice Aubree was nowhere in sight.

Lurching from my hiding spot, I wrapped my arm around Culling's throat and squeezed. Wetness slid against my fingertips. His kicks and punches struck me from all angles, as he fought for his life, but still I held tight, not letting go until I yanked him to the ground and pointed my gun in his face. "Where is she?"

"It seems my head is swimming. I can't recall." At the angling of his chin, I noticed a streak of blood across his throat.

Flipping the gun, I clocked him in the face with the stock and had his lips kissing the barrel once more. "Where. Is. She?" The words hardly pushed past my clenched teeth. I glanced up, toward the mouth of the tunnel, from where he'd come.

A click brought my attention back to Culling, and the gun he'd pulled. He brought a finger to his lips. "Shhhh. Is that ... water I hear?" His thin eyebrows winged up with his laughter. ""I wish I hadn't cried so much!" said Alice, as she swam about, trying to find her way out. "I shall be punished for it now, I suppose, by being drowned in my own tears!""

Find a way out. Drowned. He had her trapped somewhere. I steadied the gun against his forehead.

"You shoot me. I shoot you. She dies." Only the faint outline of his movement could be seen by the light from the end of the tunnel, as he scrambled from beneath me and rose to a stand, the barrel of his gun pointed at me the whole time. "Who's faster? Seems you're not quick on the draw anymore friend."

In spite of the destruction to my hand, I flipped the safety on the other side of the gun, gripped the stock, and leveled the barrel. "I wouldn't chance it."

"Hands in the air, Culling!" The shout came from a shadowed figure beyond him.

"I called for backup" I told Culling. DeMarcus, to be exact. "This place will be swarming with police and FBI any minute."

"We got Brandon Malone in custody," DeMarcus continued. "He confessed everything. We also received an anonymous chip of Julius Malone implicating you. You're done. It's over."

I didn't need to hear anymore. Backing away from Culling, I bolted back through the tunnel from where he'd had come, blowing off the shouts at my back.

At the tunnel's exit, my heart kicked up with the frantic sweep for any sign of Aubree. She couldn't have escaped over the barbed wire at the top of the fence. A staircase led to a large concrete structure, and I dashed that way and up the stairs to a small door at the top. Flipping it open, I peeked inside to darkness and what sounded like water rising toward me.

"Aubree!" I shouted. "Aubree!"

After shrugging out of my coat and kicking off my shoes, I climbed inside the vault. I'd descended no more than a couple of stairs, something hit my leg.

Jesus. No.

Slipping beneath the ice-cold water, I patted around. Limbs, an arm I presumed, floated outward, and I hooked my good arm beneath it, pushing upward, toward the surface. The body didn't budge. I tried again, but no go.

Patting down the body, I reached the legs and, finally, the boot that'd gotten caught between the ladder and a pipe.

Gripping tight to the boot, I pulled, twisting as I tugged. It wouldn't move.

With seconds ticking by and a frantic trembling beating though my body, I fumbled at the laces, loosening them, and slipped the foot out of the boot. At once the body went limp, and I lifted what I hoped was Aubree to the surface, gagging and coughing when our heads breached the water.

Up the ladder, I dragged her silent form through the hatch and back down the staircase, nabbing my coat along the way. Lying her on a bed of dirt, I tilted her head back, opened her mouth, and listened.

No breath.

Placing my lips to hers, I forced air inside of her mouth, then pulled away and pushed my palms against her chest, in quick compressions. Another blast of air and more compressions. I stopped and listened. No movement. No air.

"Don't you fucking die on me, Aubree! Don't you fucking die!" Another round of air and compressions. *Pause.* Air and compressions. *Pause.* "No, no. C'mon, stay with me, stay with me, please!"

My soul withered with each failed attempt. Numbness spread from my heart to my limbs, and blackness narrowed my field of vision. I felt light, as if I'd detached from my body, floating above the scene, urging the man performing CPR to keep going, don't give up, because fuck if I knew what I'd do without her. I was touching her but couldn't feel her, as if our connected souls had somehow peeled away from one another, leaving only shells.

As I leaned down to press my lips to hers, I stopped just short, gripping her jaw in my hands. "Don't do this. Don't fucking die. I won't have anything left if you die!"

Cold spikes of pain stabbed my heart. I forced another round of air and pressed into her chest, mentally counting off, as each second beat a reminder in my head that she was slipping farther out of my grasp. The watery blur in my eyes made it damn near impossible to see her and I frowned, concentrating on her face, searching for any sign of life.

Still nothing.

No. No fucking way. Violence and madness crept my spine, numbing my body. The world spun around me, and I screwed my eyes tight, but the image of her cold, pale face burned inside my head.

Five minutes must've passed. Who the fuck knew how long she'd been trapped before I found her? That old familiar sensation of hope fading before my eyes hit my chest and clutched my heart.

One more time. *C'mon, Nick. Save her.*

I bent forward and kissed her cold lips. "Please," I whispered against them, then I blew a mouthful of breath into her lifeless body.

Did she move? Fucking blur in my eyes made it difficult to tell. I blinked them, and her eyes flinched, mouth gaped, but only her neck bobbed, as if a cough sat trapped at the back of her throat. My chest expanded with a captured breath.

Ten seconds passed in an eternity, while her body spasmed. When her brows came together at last, water burst from her mouth on a wet cough, and I turned her to her side, while she choked and gagged, working the fluid from her lungs.

A crazy surge of laughter bellowed out of my chest, like

I'd suddenly lost my mind. Maybe I had. I could hardly breathe myself. All I wanted was to scoop her up into my arms and squeeze the shit out of her, but instead I let her work the air back into her lungs.

She rolled onto her back, and her eyes appeared heavy, still caught in a haze before realization must've struck. Hard. Her gaze fell to mine, and she broke into tears, lifting her arms out to me.

Her body shivered in mine. I shivered against her, too, but dragged my coat up around her shoulders, wrapping her in what little warmth it offered.

"Thought I lost you, Pistol Lips. Fuck." I kissed her on the forehead and pushed the hair out of her face. "Don't ever scare the hell out of me like that again."

Frowning, she let out a breathy laugh like it hurt, and she tucked her face down into my coat.

A shot rang out, and I snapped my attention back toward the tunnel where I'd left Culling and DeMarcus . "Stay here," I whispered, planting another kiss to her temple.

Her ice-cold grasp tugged my arm, and when I glanced back, she frantically shook her head, a look of terror crossing her face. "No!" A cough followed the rasp of her words.

"It's okay. I'll come back for you. I promise."

Wrenching my arm free, I took off back through the tunnel.

Grunts and scuffling told me I was close, and I stumbled upon DeMarcus slumped against the wall, gripping his arm.

I crouched to the police officer. "You shot?"

"Yeah, I'm alright," he said, his voice straining. He nodded toward a door that led back into the Ironworks basement. "He went that way. He's got my gun."

"Back through the tunnel. Aubree needs help." I didn't wait for him to answer, but raced after Culling. "Get an ambulance!" I called over my shoulder.

Inside the basement, light filtered in through the high windows, and I scanned the area, listening for sound. At a scrape of metal, I flanked right, but as I slipped through a second door, my body went light before I realized the floor'd given out from under me and I fell through the air.

A cold, hard surface crashed into my back, knocking the air from my lungs. Grit slid beneath my fingertips. I looked up to the faint darkness above me and caught sight of a shadow hovering over the hole through which I'd fallen.

"Sub-basement," Culling said with a smile in his voice. "I visited this place as a child once, with my father, and I thought how horrible it would be to fall down inside of that black hole where no one would ever find me. Who knew what was in there?"

I looked around at all of the obscure shadows, of what appeared to be containers or barrels lining the back wall, but the room remained dark—too dark to see exactly what was down there. "It's over. DeMarcus knows." As I slipped along the wall nearest me, keeping to the shadows out of sight, an odd metallic smell hit the back of my throat.

"The FBI knows. You're finished."

"DeMarcus is nothing but a fucking fly in my ointment. I have connections, and let's not forget, I had a highly motivated serial killer on my ass. Even if I didn't shoot you, your ass would land in prison, and I would personally see to it that you didn't make it past the first night. I will systematically bring every one of you fucks down. Your entire organization of rebellion, starting with you."

I caught the click of his gun as I laughed. I couldn't help it. His ignorance was more than I could stand.

"I'm glad you find humor, Nick. A man should always laugh in the face of tragedy. I laughed while I watched the pathetic story about your family. I laughed when your sweet little lesbian friend was tortured. And I'll be laughing my ass off when I finally put an end to you."

Rage kicked in at the mention of my family and Lauren, but I swallowed it down and laughed harder. "You're a stupid bastard, Culling. Conniving, but stupid."

The air in the room grew thick with tension, and as vapors filled my lungs, a cough tore from my chest, stoking the adrenaline pulsing through my veins at the dreaded sensation that we'd stumbled upon something dangerous. A place where neither one of us would stand to make it out alive.

Gaze locked on him from my vantage point, I raised my gun, left fingers threaded through the trigger.

"So, tell me. Where in the fuck can I find Alec Vaughn?" he asked, irritation clinging to his tone.

I opened my mouth to speak, but hesitated. *Why hesitate?*

I knew the truth. I always had. The night they stole everything was the same night I awoke as something darker, more dangerous. Fearless.

"I *am* Alec Vaughn. I'm Nicholas Ryder. I'm Achilleus X. I *am* this entire fucking operation."

My own words echoed inside my head.

Flashes of memory whipped behind my eyes. The fire. Ice cold snow against my cheek, and a voice telling me to get the fuck up. The hospital. Despair. Months of therapy. Whispers of Post-Traumatic Stress. A medical record. Dissociative Identity Disorder. Standing on the edge of the Penobscot building, staring down at the city, ready to jump. Alec's voice inside my head. "Revenge." Revenge. The blackouts. Aubree. Catching the sadness in her smile on TV. A bruise. A scar. A slap from Culling, away from the camera. The note she left behind for the priest at her father's funeral, the one I keep tucked in my pocket, that read, '*Save Me*'. The desperation to help her. The urge to save her. Seeing through Alec's eyes, as he stabs Marquise with the needle. Watching as he orchestrates the gruesome sculptures of those fucking pedophiles. The sounds of Jalen's screams distantly ringing in my ear as the machine crushes his arms. Punching Alec in the face, staring down at my bloody knuckles, then back to my shadow and the hole in the drywall, where I was certain I'd hit him— certain I'd hit Alec.

Out of body experiences. Almost like a dream, and I

was the observer. Disconnecting from myself and handing the reins to Alec, my doppelgänger who crossed the line I feared to tread. The one that would make me more beast than man. The one that made me question how far someone could go to ease the pain of losing so much at once.

His thirst for violence mirrored my own, but where I was bogged down with guilt, Alec was remorseless and ruthless. A cold-blooded killer, borne of my desperation to carry out the promise I'd made to my wife.

He was the dark half of me. The one who had the balls to inflict merciless pain. To punish.

"Alec is my design. The hero in a game. My revenge."

"Well, then," Culling gritted out. "That changes everything."

Flashes of light preceded the crack of gunfire.

I ducked behind a nearby barrel, but not before taking a shot to my thigh. My body, so numb with adrenaline, hardly registered pain.

Sparks flew as the bullets pinged against steel, and a flame ignited, burning a puddle of fluid just a few feet away from me that lit up the sub-basement.

After two more shots, Culling recoiled and gripped his throat, before stumbling forward and falling down into the hole.

Landing in the flaming pool, his jacket lit up like kindling. He kicked in a violent seizure, as the blaze swarmed him, and in the flames' glow, I spotted the hole in his neck where the bullet must've ricocheted back at him when he fired at the steel shelving behind me. Blood gushed into a widening pool around his head. Flames engulfed him, while he lay gasping for breath, a look of sheer horror on his face. He reached out for me, his mouth gaped to a silent scream. Within seconds, his entire body was covered in flames, and his body jerked, as the orange glow intensified, consuming his flesh like a ruthless predator.

His gurgles broke into a pathetic sort of mewling. I lifted my gun, but hesitated. Not a single part of me wanted to offer him mercy. No one had offered my family mercy.

Burn it. Julius's words beat inside of my skull.

Movement in my periphery guided my eyes to a shadowed corner of the room. Jay stepped forward, carrying his blanket, wearing his pajamas—so out of sync with the hell surrounding me, as he kept his distance, watching me.

I knew he wasn't real. Couldn't be real.

"Daddy? Are you going to shoot that man?"

It'd been a long time since I'd had waking hallucinations of my son. Tears filled my eyes, and frowning, I wiped the moisture away and double blinked.

Still, Jay stood there.

"Is he bad, Daddy?"

"Yes," I whispered. "I have to punish him."

"Why?"

"For hurting you." Falling to my knees, I let the agony tear out of my chest, breaking up my words. "And ... your

… mommy."

"But I'm right here, Daddy."

A choke of a sob escaped me, the vision of my dead son killing every corner of my soul. "No, Jay. You're with mommy."

He shook his head. "Remember? You said I was here." He pointed to his heart.

A crushing ache inside my chest nearly stole my breath, and I echoed his movement, placing my hand over my heart. "Always, Jay."

I couldn't stop the fucking tears. *Not real. He's not real.* Except, I could see his face, so vividly. The small mark above his eye, where he'd fallen as a baby and hit his head on the coffee table. The faint birthmark on his neck, which I'd told him was a special gift that gave him super powers no one else had. The blue of his eyes, like my very own, staring back at me.

"It's okay, Daddy. I'm always right here." His smile forced my own smile forth, his small frame blurred by the tears filling my eyes again.

"I'll always love you, Little Man."

"I love you, too." His form faded into the flickering light from the fire. "I'll see you in the night." His whisper carried over Culling's blood-curdling scream.

What followed was the moment that separated monster from man.

I wasn't like them.

I wasn't a monster.

Alec appeared, standing alongside Culling, smiling

down at the poor bastard whose skin blackened with each passing second. "Go, Nick. I've got this."

"Not this time, Alec. It's over."

His head craned toward me, cigar hanging between his teeth. "What are you saying?"

"I'm saying I want to start over. With Aubree. No more blackouts."

His eyes narrowed in suspicion, his shoulders bunched, and I could damn near feel the waves of anger rolling off of him. He spat the cigar into the flames and lurched toward me. "You ungrateful fuck."

"I'm sorry my friend. This is where it ends." I lifted my gun and shot twice.

The bullets passed through Alec, hitting Culling once in the skull, silencing the gurgles. With the mercy shot, Alec fizzled away to nothing.

A bright light flashed where Jay had stood moments ago, and my head snapped that way.

Flames crawled along a strip of fluid leaking from one of the barrels.

"Shit." I rocketed up from the floor, and spun on my heel, as a blaze of fire trailed at my back.

CHAPTER 52
Aubree

I couldn't remember the name of the stranger who held me down.

The building exploded before my very eyes, and the only thing I knew was, the man I loved had gone back inside after the man I wanted to destroy. From nearly a block away, the stranger and I watched the old Ironworks building crumble as its foundation caved into flames and black smoke.

The same thick black smoke that coated my airways and made a cough rip through my chest and my body turn numb.

Wake up, Aubree. It's just a dream. Wake up.

Crystals of ice climbed my spine, freezing my nerves, and in spite of the surrounding heat, I went cold. Tears clung to my eyes but failed to fall. For a moment, I was frozen in time, watching fire lash out at the air, and swallow the building and my love, in one merciless scourge of destruction.

Nick.

Not even his name could summon the sobs lingering at the back of my throat.

"She's in shock," someone near me said.

A soft bed captured my fall, but my eyes remained glued on the burning building.

"I'll come back for you. I promise." His words played over and over inside my head.

A mask slid over my face, cool bursts of air filling my lungs, and though the air was cleaner, though it expanded my chest, kept me alive, I felt like I couldn't breathe.

Fingers snapped in my periphery as though to peel my attention away from the blaze. I fought them at first, but they were persistent. A woman's voice talked to me as if I could hear what she was saying. As if I cared. As if I wanted to be saved.

Then it hit me. A gut-wrenching, soul-crushing pain. The kind that ached every bone in my body, every muscle, and made every breath an effort. The kind that made a person want to curl into themselves and die.

I couldn't say the words that slammed into my chest like a wrecking ball, crushing my heart. *He's dead. He's dead.*

No. Impossible.

I wanted run straight into the building, after him. Another part of me ached for death to swoop down and take me away. The duality left me paralyzed.

No. No way a man so strong could have such a meaningless ending. He deserved more.

The officer who'd clung to me as the first explosion thundered stood off to the side, talking with medics, voicing the answers that, in my heart, I couldn't accept.

"How many were inside?"

"Looked like a lot of East side, West side gangs. I'd say about two dozen dead on the first floor. In the basement? Two, for sure. Backup just arrived when the first explosion went off, and they didn't see anyone on the west or south exits, so, as far as I know, Michael Culling and Nicholas Ryder were the only ones on the lower level. Tunnels lead out this way, and we ain't seen nobody exit. So I'd ... I'd have to assume they're dead."

Dead.

The word echoed inside my head, a constant ring of agony clawing at my stomach. *He's not dead. He can't be dead.*

"Are you having any pain?" The medic's voice came into sharp clarity at my ear, and I turned to face her. She looked tired, with wrinkles at the corners of her eyes and dark circles lining her sockets, giving them a sunken appearance.

"What?" The word came out involuntarily, as I processed the question. Was I in pain? "Yes."

"Can you tell me where you're feeling pain?"

A stinging burned my nose, and I clamped my mouth shut as her form blurred behind the shield of tears. "Everywhere."

CHAPTER 53
Aubree

If I didn't think of him, it was only for a brief interlude. A moment of insanity when something in the world managed to distract me for a minute. I'd become a broken woman, going through motions. Empty inside.

Nearly a week had passed since the fire, and I still couldn't function.

Even then, I stared at the gray walls in the small, claustrophobic room that somehow left a metallic taste in the back of my throat, likely from all the steel housed in such a small space. The table. Guns. My nerves.

I should've been reveling in my newfound freedom.

Except, my world felt like a cage, and I was the willing captive.

I needed him. Could feel phantom sensations brush across my skin whenever I recalled the first night we'd made love. For years, I'd worn my armor, deflecting pain, but I'd become nothing more than a hollow shell, on the verge of being crushed into a million pieces.

"You said this man who kidnapped you claimed to be Nicholas James Ryder? The same Nicholas James Ryder that supposedly perished in a fire three years ago?"

The investigator, whose name I couldn't recall, sat across from me in the interrogation room. I'd sat there for hours, as if I'd been the criminal.

"Yes."

"And he confessed to being the Eye for An Eye Killer as well as Achilleus X, as a means of retaliation for what was done to his family?"

"Yes." I kept my answers brief, just as my lawyer had coached me.

"And it was your husband who was supposedly responsible for the murder of his family?"

"That's what he said."

He paused his scribbling. "That's what who said?"

I studied the pockmarks in his face and noticed the sweat bleeding into the collar of his dress shirt. Flakes of dandruff dotted his dark gray sport coat, and my eyes shot toward his greasy, unkempt mop of brown hair. To the side of him sat a Styrofoam cup, wafting out the smell of stale coffee. I'd become a vessel, soaking up observations, keeping thoughts and conversations to myself. A silent box of secrets. "Nick."

The television hanging from the corner of the room behind him showed Achilleus X, his masked face talking in silence with the volume muted. The closed caption text moved across the screen and read the same heart-wrenching message that'd played for the last two days, as news investigators pieced together a story from the destruction:

"People of Detroit. If you're watching this video, it means I'm already dead. Your mayor has broken a very solemn vow to protect and serve you. He's a murderer, a thief, and a liar. I'd intended to reveal myself, but Achilleus X is more than what's hidden behind this mask. It's more than flesh and bone. It doesn't matter who I am. I'm merely a shell to house the belief shared by all of us. Speramus meliora resurget cineribus. Detroit will rise from the ashes. Operation Culling. Operation Devil's Night. Stand down."

"It makes no sense." The investigator shook his head, drawing my attention away from the screen. "There are two completely different personalities when it comes to these crimes. It's still my theory that Achilleus X and the Eye for an Eye killer are two individuals working together."

"She's told you what was told to her." My lawyer sat beside me, flipping through notes he'd taken during the questioning. Unlike the investigator, Miles was clean cut, with manicured nails and thin-wired glasses that gave him an air of intelligence. "Are we going to sit here and keep rehashing the same questions? My client has suffered a very traumatic week."

"One more… question. Anyone that might've had some beef with your husband? A vendetta? Aside from Nicholas Ryder, who *you* claim was Achilleus X?"

Don't give them any more than necessary. Push the truth away. Don't let them see it written all over your face. I felt like a criminal, but the one true criminal had died in those flames.

I couldn't count the number of people who had a vendetta against my husband, all of them ghosts, whispering in my ear at that moment. I wouldn't allow Michael to be viewed as a victim, when he'd victimized so many people. I could provide a list of names. People who'd been victimized by Michael's violence, including our very own maid, Elise, who'd had her tongue cut out when she asked about photographs she'd once found while cleaning his office. The police had their evidence. They had their proof. Anything more would implicate the wrong person and inevitably make their saintly politician look like a martyr. "My husband made a lot of enemies in this city. You have Julius's confession."

Lips forming a hard line, the investigator dropped his gaze from mine and gave a sharp nod. "If we have any further questions, we'll be in touch. I'm sorry for your loss, ma'am."

Fuck Michael. I hated accepting any measure of sympathy for him, but that was the game I had to play.

"Thank you." I nodded, feeling light as I rose up from the chair.

I'd had vertigo a number of times since the explosion. Part of me wondered if I'd ever feel connected to the world again. If I'd ever feel whole.

Another part of me just didn't care.

CHAPTER 54
Aubree

From the dock, I stared off at the ocean that surrounded Boca Chica Island—a small piece of heaven just off Panama's Pacific Coast. Red and orange streaked across the placid surface, mirroring the sky, as the sun began to set behind me. I never missed a sunset.

With Michael's life insurance policy, I was able to pay cash for a gorgeous villa, set on over seventy acres of jungle and fruit trees, with a view of Islita Castillo off in the distance. I considered it a well-deserved treat, after months of grueling interrogations and court proceedings, for which I played only a small part as both a victim of kidnapping and a *mourning widow*.

Names had been given up by Michael's connections and exchanged for pardons and reduced sentences. Michael's dealings were investigated, his sacred office torn apart. The most heartbreaking part of it all had come during the confession of Brandon Malone, who detailed a grim and gruesome attack on Nick and his family. He spoke of the brutal torment his gang had inflicted on Nick's wife and son, the night they'd been murdered, and my heart bled when he recounted how they'd eventually disposed of them at Michael's command.

A gust of wind fluttered the note in my hand—the one I'd skimmed the night I'd awakened from being drugged. The last remnant I carried of the man I loved.

Or men, as it were.

In it, he spoke of a place he'd seen once. An island that was too perfect to be true, located just off the coast of Panama. In my new home, I'd found dense mangroves, powdery white sand, unspoiled coral reefs and hidden coves.

My own personal paradise.

I'd never planned to be surrounded by the very thing I feared, but such was life. Drowning and coming back had somehow put me at peace with the water again—enough that I found myself submerged in the silence of the ocean on nights when I felt most alone, dreaming of Nick's hands coaxing my body to orgasm. My heart felt empty but at home in the private and secluded glass house, in the thick of century-old mango trees and exotic creatures. During the day, I picked avocados and bananas. At night, I watched the moon rise over the calm, placid waters.

A couple weeks after the ironworks explosion, when I hadn't been under the microscope of investigators and specialists or bodyguards protecting me against retaliation, I returned to that abandoned mansion, where I'd been kept prisoner. I didn't expect to find the envelope.

Thought for certain they'd have found it as they dissected the house. There it lay, though, tucked inside the fireplace, where I'd left it, beneath the ash. When the noise around me finally settled, I'd read it in peace. Every word.

Nick had left me his bank account numbers—access to millions of dollars that I would never truly find the need to spend. I donated some of the money to local schools and a healing through the arts center in Panama City. He'd also given me instruction on what to say to the investigators and lawyers during the trials.

The chip held the greatest secrets. I'd taken the time to study the medical records and the heart wrenching diagnosis of his dissociative personality, thought to be a result of trauma, post traumatic stress.

There had also been two plane tickets, as though he might've changed his mind and come with me.

Darkness stole the light of day, and I reached down to my stomach, rubbing where the small bump had begun to show through my dress.

Yet another part of the man I loved, growing inside of me.

I whistled for Achilleus, my black Cane Corso, who bounded across the beach and wagged his tail, as he followed behind. Smiling, I clutched the letter to my chest, and made my way back toward the large thatched roof home just a few yards away from the dock.

Once inside, I set the letter on the granite countertop of the gourmet kitchen. The space had been designed with the most modern amenities— state of the art furnishings, mixed with a classic island appeal. Furniture had been imported from Bali, and local artists provided the breathtaking paintings hung throughout. Such an odd contradiction of civilization in an ancient world.

I ambled toward the bedroom, where a king-sized bed, handmade by woodworkers in Panama, sat empty, kempt by the maid who came by boat every other morning and shared stories of her family. She was a kind, older woman, who often brought me delicious meals. I'd never had much in the way of Latin food until I'd arrived there, and after the first bite, I didn't know how I'd gone so long without it. Food for the soul.

One of the six bedrooms in the house, far too small for anything more than a twin bed, I'd converted into an art nook. There, I spent hours trying to capture his face—the shadows and dips from his prominent jaw and chiseled cheeks, and those eyes, slicing away at my heart while they came to life on the canvas.

Pulling my hair back into a bun, I stood in front of the oversized mirror, staring at my hardened nipples. The thin, red silk dress I wore had been tied loosely in front, allowing half of each breast to peek through the wide slit. I'd become a creature of simplicity, and if not for the caretaker who lived just a few hundred feet from the house, I'd have probably walked around nude most of the day, because I could.

A faint draft brushed against the back of my neck.

In the mirror's reflection, my eyes caught on the slight gap between the thick double doors behind me. Sliding the gun from the top drawer, I spun around, tipping my head to be sure, and crossed the room, where I threw back the door to peer outside. On the deck, the hammock swung ever so slightly in the breeze, but everything appeared to remain undisturbed.

Achilleus would bark, I reminded myself.

The only other person on the east side of the island happened to be Mateus, the groundskeeper, who had his own quarters. In reality, crime wasn't an issue, but the investigations into Michael's affairs had resulted in the implication and arrest of notorious gang members and political figures. I sometimes worried they'd come after me, seeking retribution.

Closing the door, I conducted a quick, half-hearted sweep of the house, and once satisfied with my search, I set the gun on the nightstand and climbed into my bed.

From the drawer of the nightstand, I nabbed a book— *The Claiming of Sleeping Beauty*. by A.N. Roquelaure.

Sliding my fingers beneath the hem of my dress, I read in silence, skating my fingers down, between my thighs while the Prince proceeded to stake his claim on Beauty. I'd found some twisted enjoyment in the loneliness, night after night, fantasizing about Nick. My heart refused to move on.

Minutes passed, and my eyes grew heavy, my mind slipping in and out of that state of wakefulness and dreaming. Heat pulsed through my body, warming my skin, and my muscles went soft, drifting, drifting.

A whisper of touch traced my hipbone, as I lay on my

side in bed. I let out a sigh and lifted my arms above my head, surrendering to the dream that bled into my consciousness. Fingers slipped between my thighs, pushing aside my panties, and I couldn't tell if they were mine, or my illusion of Nick.

Pleasure radiated from my core, to my toes and fingertips, in delicious waves that had my hips rocking in slow, agonizing circles. God, it felt so damn good. *I don't want to wake up.* I wanted to stay in the dream, forever in the state of ecstasy, with Nick's ghostly fingers pumping in and out of me, in perfect sync with the cresting of my orgasm. As if he knew my body better than I did.

"Nick," I whispered. "You feel so … good." I fondled my breast, my tongue sweeping across my lips as the intensity built heat within my muscles.

"I watched you touching yourself. You're so fucking wet, so tight."

Oh, God, his voice was so lucid, so vivid inside my head, the sound of it alone nearly forced me over the edge, but his finger slowed again, and the haze of sleepiness lifted. Desperate, I focused, not wanting to lose the moment.

No, please. Let me have this! I *needed* this release.

My eyes flipped open. I lifted my hand, but the sensations kept on, and my muscles seized against momentary panic. Neither of my hands were anywhere near my pussy. One hand fondled my breast. The other remained above my head, something shackled about my wrist.

Yet, my walls still gripped what felt like long fingers inside me, milking them with each upward drive.

I let out a gasp.

"Come for me, Aubree."

That voice! So rich and husky, it tickled my chest. The unmistakable sound of Nick.

It's him. In my bed. He's real. Not a dream.

Squirming against him, I fought the mounting pressure, the heat inside of me surging, swirling, promising the most exquisite release.

No! No! My mind protested, wanting to be sure the man lying behind me, coaxing pleasure like a fucking boss, was really *him.*

In a desperate bid between mind and body, I tried to will away the inevitable pull at my womb, the friction against my raw and hungry flesh, the string of tension in my muscles, telling me resistance was futile. My muscles turned rigid, quivering with the effort of holding back, fighting the climb. I wanted to turn and see his face, to make sure it wasn't some slick psycho with a death wish, but the orgasm crashed over me, and all I could do was lay there, allowing it to paralyze me, take me beneath the surface.

Ripples of ecstasy zipped through my body, spreading like flames through my muscles, the chasing tingles making me dizzy. Gripping the sheets with my free hand, I bit into my arm, cursing against my skin. Back arched, muscles taut, my body acted of its own will, riding out the most intense orgasm I'd had in months.

While my mind demanded *what the fuck?*, I cried out, confessing what he already knew, as his fingers continued their unrelenting pursuit of a second orgasm, the wetness and tiny muscle contractions making quick and easy glides that created a slight suction with each pull. His thumb caressed my clit, dipping into the wetness, then smearing it across the sensitive, if not traitorous, little bud. My own moaning droned inside my head, and I squirmed, thrust, tensed against the flames building inside my muscles.

Fuck you! Fuck you! My mind screamed inside its cage while another orgasm exploded through my body, sending flashes of light behind my eyelids.

"Oh, God, Nick. I hate you. I fucking hate you." I wanted to sob into my pillow and wallow in the betrayal I suddenly felt, but those bullets of pleasure shot through my veins, a blast of cool tingles extinguishing the flames in pulses that had me smiling, in spite of my frown—a true contradiction of absolute bliss and fury tangoing inside of me.

"I can't tell you how much it excites me to hear you say my name again." His fingers slipped out of me. "I missed your taste." A growl rumbled inside his chest, and at the grip of my throat, I nabbed the gun from the nightstand, crossed my arm over my body and pushed the barrel beneath what I estimated to be a chin.

"Achilleus X?"

"Hello, Pistol Lips." His grip loosened, and I rolled on top of him until straddling his body, where his erection pressed against my ass, and pointed the gun at him.

As he pulled back the ski mask, those sickeningly kissable lips stretched to a grin. "Didn't your parents teach you to lock the doors?"

Magnificent blue eyes that I never thought I'd see again forced the angry tirade burning inside of me to die on my lips. Nick. Achilleus. Alec Vaughn. The same man rolled up into one exquisite package, gazing back at me with the kind of expression that had wetness pooling in my panties and my ass arching against his cock. The kind of thrill that only came with dreams, because what else could explain why I hadn't fallen into a pile of desolation and tears at the sight of him?

"What ... what are you?" Words tumbled out of my mouth as I mentally searched for some coherence. "I get it. I've lost my mind." I rubbed a hand through my hair, a twinge of panic crawling up my spine. "Oh, shit, I've lost my mind. I'm seeing ghosts."

Ignoring the gun, and my distress, he reached out, fingertips dancing along ridge of my dress. "Fuck ... I've never seen you in red, but I can't imagine you wearing anything else from now on. Do you always sleep in a dress, or did you know I'd come for you tonight?"

That voice. *His* voice. Like a trained dog, my thighs clenched at the rush of excitement that hit my core. My stomach knotted, as a chill climbed my spine, begging an encore to what he'd accomplished only moments ago.

Surely, I had to be dreaming. I'd dreamt that very scenario at least a dozen times, both during the day and at night, where he came to me, holding me prisoner and molesting my body for hours. I'd become the weird chick with the twisted kidnapping fetish, who fell asleep to erotic stories of being swept away, imprisoned by dark fantasies I'd never given thought to before Nick.

His touch lingered on my cheek, and if not for his stare, I'd have covered it with my hand to preserve the sensation. If he was there, *really* there, then, "Why didn't Achilleus bark?"

His brow kicked up. "You named your dog after me, I'm flattered. Apparently, he's not trained to kill intruders, particularly those armed with treats."

"That was quite an exit you made." A new burst of anger ran through my body, battled by the excitement of having him there in my bedroom, where I'd planned to hold *him* prisoner, if I didn't happen to kill him first. I hated him for making me feel the way I'd felt for so many months, but hell if my body could stay mad at him. A part of me wanted to leap into his arms. "I thought you were dead."

His gaze fixed on my lips as his jaw shifted. "I escaped. A door in the sub-basement led me to a tunnel that let out through an abandoned building two blocks down." He glanced down at the gun I kept locked on him in my refusal to believe he was alive. "Still want to shoot me?"

He'd survived. Alive that whole time?

The confusion inside my body spun like a tornado, casting out random emotions that didn't make sense. So out of place, affecting my words and my reactions. Happiness. Sadness. Anger. Disbelief. Absolute chaos twisting beneath my skin.

I wanted to scream at him, yet could only muster a smile. I wanted to kiss him, but my finger twitched at the trigger. My heart felt cold, crystalizing inside my chest with the sting of mistrust—that I'd wake to disappointment. My hands heated with the burn of a slap waiting to crack against his cheek.

I lowered the gun. The pain of so many nights, thinking I'd lost him. Nearly losing myself.

"Your body is happy to see me." He shoved the two fingers into his mouth and licked them, admittedly casting a *spine-to-pussy* shudder. He had the audacity to smile again. "Still sweet as ever."

Rage and excitement burned in my blood.

The urge to smack him and kiss him was too much! A sharp sting hit my skull as I ground my teeth. The hours of pain, tears, disbelief, grief, anger, acceptance. For nothing. *Nothing.* "All that time you were ... and you didn't ..."

Numbness webbed from my heart to my limbs, tingling in my fingertips, and I felt light—the way one does in dreams. Was I dreaming? I still didn't know for sure. Tears threatened, the rims of my eyes itching to unleash the dam of anguish I'd held back for so long. The times I cried after the explosion, I'd had to pretend they were tears for my bastard husband.

"Asshole! Do you know what this has done to me?" I thumped my fist against his chest and leaned to push off from him.

He shot upright, to a sitting position, and captured both my arms.

"Let me go!" I twisted my wrists to get loose, frustrated when his grip tightened.

"I can't tell you how many times I wanted to steal you away with me."

Breaths heavy, I stilled, silently staring at him

He released my arms, the playful glint in his eye turned to a sobering stare. "I had to keep my distance. I wanted to keep you safe. But, more importantly, I had to know that … what you felt for me in those weeks wasn't some fucked up Stockholm bullshit. Every day, I came up with new excuses why I should stay away." His gaze swept across the room down my body while his palm slid up and down my thigh. "I ran out of excuses." At my silence, the corner of his lip kicked up. "I told you that you'd destroy me, Aubree. You're my pain and pleasure. Both the prick of a needle and the buzz that dulls the ache. My addiction. I can't stay away from what I need." He squeezed my thigh, gaze locked on mine. "I can't stay away from you anymore."

The angry storm calmed inside of me. "I read the medical record. So, you … you're—"

"Yes." His warm palms continued to massage my thighs. "Of two minds, you could say."

"Are you a danger to me?"

His mouth slid into a grin, his gaze dipping downward. "Only when you're dressed like this."

I ignored the telling goosebumps popping up on my

skin and lowered my eyes from his toward my stomach, where only a small bump passed beneath my fingertips. Tears filled my eyes when his hand covered mine, and I lifted my gaze back to his.

His brows pinched together. A deafening silence lingered for what seemed like an eternity, before his jaw twitched to a smile and his eyes carried a shine. "Ah, fuck, Aubree." He pulled me into his body, clutching me against him so tight I could hardly breathe in his embrace. His lips crushed mine in a kiss so sweet, so passionate, it stole my breath. "A baby. My baby." The wonderment in his voice eased the tension in my stomach.

Through a smile and tears, I nodded. "There's no one else but you, Nick."

"It's only you for me, Pistol Lips." Rubbing the back of my nape, he smiled. "I don't know how the fuck I survived so long without you. I was losing my mind, trying to stay away."

Pressing against his chest, I sat up from him, staring down at the lines in his face, the dark circles under his eyes that spoke of sleepless nights. I stroked my thumb over his lips, and he kissed it. "I told them everything you asked. About Achilleus."

"And Alec?"

"They don't know anything about any Alec. It never once came up. In neither the investigation nor the trials."

"Good. DeMarcus must've kept that information to himself." His gaze fell to my thighs as he stroked them, distracting my thoughts. "And as far as they know, I perished in that fire."

"Why didn't you tell me about Alec?"

"Because you'd already shown me that you were willing to love the dark side of me. All of me." His jaw tightened, and he shook his head. "Telling you everything would've kept me from going through with it in the end."

"That's why you wouldn't tell me why you'd kidnapped me. Why you kept me?"

"I was afraid of you, Aubree. You're evidence of my pain. Pain I needed to purge from myself. Alec wanted to save you. I wanted to destroy you. We saw you in two different lights. He saw the truth, while I was too blinded by my pain to see anything more than the lies."

"But ... you're the *same* person. How is it possible to feel two different emotions?"

"That was the insanity I lived with night after night, while my bed remained empty, without you beside me. How could I hate you and love you at the same time? It was a duality that drove me crazy." The softening of his eyes spoke of some inner torment. "I chose to remain in denial, even as I had you right there, knowing there was something deeper than my hate for you. It was madness." He shook his head. "I'm sorry if I hurt you, Aubree. I can't change what I am, what I've had to do to cope with this pain. I couldn't imagine a life beyond Lena and Jay. I didn't want to. You forced me to see a future beyond my vengeance. And I fought it every damn day that I watched you with Culling, made up reasons to hate you, until I couldn't deny it anymore. I had to save you." His fingers curled around my hips. "Falling in love with you wasn't part of the plan, though."

"I have to show you something."

His grip fell away from my thighs, and I slid off the bed, giving a quick wave to follow me into the next room.

Once inside the hallway, I halted my steps and turned to face him. Staring into his eyes, I lifted a hand to his cheek, tracing my fingertips over the stubble there, and kissed him. "I want to help heal your past, Nick."

CHAPTER 55
Nick

With a hell of a lot of patience, I followed behind Aubree, as she led me to the door of the adjacent room.

Standing there in that red dress, she taunted every fiber of restraint I had inside of me. I knew I'd have to take things slow at first, that she'd likely hate me, thinking I was dead.

Seeing her had brought forth a dark craving from deep within me—one that would never be sated by another woman as long as I lived. I'd been blessed with two *once-in-a-lifetime* loves, and no way in hell the Big Man would give me another chance if I happened to fuck things up.

As she stood staring up at me, the slight curve of her lips had my nerves on edge. With a click, she pushed the door open and stepped aside, allowing me passage. "This is the first step to healing your heart, Nick."

My breath choked up in my throat.

The walls were glass, like the rest of the house, but unlike the bamboo that covered the ceilings throughout, black billowy fabric hung from above, with tiny bulbs of light that appeared to be sewn into it like bright stars shining down from the night sky. On the glass across the room, words had been painted in black:

The stars in the sky
Unhidden by night
Souls of our loved ones
Guide us by sight
But when dawn breaks
Bringing day's light
Remain in our hearts
And all wrongs become right.

Below it, written in silver cursive against a black splotch, it read: *I'll see you in the night …*

"I'm not a poet … I just … took thoughts from what you told me, and—" Her gaze fell away from mine.

"You did this? For …" My throat clamped shut and I pushed past the lump to swallow. Fuck, I could barely contain the tears.

"I guess a part of me hoped you'd come back. I prayed for a miracle that you'd still be alive. Even if you didn't, I thought it was a good way to honor them. To always welcome their memory in this home." Cupping my face, she stole my attention with her smile. "I'm not afraid to share your heart, Nick. If it means I get to share your life, I'll take all of it. All the parts of you. Even your pain. You healed mine by killing Michael."

"You've ignited a flame inside of me, Pistol Lips."

"Flame? What does that mean?"

"You've restored my soul. Brought me back from death and filled me with life again. Made me give a shit about more than myself. It means you'll never know that kind of pain again. You'll never know fear. And if anything so much as attempts to pull you into darkness, I'll be right here. You'll never be alone." I brushed my thumb across her cheek and kissed her with everything inside of me. Gripping her nape, I pressed our foreheads together. "I'd walk through the flames of hell for you, Aubree. Burn for you." Lowering my hand to her stomach, I skimmed my fingertips across her tiny bump, where my future bloomed inside of her. "Both of you."

She'd punched through the steel that caged my heart, sealed the gaping wound and claimed what belonged to her. I'd protect her. Kill for her. And in return, never live without her.

So long I sought retribution, and in Aubree, I found redemption.

I lifted her up into my arms, wrapping her legs around me, and pressed my lips to hers in a kiss as I blindly carried her back into the master bedroom. Setting her on the edge of the bed, I kept our mouths locked while my hands worked the knot of her dress.

Her fingers fumbled against the button of my jeans, until they popped loose, and she broke the kiss to push them off my hips, down to my knees, where I stepped out of them. Gripping the hem of my T-shirt, she yanked the garment over my head and sucked her lip between her teeth as her hands roamed my chest down to my abs.

"I can't tell you how much I missed your body," she whispered. "I just want to touch every part of you, so I know you're really here."

With my fists planted at either side of her, I caged her beneath me, ravenous and ready to devour her. Like a starving animal, I feasted on her lips, and within seconds, the kiss turned violent, greedy. Couldn't get enough of her. *More, more*, a voice chanted inside of my head. Heat shot through my muscles, as I gripped her crown, holding her still while I tasted her, the mint of her breath and the sweet sugar of her lips.

Her palms hit my chest, and I swiped her hand away. I needed her. Had craved her too fucking long to stop. *More.*

A moan vibrated against my mouth. Yes. A hand thumped against my chest.

I severed the kiss, broke away, and a coldness filled the space between us.

She sucked in a sharp inhale. "Can't breathe."

"I'm sorry, I wanted this to be gentle, but after the harrowing task of bringing your lifeless body back from death that night … my head's been in a bad place these last few months."

"The feeling's mutual. When you left me that note … you weren't planning to come back. You planned to die that night. I hate you for what you put me through."

"Hate's a strong word." Lifting her arms above her head, I pinned her to the bed and traced my lips at the base of her neck, inhaling her sweet scent—the only one that could bring me to my knees. "Are you sure you hate me?"

"Yes." The hoarseness in her voice brought a smile to my face.

Pressing into her arms, I slid my shaft against her slit, teasing her, but goddamn it, I was a thread away from losing my mind.

I'd itched for the woman's touch for months, especially on those cold, sleepless nights when I'd cut the shit out of myself, trying to push the memory of her away, until realizing in the end that I couldn't. Couldn't let her go. Like a selfish bastard, I'd gone after her instead, even knowing I'd be putting her at risk. I didn't give a shit, though, just like a junkie didn't give a shit that the next hit could be his own destruction. I needed her. Every fiber of me ached for one more hit, one more high that would settle my mind, keep the darkness from consuming me.

Kissing along her jaw coaxed a quiet moan from her lips. "How much do you hate me?" Shifting my groin, I positioned the head of my cock at her entrance, so goddamn wet, I shivered. "Tell me," I demanded, squeezing her small wrists.

Her breath shuddered in my ear. "So much."

With maddening, tiny movements, I pressed into her, but didn't breach her pussy. "Maybe I should stop."

"No!" Her breasts surged into my chest with her protest. "Please."

"Please, what?"

Her eyes flipped open, but remained hooded with lust.

"Fuck me."

"Say it again," I demanded.

"Fuck me, Nick."

CHAPTER 56
Aubree

My body came alive again, like air being forced into a corpse that suddenly blossomed with life. I not only wanted him, I *needed* him.

Food, water, air and him.

My everything.

He pushed inside of me, all the way to the hilt, while I let out a pleasured cry.

"I'm the one who brought you back, Aubree. I jumped into that water and pulled your dead fucking body out of that vault. Not Alec. Me."

The sobering thought twisted my stomach in knots of sadness, recalling the utterly shaken state I'd awakened to, with him hovering over me like some kind of dark angel, the first time I'd seen fear on his face.

"The sight of you messed with my head. I need to fuck you. In fact, it might take a few days of fucking you to get it out of my system, but right now, I need you to give me everything you've got."

The soft feathering of his lips across my throat clenched my thighs, and a whimper escaped me when he slid his tongue up my neck. Teeth grazing my jawline, he curled his fingers around my nape, gripping me, as if I had any desire to get away from him.

"Aubree, I've been so strung out, thinking about you every night, for months," he rasped. "Your taste. Your smell. Driving me insane. I want that little pistol inside of you, and as much as I fuck you, I want you to fuck me back, because you've fucked my mind."

My head slammed back into the pillow, as he short stroked me, the sensation driving me mad with lust. "Please!" Tongue sweeping my lips, I slid my hand between my thighs, shamelessly massaging my clit.

Nabbing my wrist, he trapped my arm beneath his. "Tell me what you want."

"I want you to fucking make love to me, Nick." Lifting my head off the bed, I crushed my lips to his.

"No going back after this, Aubree. You belong to me. My head might be a jacked-up mess, but my body and heart know what they want." He squeezed my wrist. "I want to strip you down, take you every night, and wake up to your beautiful face every morning, knowing you're mine forever."

"I want you, too. Both of you. All of you. As much as I'm yours, you're mine, too, Alec, Nick, whoever you are, I don't care."

His cock slid inside, filling me.

I arched into him, needing to feel every inch of his skin

against mine. With slow, taunting thrusts, he pumped in and out of me, and like always, he watched me. I watched him. We stared at each other, like two warriors about to dive into battle.

He pulled out, flipped me onto my stomach, tugged my hips in the air and drove into me from behind.

I cried out as his cock slipped against my walls, filling me in a way I'd craved for months. I angled my ass higher, rocking my hips, anxious to feel him move inside of me.

He remained still at first, breaths juddering, fingers bruising my hips. "Goddamn," he growled.

Easy glides, in and out, had me closing my eyes, smiling at the relief, as his thick cock fed my starving libido. "Yes," I breathed, reaching between my thighs to play with his balls. "Fuck me, Nick."

"Your pussy missed me, didn't it? Did you miss me fucking you?" He pushed deep, jerking me forward, and I gritted my teeth at the powerful blow from behind. "Answer me."

"Every night. I fantasized about you every night!"

"I did, too. Lost my mind with dreams of burying myself inside you." His pace quickened with his words. "I needed to touch you, to come alive after feeling dead for too goddamn long." He licked up my spine, never breaking his momentum. "I'm going to fuck you all night, Aubree. Make you come over and over. And then I'm going to fuck you again."

With his hips jackhammering into me, I clawed at the sheets, the dry cotton sapping my saliva as I bit down into the fabric. Violent, frantic, and desperate for that first buzz of orgasm, like an addict scoring a hit after months of sobriety. I needed the high. Yearned it for so long.

The growling and grunting sounds he made excited me, and I let go, crying out with each merciless slam into my body. Every pounding from behind told me how much he wished to punish me. A silent confession of how much I'd made him ache for me, turn mad with lust and need, in those months apart. I knew, because I'd felt it, too. I'd grown tired of touching myself, searching for the release only his body could give me.

He brought me to tears, not from my pain, but his. I felt it inside of me in the way he moved so frantically and then agonizingly slow. An unsettled sensation that everything could end right then and there, battling the knowledge that we had forever. Even after he'd carried out his vengeance and survived it, his pain still festered. I understood that kind of suffering, because I'd felt it myself. In spite of Michael's death, in spite of the fact that I was finally free, a wistful longing still burned inside my heart. It was the kind of crushing pain that only love could soothe. I needed to soothe Nick's heart, to heal him by handing over my very soul, my pain, the hours, minutes, seconds that I'd felt dead without him. I needed him to know the madness inside of me that'd bloomed from missing him.

"I need you. Give me more, Aubree. Everything you've got."

The pressure tightened my stomach with each stroke of

his cock that eased the ache inside of me.

He pulled out, twisting me onto my back again, and kissed me before sliding back inside.

I rolled on top of him, my nails digging into his chest, tearing at his flesh. Still fused at the mouth, I dragged his lip through my teeth and bit down. He returned the savagery, with a violent, possessive kiss, pulling my hair. We were a tangle of limbs, scratching, biting, smacking, clawing. Annihilating each other. I couldn't get enough of him, and I prayed that I wouldn't come any time soon because I never wanted it to end. I wanted to fuck him until I was weak, beaten, battered, and nothing but soft bones.

His fingers dug into my hips as I rode him. My breasts bounced with each hard slam along his cock, and lifting his head from the pillow, his mouth clamped onto my nipple.

My stomach clenched as pain pierced the sensitive flesh. The edge fringed, muscles burning. Higher. Higher.

He tugged me back into him, fingers curled around my shoulders, pressing into my bones as he guided me up and down, up and down. Pumping, pumping, pumping.

I screamed his name. A plea? It sounded as though I'd hit heaven, begging to come in for a while before I fell back down to earth.

Tingles raced through my blood, and his hot seed shot inside of me, while I called out his name, over and over and his curses bounced off the walls.

He cupped my cheeks, passion burning in his eyes,

breaths shuddering with his release. "I love you, Aubree," he said in a gravelly tone, before his lips slanted over mine. "My beautiful little pistol."

I smiled at that. "I love you, too."

A slick coating of sweat, blood and cum covered our bodies in the damp sheets where we'd destroyed each other. Happily annihilated the fuck out of one another in a matter of minutes.

"I should punish you for what you do to my body." His husky voice tickled my ear, and he collapsed beside me on the bed, tugging me into him. "But I couldn't hurt you if I tried."

Our frantic breaths finally slowed, and he slid out of bed, reaching out a hand to me. He could've guided me straight over the edge of a cliff and I'd have followed him with a smile. I didn't care—I needed to feel his body against mine again, so I took his hand.

Leading me toward the bathroom, he nabbed a loofa set in a white antique bowl atop a wooden pedestal just outside of the shower. Inside, he flipped the water on and pulled me into his body. Steam mingled with the warm scent of teak wood, and the water coupled with his hands put me into a trance, as he washed my body down. The glass of the stall, unlike inside of the house, was obscure, but had the feel of an exotic outdoor shower, with moon's light streaming in and the fresh air fusing with the steam.

Alive. He's fucking alive. I could scream the words that danced inside my head. No longer alone. For months, I'd agonized over the thought of raising his child by myself.

And I would've. My world finally felt complete. Whole.

"Part of me still feels like I'm dreaming and you're not really here." I closed my eyes as he shampooed my hair.

"I'm really here." A tweak of my nipple made me yelp, and I reached back to slap his thigh. With his arms wrapped around me, I felt small beside him. "I'm sorry I missed so many opportunities to watch you shower in here."

"A party every night. All those dirty thoughts I kept to myself. Pretty sure Mateus has enjoyed the show."

His arms stiffened around my body. "Who's Mateus?"

"The seventy year old caretaker on the island."

The tension eased. "I'll kill him," he said with a smile in his voice.

"Mister Ryder, are you jealous?"

"Only where you're concerned." His teeth nipped my ear, and he smoothed his hands over my body. "Tell me what you want, Aubree. Whatever you need, I'll give it to you."

"You. What else?"

"I'm yours." His voice turned somber. "But sometimes I'm … complicated. It's been a long time since I shared anything with a woman. I don't want to fall into old habits, but you've become my addiction. And my addictions have been known to destroy me."

I twisted in his arms to face him, my eyes at the level of his chest tattoo. "I don't want easy and uncomplicated. I want love that makes me fucking insane and irrational. I want to drown in it and never come back up for air."

I meant it. There was nothing normal or typical about our love. We should've been one hot mess of madness for all that we'd suffered, but just as a flower grows from the sky's tears, our love grew from pain. It blossomed in darkness and thrived with time.

I kissed his arm, wrapped tightly around me as if claiming what belonged to him. Lowering my gaze, I traced the outline of his tattoo. "Losing you was like a bullet straight to my heart."

"I promised I'd come back." His finger hooked beneath my chin and our eyes locked. "I always keep my promises."

"Then, promise me forever."

With a grip of my hair, he tipped my head back, leaving a trail of kisses up my throat, until he reached my ear. "I promise," he whispered.

"I love you."

"I loved you first," he battled.

"And I love you twice as much."

"Touché." A grin touched his eyes—those sparkling blue gems that I'd missed so much. "You were never meant to be mine, Aubree. But I'll take you. All of you." His hand caressed my stomach and he lowered to one knee, planting a kiss to my navel. "And any bastard tries to take either one of you from me will know insufferable pain."

I threaded my fingers through his hair. "I'm keeping you. Whether you like it or not."

He pushed to a stand, towering over me. As he bent

forward and kissed me, his arms enfolded my body like a warm, protective blanket. "I like it," he said, smiling against my mouth.

Perhaps hope wasn't such a cruel bitch, after all.

Apart, we were nothing more than two broken halves, but together, our jagged edges fit perfectly, sealed into something whole again. In the end, he saved me, and in return, I saved him.

Eye for an eye, heart for a heart.

ACKNOWLEDGMENTS

I'm no stranger to writing dark books, but this one was different for me. Nick's story crushed my heart and forced me into a very dark corner of my mind for a while, but I loved every single moment of writing it. And I have quite a few people to thank for helping me along the way ...

First, enormous thanks to my husband Trent for the many meals you prepare while I'm locked away with my imaginary friends; the times you sneak away with the kiddos so the house is nice and quiet; put up with the many occasions you'll be talking to me about something and I'll have mentally drifted off into a scene; and for the endless questions I've thrown at you about guns in the last couple of months. I love you.

To my daughters, who inspire me every day and make me a better person. I love you *infinity*.

To my mom and dad for your never-ending support. Love you both.

Julie Belfield, my wonderful friend and editor, thank you for always putting your heart into helping me clean up these stories. As long as they are sometimes, and as horrid as the first drafts can be, you never complain. You're always right there to pick me up when I knock myself down, and challenge me to venture into the dark places of my head that I sometimes fear to tread. You never sugar coat anything, and my books are better because of it.

My very talented brother, Ryan, who has inspired and encouraged me from the beginning, and designed the cover for Ricochet, thank you for all that you do. Love you!

Chris Davis of Specular Photography for capturing the perfect face to match the character.

Many many thanks to the insanely gorgeous, British model, Chris Williamson, for not only acting as my muse these last few months, but also inspiring one of the most swoon-worthy heroes I've ever written. You are the perfect Nick Ryder.

My fearless beta readers—Lana of Dirty Girl Romance Blog, Author K.L. Schwengel, and Wendy S.—thank you for going where no man (or woman) would dare to go! My early drafts are a warzone and I thank you, brave souls, for your invaluable feedback! You helped make this a better story.

To the kickass ladies from my street team, I don't know what I'd do without y'all. Your support, loyalty and encouragement have meant so much to me. The times I've had my doubts, you ladies have lifted me up and made me feel like I can do just about anything. Thank you for loving Nick and pushing me to try a new genre. Love yas!!

To Sammy C., Anne C., Angela C. (lots of C's), and Terri Rochenski, many many thanks for your endless encouragement.

To Stacy E., thank you for helping with the investigation scenes. And thank you Stephen A., J.L. McFadden and Colin Barnes for answering my computer-related questions.

HUGE thanks to all the wonderful bloggers who continue to support me and help promote my books. Words cannot express how much I appreciate each and every one of you!

And lastly, to my amazing readers, your love and support means so much to me. You are my rock stars. Thank you for taking a chance on my books, and making this possible.

XOXO

About The Author

Keri Lake is a married mother of two living in Michigan. By day, she tries to make use of the degrees she's earned in science. By night, she writes dark contemporary and paranormal romance. Though novels tend to be her focus, she also writes short stories and flash fiction on the many occasions when distraction sucks her in to the *Land of Shiny Things*.

She loves hearing from readers …

SOCIAL MEDIA LINKS:

Website: http://www.KeriLake.com
Twitter: http://www.twitter.com/kerilake
Facebook page: http://www.facebook.com/kerilakeauthor
Newsletter Sign Up: http://eepurl.com/HJPHH